She grabbed a large bowl and filled it with water. The puppies went to town, their little tails wagging, each trying to shove the other out of the way.

"Hey, I'm sorry," Ryan said.

"Don't worry. I can handle this. I'll keep them in my bathroom tonight so that the others can't get to them. They'll be safe."

"That's not what I meant. I mean I'm sorry I didn't come by the shop on Tuesday."

"You probably got tied up."

"Yeah, I've got a lot going on, but I always make room for you. You know that."

"Sure. I'm one of Jill's best friends. She'd probably brain you if you were mean to me."

He chuckled. "News flash—she hasn't 'brained me' in years. And you're my friend, too."

The way he said those gentle words sent a warm tingle down her spine. Yes, they were friends, but they had never spent much time together. At least not alone. They were alone now, and if not for the puppies, Zoey might freak out about that. Here was this incredibly handsome, wonderfully built, single man in her home on a Friday night when he could be anywhere else.

With anyone else.

Home for a Hero

Heatherly Bell & Soraya Lane

Previously published as *Reluctant Hometown Hero*
and *The Returning Hero*

HARLEQUIN MUST♥DOGS

HARLEQUIN® MUST♥DOGS

Recycling programs
for this product may
not exist in your area.

ISBN-13: 978-1-335-50744-0

Home for a Hero

Copyright © 2021 by Harlequin Books S.A.

Reluctant Hometown Hero
First published in 2019. This edition published in 2021.
Copyright © 2019 by Heatherly Bell

The Returning Hero
First published in 2014. This edition published in 2021.
Copyright © 2014 by Soraya Lane

This edition published by arrangement with Harlequin Books S.A.

For questions and comments about the quality of this book,
please contact us at CustomerService@Harlequin.com.

Harlequin Enterprises ULC
22 Adelaide St. West, 40th Floor
Toronto, Ontario M5H 4E3, Canada
www.Harlequin.com

Printed in U.S.A.

CONTENTS

Heatherly Bell tackled her first book in 2004 and now the characters that occupy her mind refuse to leave until she writes them a book. She loves all music but confines singing to the shower these days. Heatherly lives in Northern California with her family, including two beagles—one who can say hello and the other a princess who can feel a pea through several pillows.

Books by Heatherly Bell

Harlequin Special Edition

Wildfire Ridge

More than One Night
Reluctant Hometown Hero

Harlequin Superromance

Heroes of Fortune Valley

Breaking Emily's Rules
Airman to the Rescue
This Baby Business

Visit the Author Profile page
at Harlequin.com for more titles.

RELUCTANT HOMETOWN HERO

Heatherly Bell

Dedicated to Stephanie,
proud owner of the real Corky, Indie and Bella.

Chapter 1

Zoey Castillo glanced at her cell phone and hoped she wasn't being rude to her date. It was the third text in thirty minutes she'd received from her best friend, Jill Davis, during dinner. The first two had been reasonable inquiries on the exact measurements of water, coconut oil and protein to add to the freeze-dried, organic, carbohydrate-free food she gave her pets. But then the third message:

Jill: Settle a bet for Sam and me. Which is faster? A horse or a mountain lion? I say a horse.

Zoey: Hello? I'm on a date. Emergencies only!

Jill: Sorry. Tell Julian we say hello and not to worry about being late to work tomorrow morning. ;) ;)

Zoey glanced across the restaurant table at Julian, who worked as a guide at Jill's company, *Wildfire Ridge Outdoor Adventures*. Good-looking in a dark and lanky muscular way, two weeks ago he'd asked her out on a date. Zoey was excited about the first date she'd had in… Oh my god, could she count that high? Julian had offered to hold her hand and tandem zipline on friends-and-family day because she'd been nervous about doing it alone. Sweet and handsome all in one delectable manly package. It was hard to find a hot-looking guy she felt safe with. Zoey didn't understand why there seemed to be no spark and sizzle between them.

Nothing. Zilch.

"I'm so sorry," Zoey said. "Jill is my sitter tonight and she keeps texting me about every little thing."

"Understandable." Julian leaned back. "How many?"

"Three," Zoey said, then realized she hadn't counted Boo, the Great Dane she was still trying to find a home for. Just one of her many foster fails. Zoey had wound up adopting nearly all her fosters, but Boo needed more room than she had. She'd tried hard, unsuccessfully, not to get too attached. "Actually, four to be exact."

Julian went brows up. "Four? Seriously? But you're so young."

"Well, it's my business, too. I am trying to adopt one of them out. Boo."

"Adopt one out? Boo?"

Their waitress brought their plates and set them down. Steak and potatoes for Julian, stir-fried vegetables and rice for Zoey.

"I know. It's a funny name. But he's a big boy so I gave him a small name."

"That's unusual and…very brave of you." A thin line

of sweat broke out on Julian's forehead. "My mother was a single mom, so I know what it's like."

"What? Oh, no, they're not my children!" Zoey laughed at the mistake. "They're my pets."

She whipped her cell phone out and showed Julian photos of Boo, the size of a small pony, sitting majestically next to Corky, her potbellied pig and his best friend. Indie, her Chihuahua mix, and Bella, her boxer, sat nearby giving them side-eyes.

Julian coughed. "You get a sitter for your pets?"

"Not always." She sat straighter in her seat, feeling a bit attacked. "But sometimes Indie and Bella gang up on Boo when I'm not around. Indie nips his ankles. For a big dog, he's a baby and extremely sensitive."

"Uh-huh. You said he's a foster?"

"I adopted him." Zoey bit her bottom lip to keep from crying. "The owners gave him up to the shelter. I think they should have been arrested, but there's no law against giving up on your dogs."

Julian studied her sympathetically and reached across to pat her hand. But by now she could see the resignation reflected in his dark eyes. He'd just written her off into that category of single women who were single for a good reason. No problem. She'd already crossed him off her list of Men I Might Ask to Tio and Tia's Fortieth Anniversary Party. Sure, it was a small list, but it existed. Somewhere in this world there was a fellow animal lover who would accept her menagerie of pets and her raging dedication to them. They were a package deal.

After dinner, Julian said he had to be up early for work, and said good-night at her front door. Thankfully, he didn't try for a kiss but gave her a kind and warm hug. Very brotherly of him.

Zoey thanked him for a lovely dinner and watched him drive away.

"That didn't go well." She wasn't even seriously disappointed.

She decided it was probably the lack of said spark and sizzle.

Zoey turned to her warmly lit home and caught sight of Jill and Sam through the picture window, cuddled on the couch. Jill appeared to be practically in his lap and from here it looked like Sam had his hand under her shirt. *Really?* With the curtains wide open? In her house and in front of the dogs and Corky?

Who was she kidding? She wanted what they had. Passion. Vitality. Sparkle. She wanted a man whose every gaze in her direction made her quiver and shake like a 9.5-Richter-scale earthquake. Unfortunately, she already knew that man's name, occupation and address. And also the fact that the two of them ever being together was impossible—or at least unlikely.

Zoey coughed as she turned the key, grateful for the squeaky front door. She didn't want to interrupt…anything. When she heard giggles and scrambling from the direction of the family room, she figured she'd given them enough time to get decent.

"You're home early," Jill said, standing. She appeared to have been kissed and groped within an inch of her life. Her lips were bruised and her clothing a little disheveled.

"Yeah, it was a bust. He's a cool guy, but neither one of us are feeling it." As usual, Boo, Indie, Corky and Bella descended on her for pats and hugs as though she'd been gone for a year and not a couple of hours. Between Indie and Bella's yips, Boo's howls and Corky's squeals and snorts, it was a little like being swallowed by a tsunami.

"Everything went okay here. Indie tried to attack Boo's ankles but Sam just gave him that *look* he has. Indie stopped midbite."

"He's my kind of dog," Sam said. "A real warrior."

Jill pulled Zoey aside. "So…still no date to the anniversary party?"

"No, but that's okay. I can always go alone."

"Ask Ryan. I'm telling you. Ryan would do it."

Ahem. Ryan Davis, the newly elected and youngest sheriff ever to serve the small town of Fortune. He also happened to be Jill's big brother—and Zoey's secret crush. So asking him on a date mattered too much. He might say yes, which could be a problem, and he might say no, which would also be a problem. Safest course? Don't ask him.

"I don't want to bother him. He's too busy."

"He's never too busy for me. Or you."

"I'll think about it."

At the door, Jill turned to give Zoey one last hug before she and Sam left.

After letting her pets out one last time in her envelope-sized backyard, Zoey got ready for bed. She washed her face, brushed her teeth and put her long brown hair in a ponytail. Usually she wore it in either braids or a ponytail for practicality but tonight she'd worn it down like Mami did. Her aunt and uncle said she looked exactly like her mother, Veronica Milagros Caballero-Castillo, which *should* have been a compliment. And if one was merely talking looks, it probably was since Veronica made a living as an A-list movie star in Mexico. Not content to work the family pet supply store with her sister, Veronica, a California native, had moved down to Mexico after Zoey's father died. Zoey was twelve and had been left in the care of Tia Gloria and Tio Raul. Veronica had planned to be away for only a year, but she'd stayed in Mexico. For over a decade now.

Zoey might resemble the beautiful dark-eyed Veronica. On the other hand, Zoey was protective about who she would allow to adopt her rescues, and wouldn't even abandon one of her pets let alone a child.

Her *real* parents were Gloria and Raul, who'd never been able to have any children of their own. When they wanted to retire, Zoey had taken over the running of their pet supply store. She'd renamed it Pimp Your Pet and given it a complete overhaul. Business was good.

Her personal life, not so much. Well, one couldn't have everything. Best not to be greedy.

When Zoey crossed the threshold from her bathroom to her bedroom, she caught a familiar sight. Even though every pet had its own comfortable bed from Pimp Your Pet's best selection, Bella and Indie were spread out and taking up one entire side of her bed. Both Boo and Corky were simply staring from the foot of the bed, as if to say, *We told them not to do it, but would they listen?*

Good grief. "Move over, you two."

Maybe it was a good thing she didn't have a man in her life. For one thing, she had no room in her bed for one.

The next morning, Zoey woke at the usual time and stumbled to the coffee for her kitchen fix. Wait. That was *kitchen for her coffee* fix. She let the pets out for their morning business, and then started the long process of the morning feed between sips of coffee. It sounded like she lived on a farm, but she didn't. Just a small tract home in a residential area of Fortune. Still, food was life and she wanted her pets to have the best of everything. She got great discounts on the best organic foods on the market but they took time and effort to put together.

Bella and Corky were barking and snorting to be let in, so she did that, then went back to the food prep. Zoey was running out of time and still had to shower and get to the shop to open up. She added protein to the mix, chopping pieces of organic boiled chicken, and went to let in Indie who was having a yipping fit and beginning to launch himself at the sliding glass door.

All pets should be sitting on their haunches now waiting for their meal, practically salivating. It took ten minutes for the freeze-dried mix to jell together and be soft enough to eat. She always set a timer. Everyone but Boo stood at attention as if they fully expected her to forget all about feeding them. Boo had so much patience. He usually took a seat in the corner, with full faith that she'd call him when it was all ready.

She finally set the bowls down for all four animals and called Boo over. He didn't come, and it took her a moment to realize that he hadn't been let inside yet. She went to the sliding glass door and opened it, calling for him again. He still didn't come.

Boo was gone. Zoey went to the six-foot-tall wooden side gate, which she always kept closed and latched. The gate was not only unlatched but open. She didn't even employ a gardener for fear they'd forget and leave the gate open. She went around the side of her house toward the front, calling Boo's name. He was slow and couldn't get far. But there was no sign of him anywhere down her tree-lined cul-de-sac. Heart racing and thudding in her chest, Zoey ran from one neighbor to another. None had seen Boo, who—come on—couldn't easily be missed. Boo wasn't a runner and barely enjoyed a daily walk. He'd never tried to get away in all the weeks she'd had him and probably wouldn't start now. There could be only one explanation. He'd been kidnapped!

Racing back home, Zoey grabbed her cell phone and dialed 911.

"Help! There's been a kidnapping."

"Yes, ma'am, calm down. I'll send someone right over."

"Okay, thank you. I have a lot of photos. He's about four feet tall and gray."

"Gray? Zoey, is that you?" the dispatcher said.

"Yes! Boo's been kidnapped right out of my back-yard!"

"How do you know he didn't just go for a walk? Dogs like to get out every now and then, you know."

She supposed Trudy, the dispatcher, was now the authority on dogs. Really!

"Yes, I do know that, but Boo isn't a runner. I know my pets. Indie and Bella, they're runners. But not Boo. He can hardly muster up the energy for a walk. I'm telling you, someone took him!"

In that moment Zoey realized that if Indie and Bella had been outside with Boo, they would have gone with him if he'd actually escaped. They were the true runners. Which meant… Boo had been out there alone and he'd been taken, all because Zoey had forgotten about him for a few minutes. Preparing food that took roughly a decade to be ready.

"Okay, calm down there. I'm sending Sheriff Davis right over."

"No, don't. He's too busy." And she didn't want *Ryan* to see her like this. All frantic and disheveled and… manic.

"Don't worry, hon. You'll feel a lot better after the sheriff comes by and gives you a little talk. Everyone does."

Was that a sigh Zoey heard? "No, seriously, don't send Ry—"

But the incorrigible woman hung up on Zoey. Great. Now she'd not only have a rough morning, but she'd have to deal with seeing the one man who made her sizzle. The one man who made the electricity in a room spark like the Fourth of July. When she was at her worst.

Sheriff Ryan Davis. He of the dimpled, irresistible smile and wide, capable shoulders. The long legs and flat abs. The man every single woman in town had a "thing" for.

Including, most unfortunately, her.

Chapter 2

Ryan had just dispatched his deputies, all two of them, slammed a Red Bull and gone back to his office prison when Trudy, the dispatcher, buzzed him.

"Davis," he answered.

"We've got another one of *those* calls. You'll want to handle it."

"What now? Did someone get upset and call 911 because their neighbor's dog crapped on their lawn?"

He was regularly blessed with all the so-called "kooky" calls because being the sheriff in a town with a small deputy force meant he also took a patrol shift and he didn't want his staff dealing with anything but the most pressing matters. Since he was the head desk jockey, that meant he got to deal with anything that could otherwise wait.

For reasons he did not understand, he had the gift of

gab and usually had a confrontation between neighbors or spouses calmed down within minutes. Even better, it now seemed that most of the residents were clued in to the fact that if he showed up at their doorstep, their call was considered a nuisance. The embarrassment of that knowledge usually meant his visit was short and sweet, though he still occasionally got asked inside for a cup of coffee and some conversation. Occasionally a sexual favor or two.

He always declined. The conversation and sexual favors, not the coffee.

"Zoey Castillo. Says her dog Boo has been kidnapped. He probably just got out and she can't find him."

He resisted the urge to snap at Trudy. "It might not be a kidnapping but it could be theft."

Maybe it wasn't his highest priority, but this week had him facing a city council meeting where he would listen to the concerns of citizens who wanted a crime update and a meeting with the city planner. Excuse him if he could use a little pick-me-up. The sight of beautiful and sweet Zoey would lift his spirits. A single woman who wasn't on the make and interested in lassoing him like a wild buck. At thirty-two, he'd had enough of that.

"I'll head over there and check it out."

"Good luck, sheriff. God bless you. You're a saint."

Hardly. Was he a saint because every time he laid eyes on his little sister's best friend he wanted to kiss her full and sensual lips? Would a saint notice every curve of her body and her perfectly shaped behind?

No. He was no saint and he didn't appreciate being put on a damn pedestal again. But the residents of Fortune had put him there. He simply understood restraint. Boundaries. He understood the importance of order to avoid chaos. Having been an officer in the army, he'd learned plenty about duty and obligation. Leadership. That didn't make him a saint. Far from it.

When he arrived at Zoey's a few minutes later in his Jeep, she was sitting on the top step of her small porch. Hair in a ponytail, wearing dark sweatpants and a loose T-shirt with a saying written on it that had him losing his focus for a moment. She held one of her many dogs. This one a little ankle biter named Indie. She might have slept in those clothes, and he metaphorically shook his head and tried not to picture her sleeping. With or without clothes. Of course, his preference would be for the latter.

"Hey," he said as he walked up to her.

She stood, cuddling Indie. "Sorry, Ryan."

To his horror, it looked like she'd been crying. Her eyes were red rimmed and her cheeks tear streaked. Two seconds into this call and she was already killing him.

"Sorry for *what*?"

"They always send you out for the nutcases."

"Not this time." He straightened and met her gaze. "If someone took your dog, this is a robbery."

"Exactly!" Her brown eyes flashed in a way that shouldn't affect him the way it did.

Long ago he'd decided to take a hands-off approach to Zoey. He'd always been attracted to her, but she was sweet, innocent and vulnerable. He neither needed nor deserved any of those things in his life.

"Show me where this happened."

She led him to the side gate, stepped inside the yard and set Indie down on the lawn. "He's upset. Almost as much as Corky. It's like when you think you hate someone, but don't realize until they're gone how much you'll miss them."

He inspected the gate latch, which didn't seem to have been bent or broken in any way. "And this gate was latched."

"Yes, I... I think so." She pulled her lower lip between her teeth. "I always latch it."

He shut the gate and stood on the other side. "Do me a favor and latch it now."

When he heard it snap into place, he reached one arm over and easily unlatched it. It would have to be someone at least six feet tall or more, but...

"Even if it was latched, it could have been easily unlatched from the outside."

"See? Someone *did* take him."

"You're sure someone didn't just leave the gate open? Your gardener maybe? Boo didn't just get out and go for a walk?"

"I don't have a gardener and Boo doesn't like walks. I searched the neighborhood. No one saw him and he couldn't have gotten very far on his own."

O-kay. So he had himself a little mystery on his hands. One he'd probably solve in a couple of hours, but nevertheless he welcomed the challenge.

"Do you have any idea who would have taken him?"

"Obviously someone tall." She glanced behind him to the gate and worried a fingernail between her teeth. "But I don't know who would do this. Or why."

"Wasn't he one of your adoptions?"

"Yes, and I've been trying to find the perfect home for him."

He could see why that would be a chore. The dog

was roughly the size of a small horse. "You were actually trying to *give* him away and someone steals him?"

That made no sense. Why steal the dog when they could have him for the asking?

Maybe someone who didn't know that Zoey was trying to find Boo a home. He had to wonder, too, why this was such an issue when it seemed Zoey's problem had been solved. The dog had found a home. But he knew better. Zoey wouldn't rest until she knew that the dog was in a *good* home. One of her most endearing, as well as frustrating, qualities. She'd tried several times to get some of his friends to adopt Boo, he assumed so she could keep an eye on him, but no one had the room. Neither did Zoey, a fact that didn't seem to matter to her.

The radio squawked on his shoulder. "Davis."

"You're needed at city hall."

He winced. "Why?"

"Some kind of press conference."

Nothing like last minute. Their current mayor excelled at last minute. Ryan had gone to school with the man so he felt qualified to judge.

"I'll be there."

Zoey had already picked up Indie and walked toward her sliding glass door. "See you later."

"Wait a second." He waved her over.

"You have to go."

He hated that she would have to wait, but that didn't mean he wouldn't take this seriously.

"Here's what I want you to do. Make a list of anyone you can think of, anyone at all, who might want to take Boo. I'll send a deputy over to file a police report. I'll find him for you, Zoey. Don't worry."

She gave him a heartbreaking smile and nodded. "Thank you."

"It's my job."

Helping her, of course, would be a special honor but she didn't have to know that. Zoey had always struck him as someone who liked to blend into the background. Hide in the shadows. Amazing how well she'd managed, too, considering she was a knockout. A ten on his scale. He figured she hid well because of the way she dressed and because she often wore her hair in braids. She didn't wear makeup like his sister and other women he knew.

Plus, all the animals. She wasn't the crazy cat lady but some called her the pet whisperer. Jill swore Zoey had an uncanny ability to determine each person's perfect pet match. She was a bit younger than Jill and even younger than him. Unlike Jill, Zoey was innocent and shy. He couldn't help thinking *virginal*, but that likely wasn't true anymore. Not that it was any of his business. He made an effort to redirect his thoughts. But then again, as long as his thoughts remained just that, *thoughts* and nothing more, who would be the wiser?

He had a job to do, and she was a resident like all the others who deserved no less attention.

Though he loved serving, he wasn't thrilled living life so publicly and wished someone else with enough so-called stature had expressed an interest in being sheriff of Fortune. Ryan had agreed to run at the request of the mayor—they'd had a special election after the last sheriff had been run out of town following a small-town scandal, and no one had been primed to take his place. So, though Ryan had been working as a detective up north in Oakland, he was quickly recruited by the powers that be to move back to Fortune, his small hometown, and run for sheriff. All politics. He'd easily won the election in a landslide.

He blamed the medal.

The medal of honor that the United States government had bestowed him, which he was still trying to earn. He'd done what he had to do to save the lives of the men that were under his command. In his opinion that didn't make him a hero. His life had never been the same after the medal, for more than one reason. A parade on his return was one of those reasons. Being called a hometown hero was another.

After the service, he'd naturally fallen into law enforcement and a job as a detective for the homicide division. Living and working in Oakland had at least afforded him a certain amount of anonymity, but in Fortune, everyone knew him and his family. Everywhere he went residents bought him drinks and meals. Thanked him for his service. Some wanted to talk about the medal. He never did, preferring to leave that part of his life where it belonged.

In the past.

In the hot and arid desert of Iraq.

Chapter 3

After printing and posting *Lost/Reward* flyers on every block around her neighborhood, and calling every shelter within thirty miles in case the thief grew a conscience and brought Boo in, Zoey finally got herself to work and opened up her shop. The UPS guy had left a couple of shipments blocking the front door, so she pretty much had to shove and push to squeeze by. Then she dragged the heaviest box inside inch by inch. By the time she was done she was out of breath.

The smaller box was from her mother. Zoey opened it up and read the small note inside.

Querida:
Use this facial cream every night. You're getting older and it's never too early to start. One day you'll be like me and at fifty won't look a day

over thirty. You must come and visit me again. What's it been? Five years? Hope you and Tia and Tio are doing well.
Mami

It was more like ten years and not five, but Mom still apparently lived heavily in denial. She'd forgotten about Tia's fortieth anniversary next week but maybe she'd send something later. Zoey shoved the box aside.

Veronica wanted Zoey to visit, but the last time she had, Zoey was fifteen. It had been a living nightmare to be around so many people who constantly fawned over her mother. There were dinners and parties and way too many crowds and cameras. One evening, Zoey had dressed up for a party like her mother so they could be "twins." Veronica's idea. Zoey had worn the same black clingy plunging neckline dress, her hair down, and some cute strappy heels she'd nearly taken a pratfall in.

That night Zoey had some unwanted attention from Mami's creepy director. He'd leered, said ugly comments no fifteen-year-old should hear from a man twice her age. Thank god she'd been rescued by a producer looking to talk to Jorge privately. Later, when he suggested Zoey play Veronica's daughter in one of her next *peliculas*, Zoey impersonated the paint on a wall.

Her mother had simply smiled and said: "But, Jorge, I don't look old enough to have a teenage daughter. It's too unrealistic and no one would believe it."

Ha! She wondered what her darling mother said now that her daughter was pushing twenty-seven.

Zoey opened the next box. The heaviest shipment turned out to be her Pimp Your Pet brand dog and cat tees in assorted colors. Neon pink, neon green, neon blue. On closer inspection, however, the shirts read *Primp* Your Pet. And in very small, practically unreadable letters. The design she'd seen online looked nothing like this. Definitely *not* what she had ordered. Oh, good Lord, would this Monday stop already? How was she supposed to function after Boo had been kidnapped right out of her yard? Where was he and was the disgusting, pathetic criminal even treating him right?

To make matters worse, this morning Ryan had shown up looking like a GQ magazine cover, law enforcement division. Golden hair in need of a cut curling at his neckline, intelligent green eyes that didn't miss a thing. He wore a different uniform than the regular officers. Dark boots, khaki pants that fit his fine butt like they were tailored to it and a white button-up shirt with sleeves rolled, showing off strong forearms. He had his gun strapped to him in one of those black leather side holsters. Was it wrong to be turned on by that? Probably. And her, wearing sweats and a gag T-shirt that read, I Do Everything Doggie-Style.

Yeah, she hadn't realized that until after the fact. Face palm.

She pulled out the invoice charging her far too much and dialed customer service. After getting through all the commands she finally reached a live person. This person thought he was a comedian.

"Actually, don't you think *primp* your pet sounds much better than *pimp* your pet?"

"That's not the name of my store. It's *Pimp* Your Pet. As in outfits and everything a pet needs. But I don't *primp* pets. That would imply I'm a pet grooming place and I'm not."

"We'll agree to disagree. I think it's cute. How about we split the difference and I credit you for half the shipment? It will be like a little inside joke. Pimp and primp. Maybe you could make it a contest. Which is better? Win a bag of food or something."

"No, I don't think so. It's all wrong."

"Alright then, calm down *lady*."

That was the second person this morning telling her to calm down. She would not calm down! "I am not a *lady*, sir. Take these stupid shirts back before I come find you and shove them down your gullet."

"No need to get crazy. I'll send you a return address shipping label. Guess what? The shipping's on us!"

"How generous of you."

She took extra pleasure in pressing End Call by digging her index finger into her phone and pretending to push on the guy's Adam's apple. Crush. Oh, whew. She was not usually so violent, but it sometimes felt like a latent anger had simmered inside for…years. Taking deep breaths, she picked up Annie, the store cat, from her box near the register and gave her a cuddle. Zoey kept the gray Russian Blue at the store because she was so friendly with customers and let anyone give her a rub. Of course, Boo was also friendly with customers as well as every living thing on planet Earth, but he blocked the aisles and young children feared him.

Someone else out there knew that he was a good dog, despite his size and general appearance. That someone had taken him without asking. Zoey already missed Boo and it hadn't been more than two hours.

As the morning progressed, her customers filed in one after the other. Mrs. Nesbitt for her specially ordered cat food, Mrs. Williams for her parakeet's food and someone with an elderly dog searching for diapers. After sniffling with the nice man over aging dogs, and giving him a much-needed hug, she helped him find what he needed. Monday mornings were not her busiest time and so she attempted to occupy and distract herself by switching displays. She was in the middle of moving the cat socks to aisle two when Joanne, owner of the bridal shop nearby, came in with her friend Hudson.

He was the firefighter lieutenant Zoey had matched with a cute cockapoo a week ago and gifted him a few supplies to tide him over. Normally, one wouldn't think that a big brawny firefighter would be a match to a cockapoo but Zoey had seen something tender in Hud that maybe no one but she and Joanne saw. Zoey had been right, too. Another match made in doggy heaven. Her success rate was astronomical, but she didn't like to brag.

"Hi, guys." Zoey left her display. "What can I help you with?"

"Hud needs help." Joanne eyed Hud with a look of pity and patted his biceps. "He always does with the ladies."

"Hey!" Hud protested, but he grinned at Joanne.

He didn't look like the type to ever have trouble with the ladies, unless the trouble included kicking them out of his bed. That might be a problem, she could see.

"Oh no, is Coco not doing well? What's wrong?" Zoey asked.

"I don't like that name, by the way." He ignored the question and scowled in Joanne's direction. "Why do you get to name my dog?"

"Because I have better taste than you do." Joanne batted her eyelashes at him.

"Who says? Rachel is a great name."

"Your childhood addiction to *Friends* and uber-crush on Rachel is rearing its ugly head again."

"So what? She's hot."

"Rachel is a great name for a woman, not so much for a dog. Think of it as a best friend's right. I get to name your dog so you don't look stupid calling her in every night. *Rachel! Rachel!* People are going to think you lost your woman again."

"And Coco is not going to make me sound dumb? Face it. You're trying to take away my man card."

Zoey cleared her throat. Sometimes it felt like people didn't notice she was still standing there. Sometimes that worked for her. Other times, like now, not so much.

Joanne turned to her. "Hud is going to need a few more things. Where are the fancy collars?"

Zoey led her to the right aisle and Joanne flitted around, picking blingy collars in pink and heart-shaped name tags. Hud grumbled as he let her pick out everything and put it in the basket he carried. Joanne had good taste. When Zoey rang him up, Hud had spent three figures and almost made up for Zoey's craptastic Monday. He pulled out his wallet, extracted his American Express and threw Joanne a look that only a best friend could get away with. But when they left the store, they were both laughing and smiling as she put her arm through his.

"Have a great day, guys!" Zoey wasn't sure they'd heard her.

She'd finished rearranging the cat sock display and called it a win when she thought she smelled smoke. She carefully went around every aisle, sniffing in every corner. Bringing in her dogs would have been handy today. They'd smell a fire two miles away. Annie slept calmly and surely would sleep through Armageddon. Zoey turned down the music piping through the store in the background so she could concentrate and smell better. But it wasn't until she saw Fred from Fred's Auto Repair running outside and then back into his shop with his arms thrown up in the air like a crazy person that she thought to go outside. The acrid and strong smell of fire was much stronger there and it felt as though a stone lodged in her throat. Pimp Your Pet was in an older strip mall in town at the bottom of Wildfire Ridge.

They hadn't had a wildfire there in years, and Zoey prayed they wouldn't have one now. Jill had her brand-new business on the ridge, and she and Sam were building a home there. This could be a disaster. Zoey walked outside to get a better view of the ridge and saw black smoke and flames rising out of the dumpster ten feet to the side of the last building. Customers and shop-keepers were standing nearby, simply watching. Fingers cupped over mouths. Jaws dropped. Hands to chests. Smoke anywhere during wildfire season struck dread in every resident.

And Hud had been here no less than thirty minutes ago. Amazing timing, Monday. Way to go.

"Has anyone called 911?" Zoey called as she pulled out her cell phone.

"Yes, Fred did," Susie, owner of the nearby Hair-Em Salon, said. "I hope they get here quickly. The flames could lick the side of the building soon."

"You know this is happening all over town, don't you?" This was from one of Susie's clients, hair covered in foils. "Some rabble-rouser is setting fires in dumpsters. Getting his kicks that way."

The next second, Zoey heard sirens in the distance.

The Fortune Fire Department descended on them, engine truck, ladder truck and the whole enchilada. It didn't take them long to get the fire under control with their powerful hose. But the smell of smoke and soot, Zoey realized, would probably hang in the air for days if not weeks.

It was official. Next week she would start her week on a Tuesday.

Ryan had taken care of the last-minute press conference, only to get a phone call late in the afternoon from the city's arson investigator, Lou Walker.

"We had another dumpster fire. I won't know conclusively for a few more days, but found a similar rag which could have carried the accelerant."

Ryan feared that this arsonist would escalate and wind up eventually setting the ridge on fire. So far the fires, which had started a month ago, had been small. All easily contained by the FFD, and all with some type of accelerant involved. All in dumpsters. Ryan suspected a teenage firebug, and so did Lou, but they couldn't be certain. The number one reason for arson was to cover up a crime but these fires, several in neighborhood park dumpsters, another in a school's dumpster, hadn't fit that profile.

"Where was the fire this time?"

"The Candy Lane strip mall downtown."

Ryan gripped the edge of his desk. That was the location of Zoey's shop. "Everyone okay?"

"Our guys put it out in record time, so yeah. No damage to the building either. But I don't have to tell you this could work out to be a serious problem. The politics of this deal are all yours. And the mayor's. I've already given him a heads-up."

"Yeah, thanks." As usual. He scrubbed a hand down his face.

Though it might not have sounded like it, he did appreciate the alert on the latest. When news got out that they had an arsonist on the loose, Ryan would have a major headache dealing with the small-town press and locals. But, as Lou mentioned, that was his problem. Always. It was his job and that of his deputies to investigate and follow leads. So far, they had nothing. He hoped they'd catch the arsonist before he did any real damage or, God forbid, hurt someone.

He hung up with Lou and shifted gears. Time to end his day. One of the few advantages of being the sheriff was the mostly regular office hours. He usually got out of here around six in the evening. It gave him time for his pet projects, like the fixer-upper he'd bought and, with Sam's occasional help, was working to renovate, and also the group for at-risk kids he and Aidan McIntire, one of his deputies, had formed in partnership with the Boys and Girls Club. Also gave him time to hit the gym, and theoretically plenty of time to date someone, at least according to his sister, his mother and Renata, his admin.

But given the way his short engagement to Lauren had gone down in flames last year, he wasn't interested in a commitment again anytime soon.

He filled the downtime hours fine, which was preferable to the overtime shifts he'd pulled at the Oakland PD. There he'd never had a moment's peace or a minute to himself.

Renata was locking up her desk. "Breaking any hearts tonight?"

"Nope," he said for the eleventh hundredth time. "Looking for a dog."

"A dog?" Her forehead wrinkled. "I thought you couldn't have pets in your apartment."

"It's not *my* dog."

He'd checked and the stolen property report had been filed by Aidan. But Ryan knew that a stolen dog was very much at the bottom of the list of the department's list of priorities.

She put her hand to her heart. "Looking for someone else's dog in your spare time. Maybe Trudy is right . You ought to be canonized."

He shook his head. "Save it."

Refusing to accept his impending sainthood, Ryan walked her out, then climbed in his Jeep and made the drive home to his apartment to change and lose the gun. He hit the pavement thirty minutes later, having planned his jogging route in advance. He lived a mile from Zoey, and figured he could start on his street, circle up and end up on Zoey's street. As he jogged, he looked for dogs the size of ponies. Figured Boo would stick out, although if someone had stolen him they would likely be hiding him for a while, if they were still in Fortune.

As a kid, he and Jill had owned beagles, each of which got out about once a month. Usually the dog was located a few streets away, following a track only it could smell. Just once had they not found a dog immediately, because a kid had taken him back into his yard for a play date. As the evening hour had marched on, Jill had a meltdown, certain the dog would never be found again. Eventually they'd received a call. But Ryan always thought it had helped that their house phone number was on a collar that also read Reward.

Jogging past Zoey's house, he noticed her car in the driveway. He'd have to ask her whether the Great Dane's collar had her phone number and the rather important word, *Reward*. Personally, he thought it prevented some greedy people from keeping random pets for their own.

One could hope.

With no sight of Boo anywhere, he ran another mile just for kicks then headed back. Sweaty and out of breath, Ryan slowed and began the cooldown. He fished for his cell phone in his pocket and dialed Zoey.

"Hello?"

He could hear a dog yipping and yarking in the background. Was it too much to hope…? "Did he show up?"

"Of course he didn't show up. Someone stole him. Quiet, Indie!" she said. "I'm trying to talk on the phone."

As if the dog understood, there was sudden silence on the other end. Impressive.

He took another breath of cool evening air. "Thought there was a chance of, you know, buyer's remorse."

Zoey huffed. "Whoever has him won't want to bring him back once they realize what a wonderful and well-behaved dog he is."

"Did his collar have any information on it?"

"It had the store's phone number."

"Anything else?" He took another breath. "Like, maybe offering a reward?"

"No, but he's chipped in case he gets brought into a shelter. I should have thought of adding a reward. People are so greedy sometimes." Her voice lowered. "Why are you calling me right now? You sound…busy."

"What do you mean?"

"You sound a little out of breath and…um, maybe you should get back to it."

Huh? It took him a minute to realize Zoey thought he'd called her right after he'd had sex, and he laughed out loud. Everyone in this town thought he had far more game than he did.

He tried not to snort. "I went for a run."

"Oh, sorry. I just thought you sounded like…like…"

"Like I just had sex?"

Dead silence on the other end of the line. He could almost hear her pets' breathing. After a moment, she finally spoke. "I didn't mean…what I meant was that you…"

"Just so you know, right after I have sex the only thing I'm thinking about is *more* sex. There could be a nuclear attack and I'd still be thinking about sex."

"I'm sorry. I didn't mean to imply you'd have sex with someone and then call me. Why would you be thinking about me and sex at the same time?" If it was possible for a voice to blush, Zoey's just had. "What I mean is…oh my god… I just realized it's still Monday."

He had no idea what that meant but this might be a good time to stop talking about sex with someone he'd never have sex with. *Inappropriate, Sheriff Idiot.*

"Never mind. I kept my eye out for Boo on my run and no sign of him anywhere. Listen, did you make that list I asked you to make?"

"Yes, I've got the names of people who came to look at Boo but I really don't think any one of them would take him. They're all good people, and after seeing his size they all pretty much agreed with me it wasn't a good match."

"You're telling me no one was upset?"

"That I didn't think they were a good fit to Boo? No.

I think my reputation in town precedes me. Everyone knows I'll find them a perfect pet. They simply have to be patient."

Of course he understood the theory that Zoey could choose a person's kindred animal. And in the case where the kindred animal itself couldn't be a pet, she found the next best choice. Jill swore by her friend's expertise. He wouldn't know. Once, he'd asked Zoey what his kindred animal was, wanting to play along. It was a good party game and for someone who normally hated any kind of attention, Zoey did well with it. But when he'd asked she'd simply avoided his gaze and found something else to do. He hadn't pressed the issue. She usually behaved as if she had no time for him. Besides, what if his kindred animal was a rat and she was afraid to tell him? He didn't think so, but what the hell did he know?

"Someone may have wanted the dog. Even if they weren't a good match. We have to start somewhere."

"You're right."

"I'll come by the shop tomorrow to get your list."

"Why are you the one helping? Aren't you too busy with other sheriffing, um, stuff?"

How to tell her that with a possible firebug on the loose, his small staff of deputies would have their hands full. This case would languish unless someone wanted to work it in their free time. That someone would be him, because…well, *Zoey.*

"Nah. Consider me your one-man task force."

"Oh." A slight pause, then Zoey spoke again. "Thank you."

"Good. See you tomorrow."

He hung up and wondered what the hell was wrong with him. He was really looking forward to tomorrow.

Chapter 4

By Friday, Zoey was out of her mind with worry. Corky was nearly despondent, searching the house and yard for his giant friend. Whining and snorting at the gate, as if he could still catch Boo's smell but had no way of following. Ryan hadn't come by the shop on Tuesday or any other day that week, but she didn't blame him. He was busy with the city's business. She figured he'd only agreed to help her because she was Jill's best friend.

By now, she'd called everyone she knew to call. All the pet rescue organizations she'd worked with over the years. All her connections over social media. On Ryan's advice, she'd been over the list once, twice, and maybe a dozen times. Names and phone numbers of people who had expressed interest in adopting Boo. Only six names on the list, and only one from out of town. She thought about calling them herself, but what could she say?

"Did you by any chance steal Boo?"

Who would admit that? Either way, she was certain no one would appreciate being accused of such a terrible crime. Personally, she'd be highly offended. It was one thing to want something desperately. She could definitely relate to that feeling. But it was quite another to take it and to hell with the consequences.

At the end of the day, Zoey locked up the store, went home for the feedings and to cheer up her pets.

"Don't worry, Corky—we'll get him back."

Corky squealed. That meant, "I have full faith in you."

Tonight she had her standing dinner invitation at her aunt and uncle's house. Given that her two best friends in the world were now in firmly committed relationships, Zoey had all the social time in the world and a free calendar most every Friday night. It was sad. Zoey secured the pets inside safely behind their dog-proof gates, since she didn't plan on being long, and she walked the three blocks to her aunt's home.

Plum trees dotted the streets in this older and established neighborhood, flanking the substantial cracks in sidewalks. The roots of some trees had come up through the concrete years ago on their quest for water.

Her Tia Gloria's home stood framed in the soft glowing light of impending sunset. Home. She'd grown up here. Had her first skinned knee on this very sidewalk. She'd had her first broken heart inside these cozy walls. Her prom dates had picked her up here and played twenty questions (otherwise known as The Inquisition) with Tio Raul. She'd still be living here if a couple of years ago she hadn't decided that in order to be a real grown-up she had to move out of her childhood home. Spread her wings and all that.

She'd managed to get a few blocks away, which in her book was progress. The Castillo-Lopez family was large and tight and Zoey had been homesick for weeks. But now she'd been away from home for three years and managed just fine, thank you very much. She had far more animals now than her aunt and uncle had ever allowed her to have, or even approved of, which was the privilege of being a grown-up.

"*Querida*!" Tia greeted Zoey at the door. "Just in time. The rice and chicken are almost ready."

"Ten more minutes for the rice," Tio called from the kitchen.

Seemed it was always ten more minutes. But Tio's Spanish rice and chicken were always worth waiting for. Tia did all of the cleaning and most of the cooking but this was his one dish and a favorite of Zoey's.

"Any news about Boo?" Tia walked with Zoey to the living room, where photos of Zoey growing up adorned the fireplace mantel.

One would have thought they'd also have photos of Veronica, and there was one photo of Zoey around age five with her parents. But the rest of the photos of Veronica, as she blossomed and eventually became a full-blown movie star, Tia kept in scrapbooks. She was Mami's older sister by fifteen years, so to say she was proud was an understatement. But she'd always understood that the last thing Zoey needed to see at home were photos of the glamorous Veronica. She and Zoey were so different at times it was difficult to believe they were related.

"Nothing yet." Zoey took a seat on the flower-print couch. Same one she'd sat on for years.

Her aunt and uncle had given everything to family and their business. Now that they'd semiretired and let Zoey take over running the pet store, they had more time but the same amount of money. They took great care with every penny and Zoey respected that. It was the reason she hadn't been allowed to have more than one pet of her own at the house.

"Have you heard anything from your *mami*?"

Tia still referred to Veronica as Mami. Even if clearly Tia had been her actual *mami*, Zoey called Veronica her mother simply out of respect. It was just a nickname and didn't mean what it should to Zoey. To her, Veronica wasn't a soft place to fall.

"I got a package just the other day with some face cream. She asked after you and Tio."

"How kind."

"The face cream or asking about you?"

"Not the face cream." Tia grimaced. "I hope you're not thinking…"

"What? Am I crazy?"

"Because you're not even thirty. Plenty of time to worry about wrinkles."

"If ever. You never worried about that sort of thing."

"Well, I wasn't the beautiful one. That was Veronica."

"No, no, *mi amor*." Tio walked into the living room. "I married the beautiful sister."

"Raul." Tia waved her hand dismissively and blushed like a schoolgirl.

Oh, to have that. Zoey wanted a man to see her as the beautiful one, the way Tio saw his wife. Tia wasn't classically pretty, but the only thing that mattered was the way he saw her. And Zoey wanted someone to see her for who she was inside. *Maybe someday.*

"Is the rice ready?" Zoey asked.

"Yes…" Tio said.

Zoey and Tia rose.

"In ten more minutes," Tio continued.

Zoey plopped back down. This was the family joke. The rice always needed ten more minutes. If it cooked too long, it absorbed all the tomato sauce. Not long enough and it was too soupy.

"Do you have a date to the party yet?" Tia cocked her head to the side, all innocent-like.

"You know she doesn't have a date," Tio said. "Has she asked me to check him out? No. Of course she doesn't have a date."

Right. Zoey hadn't ever asked Tio to check out her dates, and since moving out she'd used the benefit of having her own home to make her own choices. Which hadn't worked out that well, come to think of it. Her last boyfriend nearly two years ago had been a piece of work. He'd used Zoey's kindness against her, borrowing hundreds of dollars he desperately needed to buy medical insurance, he claimed, then promptly leaving town. The boyfriend before him had claimed he loved small-town life and Fortune. Then he'd picked up and moved to Los Angeles with little explanation of why he'd changed his mind.

Yep. She sure could pick 'em. "Not yet. I had a date last Sunday. I don't think it's going to work out, though."

Best not to mention that her date had been skeeved out by all her pets. Tia already thought that Zoey should have fewer animals and make room instead for a man and, someday, children. But what kind of mother-to-be would give up on her animals? Each one of them had required rescuing at one time or another and she'd been there for them. She wasn't ever going to abandon them.

"Someone will come along." Tia patted Zoey's hand. "You still have a couple of weeks."

"She's a beauty, inside and out, this one. Any man should be so lucky as to marry her someday," Tio said as he walked back to the kitchen.

While that was good to hear, this was the man who had mostly raised her talking. If Jill was right, and she was more often than Zoey cared to admit, she was going to have to put herself out there. Buy sexy lingerie. Learn how to flirt. Read Cosmo or a book about sex. After many years of working hard to blend into backgrounds, she was somehow supposed to call attention to herself to get a man. Attention she still didn't feel comfortable receiving, especially if it was based on her looks. Sometimes that kind of attention could get out of hand. Fast. It could accidentally come from a man you weren't trying to impress, while the man whose attention you wanted didn't even notice.

After dinner and a movie with her folks, Zoey walked home in the soft ebbing light of a long summer evening. The moon was bright and full, fighting for top billing with the slowly setting sun.

Give it up, sun. The moon is here.

Zoey loved the moon, which made her the odd one among her closest friends. Her friends preferred the sun. She also liked rainy days instead of the bright, burning heat waves of the summer. They didn't see rain often enough in Fortune Valley. She loved the rain so much that she'd written *I love you* on the windowsill of her childhood bedroom, where the raindrops occasionally touched if she opened her window wide enough to let them in.

But Zoey was different from her friends in another, more disconcerting way. She was the only one of her friends whose mother was a movie star. A distinction she didn't particular appreciate and one she tried not to think about most days. And after that last visit, when the director had been inappropriate, then suggested Zoey play Veronica's daughter in a small movie role, Zoey didn't want to go back. She'd never told her mother about the director's indiscretion because Veronica would have probably made some flimsy excuse for his behavior.

Zoey turned at the corner of her street and spied a familiar looking Jeep in her driveway. Ryan sat on the top step of her stoop, long legs splayed out, arms stretched between them. A cardboard box sat next to him. It took everything in her not to stop and simply gawk at his solid body sitting in front of her house as if waiting for her. And on a Friday night. Didn't he have a date or… something? His dark blond hair caught a glint of the moonlight as he bent toward the box. It was too long, she realized, curling at the neckline as if he didn't put that much stock in his appearance either.

A while ago while they were working together at the coffee shop in town, The Drip, Jill had devised a complicated rating scale of good-looking men she referred to as the Chris Scale. It was based on all the famous Chris men: Evans, Hemsworth, Pratt. Zoey didn't know how to tell Jill, but her brother Ryan blew the scale. He was off the charts, but Zoey imagined Jill couldn't see that. Ryan shoved a hand through his hair then held up his wristwatch to the porch light. Still, he hadn't noticed her. She knew she had that way about her. Quiet. She reminded herself that she wouldn't ask Ryan to be her date so she didn't have to be nervous. He was going to help her find Boo. She picked up her pace, emerging from the shadows, and he turned toward her with an easy smile.

Then the box barked.

Ryan put his hand in it and came out with a puppy. Its tiny pink tongue licked Ryan's face.

"Look what I found."

Zoey fairly ran the rest of the way. Inside the box were four irresistibly cute black-and-white puppies. One had a black patch over one eye. They looked too young, six to seven weeks, and barely old enough to be separated from their mother.

"Oh, where did you come from, babies?" She took a puppy, upon closer inspection a girl, and brought it to her face. "You're adorable, you know that?"

"Found them on the side of the road three miles out of town. The box had Free to Good Home written on it. Seems someone abandoned them."

Her heart seized in the dark way it did whenever she heard of an animal being hurt or abused.

"Who would abandon you?" She spoke to the third puppy, trying desperately to climb out of the box and join the others.

"I have no idea, but I knew you could find good homes for them. I couldn't just leave them there."

She rubbed her cheek against the soft fur. "Thank you. I'll take them to work with me tomorrow. I have a short list of already pre-approved homes waiting for a puppy. I doubt they'll last till lunchtime."

"Unless you decide to keep one." He winked.

Oh, wow, he really shouldn't *wink*. It gave him a devastatingly boyish look along with that one hundred percent strong alpha male presence. Then there were the dimples. Like a double whammy to the heart.

She shook her head and forced her mind back to his suggestion. But Zoey had reached a sad truth a few years ago. She alone couldn't save all the animals. It was why she worked with rescue agencies and did fostering. Her attention was spread thin enough with the animals she had. Heck, she'd lost one possibly due to being spread too thin. Responsible pet ownership was one of her core beliefs.

"I can't. A puppy is too much work, and I already have three pets. Four if you count Boo." She picked up the fourth puppy and snuggled both of the ones in her arms against her chest.

"Right," Ryan said, ducking to avoid his puppy's efforts to make out with him. What a smart little dog. "I would take one, but—"

"I know. You live in an apartment."

"Plus, I still don't know my kindred animal. Are you ever going to match me up with a pet?" He gave her a lazy smile.

Oh, geez. Far too embarrassed to reveal his kindred animal, she'd been skillfully avoiding that for years. Plus, his wasn't a pet. It was a wild animal.

"No point in doing that until you move from the apartment." One point and the save for Zoey!

"Guess you're right." He stood and met her gaze. "But someday you'll tell me."

"Y-yes. Sure I will."

Someday, when he was safely in a committed relationship. Then she'd tell him that they both had the same kindred animal, and they'd have a good long laugh. She, of course, was a mama bear. No surprise to anyone who knew her. Ryan was a grizzly bear. Large and protective. And she and Ryan were the perfect match, if one were simply talking kindred animals. Which they were not.

The whole kindred animal thing was silly, she understood, and a good icebreaker. Zoey was simply good at matching people with animals. Her gift. And she and Ryan, far from being a perfect match in real life, were about as different as two people could be. He was comfortable in crowds, talked easily and confidently with people, and had an ease about him that she envied. Everywhere he went, people gave him all their attention. Ryan was a born leader.

He was a little like the sun.

"Help you inside with these?" Ryan picked up the box and balanced his wriggling puppy by carrying him like a football.

Zoey opened the front door and Ryan quirked a brow. "You don't lock your door?"

"I just went to my aunt's house one block down."

"Do me a favor and start locking your door. All the time."

It sounded like an order. He'd say the same to Jill and Zoey realized that, so why did her heart skip a beat?

"Um, okay," she said because, c'mon, he'd brought her *puppies.*

Worse, he was right. She had precious property in her home and should be more cautious, even if she was just down the street. The fact that she lived in a safe neighborhood in a small town obviously didn't mean that a criminal hadn't taken something valuable from her.

No sooner had they walked in the door than their greeting committee welcomed them with barks, yips and snorts. They knew she'd brought someone furry into the home and they were naturally curious.

"Calm down, guys," Zoey said, trying to keep one puppy from wiggling out of her arms. "We've got company."

Ryan set the box down and took the second puppy from her. She gathered towels and warmed them in the microwave as Indie, Bella and Corky pressed their noses against the doggy gate. The poor puppies would be lonely and missing the warmth of their mother. She grabbed a large bowl and filled it with water. The puppies went to town, their little tails wagging, each trying to shove the other out of the way.

"Hey, I'm sorry," Ryan said.

"Don't worry. I can handle this. I'll keep them in my bathroom tonight so that the others can't get to them. They'll be safe."

"That's not what I meant. I mean I'm sorry I didn't come by the shop on Tuesday."

"You probably got tied up."

"Yeah, I've got a lot going on but I always make room for you. You know that."

"Sure. I'm one of Jill's best friends. She'd probably brain you if you were mean to me."

He chuckled. "News flash. She hasn't brained me in years. And you're my friend, too."

The way he said those gentle words sent a warm tingle down her spine. Yes, they were friends but they had never spent much time together. At least, not alone.

They were alone now, and if not for the puppies, Zoey might have freaked out about that. Here was this incredibly handsome, wonderfully built single man, in her home on a Friday night when he could be anywhere else.

With anyone else.

"You have that list for me?" He looked up from where he squatted next to the puppies.

"Yes. I'll get it." She went to pull the list out of her backpack. "I thought of everyone."

His fingers brushed against hers as he took the list, and just that simple touch elicited a deep pull of longing in her belly.

Don't be ridiculous. I'm not going to crush on him again. I used to dream about what it would be like to be kissed by Ryan Davis, but that was years ago and I got over him.

It's just that he was being so kind. He could have left when she wasn't home instead of waiting for her. He should have rushed out after dropping off the puppies. But he was still here and hanging out. Helping her. The much younger Zoey would have taken this and imagined all types of scenarios which in the end all meant he was secretly in love with her.

"I think I'll go ahead and set them up now."

He picked up all four puppies at once. "Where to, boss?"

Was there anything more attractive than a handsome man wrangling puppies in his big and capable arms? If there was, Zoey didn't know about it. She was forced to lead him into her bedroom and the master bathroom adjoining. Thank goodness she still kept her home as clean as Tia had raised her to do. Zoey couldn't cook anything but sandwiches and macaroni and cheese from a box, but she kept an immaculate house. Lining her tub with the warm towels, she motioned for him to set them down. He did, and then they were both kneeling, elbow to elbow, petting the puppies.

"You should name this one Patches." Ryan rubbed the belly of the puppy with a black spot over one eye. He'd rolled over on his back and closed his eyes in puppy bliss.

"We don't get to name them."

He was so close to her in this tight space that she felt his hot breath fan across her neck. That deep pull in her belly wandered farther south.

"Just for now, I mean. For fun."

Fun? He wanted to have fun. With her.

"Alright, then I'll name this one Bear." She reached for the fluffiest one, bumping Ryan's shoulder. "He seems to be your favorite."

"How did you know?" His brows went up. "He was the one barking the loudest when I found the box. As if he was yelling at me. Daring me to walk away from them."

"What were you doing when you found them?"

"Looking for Boo."

"You were?" And here she had imagined him busy every night with whatever it was he did after work. She never imagined he'd still been searching.

"Sure. I look during the day when I'm around town on business and at night when I'm running."

"You *run*? On purpose?"

He cocked his head and grinned. "Yeah. With no one chasing me."

"You are a sick man, Ryan Davis." She shook her

head, then turned to him to smile and caught him studying her.

"You have no idea." As if he'd done something wrong, he rose to his full height quite suddenly, and she followed suit. But Ryan didn't quite clear the curtain rod over the tub.

She winced. "Are you okay?"

He rubbed the top of his head and all that beautiful thick golden hair. She wanted her hands in his hair, checking to make sure if he was okay, naturally. Also, to know if his hair was coarse or soft to the touch. But she didn't dare.

"I'm good. Maybe that will knock some sense into me." He moved toward the door. "I should go. You're situated."

She didn't want him to leave but couldn't think of a single reason he should stay. And if she asked him to stay, he'd certainly want to go. Immediately. He wouldn't want to encourage any more of her silly crushes on him. Ryan was too kind, too good to lead her on. And she was far too smart to fool herself. Far too wise to take what she wanted without considering the consequences. In this case, there would be a broken heart.

She closed the bathroom door and followed him to the front door. "Thank you again."

"What are you doing tomorrow?"

"Besides finding homes for these puppies? Working at the shop."

"I'll come by the store tomorrow after I call the people on the list you gave me."

"What are you going to ask them?" She couldn't

imagine any way that wouldn't wind up sounding like an outright accusation.

"You let me handle that."

He stepped outside, confidence in every easy move he made. She watched from the window as he strode to his Jeep, climbed inside and drove off.

She hitched in an uneven breath. It was all going to be okay. She wouldn't get all caught up in him simply because they were going to spend a little time together. For Ryan, this was all clearly in the pursuit of justice. But she was a little worried because Ryan was such a good guy and he meant safety to her. She knew Ryan would never touch a woman without knowing she wanted him to. He'd never take advantage of Zoey, and even if there were two sides to that coin, she appreciated that.

The puppies yipped from behind the bathroom door. "I'm coming, babies."

She had to calm the puppies down and then reassure Indie, Bella and Corky that they hadn't been forgotten.

Chapter 5

"Please, Mommy? *Please*?" the little girl whined. She was petting Bear with adoration in her eyes.

It had been a bit of a mistake to bring the puppies to work, as most were spoken for. But she couldn't leave them unattended all day. They were babies who required constant care. She'd started alerting everyone on her special puppy list last night. Most were thrilled and excited to finally get their puppy and the first owner had dropped by and made her choice when Zoey opened the doors this morning. The second came shortly after, and now only Patches and Bear remained.

"No! I told you no more puppies! The last one destroyed our house," the mother said, yanking her daughter's arm and pulling her away.

The child winced and so did Zoey. She wouldn't have let that woman adopt a puppy if her life depended on it.

"I'm sorry, honey," Zoey said softly to the girl. "These already have forever homes."

"Then *why* would you bring them in here to *torture* the children?" the mother asked, her anger overshadowing everything.

Zoey blinked. "I… I…had to…"

When people got ugly and up in her personal space like this, Zoey lost her words. This was her store, and part of her adoption process included outfitting the families with everything they would need to get started. Food, bed, collar, leash, a Pimp Your Pet tee. On her dime. But the words wouldn't come. Just then the bell over the door chimed and Ryan stepped inside. He saved her from talking, as the woman dropped everything, turned into someone less hostile and flashed him a toothy smile.

Zoey was going to go out on a limb and guess the woman was a single mom.

"Hello, Sheriff Davis," she said with saccharine sweetness. "How are you today?"

"Good, thanks." He whipped off his aviator shades and propped them on his head. "And you?"

She placed a hand on her daughter's shoulder. "Chelsea was impressed with the talk you gave at her school. She wants to go into law enforcement now."

"Is that right?" Ryan smiled down at the little girl.

"You have a big gun. And my mommy is single," Chelsea said.

Zoey choked back a laugh and this meant biting her lower lip so hard it hurt.

The mother laughed and tossed back her long blond hair. "This isn't the time or place, sweetheart, though it is true."

"You all have a good day," Ryan said, moving past them, clearly unfazed.

The woman rushed out of the store without buying a thing.

"How are our puppies today?" He came behind the register and bent low to pet Patches until Bear pushed him out of the way with his heftier size.

"Two have already been adopted and just Patches and Bear are left. Their owners are coming as soon as they can."

"You work fast."

"Well, I had a list." She cleared her throat. "Any luck with Boo?"

"Not yet." He rose, cuddling Bear. "But don't give up."

"Of course not."

She never would. Not until she at least knew Boo's fate. She could only hope he'd somehow wound up in a good home. She told herself every night that he had. It was the only way she could sleep.

"Sheriff Davis." Mrs. Richardson, a store regular, approached. "I'm glad you're here."

"Just checking in with all the business owners about the dumpster fire," he said, putting Bear down. The puppy whined in misery. "It's important that we get as much information as possible on who may have been in the area."

"I have a very serious problem to bring to your attention. My neighbor's poor dog barks all night long. His cruel owners leave him outdoors every night. Now, other than giving them a stern talking-to, shouldn't there be a law against this, gosh durnit?"

Ryan didn't seem to mind the complaint. Instead,

he moved to the side to have a conversation with Mrs. Richardson. A rather one-sided conversation, as he mostly nodded in places. Did residents bother him like this about every little thing?

As it happened, Zoey agreed with Mrs. Richardson, but on the other hand, some of her customers were whispering that there was a firebug in town. An arsonist setting fires way too close to wildfire season. Poor Ryan probably had a whole lot on his plate, although some of it might seem like a nuisance to law enforcement. She guessed this was what he got for working in their small town. But everyone clearly adored Ryan. The entire town had thrown him a parade when got home from Iraq. All Zoey remembered about that day was Ryan looking miserable and Jill next to him, his cheerleader, smiling and waving from the antique car.

Zoey didn't know too much about how Ryan had made the decision to come back to Fortune a few years ago. Jill said their parents had begged him to relocate closer to them, but in the end it was the need for a new sheriff that got him back to the south Bay Area. He'd won the election in a landslide. Zoey guessed that was in large part to the fact that he was literally their hometown hero.

She rang up a few sales and glanced at her phone. No calls, texts or messages. If she had to hang on to one of the puppies an extra day, she wouldn't mind at all. Maybe she could get Ryan to come over and help her...

Her store phone rang. "Pimp Your Pet. How can I help you?"

"Hi, Zoey. I got your message." It was Yvonne Cruz, who had asked a year ago to be matched with the perfect puppy.

"Your forever pet is waiting for you," Zoey said.

"About that. I can't. I'm sorry."

"What? Why?"

Sometimes it happened. People got tired of waiting and went elsewhere. She couldn't blame them.

"We're pregnant," Yvonne gushed. "And right now the thought of a puppy is just too overwhelming. I feel like I wouldn't be able to give it as much attention as he deserves."

This was exactly why Zoey screened her adoptive parents carefully. Yvonne would have been a responsible pet owner. Too bad.

"I understand." She hung up with Yvonne, grateful she'd been honest.

Zoey had another idea. Maybe Jill would take a puppy, even though she and Sam were living in a trailer on Wildfire Ridge while they built their dream home nearby. But they already had Shakira the rabbit and Fubar their dog in tight quarters. Maybe Carly, her other best friend…

"I'm here! Where's my baby? Let me see!"

Mrs. Smith, a widow who had patiently waited a year for Zoey to find her the right puppy, walked inside.

"Perfect!" Zoey sang out. "Come see who we have here."

Mrs. Smith got to immediately snuggling with Bear, who really was a pushy little guy.

Done with his resident outreach, Ryan came back and picked up Patches for a cuddle. "I'm kind of fond of this one."

"You get to choose," Zoey said to Mrs. Smith. "And then you get to pick out a bed, food, collar and leash, all paid for by Pimp Your Pet."

"That's so generous of you." Mrs. Smith smiled and gazed at Zoey from behind her lowered glasses. "All from the same litter?

"Guessing that," Ryan said, as Patches licked his face. "Found them on the side of the road."

"Who would do such a thing?" Mrs. Smith said.

Zoey would have to guess a monster, but she didn't answer because she was watching Patches nestle in Ryan's arms. It was possibly the most attractive sight she'd ever seen in her life.

"Actually," Zoey said. "They're both available now. The other person can no longer take a puppy."

Ryan quirked a brow. She wished he didn't live in an apartment. Would it be crazy…no. He had too much to do without adding a puppy to the mix. But she trusted him to be a good pet owner. Watching him with the puppies she'd seen his tender side and it clearly ran deep.

"Actually," Mrs. Smith said. "If you think it's alright, I hate to separate them. They've been together all of their short lives."

"You would take both of them?"

It would be ideal, but most owners weren't ready for two. Zoey had always disliked the idea of separating siblings. As an only child, she'd never understood her friends complaining about their brothers and sisters. It would have been wonderful to have a built-in friend. A protector and cheerleader.

"I certainly have the room. And now I have the time, too." Mr. Smith had been gone for a year. She put Bear down and took Patches from Ryan. "Aren't you precious?"

Within a few minutes, Zoey had helped Mrs. Smith choose everything she would need, including a big box of training pads. It was a few hundred dollars' worth of merchandise and if Tio and Tia knew she did this occasionally, they wouldn't be too happy. But somehow Zoey always managed to make it up in sales. The happy new owners spread the word about the friendly pet store in town. Word of mouth was powerful and her best marketing tool.

Ryan helped carry out the boxes to Mrs. Smith's car while Zoey watched from inside, waving. Another doggy match made in heaven. Why did she feel like crying? She bit her lower lip till it felt like it might bleed, but it was no use. It only took Ryan walking back in the store, his furrowed brow questioning, to have her dangerously close to overflowing.

"What's wrong?" When she didn't answer, he lowered his head and peered from under long lashes. "You're going to miss them."

She pressed her lips together and nodded, not trusting herself to speak. Stupid emotions. Her resolution earlier this year was to be tougher and not so softhearted. So far it wasn't going well.

She wasn't pathetic.

No way.

But she had to be tougher.

"Hey." Ryan drew her into his arms. "Aw, Zoey."

She wound up pressed against his hard chest, trying to hold the tears back. And, oh my lord, he smelled so good. He felt even better, his arms strong and tightening his hold around her waist. A heat spread through her, wrapping around the backs of her knees and weakening them till they felt like dust. Suddenly she forgot to cry because she was distracted by another more intense emotion. Attraction, pure and simple. No longer a simple crush on a good-looking man. She didn't want to recognize that feeling, but there it was. Lust. Need and desire. Also a hefty amount of tenderness and affection for him. For the way he'd saved the puppies and loved on them even for a short time. For the way he was oblivious to the women who fawned over him.

She pulled back, her fingers skimming up his long-sleeved white button-up, feeling steely biceps just to touch him one last time. "I'm okay."

With one finger, he tipped her chin up. "Don't make me sorry I brought you the puppies."

"No, of course not. I knew I had to let them go. It's just…tough to say goodbye."

"Especially for a soft touch like you."

Yeah, that was her. Soft. But she didn't want to be anymore. She was tired of that Zoey and now wanted to be stronger and not just when it came to animals. The new and improved Zoey should have told the mean mother not to wrench her daughter's arm the way she had. Not to speak in a voice that scared animals and children. Should have told her that parents, especially mothers, should protect their children. Not feed them to the wolves.

The door chimed again and who should it be but the return of Mean Mom. Her gaze slid down Ryan's body as he continued to hold Zoey without moving, and her upper lip curled.

"I forgot the cat food."

Zoey pulled out of his arms, guilty she'd given Mean Mom the wrong impression. It wouldn't be fair to Ryan, even though she hoped he wouldn't be attracted to this woman. Still, there was no accounting for taste.

"This weekend." Ryan pointed as he backed up to the door.

"This weekend?"

"I'll pick you up and we'll go check out a local breeder. Pay them a visit."

"You think they took Boo?"

It hadn't even occurred to her. There used to be a few breeders in town, but there was only one breeder left that she knew about. Backyard breeders raised pure-breds and sold them for fifteen hundred a puppy or more. Zoey was a huge Adopt, Don't Shop advocate but not everyone in town was willing to wait for the right match.

"No, but I checked out all the people who'd wanted to adopt Boo and been turned down. Nothing." He squinted just before he slipped the shades back on. "I know this is a long shot, but maybe they've heard some-thing. Kind of running out of options."

"I see." Zoey wanted to cry all over again. This time for Boo. Would she ever see the big guy again? "Thank you for trying."

"Hey, I haven't given up yet. We'll try this. If noth-ing else, we might get a lead."

A lead. Well, this sounded like detective work. But she figured, as a small-town sheriff, he'd prefer this to some of the other petty stuff he occasionally had to handle. Last week she'd heard Mr. Boris took scissors to Mr. Olaff's lawn, claiming it wasn't perfectly even. Mr. Olaff then took scissors to Mr. Boris's lawn. Mr. Boris called 911.

"Better go check in with Fred at the auto repair. He wants to make sure we're doing everything we can to catch the person who started the fire in your dumpster." He took a step forward. "You didn't see anything that day, did you? Anyone suspicious hanging around outside?"

But that was the day she'd lost Boo. The day Ryan had shown up to help. The day she'd had a delivery of messed-up dog tees and skin cream from her mother.

She wouldn't have noticed if the Unabomber had been loitering.

"It's one of the skateboarders, I'm telling you!" Fred shook his finger. "I've been in this same spot for thirty years and change, and all I can say is every year it gets worse. Littering, even with a dumpster nearby, smoking, god knows what else. I saw that no-good kid, Ethan Larsen, hanging out by the dumpster, pants almost down to his ankles for the love of Pete. Right before the fire."

Ethan was one of the kids Ryan worked with at the Boys and Girls Club. He had been having a tough time since his mother got remarried to a city councilman. Ryan had been trying to reach out to Ethan with small steps but he hadn't gotten very far.

"You sure it was Ethan?" Ryan pressed.

"Absolutely."

"Was he alone?"

"Alone?" Fred scratched his chin. "I think so. Either that or with his best friend."

So much for being absolutely sure. Ethan had no best friends. "What friend?"

"Do I have to do all your work for you?" Fred scowled.

"Thanks for your help, Fred." Ryan nodded and headed out the door.

He'd talked to every shop owner in the strip mall. Not

one other person had seen Ethan in the vicinity, which made Fred's ID increasingly suspect. Ethan was a troubled kid. He'd done a bang-up job of winning friends and influencing people when he tagged the wooden fence on the outskirts of Fortune with a marijuana-plant design. He was a classic teenage vandal, but he didn't strike Ryan as fitting the profile of a pyromaniac.

There were four to five different types of arsonists, and though the most common was arson to cover up a crime there were also pyros who simply got off on setting fires. And the great majority in that category were young Caucasian males. They were of below average to average intelligence, often with difficult home lives. All of which described Ethan, but that didn't mean he was the perp.

Still, he'd keep his eyes open and talk to Ethan next time he saw him.

Chapter 6

"For the last time, I'm *not* going to ask him," Zoey said into the phone.

"But I already did and he's free," Jill said.

"Oh no, you didn't!"

"I didn't ask Ryan to *take* you to the party. I just mentioned there *was* one and wondered by chance if he had any plans. He said he didn't."

Zoey broke out in a sweat. "You are so not helping."

"Look, if you're already going to spend the day together—"

"Looking for Boo!"

"I'm just saying, if there's a lull in the conversation somewhere, you might mention it."

Zoey understood why Jill kept pressing the issue. As a best friend, she was simply doing her duty to get Zoey a passable date and Ryan was more than passable. But

Zoey's sense of pride meant she didn't want him going with her as a favor. She could get her own date. Or not.

"I just don't see the big deal. It would be like going to the party with your big brother," Jill went on.

Zoey couldn't entirely blame Jill for being so clueless. Zoey wanted a date with Ryan to be nothing like going out with a big brother. But Jill had been tied up with Mr. Hot Marine for the past two months. Pretty much oblivious to the world. And to be fair, Zoey had never shared her huge attraction to Ryan with Jill.

"Okay. I said I'd *think* about it."

Zoey hung up with Jill then let the pets out, went through the morning feeding, had her coffee, took a shower and dressed in her coverall denim shorts, pairing them with a short-sleeved tee. She braided her hair so it would be out of her face and wore her reliable Chucks for ease of walking. They'd probably be doing a lot of that today. While she waited for Ryan, she recited over and over the reasons she shouldn't be nervous.

1. I'm not asking him to the anniversary party.

2. He's obviously not interested in me.

3. We might actually find Boo today.

That last one filled her with hope. Maybe tonight she'd be feeding Boo and watching as he and Corky silently judged Indie and Bella for hopping up on Zoey's bed.

When Ryan arrived in his Jeep, dressed casually in jeans that weren't too tight but nevertheless accentuated his great butt, Zoey was primed for him.

She'd psyched herself up to the point where she seriously didn't care that his T-shirt had short sleeves that strained against impressive biceps. Paid zero attention to the sexy tribal tattoo that wound around one biceps.

Also she was completely unaffected by his opening the passenger door for her like a gentleman, and of the fact that if Tio Raul were watching he'd probably award Ryan a second medal of honor.

Yes, Tio and Tia already adored Ryan. Who didn't? He was kind of perfect but in that careless way that made Zoey sense he didn't really try. So as he drove them to the outskirts of Fortune and the few farms left in the area, she concentrated on paying no attention to the fact that the wind coming through his rolled-down window whipped through his hair and gave him a tousled, just-rolled-out-of-bed look.

Yep, she paid no attention at all.

Chapter 7

Ryan pulled on to Monterey Street and glanced at Zoey sitting next to him. She was dressed down as usual, in her short coveralls and Chucks. It was almost as if she worked hard to look plain.

It didn't work. Because Zoey Castillo could never quite accomplish fading into the background. At least, he'd never thought so. The dark-haired, dark-eyed beauty was the kind of woman who he imagined wouldn't look any different the night before than she did waking up in the morning next to her lover.

Her lover. Well, there was a word he didn't ever associate with any of his sister's friends. There was a first time for everything.

"I didn't call ahead, so Max is not expecting us."

"Are they still breeding Great Danes?"

"And goldens. Unfortunately I heard a rumor that

they might be overbreeding." He cleared his throat. "What's new with you?"

"Nothing other than this kidnapping case."

Fail number one.

She wouldn't be volunteering any information on the anniversary party. But Jill had dropped mention of the party in passing.

While it was true that he was a great casual "big brother" date, he also wanted to spend more time with Zoey, and their case was coming to an end. If they had no leads today, he'd run out of options. She would simply have to wait and hope that the person or persons regretted their decision and returned Boo. Or somehow got caught.

And though Jill had warned that he shouldn't start anything up with Zoey unless he was ready to, in her words, "put a ring on it," Jill had encouraged him to ask Zoey about the party. He'd promised to think about it.

But hell no, he wasn't ready to put a ring on anyone. He was soured on the idea of marriage, even if he admired those who got it right. His father the doctor and his mother the scientist had been married for thirty-five years and rarely been apart. They set the bar high, as they tended to do with everything. He'd been born into an overachieving, goal-oriented family and he was no different.

But not long ago, Ryan had come to a realization. Falling in love was not something he could achieve or earn. True love should be given freely and without conditions. And so far, in his case, it seemed to be MIA.

Jill seemed to be on the right track, for which he was grateful. Sam was a good man, a former marine.

He would take care of Jill or die trying. One less thing for Ryan to worry about.

"We haven't really had a chance to talk since the Christmas party at Carly and Levi's," Ryan said.

"I've been busy with the store and stuff."

"Your aunt and uncle are having an anniversary, I hear."

"Um, yeah. Forty years, can you believe it?"

"You got a date for that yet?"

"What?" She turned to face him.

"A date. You know, someone to go with."

"I… I don't have a date but that's okay. I might go alone."

"I'm free that weekend."

"You're probably busy."

They both spoke at once.

He laughed. "No. Want to take me?"

"Why? You want to go?"

"I give great date."

She blinked. "I h-hope Jill didn't talk you into this. Really, I'm okay. I can go alone if I don't find a date. Maybe I'll ask Julian."

Not Julian. Sure, he was a nice guy, but Ryan wasn't sure Julian was good enough for Zoey. Then again it was difficult to picture anyone who would be. He'd heard that Zoey and Julian had been on one date. One. No follow through. It didn't sound like a love match. At this point, it was every man for himself.

The other night when he'd brought over the puppies, he'd felt a connection with Zoey. Strangely, being in that small bathroom with her wrangling puppies was the most fun he'd had on a Fright night in a while. And it had felt oddly intimate somehow. He'd had…thoughts.

Thoughts like how she'd react if he leaned down and kissed her. Just then he'd bonked his head on the shower curtain rod and talked himself out of it.

But he didn't see any harm in taking Zoey on one date. He'd get to spend more time with her, talk over the dognapping case and anything else that might develop.

"You don't want to ask Julian or anyone else. I'm the perfect date. Just ask Carly. I took her to a wedding before she met Levi. I like parties, know how to be a gentleman and I'll even dance if you ask nicely. Did you know I can do a backflip? But I need to have a shot of tequila first."

"You took *Carly* out?"

"Just that once. Yeah, it was no big deal. She was between boyfriends. I was between girlfriends."

She seemed to be mulling it over and what felt like roughly a decade later, finally spoke. "That would be great. If you're sure."

"Wouldn't have offered if I wasn't."

"Thanks, buddy."

He bristled at the friendship designation, wondering why it bothered him. It was accurate.

"No problem. Think nothing of it."

He'd take her on this date, behave himself and that would be the end of it.

Max Pina greeted them at the front door of his modest-sized home on a three-acre parcel of land not far from Ryan's own fixer-upper. Before retiring, Max had worked for the post office. Since then, he'd been breeding purebreds and had settled on Great Danes and golden retrievers. He raised them to eight weeks and then sold them. Some of the goldens were snatched up by programs that trained therapy dogs. It was all a respectable operation and Ryan had no doubt Max was a straight arrow despite the rumor. However, he might know something.

And hell, they had to try. He'd do anything to wipe away that look of anguish in Zoey's deep brown eyes.

"What can I do for you, sheriff?" Max asked. "Surely I didn't get any more noise complaints."

"You got any puppies for sale?" Ryan asked.

At his elbow, Ryan could feel Zoey's gaze trained on him. He wasn't interested in a puppy. It just so happened that Max was a dyed-in-the-wool libertarian who could recite the constitution backwards and forwards. Off duty or not, Ryan wasn't getting on his property without a good reason. He didn't hold it against Max, or anyone else for that matter. Being the sheriff, or any member of law enforcement, carried with it ramifications he'd dealt with for years now. The number-one problem was that some people tended to censor themselves around him, in or out of uniform. A law enforcement label, sheriff or detective, tended to go with you wherever you went, and caused people to clam up.

"Matter of fact, just had a litter four weeks ago. Have to say that four of them are spoken for but I have a runt. Of course, they won't be ready to go for another few weeks."

"That's fine."

Max turned to Zoey. "You here to help him?"

"Yes," Zoey said, playing along.

"Good choice," Max said with a nod as he stepped outside and led them to the side gate of his backyard. "I appreciate you bending your rules about adoption to consider one of mine."

Outside, Max led them to a fenced-in area where they

found an older golden dozing surrounded by five small sleeping puppies. Younger looking than the ones he'd found on the side of the road. As they approached, the mother lifted her head as if to issue a warning. Don't come any closer.

"So sweet," Zoey said, almost reverently. "In the animal kingdom, it's instinctive to protect your own."

"She's always a good mama," Max said. "Fourth litter for her."

As Zoey and Max talked, Ryan casually surveyed the area. He hadn't expected to find anything here and he'd been correct. This day would turn out to be more or less an exercise in showing her that he'd tried. Done his best.

"You heard about Zoey's missing dog?" Ryan asked.

After Zoey explained the situation to Max, the man's eyes narrowed and his scowl deepened. "Sumabitch. Some people. Did you check with all the shelters?"

Zoey nodded. "He's a good dog. Someone knew that."

"Let's hope the idiots are taking good care of him, at least. I stopped breeding Great Danes. Too many health problems."

"If you hear anything, will you let me know?" Ryan asked.

"Sure will." Max turned to Zoey and slipped an arm around her shoulders. "Sorry this happened to you. It's not your fault, you know."

It seemed to be what Zoey needed to hear. She brightened slightly, her brown eyes shimmering.

"What do you think of my runt, sheriff?" Max asked, waving to his litter.

"Need to think on it some more, but he is beautiful."

"Don't think too long."

As they were leaving, Max offered another thought. "Don't think this will amount to anything, but rumor is there's a puppy mill just outside of town. When people will do anything for money, well, you just never know. If I hear anymore, I'll let you know."

Ryan had no idea what a puppy mill could be but it didn't sound good.

"Puppy mill?" he asked Zoey as he started up the Jeep.

"That's when an irresponsible breeder is in the business strictly to make money. They mass-produce dogs, which leads to serious health problems. As of last year, puppy mills are illegal in California."

But Ryan realized this didn't mean all breeders would stop the practice. One tended to see that problem a lot when money was involved.

"I'm sorry, Zoey," Ryan said. "I don't know what else we can do."

"Don't be sorry," Zoey said. "You've done more than I ever expected."

"I wanted to do more."

He always did. It was like a sickness with him. Even when he told himself that he couldn't be all things to all people. Not everyone could be saved, no matter how hard he tried.

He dropped off Zoey in front of her home a few minutes later.

"See you next week?" Zoey asked, climbing out. "I'll call you with the time later. Don't worry, dress is pretty casual."

"Actually, I'll see you tomorrow at the pet wash."

Her brow furrowed in confusion. "You're bringing Fubar?"

Fubar was Jill and Sam's dog, a very cool three-legged dog with a ridiculous name. Ryan could see why Zoey might think he'd bring Jill's dog. He didn't own a pet and the pet wash was a way to raise money for Pilots n Paws, the organization that used volunteer pilots to fly pets to their forever homes. The pilots from Magnum, the small regional airport nearby, participated in the program. This would be the second annual event. Zoey donated all the pet shampoo, tubs and other necessities. But the washing of the pets was done by shirtless pilots as a gimmick. Suckers.

"Our department got together and raised some money for the cause. It's a big check." He winced.

"How much?" Her curious brown eyes sparkled in the sunlight.

"No, I mean it's one of those huge fake checks, which I'm assured is backed by a real one."

"Oh. Guess I'll see you tomorrow."

With that she turned her back to him and walked toward her front door. And damn if he didn't enjoy every minute he watched her cute butt wiggle away.

Chapter 8

The next morning bright and early, Zoey set up for the pet wash in front of her shop. Indie, Bella and Corky had come along, of course, and would get their own baths. Zoey always contributed to the cause.

They'd sectioned off the parking lot and Zoey set up the three stations with tubs and bottles of shampoo. Susie from the Hair-Em Salon had used her sinks to fill buckets with warm water that they could use to fill the tubs. After she'd blow-dried the pet's fur, she would place a bow tie or ribbon on them and take a photo that would later be uploaded to the website. Last year the event had occurred at the airport but since the regional airport was under construction, they'd switched locations. Luckily, all of the shopkeepers were fully supportive of the charity and brought their own animals.

Zoey loved the pet wash but she'd be nervous this

year because of Ryan. Especially now that he'd offered to take her to the anniversary party. She would be intensely aware of his every move today, even more so than normal.

"Where's Carly?" Zoey asked Jill when she arrived, Fubar in tow.

"She woke up feeling sick so Levi is staying home to take care of her and watch the baby." Jill pointed to Sam a few feet away. "I'm lending my own piece of man candy, you're welcome very much."

Zoey observed as Sam stripped his tee off near one of the tubs.

"Oh my god," Zoey said, trying not to drool.

Jill smiled. "I know, right?"

Zoey shook her head, wondering what Ryan looked like without his shirt. Probably better than Sam, and that was saying something. She dumped a bucket of warm water into a tub. Jill followed.

"Thanks a lot, by the way," Zoey said, scowling a little at Jill.

"Um, you're welcome, but not sure what I did. Pretty sure it was awesome."

Zoey barely restrained herself from rolling her eyes. "Not this time. You got Ryan to offer to take me to the party, didn't you?"

Jill put her hand on her heart. "I did not."

"Well, you told him about it and he offered."

"Oh, yeah? So, did you accept?"

"Of course."

"That's good. He took Carly to a wedding."

"I know." Zoey was aware that Jill was not matchmaking. She wasn't very good at that, anyway.

"And look what happened there."

"Why? What happened?"

"She met Levi right after that."

"So…what? Ryan is some kind of good luck charm for meeting Mr. Right?"

"You never know. Maybe he's your charm. Some dude is going to see you at that party with Ryan and notice you for the first time."

Zoey swallowed hard. She would have hoped that man could be Ryan, but obviously Jill didn't share her thoughts. Anyway, it would be crazy. Six years older, he was so much more experienced than Zoey in every way. She was his little sister's best friend and it would probably take a seismic shift for him to see her in any other way. And Zoey wasn't a fan of the ground shifting beneath her feet.

"He's the perfect date to my friends," Jill said. "A complete gentleman. Won't drink too much, and won't make a move on you."

Yeah. Great. Just what the doctor ordered. "Okay, okay. You already sold me on him."

Once owners and their pets began to arrive, the lines moved swiftly. Pilots Stone Mcallister, Matt Conner and Sam took care of the washing. Shirtless. It meant a great deal of donations to the cause. Jill helped with the blow-drying, Zoey gave her pet massages and Susie put on the final touches of ribbons or bow ties. Zoey had been so busy that she hadn't even noticed when Ryan arrived. But at one point she turned and there he was. Ryan was so good at representing. He was like a walking advertisement for law enforcement.

She was cleaning up her station when Ryan appeared at her elbow. "Hey."

"Hi. Did you bring that big funny check?" She tried a smile.

"Yeah, it's propped over there." He pointed. "You got a minute?"

"Um, sure." She dried her hands and followed him to the storefront of Pimp Your Pet where a photographer stood, working his digital camera.

"The newspaper wants a photo of me handing over the check to someone involved in the pet wash."

"Oh, okay. Maybe one of the pilots or their wives." She turned in a circle. "They're around here somewhere."

"They're all pretty busy and the guys don't have their shirts on. I'll just hand it to you," Ryan said. "You're a big part of this pet wash."

"Yeah, but…b-but this is all for Pilots n Paws."

"Not a local organization. And Magnum Aviation couldn't do any of this without you. This is all community stuff. You know, rah-rah Fortune."

"But…"

Speaking of the ground shifting under her feet. She did not want her photo taken. Not that it mattered to anyone else but she wasn't presentable for a photograph. She wore denim shorts, her favorite rain boots, a T-shirt that, due to the German shepherd that had shaken his wet fur all over her, was still wet. Her hair was in a ponytail, other than the stray fly-away hairs, some of which were plastered to her forehead. Lovely.

Ryan grabbed the check and the photographer set up the shot. Ryan stood next to her, the huge check in front of the two of them, his much larger form making her feel tiny. Then the photographer signaled Ryan over with a hooked thumb, and Zoey thought maybe she was about to get out of this. Surely the photographer understood someone else would be more appropriate. Someone dressed. Like, in a dress. While they conferred, she waved her arms, jumped a little and tried to catch Jill's attention. But she was ogling Sam. Did she not get enough of that in the privacy of her own home? It took a few more waves over her head until Jill finally caught sight of Zoey.

Help. Get me out of this, Zoey mouthed.

What? Jill mouthed back and squinted. For the love of dogs, could she not read lips? Zoey enunciated and everything. She tried again, but then Sam grabbed Jill by the waist and it was all over.

Zoey sighed. The photographer was explaining something to Ryan and it appeared to be somewhat important given the way he leaned in and gestured. Ryan nodded and glanced back to Zoey. His eyes widened, but then he gave a slow smile. It made every part of her light up like a Christmas tree. Like a wet Christmas tree. That meant electrocution, probably.

He strode back to her and repositioned the check so that it covered her chest. Another easy smile. "We're just going to put this right here."

That's when she glanced down at her T-shirt and noticed her nipples protruding through the flimsy damp cotton, giving all who cared to see a free show. Horrified, she thought about running, thought about screaming, but she had cover right now. She was going to take this check with her after the photo and if anyone tried to stop her *then* she would scream.

Ryan pulled Zoey in close, making the lights of her metaphorical Christmas tree blink in a possibly seizure-inducing pattern. He had one arm draped oh-so-casually over her shoulder and the other hand was holding the check. He hadn't asked her to but she was also helping to keep this giant check positioned in place. Just try and stop her.

"Thanks, Zoey. You're a real sport." Ryan turned to her when the photos were all taken.

Well, crap, he might as well have patted her head. "You're welcome."

"I can take this now." He pulled on the check. He was smiling again, his left dimple showing. Was he having fun with her?

"Oh, no you don't." She held it in front of her like a shield.

"Zoey," he said, and his eyes smiled.

She turned, walking with the check in front of her. "You'll get this check back when I'm good and ready. After I change."

Ryan was pulled aside by another concerned citizen so he couldn't follow her.

"That was cute," Jill said, coming up behind Zoey. "Why are you walking like that?"

"Because I don't want to flash anyone else!"

"Huh? Are you naked under there?"

"It's wet T-shirt contest time down here." She lowered her gaze to her boobs. "One of the dogs splashed me and got me big-time."

Jill covered her mouth with her hand, making no real effort to hide her laugh. "Oh my god."

"The photographer noticed and made Ryan move the check to cover me. Otherwise I'd be in the next edition of the *Dispatch*, my two nipples waving hello to the world!"

"Oh, c'mon. You're exaggerating. How bad can it be?"

Zoey deadpanned and then lowered the check so only Jill could see.

Again, she covered her mouth. "It's not that bad." Her eyes grew wide but then she smiled brightly. "Aren't you wearing a bra?"

"Yes! It's much worse than I thought!" Zoey walked to her shop, the check in front of her. She was never going to wear this kind of flimsy sports bra again. To hell with comfort. "I'm going to change."

"Don't worry. I bet the photo is really cute and the check covered the boobage. It should be in the *Dispatch*'s Wednesday edition."

"Great. Me, Ryan and my boobs."

She was going to be in the local newspaper with Ryan. She turned to see him, now surrounded by a group of residents, smiling, at ease, confident. And boy if that wasn't a familiar sight to Zoey. She'd watched from the sidelines many times while Veronica took the spotlight, surrounded by fans, admirers and movie producers. Smiling easily, oozing confidence and sexuality.

But there was one marked difference between the two. Ryan was doing a job for the community, a job he seemed to genuinely enjoy. Zoey never got the sense that he liked being the center of attention and fed off the allure. More like he accepted it because he cared so much about the community. Family. His hometown.

Because that's what you did for the people you loved. Anything.

After Ryan finished the morning roll call with his deputies on Wednesday morning, he made it back to his desk to find a copy of the *Dispatch* lying front and center. It was open to the middle section with a photo of him and Zoey at the pet wash holding the giant check.

At least the photo didn't display the perky breasts that had been straining against the wet T-shirt. Good thing the photographer, an older man who probably thought of Zoey as he would his own daughter, had noticed. Ryan had not until that moment, but he'd be lying to say he didn't appreciate getting the heads-up. Missing that would have been criminal even if it had fueled more highly inappropriate fantasies on his part.

What he hadn't noticed until now was the smile on Zoey's face as she looked up at him. It wasn't what he'd expected, since a moment before that she'd had a stunned look in her dark eyes when she'd glanced down at her shirt. She'd been embarrassed. Humiliated. A little irritated with him for teasing her, which was fair.

His cell phone rang and he picked it up without looking at the caller ID, in full sheriff mode. "Davis."

"Hello, handsome," a syrupy sweet voice on the other end of the phone said.

Lauren. That sweet syrup was the outside covering for steel and he damned well knew it. She didn't have a kind bone in her body.

"Hey, what is it? I'm busy here."

He didn't like talking to Lauren, but he hadn't closed down all communication with her, in case he ever wanted to come back to Oakland looking for a job. Best not to burn a bridge. She had pull and contacts and wouldn't hesitate to use them. His job was to make sure he'd never need them.

"I need your advice on a case I'm trying."

At least this was new. She hadn't called him about work-related stuff for some time and she'd never asked for advice when it came to her cases. "Go ahead. How can I help?"

"I have the authority to offer my perp a plea. It's incredibly generous and I'm sure they'll take it. But I don't know if I should do it. Maybe just take my chances in court, you know?"

Lauren loved to fight and she absolutely hated losing. He sensed a trap. "Hard evidence?"

"Circumstantial."

"Then what's the problem?"

"He's a bad guy. Just because I don't have enough to convict him doesn't mean he's innocent."

And it also doesn't mean he is guilty of this particular crime.

"Why are you bothering me with this? You never wanted to tarnish your perfect conviction record. This could do that. So why *not* the plea?"

"I don't know. Maybe I'm trying to do the right thing. I want justice for the victims. It's not all about winning, you know."

"It almost sounds like you'd been listening to me." He snorted.

"What can I say? You were right. I get it now. Any chance you'll come back to Oakland and help fight real crime?"

"Why? You think we have fake crime here?"

"Property line disputes and DUIs?"

"Try arson."

"Hmm. That is at least a little challenge. Then again you're not the one doing the investigating, are you? I'm sure by now you're getting bored with all the meetings and media stuff."

"I'm good, thanks for asking."

He got the idea that she didn't care about his state of mind as much as she was simply curious. Fishing. When he'd decided to run for Sheriff, she hadn't wanted to relocate to the small town of Fortune. Not so that he could run. Not for any reason. She'd found the thought of commuting to Oakland equally horrific, not that he blamed her for thinking that way.

But the point was, if he'd been in love, no one would have been able to talk him into coming back to Fortune without her. If she'd been in love, she would have followed him here or they'd have worked something out.

She gave a long sigh. "You think I don't care but you're wrong. Was I wrong not to give up my career for you? I love you, Ryan, but you wouldn't have done that for me. Admit it."

He didn't miss the fact she wasn't speaking about her feelings in the past tense. A sense of unease settled in his bones. They were more than done and he didn't get the need to rehash the past yet again. Lauren's idea of love had come with conditions. That wasn't love. It was control.

To fill the silence, he cleared his throat. "Need anything else?"

"I wondered if you're ready to come back yet."

"Come back."

"Back to Oakland where you can make a real difference."

"I'm not coming back, Lauren." He didn't add that if he ever did, it wouldn't be for her or because of her.

"Don't be a dick. Think about it. You know you could never be happy in such a small town where everyone knows about the medal."

The medal. He'd never talked to her about that, but

at some point it had become obvious that she knew. After all, he'd had a thorough background check before coming on board with the Oakland PD. She'd made an incendiary comment about how they awarded medals for anything these days, and he'd realized she'd known all along.

"Got to go."

He disconnected with Lauren, swallowed some nasty coffee—neither he nor Renata had yet figured out how to use the new coffee maker—and took another look at the photo. It had been taken at the exact moment Zoey looked up at him. While he smiled dutifully for the camera, she smiled up at him. She'd been wearing the tee, denim shorts and pink rubber boots with kittens all over them. Her hair in a simple ponytail. Still breathtaking.

But it was the expression on her face that struck him. If not for the picture frozen in time, he might have missed it. The camera had captured Zoey gazing at him with a desire that he hadn't noticed until now. He shook his head to clear it. Work was doing a number on him.

Later that evening, after work, Ryan and Aidan had a rousing pickup game of basketball at the Boys and Girls Club. They were tied forty-five to forty-five when Ethan dunked the ball and ended the game with a win for his side. At six-five and only fifteen, dunking was not difficult. He towered over the rest of the boys—hell, he had a few inches on Ryan. Despite his popularity on the court, he didn't play on the school team. He kept to himself and didn't have many friends. The Boys and Girls Club, according to his grandmother, was his only social outlet.

As planned, Ryan and Aidan gathered the kids together before dismissing them.

"Any of you hear about the dumpster fire?" Ryan asked.

"Yeah," one of the boys said. "My mom was getting her hair done when the fire truck came."

"That's not the first fire we've had around here in the past few weeks," Aidan continued.

"Since most of you are from Fortune, you know that we're about to go into our wildfire season. The hills have been brown—" Ryan said.

"Golden," a smartass in the back said, referring to the positive way some liked to refer to their arid hills.

Ryan continued. "If you see something, say something. We're all a part of this community and we need to watch each other's backs."

"That's right," Aidan said. "Any one of you need me or Sheriff Davis, you know where to find us."

A small talk about fire safety followed, a reminder of the dangers of a single flame. Ryan noticed several bored looks while some schooled their expressions into at least the appearance of interest. Before they all disbanded, and as Aidan was gathering the balls, Ryan pulled Ethan aside.

They hadn't talked since the previous week when he'd been scheduled to go for a visit with his father. The kid hadn't been thrilled to give up a weekend for a man his mother called the "sperm donor." Ryan knew the family. His stepfather was a city council member Ryan dealt with occasionally and his mother worked at the local bank. Still, it seemed to be his grandmother the kid was closest with.

"Hey," Ryan called out.

Ethan turned, his eyes registering the usual boredom. It was as if he'd already checked out. Even when dunking he didn't celebrate nearly as much as his teammates did. Simply to be on Ethan's team meant having a post up player at every game and an almost certain win. This never seemed to matter to him.

He stopped his lumbering slow walk, which always looked as if it took every ounce of energy he possessed to move at all.

"How was last weekend?"

He lifted a shoulder, the equivalent of *meh*.

Give me something, kid. Anything at all. Let me know you're in there.

But difficult though it was to believe, Ethan had the same thousand yard stare Ryan had seen in the returning soldiers he'd mentored after his return stateside. Same vacant look. Unnerving.

"Everything okay at home?"

He nodded.

By now Ryan had grown accustomed to the fact that most people, let alone teenagers, would not confide in a law enforcement officer. No matter what. Whether it was fear of the reaction or fear of the outcome he had no idea. But it was frustrating when all he wanted to do was help. Communicate. Build bridges.

But he couldn't help feeling that he wasn't making any headway at all.

Chapter 9

Zoey got to work earlier than planned on Wednesday, after having paid for and cleared out all copies of the Dispatch from the stand in the Candy Lane strip mall. Because, yes, she'd *heard* about the embarrassing photo. Had received a call from Jill that morning, and another one from Carly. Carly remarked on the adoring look in Zoey's eyes and asked whether she was back to crushing on Ryan again. Because she and Ryan looked *adorable* together. How sweet. Even Tia called to tell her she'd taken such a great photo and that she looked more like her mami every day.

"Is there a reason you need all those copies?" Fred asked from behind her. Though he'd framed it like a question, it sounded more like an accusation.

"Yes." She tilted her chin and handed Fred a copy. "Here you go."

"Thanks." He scowled back at her.

The storefront bell jingled as she entered her shop, balancing approximately thirty copies of the *Dispatch*, give or take. Hannah, her part-time worker, greeted her with a smile.

"I know you, so I already got a copy. Too late."

"There's at least thirty people that won't get one."

Zoey went behind the register where she dumped the newspapers with her backpack. But as she turned to the register, she saw a copy of the *Dispatch* sat opened to the page with the photo of her and Ryan. Hannah had drawn a heart near Ryan. It was worse than Zoey had imagined. In the photo, she stared up at Ryan, smiling, a dreamy expression on her face. She couldn't have been more obvious about her intense affection for and attraction to him. He, of course, was oblivious as he smiled easily into the camera.

"Oh, god." Zoey face-planted on the counter.

"I think we should frame it," Hannah sighed. "He's so freaking dreamy. I have a thing for older men."

"He's not that *old*."

"No, I know. If he was a dad, he'd totally be a DILF."

"Tell me the truth. Am I that obvious in this photo or is it just me?"

"Oh, you're obvious alright."

Oh, man. Ryan would see this photo and might realize her feelings ran much deeper than the friendship he'd offered. The jury was out on whether there would be more metaphorical head patting, or whether he'd simply avoid her. But he couldn't avoid her. They were going to a party together.

This was all so terrible.

"Do you think everyone will know?"

Hannah picked up the paper again and inspected it. "I don't think everyone will know. Had it been me in that photo, *I* would have been more obvious. Do you see here, how his body is kind of turned in to yours? Yours is also angled naturally toward him. It's just the angle of your face that's the problem. And the head tilt. *And* the dreamy smile."

"He caught me at a bad time. A minute before I'd looked directly at the photographer. But of course he wouldn't take *that* shot!"

"I don't know what you're upset about. You look really cute together."

And that was part of the problem. The picture spoke to her, teasing her heart and other tender pink spots. She couldn't put her finger on it, but the way he stood next to her was…protective. Dared she even think it? Caring. The only words that came to mind. In some unknown way to her, they fit. The two of them seemed right somehow.

Maybe now that this photo had spoken for her, she should just roll with it. Take a chance. Whatever happened, it couldn't be worse than this public display of her affection for him. It felt like a very private moment had been broadcast for the entire town to ogle.

"Any luck finding Boo?" Hannah wisely changed the subject.

Not to a much better one.

"No. We've tried everything. All we have left is to hope that the person who took him has regrets and takes him to the shelter where the chip will be read."

"Or maybe he'll get out on his own, make a break for it."

That sounded like another dog. Boo was easy and

content to lie around all day. But she could hope. "Yeah, maybe."

The phone rang and Zoey picked it up, grateful for an opportunity to stop mooning over Ryan. "Pimp Your Pet, how can I help you?"

"*Hola, querida,*" Tia said. "I have good news. Tio found you a date. The man checks out and everything. Works at the post office. *Very* good man."

"I'm sure he is, but I already have a date."

"Raul! She already has a date!" Tia gushed.

"Don't make it sound like I never have a date." She wasn't pathetic. She had dates now and again, just not any great ones.

"What man? I haven't spoken to him, have I?" Though he was not on the line, Tio's thundering voice could be heard through the phone.

Zoey took a breath. They'd forgotten she was twenty-six years old and not sixteen. "Tell Tio he already knows him. It's Ryan. The sheriff. Surely *he* checks out?"

"Oh, the sheriff! *Ay, muy guapo.* Raul, it's the sheriff she's bringing! Mr. Davis."

"Ryan," Zoey corrected.

"He's a *very* good man." For the love of dogs, Tio sounded as though he were on a megaphone over there. "I approve."

What? Without the inquisition? Zoey did the eye roll thing in Hannah's direction. "I'm so glad."

It was just one date. It wasn't like he needed to be cleared with Homeland Security—though, come to think of it, he probably had been.

"Don't get too excited about this. He's just my friend."

"Who said I'm excited?" Tia said. "Let's go shopping for a dress!"

"I have to wear a *dress*?" Zoey squeaked out.

"*Mija*, we've been married forty years. If that's not a special occasion, I don't know what is. What do you think?"

She would need a damn dress.

It took three stores and five dresses for Tia to locate a dress she liked for herself. Despite what she'd said about not being the "attractive one," Tia chose carefully and finally found a dress that met with her approval. The dress was wine-colored taffeta with a sweetheart collar and fell just below her knees. Zoey thought Tia looked beautiful *and* classy. That look was difficult to achieve in her opinion, but Tia nailed it every time.

Zoey found her own dress immediately, but Tia made her wait because "there might be something better" and they'd just circle back if they didn't find it. After the second store and the second "right dress," Zoey wised up. Clearly, *she* couldn't find her dress until Tia had found hers.

Coincidentally, she found another perfect dress immediately after Tia found hers. It was summery, a simple A-line, and hit just above the knee, which Tia insisted was completely appropriate for a "young lady."

Zoey liked that it was blue.

"The sheriff will have the best date at the party," Tia said. "You look beautiful in that modest dress. It shows off your figure."

"You think so?" Zoey turned in a circle.

Maybe she'd wear her hair down for the party. Style it, if she could manage to the way Susie at The Hair-Em did. Zoey always looked ten times better on the day of a haircut.

"Do you like him? I know he's Jill's brother, but he'd also a single man." Tia waggled her eyebrows.

"I like him, but I don't think he'll ever see me that way."

"You never know until you try."

The night of the party, Zoey paced her living room. She'd found another sitter for her dogs, this time her next door neighbor Mrs. Martinez. She had a strange cat named Bonkers who, oddly, thought he was a dog, too. Therefore, he wasn't at all scared of Zoey's dogs and had some kind of weird crush on Corky. This would be good for the small pig because he was still missing Boo.

Ryan was due any minute, and Zoey suddenly wondered if the dress said more than she wanted it to say. Did the fact that the hem was just above the knee *mean* anything? What about blue? Was this a talkative dress, or would it just allow her to have a nice time tonight?

Tia's words repeated themselves over and over in Zoey's mind. How many times had she told a prospective owner that a cat really was their perfect pet match?

She usually got plenty of arguments: I don't like cats; they're mean; they're too independent.

How do you know until you try? Zoey would always ask.

And it always worked out.

Naturally it wouldn't be that simple for her. But she could try.

She had to relax and stop overthinking. This night was all about Tia and Tio, and she didn't want anything to take the focus off them. Family was coming from as far as Hollister and pretty much everyone they'd ever worked with while running the pet store for decades would be there.

It meant that half the town was invited, so the party had to be held at a rented hall in town. The catering had been done by a friend of Zoey's, Kayla, who was a wonderful chef and baker. It would be good to connect with old friends and family tonight, and Zoey needed to put her energy there and not on what it would be like to be out on a date with Ryan Davis. She would be on a date with Ryan. A fantasy she'd replayed often enough in her head even if clothing, of any type, hadn't been involved.

After she'd changed from a pair of cute wedge sandals that gave her height and were easy to walk in to a pair of flats that would be easier to dance in all night (should the case arise), then back to the wedges and finally back to the flats again, Ryan arrived. Looking at him, she'd have bet *he* hadn't agonized over anything tonight. Still, he looked amazing in black slacks and a blue button-down. Blue.

"Hey, we match," Zoey said inanely as she stepped outside.

"Told you I give great date," Ryan said as he opened the passenger door for her. "I planned that."

"Really?"

He chuckled, coming around to slide into the driver's seat. "No. Just teasing you."

Of course. There would probably be a lot of big-brother teasing tonight, maybe even some head pats. It was her fault. She hadn't ever done anything to show him that she'd like the trajectory of their relationship to change. If she wanted a shift it had to start with her. Tonight. Ryan would otherwise be the perfect gentleman.

"Jill said Carly met Levi a few weeks after your date with her," Zoey said to fill the silence as he drove.

"Yeah, I guess that's true."

"Are you a good luck charm, sheriff? One date with you and then a girl meets the man of her dreams?"

This was her feeble attempt at flirting, but it didn't seem to go over well.

He didn't answer for a minute but simply cast her a sidelong glance before he turned his gaze back to the road. "I live to serve."

While that had her wondering how many women he'd "served," she understood it wasn't what he'd meant. Best to get her mind out of the gutter.

The hall was filling up by the time they arrived and, no big shock, Ryan was stopped several times by residents wanting to say hello. Zoey was surprised when he took her hand after a few pleasantries and drew them away from all the well-wishers. His big warm hand swallowed hers and gave a sharp and thrilling tingle. Inside, there was a nice-sized dance floor and a DJ. Dessert and wine bars were set up in opposite corners of the room. Large banners read, Congratulations Gloria and Raul… A Partnership Forty Years in the Making. Balloons were everywhere.

They walked hand in hand to the courtyard outside, which was strung with fairy lights.

"This is great," Ryan said, letting go of her hand. "No less than they deserve for hanging in there forty years."

She smiled up at him and batted her eyelashes. One lash got stuck. She blinked and had to use her finger to push it back out of her eye. Stupid mascara. "D-do you think you could do it?"

"Is that a trick question?"

Embarrassed, she tucked her hair behind her ears. "I'm not sure I could. Forty years is a long time."

"Long time to put up with someone else, that's for sure. I'm not the best person to ask since I didn't even last six months in an engagement."

"Maybe she just wasn't the right one."

"No maybe about it." Ryan glanced around the room. "Where are the folks, anyway? I want to say hello."

With the sea of people in the room, for a minute it was hard to locate Tia and Tio. But it should have been easy enough to do. They were the couple flitting about the room together, making sure everyone else was having a good time.

"Mr. Sheriff!" Tia said as she approached them, arms wide. "Have a wonderful time here tonight."

"Yes," Tio added, clapping Ryan's back. "We want to celebrate with all our friends and family."

"Congratulations." Ryan shook Tio's hand and accepted Tia's hug. "But this is about you. You two should enjoy this night."

He'd taken the words right out of Zoey's mouth. For once she wanted her hardworking folks to relax and enjoy the evening. But she also realized that this was what gave them joy, simply being surrounded by loved ones and tending to their needs instead of their own. Their only need was each other.

The DJ played a Selena ballad, *"I Could Fall in Love,"* and Tio drew Tia to the dance floor. "This is our song, *mi amor.*"

"Love those two," Ryan said as the older couple drifted to the dance floor and joined the crowd.

"I'm so lucky they're my family."

"Want to dance?" Ryan smiled and a single dimple appeared in his cheek.

Gosh, if he gave her a smile like that again she'd

do almost anything. But it might be bad luck to dance with him to a song in which a woman sings about falling head over heels for a man, right or wrong. Turned out Zoey didn't have much of a choice in the matter because Ryan gently took her hand and lured her to the dance floor. He pulled her close and strong hands settled on her waist.

Enjoying being pressed up against him this way, she curved her fingers around the nape of his neck because that was what couples did when they danced. She only glanced up at him once and it was all too much. He was so close and he smelled so wonderful. Feeling shy, she brought her chin down, which meant she stared at his neck for a while since he was nearly a foot taller. How she wanted to kiss that neck and bury her face in it. She must have dreamed of kissing him at least a hundred times.

I could fall in love Selena crooned, a heartsick woman. *And I know it's not right...*

Snap out of it, Zoey!

She had a sudden random thought that should accomplish her purposes. "Did you dance like this with Carly?"

She expected to hear him say yes, because of course they'd danced together, and he probably danced like this with everyone. Why not? He was a wonderful dancer.

"No." Then he pulled her even closer.

Okay, so much for snapping out of it. Much closer to him and she wasn't going to be able to move. And she didn't want to. Pulling together every last reserve of courage she owned, Zoey tipped her chin to look him in the eyes. Very beautiful green eyes that weren't smiling and teasing her with a joke. He wasn't lying. Tonight was different for him somehow. Just as it was for her. She couldn't look away as something shifted and the air turned to a thick coil of electricity between them.

She fixated on his lips. "Ryan—"

A commotion at the entrance to the hall caused Zoey to turn to see who had arrived. Possibly the mayor, who of course had been invited, and would want to attend simply to reward Tia and Tio for being such a vital part of the community for so many years. But it wasn't the mayor. Zoey saw someone who had not been expected tonight, or any other night, at least not in Fortune.

Not at all.

Chapter 10

Ryan wouldn't have had to be looking deeply into Zo-ey's brown eyes to know something was wrong. He sensed it in the way her entire body stiffened in his arms and she stopped the rhythmic movements of her body brushing against his and driving him crazy.

"She's...she didn't..."

"What's wrong?" he asked, following her gaze to the group of people who had entered.

At the center was a woman dressed in a sparkling floor-length black gown. She looked as if she was about to present an award at the Oscars. Total dress code over-kill.

"It's my *mother*," she said with all the enthusiasm of a prisoner headed to death row. "She didn't say she was coming."

"Surprise, huh?"

"She excels at them."

Zoey's mother was flanked by a couple of well-dressed men in dark suits who followed her every move. *Bodyguards?* He hated to break it to her but this was Fortune, and she wouldn't need a security detail. She opened her arms wide to Gloria and Raul, covering them both in kisses.

"I can't believe you made it," Gloria said. "How wonderful."

"There's no way I would miss this occasion. I wanted to surprise you both. Surprised?"

More kisses and hugs followed. Clearly Gloria and Raul were ecstatic to see Veronica. Meanwhile, Zoey had turned to stone next to him. He squeezed her hand. Ryan understood that Zoey hadn't been close to her mother since she moved to Mexico years ago to pursue an acting career. But the tension and hostility that he felt radiating from her surprised him.

Veronica approached, one of the men following close behind her. "Zoey! How I've missed you. It's been too long. You remember Jorge?"

"Hi, Mami," Zoey said, though it sounded muffled when she was pressed up against Veronica's ample chest.

The older man with a salt-and-pepper goatee shook Ryan's hand and introduced himself as Veronica's fiancé. When he moved toward Zoey, Ryan didn't miss the way she took a huge step back. Fortunately that meant her back bumped into him giving him the opportunity to haul her closer while he tried to decipher what this meant. Because she'd flinched when Jorge approached. There was no doubt about it. He was sure anyone paying attention would have noticed.

"It's so nice to meet you. I'm Veronica Milagros Caballero-Castillo, Zoey's mother."

Veronica, who apparently didn't believe in brevity, smiled, shook his hand between both of hers and then embraced him. Clearly, Zoey's mother was a hugger. He didn't mind. It struck him that her entire demeanor, but particularly the way she dressed and presented herself, was the opposite of Zoey.

"Nice to meet you both. I'm Ryan Davis."

"Zoey, you didn't mention that you have a handsome boyfriend," Veronica said, running her hand down his arm. "He's—"

"The *sheriff*," Zoey interrupted.

"And Zoey's friend." He was irritated that she would relegate him to his job and nothing more.

He hadn't thought it was just him who'd had a moment on the dance floor. A moment when she'd lowered her defenses, stared him in the eyes and let him in just a little bit.

"The sheriff, oh my," Veronica said. "You're good-looking enough to be an actor. Isn't he, Jorge?"

"Absolutely." Jorge spoke in a heavy accent.

"He's too busy protecting the people of Fortune," Zoey said with such force that everyone stared, speechless.

Apparently only now realizing the hostility in her delivery, if not her words, Zoey pulled out of his arms. "I'm sorry," she said and stalked away.

"Oh, no," Veronica said, watching her walk away. "What did I say?"

"Don't worry." Gloria put an arm around Veronica. "She's never been good with surprises. I'm sure she will explain later, probably with another apology."

"I'm going to go talk to her," Ryan said and followed her.

She'd headed to the courtyard, a good idea if she needed to cool off. Also a good idea for the privacy he'd need to ask her a few questions. Because he'd seen a woman flinch in front of a man once before, and it hadn't come with a good backstory.

For a moment he stared at her figure in that sexy blue dress she wore, her back to him in the darkness, the blinking outdoor lights creating random shadows in her dark hair. Not for the first time he noticed that Zoey was incredibly beautiful. She tried hard not to be but there wasn't much she could do about it. Her beauty was classic and understated. Rare. But she wasn't the type of woman to enter a room and cause heads to turn. Instead she was the woman you noticed after a while and then wondered how you could have possibly missed her.

She turned to him. "I'm sorry. I didn't mean to be so rude."

"You didn't do anything wrong." He drew closer until he was only inches from her. "Want to tell me what happened?"

Her lower lip quivered and she seemed to fight back tears. "For once, I don't want my mother to walk into a room and steal all the attention from her sister. She's been doing that all of her life and on a night like this I thought maybe she'd be kind enough to stay away."

"So that's what this is about. You're upset for your aunt." He took her hand, tugging her even closer. Her arms immediately came around his waist.

She nodded. "Mami always needs to be the center of everything. And that *man*. Jorge."

"Yeah?" he said, hoping she'd go on without him having to play twenty questions. That always went so well.

"I don't like him much. She shouldn't have brought him here."

"Her fiancé?"

"I didn't know he was her fiancé. He used to be her movie director."

He tucked a stray hair behind her ear. "And you know him."

"Yeah. I know he's creepy."

He tensed, every muscle in his body at high alert. Rigid. "Tell me."

"No. I don't want to talk about it."

While he silently wondered if his sheriff's badge was also going to be an obstacle between him and Zoey talking honestly, he thought better of pushing her. But damn he was so over people he wanted to help not talking to him. Not wanting to share with him what was wrong so he could fix it.

And there was always the possibility that Zoey didn't want or need his help. "I'll keep him away from you."

"That's all I can ask."

He tipped her chin to meet his eyes. "Actually, you could ask a lot more from me than that."

"R-really?" She blinked up at him. "Like what?"

"Anything you want. I think you know that tonight, this thing between us, is different. I took Carly to a wedding but we didn't dance the way you and I just did. And I didn't follow her outside just so that I could be alone with her."

"I like hearing that." Her hands drifted up to his neck.

"Then tell me I'm not alone here." He focused on her full sensual lips, the bottom one slightly pouty.

She shook her head. "You're not. I've always—"

But she didn't finish that sentence because he covered her mouth in a kiss. He'd meant it to be a short, sweet kiss. Testing the waters. But the way she responded to him revved him up as much as when she'd moved against him on the dance floor. He couldn't have imagined in his wildest fantasies that he and Zoey would have this kind of explosive chemistry.

Whatever her skill level, she made up for it in enthusiasm. And she wasn't just enthusiastic, she could kiss a man's lips off. A new song now played, and the sound of Thomas Rhett singing "Die a Happy Man" drifted outdoors into the cool summer evening. Ryan could definitely die a happy man at this moment.

He broke the kiss before it got out of control but even then all he managed to do was stare into her eyes. They weren't as dark as her hair, but a lighter brown with hints of copper in them.

"Is this really happening? Because I think I'm dreaming." Her smile was tentative and her eyes soft and glittering.

He pressed his forehead to hers and reminded himself to cool down. Her entire family and half the town was inside and he'd have bet money their privacy wouldn't last much longer.

"*Querida*," a soft voice said from behind them, assuring him he'd have won that bet. They both turned to see Veronica. "Can I talk to you…now?"

Ryan squeezed Zoey's hand and waited. He wasn't going anywhere until she told him to go. He didn't care if Veronica was her mother. Something, he still didn't know what, had happened to Zoey and he had a strong suspicion that no one had protected her. That would stop tonight.

"Um, okay." Zoey's hand rose to touch his arm gently and she looked up at him. "I'm fine, Ryan."

"I'll be right inside."

Zoey couldn't breathe. First, Ryan had kissed her, he'd *kissed* her, and that kiss exceeded her biggest fantasies. His kisses matched the way he looked: breathtaking. Now Veronica stood before her, staring with a mixture of confusion and awe. Because, hello, *Ryan.*

"I'm sorry I was rude," Zoey began. She'd been raised to respect her elders and she always had. Even when they were wrong.

"No need. I've missed you so much, and I don't want us to be mad with each other. What can I do to make this better?"

Stop stealing the show. Let Tia shine for once because she deserves it even if she doesn't want it.

Keep *that man* away from me.

Protect me.

"Did you have to bring him?" Zoe said.

"Who? You mean Jorge?"

"Yes, *Jorge*, and since when is he your fiancé?"

"That all happened recently, and I wanted to tell you in person. We've grown so close over the years. All the movies we've made together. He's been there for me. Paved the way. Defended me from jealous co-stars who wanted my parts. You understand. I see that your young man is quite protective, as well."

Zoey almost gagged over the comparison between the two men. Ryan was nothing like Jorge. "I don't think Jorge is protective of you."

"Well, you don't really know him yet."

"I met him when I visited you."

"Yes, that's right. Just that once. It was right after I'd finished filming *Mujer Bonita* and we were celebrating. All those parties."

Zoey took a big breath and wished for strength. "I remember that party, the one where you wanted us to dress alike."

Veronica smiled. "What a wonderful time that was."

That was the way she remembered the evening, the last time they'd been together before tonight. She looked happy. Serene. She had no idea. But frustrated and angry as she was with her, Zoey still loved her mother.

Now wasn't the time to tell Mami the truth. She'd surprised Zoey tonight, showing up so unexpectedly, and she wasn't ready for this confrontation. She'd held on to her secret for so long already, and she wasn't cruel enough to tell Veronica at this wonderful celebration that her fiancé was a creep.

If only Zoey had said something to her mother sooner, then maybe Veronica wouldn't be engaged to him now. But Zoey had waited too long, and she had herself to blame for that.

Telling Veronica now might cause a scene. And Zoey didn't want Ryan to know. Not tonight. Once he knew, what would he think of her mother for failing to protect Zoey? Nothing good.

Ryan. He stood just inside. She could see his strong back to her, head bent, shoulders rigid as if standing guard. No doubt he would keep Jorge away from her tonight no matter what it took. The knowledge of that made her fall a little for him.

"I'm sorry if I said something to offend you," Veronica continued. "Was it the fact that I complimented your boyfriend? I know how sensitive you are, and I didn't mean to embarrass you."

"He's not my boyfriend."

"Are you sure?" Veronica winked. "I saw you two on the dance floor and you were about to kiss."

"Maybe." Despite everything, some part of Zoey wanted to talk to her mother about Ryan. Crazy. "He's so… I really like him."

"I want to know more." Veronica took Zoey's hands in hers and squeezed. "But later, because he's waiting."

"Okay. But…please, do you think you could let tonight be more about Tia Gloria? She never gets any attention when you're around."

"I'll try." Veronica smiled. "I always do, but she doesn't like the attention. She's just like you."

Zoey didn't think her mother had ever given her a bigger compliment.

As Zoey and her mother walked in together, Ryan turned and immediately took Zoey's hand. "Everything okay?"

"Yes," she lied. "Can we dance again?"

"We're going to do whatever you want," he said and pulled her to the dance floor.

Chapter 11

The rest of the evening was spent dancing with Ryan, dancing with Tio when he cut in, and enjoying the dessert bar (Kayla's salted caramel brownies were addictive) all while skillfully avoiding Mami's entourage. They mostly kept to each other the rest of the night, all at the large table closest to the wine bar. Whenever she glanced in her mother's direction and saw her holding Jorge's hand, Zoey's gut twisted. Regret washed over her. She had to tell her mother.

Toward the end of the evening, Veronica asked the DJ for the microphone and recounted story after story of Tio and Tia. How they'd met, how long they dated before Raul asked their father for Gloria's hand in marriage. The often laughable ways in which their father made Raul prove his worthiness to marry the family's eldest daughter. All of that was quite nice and Zoey enjoyed hearing the stories she'd heard again and again from a different perspective. Veronica finished her speech by making a toast to the most loving couple she'd ever known.

"To Gloria and Raul, the center of each other's hearts. May they love and laugh together and forever!"

Tio grabbed his wife in a clinch and laid one on her. So sweet to see Tia blush.

On the way home, Zoey stayed quiet while Ryan drove, simply trying to process everything. She was attempting to deal with all the fresh emotions that Ryan's kiss had brought out of her. She believed he'd meant the kiss, too, and had not just been caught up in the moment or the song. While she had no idea when his feelings had changed for her, maybe that part wasn't important. The significant part was that they had and he saw her as more than a friend. He'd proved that tonight.

He'd danced with her, kissed her, stood up for her and made her feel like the only woman in the room.

When he pulled up to the curb in front of her home she was so nervous her voice shook. "Do you…do you want to come inside?"

"Yes."

"But I have to pick up the dogs from my neighbor first. She dogsat for me tonight."

"I'll go with you."

After speaking with Mrs. Martinez for several minutes, most of which the woman spent grilling Ryan on whether or not a traffic light would ever be installed at Fruitvale and Cherry, Zoey carried Indie in her arms and Ryan took the leashes for both Bella and Corky.

"I'm sorry about Mrs. Martinez. She's usually very

nice, but I had no idea that traffic light was so important to her. This kind of thing happens a lot, doesn't it?"

"Residents wanting to talk to me about everything from city planning to petty crime?" He nodded. "Small town. I'm not the badge but it still goes before me, everywhere I go."

"That doesn't seem fair." She unlocked her door, opened it and set Indie down inside. He took off, headed in the direction of the bedrooms.

Ryan crossed the threshold with Bella and Corky, then bent to unleash them. "You did it tonight, too."

"I did not."

She racked her brain to think of a moment when she'd asked him about anything other than whether or not he wanted to dance. Or whether she could have a bite of his caramel-chocolate brownie after she'd finished hers, because yeah, *that* had happened. Twice.

"When you introduced me to your mother as the sheriff." He straightened to his full height. "Instead of your friend. Or, you know, your date."

Damn, she had done that. She lowered her gaze. "I didn't realize. I'm sorry."

"It's okay. I've worked in law enforcement awhile so I got used to it. No one wants to see me until they need me. As an added bonus, people often won't talk honestly to me for fear of being judged."

She'd never thought of it in those terms. "Except for all your friends, of course, and Jill. And me."

"You? I'm hoping."

This moment seemed so surreal she almost wanted to check her pulse. Ryan was gorgeous, his lean, hard body utterly perfect. Wide shoulders tapered down to slim hips. She'd bet he had abs of steel. She wondered if he'd be too shocked if she asked whether she could lick him from neck to abs. Because he looked that yummy. To keep busy, and also keep from professing her undying devotion, she walked to the kitchen and poured them both glasses of iced tea from the pitcher in her refrigerator.

"You don't like being the sheriff?"

He'd come back to Fortune to run for Sheriff, and won easily, so she hated to think he wasn't enjoying the job.

"Hell, no."

This shocked her. Because Ryan was so good at the schmoozing she would expect him to enjoy it.

"Is it because everyone is always bugging you?"

"Mostly because I never wanted the job. I only won because of the medal. But I never asked to be anyone's hero. I still got a homecoming parade I didn't deserve."

"But you *are* a hero."

"No." He shook his head. "That's only one version. I don't appreciate anyone putting me on a pedestal. Too easy to fall off. My plan is to find someone to take my place before the next election."

Another pebble of anxiety lodged in Zoey's throat. "What will you do then? Go back to Oakland?"

"To my ex who wouldn't come with me when I moved to Fortune? No, that's over."

"Oh, that's good." She rethought her comment. It wasn't "good" that Ryan's fiancée hadn't loved him enough to move to Fortune with him. "Um, I mean... what I mean is, I for one would love you to stay. And so would Jill."

A dimple flashed in his right cheek but he didn't speak.

She cleared her throat. "If you don't want to be sheriff, what do you want?"

"Good question. For a while now I've been interested in restoring old homes. I started in Oakland but there's not much available. The real estate tycoons scoop them up because of their land value alone, and I didn't have much spare time to chase down deals. But I finally closed on a property last week. Sam and I have been talking about starting up a business. He's almost done building their home on the ridge and the guy knows what he's doing. So do I, by the way."

She could see Ryan with a tool belt around his waist, a hammer in his hand, sweaty, on the wrong side of a shave. A little drool pooled in her mouth just imagining it.

"Our plan is to lease the homes we rebuild to veterans."

Jill had hired veterans as guides for Wildfire Ridge Outdoor Adventures, which was how she'd met Sam.

"Runs in the family, doesn't it?"

"Jill might be a pain in the ass, but she has some great ideas."

"So do you."

He gave a slow smile and set his glass down on the counter. "Come here."

She went straight into his arms with zero hesitation. Those arms tightened around her waist and pulled her closer. His head dipped and he very naturally met her lips in a sensual kiss. His tongue pushed against her teeth and she opened for him. It was all so good, so perfect, that she tightened in anticipation. Ryan continued to kiss the life out of her. He made love when he kissed.

Hot. Intense. Intimate. It was fair to say she hadn't ever been kissed like this.

Corky snorted and Zoey suddenly remembered where she was. Then Ryan stopped the slow teasing of his tongue.

"Let's go in my room," Zoey said, urging him toward it.

"Yeah?"

It didn't take much effort to move him so she realized he was fully on board as he followed her into the bedroom. Zoey closed the door and then was pressed up against it by Ryan's hard body. Pinning her there, one strong arm braced on either side of her, he seared her with open-mouthed kisses down the column of her neck to meet her shoulder. Said shoulder tingled and heat wrapped itself around her spine, sliding down to the back of her knees. He could probably kiss her nose and light her on fire.

"God, Zoey, you're so sexy," he said after branding her shoulder with a kiss.

"So are you." She began unbuttoning his shirt while he laid kisses everywhere he could touch.

When he shrugged out of his shirt she got an eyeful of the most incredible chest she'd ever seen up close and personal. He was all hard planes and brawny muscles. She let her fingertips trail up his tempting forearms to his biceps, luxuriating in their strength.

"I can't stop touching you," Zoey breathed.

"Don't."

Not one to disobey an order from the sexiest man on earth, she didn't stop. He'd unzipped her dress so that the top of it was loose enough to pull down to her waist. There was pure heat in his eyes as his thumb traced the lace of her black push-up bra, then followed the path with his tongue.

Zoey moaned. "Don't you dare stop."

"Bed," he ordered.

"Yes, please."

He hauled her into his arms and walked them to the bed. She wrapped her legs around him, feeling his hard length between them. Ryan dropped her to her back, his body covering hers, braced perfectly above her. Seeing as she had only one half of the dress on, Zoey wiggled beneath him and he helped her remove the dress completely. Judging by the blazing expression on his face, he approved of the black thong that matched her bra. He approved so much that he knelt on the side of the bed and was slipping them off her when Zoey heard the panting.

Panting was good but it clearly wasn't coming from Ryan. Behind her. She crooked her head to find Indie and Bella on the other half of her bed, watching them with open curiosity.

"Oh, god!" Zoey said.

"I haven't even started yet, babe," Ryan said from between her thighs.

"My…my dogs."

Why, oh why did she have to notice them now? Couldn't she have noticed them a few minutes from now?

Ryan rose and finally clued in to what was going on. "I see what you mean."

Indie yawned like they were boring him.

"I don't feel comfortable with them here right now."

"Neither do I," Ryan said with a lazy smile. "I only want my performance rated by you."

"I'll be right back." Zoey grabbed her robe and threw it on because her pets had never seen her naked and she hated to start now. "Off."

Indie hopped off and came to sit at Zoey's feet. Bella, for her part, clearly thought Zoey must be talking to someone else.

"Bella! Now! Off." Zoey slapped her thigh for emphasis.

Bella wasn't having any of it. It was as if she'd forgotten all of her training. Zoey was about to resort to bribery with some leftover bacon from the kitchen when Ryan spoke in his deep masculine voice.

"Off."

Bella whined like she was utterly wounded and jumped off the bed. Zoey led them to the front room where Corky was calmly sitting on a bed. With Boo gone, her pig was now her best-behaved pet. Zoey pointed to their respective dog beds, and Indie and Bella reluctantly climbed on with dual doggy sighs.

"Please behave. I've got this very special man in my bedroom and… I really, really like him. So…no barking unless the house is on fire."

With that she backed up the hallway to her room, keeping her eyes trained on them. She pointed to her eyes as she moved. They didn't budge, watching her like she'd lost her ever-loving mind. Well, maybe she had. If so, she was enjoying every minute of her insanity. She reached her bedroom and not so subtly yanked the door open and shut it again. Tonight, of all nights, she would relish her privacy.

Ryan was sitting on the edge of her bed, shirt back on, fully clothed. Disappointment hit her like a weight.

He stood. "I should go."

"What? Why?"

"Zoey." Coming close, he tugged on a lock of her hair. "We're rushing this."

"You didn't say that a few minutes ago."

"A few minutes ago I wasn't thinking. Neither were you."

She took great offense to those words. "What are you trying to say? If you think about this, you won't go through with it?"

"No. Listen," he said, pushing her robe up over a bare shoulder. "I want both of us to take a day. This isn't a rejection."

"Tell me. Did I do something wrong?"

"No, babe. You did everything right. Too right." He traced the edge of her lower lip with his thumb. "You make a man forget…everything."

"Good, then I want you to forget about leaving."

He chuckled. "You are even sexier when you're pissed off."

"Buddy, you haven't seen anything yet. I'm Hispanic, remember?" She put her hands on her hips, just shy of stomping her foot for emphasis. "Hot-blooded."

"You don't have to tell *me* that." His voice was smooth and deep. Sexy.

She may have blushed. They'd been so close, his mouth on her nipple, his head between her legs. He knew a lot more about her than he had a few minutes ago. And she now knew that his hair was soft and thick, not coarse. He smelled like leather and man. And she loved the way he kissed.

"I don't understand. We were both having a good time. I'm sorry about my dogs, but—"

Ryan, still so close she could feel his heat, framed

her face. "If this was just about getting naked and getting off, you know I could do that. But we both know this is something more."

She couldn't argue, and the knowledge of his feelings went all the way to her heart. Hard as it was to hear at that moment, she appreciated his thoughtfulness.

"I'm going to go now but I'm calling you tomorrow."

"You better."

"And you better answer the phone."

He closed the bedroom door behind him, and she heard him leave. Indie and Bella whined after him. She understood the feeling since she too wanted to whine and moan. All the pain and frustration of the night came out in full force. Mami. Jorge.

Ryan, making it all hurt less.

Zoey pushed her face into her pillow and let every ounce of sexual frustration go with a muffled scream.

Tomorrow couldn't get here soon enough.

Chapter 12

Wondering who had ever decided that lime-green was a great color for a kitchen counter, Ryan viciously slayed it with a sledgehammer and watched it crack. Repeat. Demo could be fun. Usually manual labor burned off frustrations of every type. But today he was trying to get rid of his sexual tension and hard work wasn't helping as much as it did when he was exasperated with the city council or the mayor. Or the residents who thought he alone could control where, when and whether a traffic light got installed. Looking at you, Mrs. Martinez.

Smash.

Last night he'd nearly gone back to Zoey's house three times, once literally making an illegal U-turn on Main Street, fortunate one of his deputies hadn't caught him in the act. He would have hated to explain that one. Eventually, he'd made it back to his apartment, where he'd had a good long laugh at himself. It was official. The safe and easy job had driven him crazy. Why else would he have left the arms of the hottest woman he'd ever been with, hands down?

Swing. *Crack.*

Because you know better, his conscience answered him.

Boom.

Everything he'd said to her was logical but logic didn't work when it came to her. Still, he would not simply screw her on the night of her aunt and uncle's anniversary party and move on. He would not screw her and run into her at the next party Jill gave. But what he'd been through had soured him on relationships. He honestly believed he'd be better off single. Maybe his expectations for a relationship were too high.

He'd already been with a woman who seemed to be compatible with him in every way and it hadn't worked. When he'd come to the realization that he and Lauren had never loved each other at all, or enough, he'd questioned everything he'd come to believe. Was he going to make the same mistake twice? Why the hell wouldn't he, until he understood what had gone wrong in the first place?

There was a lot wrong with this particular situation. Zoey was vulnerable, and whether *she* realized it yet or not, she had him on a pedestal. Her best friend's older brother. He'd known that Zoey had a crush on him since the first time they'd met years ago. But then he'd gone to West Point and subsequently to war. He'd visited Fortune often, but after getting out of the service he'd relocated to Oakland. It had been a better place for him to be.

Zoey was a sweet girl, his friend and his sister's friend, who happened to be beautiful. Now, he'd *noticed*. He wasn't going to be able to ignore her ever again. How was he to navigate this terrain? Despite everything, Saturday night he'd been minutes away from burying himself deep inside her and to hell with the consequences. He wanted what he wanted, and damn everything else.

And that scared the shit out of you.

Slam.

Crack.

Yeah, okay, there was that.

He heard a car door slam and turned to see his soon-to-be brother-in-law, Sam Hawker, walking toward the house. Because of his position as a single man with few personal commitments, Ryan had put up the cash and worked out the loan with the local bank. Not VA financing since he didn't plan on living in the house, but he'd worked out some good terms. He believed that a couple of people might have called in some favors for him, and for once he didn't mind. This wasn't about him. It was about earning the medal. Working hard to honor those that didn't come back. Sam sure as hell understood. On some level, he was doing the same.

Sam walked through the open door and straight into the kitchen they'd decided to work on first.

"Man, you weren't lying. This place needs help. It's on life support."

"Let me show you our patient."

Sam shook his head. "A real fixer-upper."

He wasn't exaggerating. But even though the place looked close to being condemned, most of the work was cosmetic. The foundation was solid. Ryan had been able to buy it because he knew the owner. On a half-acre parcel of land on the outskirts of town, with a view of Wildfire Ridge, the land by itself was valuable.

All of the older homes, the first in town before it incorporated, were separated by acreage, rare in the area. Real estate developers salivated over parcels this large, where they could squeeze four homes in the place of one. But when Art had heard about what Ryan planned for the property, he'd worked out generous terms. He carried owner financing and the bank financed the rest. Sam would provide most of the muscle and labor along with Ryan.

Ryan still intended to introduce himself to the neighbors and explain what they were about to do but there was no real rush. They would be working here for some time before anyone could move in and make it their home.

"You guys still on the lookout for Boo?" Ryan asked.

Both Sam and Jill had been, just in case someone had cruelly dumped him on Wildfire Ridge. Considering there were still mountain lions on the ridge, Ryan didn't want to just ignore the possibility.

"Every day, but still nothing."

"Damn." Not what he wanted to hear. At this point Boo could be anywhere.

"How's Zoey doing?" Sam understood how attached Zoey had become to Boo.

"She's okay." Ryan hoped that, at the very least, he'd taken her mind off Boo for a few hours the previous night.

She had seemed to enjoy the evening, the dancing, and later…well, she'd enjoyed that too.

From the bucket of tools he'd carried in, Sam pulled

out a large mallet. "Gotta tell you, brother, this is my favorite part of construction."

"This is the opposite of construction."

"Exactly." Sam nodded. "Tearing it down. The fun part."

"Go for it," Ryan said, wiping his brow. "Taking a break. Got a phone call to make."

He stepped outside into the warm late summer day and spied his closest neighbor in the distance, walking a small dog. And he could see that the property on the corner had a stable and a small barn. The zoning was different in this part of town, and some farm animals were allowed.

Zoey answered after two rings.

He began with the truth. "I'm an idiot."

"Don't expect me to disagree."

He chuckled. "Am I forgiven?"

"Yes, because you were right. We probably shouldn't rush into anything."

"Yeah? I hate being right."

She laughed softly. "No you don't."

"All things being equal, I wish I'd stayed."

"It was the right thing to do."

"You're not mad?"

"I wouldn't say *that*."

"Uh-oh."

"Disappointed. But you can always make it up to me."

Damn, her sweet voice alone turned him on. "That's...not a bad idea. If you're sure."

"Sure about what?"

There were no guarantees in life. None here that they wouldn't stomp on each other's hearts and barely be able to look at each other afterward. He couldn't even stand the sound of Lauren's voice. It grated on him, not because of any hurt or pain that remained, but because of a complete annoyance at himself. He'd been about to get married, which would have been the biggest mistake of his life, and he'd made enough of those.

"About me. I'm probably not who you think I am."

"Why? Who are you?"

Allow me to introduce myself. I'm Ryan Davis from the over-achieving Davis family. Just call me a reluctant hometown hero. I've worked hard all my life to prove something to myself. To my family. To my country. At some point I realized it was never going to be enough. And now I'm exhausted.

That's what he should have told her.

Instead, he said, "I'm just a regular guy. No one special."

There was a moment of silence on the other end.

She spoke softly. "You don't ever want to be special? To anyone?"

Framed that way, it struck him with a force he hadn't expected. Hell, yeah it would be great to be loved and appreciated simply for who he was and not for what he'd achieved.

He cleared his throat. "Well, yeah. Of course. Someday."

"It just so happens that I'm looking for a regular guy. Why can't we just see where this goes?"

He almost choked but then laughed. This was close to the same line he might have used with anyone but Zoey. *Let's see where this goes.* No expectations or pressure. Maybe he had to stop treating her so differently. She was a grown woman. Someone who might even be angry to know that he thought he had to protect her and treat her like she was fragile enough to break.

"You got it."

"Want to come over for dinner tonight?"

"Where do you want to go?"

"No, I mean I'm cooking."

Staying in. What a concept. He might even get to finally find out what his kindred animal was. "Name the time."

After getting the details Ryan hung up with Zoey, then went to find out what was wrong with Sam. He'd just let loose a volley of curse words from inside the house.

That couldn't be good.

Chapter 13

Zoey's rice and chicken casserole was a disaster. A complete and total wreck. She'd overcooked the chicken and undercooked the rice. Somehow she'd burned the tomato sauce, too. It always looked so simple when Tio made it, and she'd wanted to cook a traditional family dish for Ryan and not make sandwiches or something simple. No, she'd had to decide tonight was the time to try something new. Huge mistake!

She phoned Tia, hoping for some help. "I need a food intervention."

Zoey explained and Tia reiterated the information word for word to Tio, who shouted back with his megaphone voice. "I'll make some and bring it over."

"Really?" Seriously, Zoey had lucked into the best uncle in history. "You don't have to do that."

"He wants to," Tia said, as the sound of banging pots

and pans could be heard in the background. "I'm glad you called. What on earth happened between you and your mother yesterday?"

"Why? What did she tell you?"

"Nothing."

"I… I was upset that she showed up the way she did. In that dress. Stealing all the attention away from you. It was your night."

"Don't be silly. I didn't mind. You know I hate being the center of attention."

"Even on your fortieth wedding anniversary?"

"Yes, even then. I always like seeing Veronica even if she's usually overdressed. That's just her way. Did you apologize to your mother?"

Tia had taught her to respect her elders and would expect nothing less. But then she didn't know about Jorge yet. "Of course."

"She's staying in the area for a little while."

"Yeah?" That surprised Zoey. She didn't think Veronica would want to stay long in a place where she wasn't famous.

"Apparently there's a Latino festival in Salinas and their movie has been nominated for an award."

"What do you think of her fiancé?" Zoey began.

"I'm surprised."

"You are?"

Zoey wanted to tell Tia what he'd done. She always had. But that would only make her aunt feel guilty that she'd let Zoey go visit Veronica in the first place. Tia hadn't wanted Zoey to go, worried Veronica wouldn't have time to properly supervise her daughter, but had relented when she begged. And Tio? God only knew what he would do. She feared he would wind up in jail, arrested by none other than the man she wanted to date.

Holidays would be weird after that.

"Why marry now, at her age? It's not like she can have any more children," Gloria continued.

"Maybe she loves him."

The thought made Zoey's stomach burn.

"I don't think so. She's only ever loved one man, your father. Sometimes there really is only one person on earth for us. Your Mami at least had him for a little while."

That sounded so romantic, but it also frightened Zoey. What if she never found her person? She'd meant it when she told Ryan she wanted to see where this thing between them went. But it might not go anywhere, and even if it did he could always change his mind.

She didn't want to be single, the "dog lady," just her and all her pets alone in this house forever. Growing old running the pet store and having no one to hand it down to. Her pets were like her children, but they could never run a pet store.

Tio arrived right on time with the casserole and after he gave directions on how to warm it up, he kissed Zoey on the forehead and left to take Tia out to dinner.

Zoey hopped in the shower, fed her pets, made sure they'd been out to do their business, and just before Ryan was to arrive she warmed up the casserole per Tio's careful instructions. The smells of tomato sauce, garlic and chicken filled the kitchen and she set the table. She wanted this evening to go well, or as well as it could considering how the previous night had ended. Hopefully she'd calmed down Ryan's nerves so that he didn't think she'd expect him to slay a dragon or two for her tonight. Cue one more thing she now understood about Ryan. He just wanted to be a normal dude, which was the very opposite of the way everyone saw him.

Her kitchen table was set with a vase of yellow-and-white daisies in the center and her one and only tablecloth, decorated with dogs chasing butterflies. She declared the setup a success. It was only then that she thought to look down at what she wore. Cut-off denim shorts and a T-shirt that said Enjoy Responsibly in bright red letters across her chest. A gift from Carly purchased on one of her New York City trips. Deciding she didn't want Ryan to think he'd ever enjoy her boobage irresponsibly, she tore it off in her bedroom and, since she'd already done that, she took the shorts off too. A dress sounded good. Or…maybe not a dress, considering she only had two. One made her look sixteen and the other she'd worn to the anniversary party.

When the doorbell rang, she'd just slid on an indigo-blue blouse and her favorite pair of jeans. No need to get fancy. This would be a relaxing evening in which, with any luck, she would soon have hot sex with the man she'd fantasized about for years.

No big deal.

The dogs barked and Corky snorted the announcement that someone had arrived and was at the door, in case she didn't already know. Of course, Indie and Bella followed her to the door to "help" her open it. A while back, Corky had decided that he wasn't interested in being part of the welcoming committee. So had Boo, who had preferred to watch calmly and regally from his perch next to his best friend.

She opened the door to Ryan, and it was clear he'd been thinking casual, too. He was dressed in a plain black long-sleeved tee rolled up and showing off taught and sinewy forearms. Black jeans and dark work boots. He'd showered recently, evidenced by his dark-blond hair, still slightly damp.

"Sorry I'm late," he said, bending to pet Indie and Bella. "But Sam found a plumbing issue."

"You're late?" She'd been the one to lose track of time. "Oh no!"

She ran to the kitchen but it was useless. Now Tio's casserole had gone the way of her own. The tomato sauce was all but gone and the rice appeared sad and defeated. Zoey turned to Ryan, who'd followed her into the kitchen.

"I ruined dinner." She bit her lower lip. "I'm sorry."

He cocked his head. "You made dinner?"

"What do you mean? I told you I would."

"Yeah, but..." He ran a hand through his hair. "I didn't think you meant it and so I grabbed a burger before I headed over."

"What? Why?"

"Experience? Usually no one cooks for me." He lifted a shoulder.

"Not even your mom?"

"Especially not my mom. She gives new meaning to the term 'science experiment' when she's let loose in the kitchen."

You poor deprived man, Zoey almost said out loud.

Zoey cooked, she just wasn't all that great. But she could do the easy stuff. For Ryan she'd wanted to go the extra mile and she'd wound up crashing. Poor Tio. All his efforts gone to waste.

"Is it that bad?" Ryan hovered near the pot. "Still smells good."

"Are you still hungry?"

"I'll always eat, but eating before just ensured I wouldn't starve."

It was amazing how little they actually knew about each other. Like Tia, Zoey would never let a man starve. She couldn't even stand for them to be hungry in her presence. Zoey chopped up some other leftover chicken in the fridge and spread it on sourdough bread for sandwiches. As it happened her expertise was sandwiches and she took great care to make them special. She added nuts and grapes and bits of celery to the chicken.

They ate at the beautifully set table as the dogs and Corky watched from a safe distance, panting and snorting. Indie and Corky begged openly but Bella always used the hard-to-get approach. The *I don't care, but secretly I do care* way. Zoey never fed them scraps. Despite that, they never seemed to give up hope.

"Meant to ask you last night," Ryan said. "What's with your mother's fiancé?"

"What do you mean?" Her stomach dropped. She should have known he'd ask.

"Zoey, come on. You flinched."

"I did?"

"When he came close to you. You backed up a step and you flinched. In my experience, that's never a good thing."

Of course he would notice. He'd already asked once and she'd avoided answering. She remembered what he'd said at the party about people not opening up to him for fear of judgment. People only wanting him around when they needed him. She didn't want to be like those people.

"You have to promise not to get mad."

He leaned back in his chair, palms on his thighs. "I can't promise that. How about if I promise I won't act on it?"

That was actually better.

"Okay. When I was fifteen, I went back to visit my mother for the summer. I was excited because I hadn't seen her in about three years. I missed her terribly, even though I loved living with my aunt and uncle. But she was beautiful and in the movies. So glamorous. We had all the photos she'd send over. In Mexico, my mother is as famous and beautiful as Angelina Jolie is here. At fifteen, that was very exciting to me. Stupid."

"No, it's not."

"One night we went to a party and she thought we should dress alike. She thought it would be funny to be like twins. And I loved the idea of playing the glamorous movie star for just one night. So I wore a sexy black evening gown like hers with a leg slit up to my thigh. Strappy heels. Makeup. My mother's makeup artist did it all. I looked pretty good, I thought. And at the party everyone was so kind. Nice. Except for my mother's director. Jorge. He sort of took me to the side away from everyone else. I thought he'd been drinking too much, but I've been raised to respect my elders and I went with him. You can probably figure out the rest."

He reached for her hand and stroked it. "I need you to tell me, babe, because I have a pretty active imagination. And I've seen a lot of victims."

"Oh, no. I'm not a *victim*. He didn't rape me if that's what you're thinking. Someone came to find him and he stopped…*pawing* at me. But he did touch me and made my skin crawl. And…the things he said to me…no one had ever talked to me that way. It was disgusting."

Ryan worked his jaw and narrowed his eyes. Clearly he wasn't happy but he had to be relieved the worst hadn't happened. "No wonder. The guy is what...thirty years older than you? And you were *fifteen*. Fifteen."

"Yes, and as I got older I realized more and more how awful it was."

"You never told your mother."

"How do you know?"

"Just a hunch."

Zoey lowered her gaze. "I can't stand the thought of her marrying him without knowing."

"Are you going to tell her?"

"I should."

"Let me guess. You don't think she'll believe you."

"Okay, how did you know *that*?"

He studied her from underneath his eyelashes. "Not my first rodeo."

That brought up images she didn't want in her head right now. Crime was much worse in a large Bay Area city like Oakland. After two tours in Iraq, she would have thought he'd seen enough. If he had to be in law enforcement, better that he be here in a small town where normally nothing horrible ever happened.

The job had at least brought him back. She couldn't regret that even if the office was a political one. When someone else was elected to take his place, he'd be much more compatible with her. She could already tell. Like her, he seemed to like quiet evenings at home. He didn't like all the attention either. They were so much alike.

They were bears. Mama Bear and Grizzly Bear. She should really tell him. Maybe if he asked her again.

Once they'd finished eating, Zoey took their plates to the sink. Since the ruined dinner had been intended to be the center dish, she hadn't planned for a special dessert.

"I have ice cream."

Suddenly Ryan was right behind her, strong arms around her waist, his head bent to her neck. Her entire body tingled in anticipation and she froze in place, afraid if she moved a muscle she'd ruin this. She'd miss something.

"I hate that happened to you, babe. Hate it," he said softly and his warm breath fanned across her cheek.

He spoke so tenderly and with a deep and rich voice that sent tingles down her spine. His warm callused hands slid up and down her arms.

And she was lost.

"I should have slapped him. I could have stopped him."

She didn't feel the need to add, as well, that she refused to be a victim. It could have been much worse. Didn't make it okay.

"Baby, don't ever let me hear you say that again. It wasn't your fault."

"It was a long time ago."

"Doesn't matter. I'm going to make sure no one ever hurts you again."

No one had ever said anything like that to her. If anything, some of the men she'd dated (and she used the term men loosely) she'd required protecting *from*. Just to know that Ryan wanted to protect her, even if she didn't need him to…she didn't have words.

"Ryan." She turned in the circle of his arms.

He studied her with those deep green eyes. So serious. "Yeah."

"Your kindred animal is a grizzly bear." She touched

the short dark-blond bristles along his jawline as the words came rushing out of her.

"Get out. I was afraid it was some kind of rodent. Why wouldn't you tell me before?"

Her breath hitched. Okay. Not quite ready. Yet. "The timing had to be right."

He grinned, seeming to accept her half-truth. "So what kind of pet is my best match?"

She went up on the balls of her feet and wrapped her hands around the nape of his neck. "I've been thinking about this for a while and it's a German shepherd. They're protective dogs and can be both fierce and gentle."

"We had one in our unit. He failed out of aggression training courses. Too gentle to go on patrol but he was a great scout and bomb sniffer, and a great morale booster." Ryan tugged on a lock of her hair and then threaded it between his fingers.

"Aw. What was his name?"

"Ajax."

"Why don't you ever talk about that time?" She asked this softly because she'd had the feeling for a long time that Ryan had never been quite the same after Iraq.

"Not many great memories there."

"There's Ajax."

"True enough."

"Do you really hate the medal?"

She was pushing a little, but she'd always been curious. Zoey had once considered looking it up on the Internet to learn all the details. But she'd been too afraid of what she might read. She'd never been one to focus on anything violent or tragic and some things could never be unseen. Jill had warned her not to discuss the medal in front of Ryan, or ask him about it. Her reasoning? *It makes him sad.*

So like everyone else, Zoey had tiptoed around the issue. To protect him. But she'd recently discovered that shielding people didn't always work out the way one planned. Sometimes it led to strained relationships and pent-up anger. Distance and mistrust.

There was a flash of what looked like surprise in his green gaze as he studied her. He probably hadn't expected that she, of all people, would bring this up.

"I don't deserve it, for one."

"Pretty sure they wouldn't have given it to you if you didn't." She brought her hand down to his forearm and squeezed. "Why don't you deserve it?"

This time his brow knotted in confusion. Had no one ever asked him, or was this a dumb question?

"I lost one of my men."

"Oh, I'm so sorry."

"Yeah, I...we were on patrol and came upon a very tense situation. We took on heavy fire and four of my men were badly injured. I was able to get us out of that situation, dragging them all to safety, but it was too late for one of my men. Lost him to massive trauma." He pressed his forehead to hers.

"God, Ryan." She gripped his arms tightly. "So you saved all the others?"

"I helped, yes."

Of course he wouldn't want to take all the credit but by now Zoey understood those medals weren't handed out to just anyone. Ryan was the kind of man who wouldn't abandon those he was sworn to protect, even under the worst of conditions. But he regretted the one he'd lost and in Ryan's mind he'd been rewarded for failing him. She understood far better than he realized. It happened every time she considered that, for every animal she rescued and placed in a forever home, three or four of them would not be saved. Those were the odds.

"Thank you for telling me."

He was so close that she could see a single brown speck in one of his shimmering irises. She concentrated on his full, sensual mouth, which suddenly tipped up in a half smile.

"Kiss me," she ordered tentatively.

"Yes, ma'am." He obliged by taking her mouth in a deep and searing kiss.

When he broke the kiss, it was to study her with sharp eyes, his hand firmly grasping the back of her head. "I'm not messing around here, Zoey. Believe that."

She believed him.

Chapter 14

Everything moved quickly after Ryan's sizzling hot kisses and tender words. He swooped her up in his arms and carried her in the direction of the bedroom. For a moment, he stopped moving.

"Hurry up. Why are we stopping?" She spoke into his warm neck.

"I'm counting. Yeah, three. They're all accounted for." He kicked the door to her bedroom open and closed it with his back, all without dropping Zoey. "Don't want any interruptions tonight."

Neither did she. Not when he looked at her like he was about to eat her alive. "No interruptions."

He slid her down the long length of his body, and she stayed close, wanting to stay glued to him like a second skin. While he bent to kiss and lick her neck, and made his way to the tender spot behind her ear, she slowly tugged him toward her bed. When the back of her knees hit the mattress, she fell onto it and he followed her, covering her body with heat. A warm surge of pure desire spiked through her and she pulled off his tee, trailing fingertips down the long and lean muscles of his chest to his abs. He groaned.

He was so gorgeous, a light smattering of golden chest hairs on his brawny chest. So perfect. Speechless for a moment at his male beauty, she finally found words. "I want you so much."

"Want you too," he said and pulled off her blouse.

She managed to wriggle out of her jeans with him braced above her and assisting, smiling as though he enjoyed the show.

"I love the way you move." He stood to unbutton and slowly remove his jeans.

As he did so, he turned slightly and she got an eyeful of what she'd pictured for so long in her fantasies. It didn't disappoint. He had strong muscular thighs and a steely butt. He was hard all over, too, which became obvious the moment he was down to his tight boxers, ready to spring out of them. It felt good that she'd done this. That she excited him that much. She did everything but lick her lips in appreciation.

Ryan quickly took the lead and reached behind her to unsnap her bra. Her breasts spilled out into his hands and he almost reverently grazed a thumb over a nipple, then drew one gently into his mouth. He sucked softly and tugged until she moaned, going from a light touch to something a little harder and wilder. When he stopped, her nipples were hard pink peaks and she was damp between her thighs. He continued kissing and licking his way down to her abs and her thighs. Then he kissed between them and she gasped in surprise. A man had never put his mouth and his tongue to her most sensitive folds, but Ryan continued to lick and tease mercilessly. She writhed beneath him and fisted the sheets, and when she was unable to hold back any longer, she bucked and cried out.

This might be why her girlfriends liked sex better than she did.

Zoey wanted to do the same for him. She didn't know that she was any good at this, but she believed her instincts were there. She wanted her mouth and tongue on him licking him like a Popsicle. When she reached for his hard length to ready him, Ryan moved her hand away.

"Plenty of time for that later."

He removed a shiny packet from his wallet and ripped it open with his teeth. She could have come again just watching him slip it onto his hard length, never breaking eye contact with her. He stroked himself once, and watching him, her body vibrated and hummed with heat. She didn't think in all her life she'd ever needed anyone like this. Braced above her, Ryan entered her in one long and deep thrust that made her moan all over again. He moved inside her with slow and steady strokes that had waves of pleasure pulsating through her.

Oh, boy. She was going to come again. This never happened to her. He loved the way she moved? It was nothing compared to the way he gyrated his hips in a rhythm that was giving her more pleasure than she'd ever had. She was slick with sweat, both his and hers. Their bodies were sliding against each other, connecting, and strangely this felt even more intimate than what they were doing. She closed her eyes at the onslaught of intense pleasure as another wave built and crested. It was going to happen. She couldn't stop it now, almost as if her body was no longer under her control at all.

"Look at me," Ryan said. "I need you."

She opened her eyes to see him finally lose his tight control. His eyes glazed over and he began to pump harder and faster as if he couldn't hold back any longer. Couldn't slow down. She didn't want him to. She was ready for him. Gripping his shoulders, she met him thrust for thrust as he went even deeper. Her body tightened and shook as she came again, bucking against him with a fierceness that shocked her. Ryan followed her over, groaning and cursing.

Both of them out of breath and panting, Ryan rolled onto his back and tucked her in beside him.

He kissed her temple. "Wow."

She hoped this was a good wow and that she hadn't done something wrong. Because for her, it had been glorious. "What do you mean? It was good, right?"

"It wasn't *good*, it was amazing." He kissed her neck. "You're a wild woman."

Her? A wild woman? Probably not, but it was still nice to hear it from him. "Is it true? Do you need me?"

She was afraid he'd said that in the throes of passion, which she could understand. Still, she wanted to believe it because she needed him. Badly.

"Yeah, I do." He tipped her chin to meet his eyes.

"I mean, it's really okay if you said it just because you were feeling so good."

Totally understandable.

"No, that wouldn't be okay," he corrected her. "I'm never going to tell you anything I don't mean. Especially in bed."

Her breath hitched. He always managed to say the right thing. "Same here."

"Then we're on the same page."

A page she didn't want to turn. They lay together for a few minutes, cuddling, and then Zoey propped herself up on one elbow.

"I want to do it again."

"Look at that—you read my mind."

How else would she learn to be good at this if she didn't get a chance to practice? She pushed him back down and lowered her head to do what he hadn't let her do before.

This time he didn't stop her.

Chapter 15

Reluctantly, Ryan left Zoey in her bed around midnight. He had work in the morning, and not having expected *this* at all, he had to get home to actually get some sleep. Without a doubt, he'd get no sleep next to Zoey. He needed to change into his uniform, grab his holster and gun. If not for that, he was certain he would have stayed all night or until she kicked him out. He wasn't one to stay the night the first time with a woman, ever, but apparently three times inside Zoey hadn't been quite enough for him.

Her enthusiasm had him reeling since the degree of it was unexpected. She'd wanted badly to please him, waited for him to instruct her, and he had. She was sweet and soft and he'd honestly never been with a woman who made him feel like this. The intensity shocked him. He might have expected to feel a more controlled attraction to her, something easy. Simple. But she'd woken him up. Reminded him of all he'd been missing. All that he still wanted. Maybe he'd been doing this relationship thing wrong all along. The trick might be finding someone different from him. Opposites attract and all that crap. The important thing was that he'd just discovered they were hugely compatible in at least one significant way.

And he didn't know how he'd missed something else about Zoey. She was as loyal a person as there could be. There were few who appreciated loyalty more than a former officer. Being with her was close to the equivalent of someone having his six all the time.

She also appreciated him for who he was.

And he'd talked about the medal for the first time in years. To *Zoey.* That had been completely unexpected. Both her question and the fact that he'd answered. It had something to do with the way she'd lowered her own defenses with him to share her own private pain. Fair was fair.

So he'd given her the whitewashed version. *Tell someone*, a counselor at the VA had told him shortly after he'd come home. *Anyone. Believe me, it will help.* But he hadn't. Not for years. Even as he worked through all his trauma to be a whole person again. To function. Work. It stayed in the back of his mind behind a brick wall. If he didn't talk about it, maybe it didn't exist. Didn't happen.

He slept lightly for a few more hours at home, then showered and dressed in his usual white button-down with khaki slacks. He holstered his gun and strapped it on. The drive to the station might be the easiest part of his day. In Oakland, he'd had to battle with traffic to the point that he was already pissed when he arrived to start his day. But the very worst part of his job had been the victims. Domestic violence, rape, murder. He'd met enough rape victims to know before she even told him that Zoey wasn't one of them. A relief to have this confirmed, anyway. Zoey's eyes weren't vacant and empty like many of the victims he'd known.

Despite that, he still wanted to kill Jorge. Okay, kill might be an exaggeration. What he wanted to do, but wouldn't, was scare the man spitless. He wanted to slap cuffs on him and haul him to the jail, book him, then admit he'd made a mistake and let him go. He'd bet the guy would wet his pants. Men like Jorge were all the same. They liked forcing their strength on the most vulnerable.

But Ryan wouldn't use his office to press his advantage. However, if he happened to see Jorge some night when he was off duty, alone, well, who could say what might happen? Certainly a stern talk about boundaries. A talk about how men shouldn't intimidate women in any setting, but especially not a child. And at fifteen, Zoey had been a child. Any teenage girl would have wanted to dress like a glamorous movie star for the evening. The way she'd dressed should have had nothing to do with it anyway.

Opening the door to the station, he could smell the coffee brewing.

"I finally figured out the new coffee maker," Renata said. "Tell me what you think."

He accepted the mug of coffee she gave him and took a swallow. "Yeah. That'll do."

At this point she could have served him liquid mud and this mood wouldn't be ruined.

She handed him some phone messages—in their

town if residents called the sheriff they spoke to a live person and not a machine. "Nothing urgent."

When the first-shift deputies came in, Ryan had their usual meeting and distributed call-to-action items. No more developments on the suspected firebug in town and no more fires either. All good news. The cruisers left the station and Ryan settled behind his desk to check email. A few minutes later, he heard a familiar voice and looked up to see his sister standing in the doorframe.

"Hey, you."

He stood. "Hey. What are you doing here?"

"I had to drop off some paperwork on permits so I thought I'd stop in and say hi." Jill glanced at his empty desk. "Am I interrupting anything?"

"Nope." He waved her inside. "What's up?"

Jill filled him in on her business on the ridge and the status of the home Sam was building for them. Even though he'd heard the latest from Sam yesterday, it was interesting to hear his sister's perspective. She ended by asking him about the anniversary party.

Should have seen that coming, genius. He cleared his throat. "Yeah, that was a great party."

"I told you. I guess Zoey didn't crush on you too hard."

It would have to be said eventually so he might as well do it immediately. "Yeah, see. Here's the thing."

"Oh, boy." Jill's eyes got wide. "What did she do?"

Everything.

He scrubbed his chin, an occasional nervous tick of his. "You might as well know. Zoey and I…we're a thing."

Jill's expression went from worry to shock to anger to shock and back to worry again. It had to be exhausting to be her.

"Ryan. She's my best friend."

"I know."

"You can't hurt her, or I'll have to kill you."

"I won't but thanks for the vote of confidence."

Jill frowned. "I'm sorry, but didn't you say that you're not ready for a serious relationship? That you don't believe they work?"

"I did say that, and yet you, Mom and nearly everyone in town has a niece, granddaughter or daughter that I absolutely need to meet. And last I checked you didn't want me to deprive a child of my dimples."

"That's true, but Zoey…she's so sweet and innocent."

Well, he'd fixed that, hadn't he?

"She's not *that* innocent."

"Oh, god!" Jill plugged fingers in her ears and started singing. "*La la la*, I can't hear you. *La la la*."

He smiled in spite of his innate desire to tell her to get out of his personal business. "Okay, Lady Gaga, you need to get going. Your brother has sheriffing to do."

As he led Jill toward the exit, she stopped, unplugged her ears and turned to him. "This is amazing. When you took Carly to a wedding, she met Levi right after. Now you took Zoey to a party and she met…you."

"Yeah, that's super."

"You know, I really think I might be good at this matchmaking thing."

"No you're not. You're not a matchmaker."

"I could be." She straightened, chin up.

He knew better than to argue with her. He patted her back. "You can do anything you want, Jilly."

"That's right!"

"Sheriff, it's Trenton LaRue on line one," Renata called out.

"Got to take this," Ryan said as Jill waved goodbye.

Trenton was his best prospect for taking his place in the next election. It was still six months away, but Ryan had been searching for his possible replacement since almost day one. Actually, it had been day two, when he'd intervened in some kind of parade that Renata wanted to arrange for him. Another parade! Hometown hero wins in landslide! Uh, no.

The parties after his election had been enough. Despite what everyone believed, he didn't enjoy being the center of attention. It was simply that he understood how to handle it, having been an officer. He understood leadership and the chain of command. It didn't mean he enjoyed it. Not anymore.

It had been logical to approach the current deputies first, but they weren't interested in running, even when he explained that he wouldn't run against them. Even when he explained he'd endorse them. It had been a nogo. But Trenton would be different. They'd been in Iraq together and Ryan knew he could trust Trenton with his six anytime, anywhere. Best, Trenton had been working as a police officer in Denver and wanted to make a move to California. So when his request had been approved to add one more deputy to the force, Ryan had contacted Trenton immediately.

Fortune's town rules stated that Trenton had to work as a deputy for Fortune for at least three months before running for sheriff, with Ryan's full endorsement.

"Hey, dude," Ryan said. "Hope this is good news."

"It's a go," Trent said. "I'll be there in about three months to check the area out."

"Good, I'll schedule your interview."

"So what's it like, being the sheriff?"

One piece of information Ryan hadn't yet shared with

Trent was that he'd like him to run as his replacement when the time came. Either way, though, he needed another deputy and Trent needed the work. No sweat if Trent wouldn't do it, but Ryan had a feeling he'd welcome the opportunity.

"It's a great position for an upwardly mobile individual."

Trent practically had a coughing fit on the other end of the line. "Cut the BS."

"Yeah. Won't lie to you—it's slow here. Most of the time I'm dealing with residents who think I control the oxygen in this town."

"You don't?" Trent chortled.

"There's work to be done but it's not the adrenaline rush you're used to."

"Right now, bud, I could use a break from the daily adrenaline fix."

"No doubt. I take our nuisance calls so that my deputies can take care of the real work."

"You're a prince. Always knew that."

"Yeah, yeah."

"What kind of nuisance calls?"

"Residents calling because a neighbor's dog defecated on their lawn. Noise disturbance calls when someone's TV was too loud. Someone revving their engine too loudly next door."

Zoey calling 911 because her dog had been stolen.

Trent whistled. "Whoa. That's a slow day."

It wasn't that Ryan minded the slow days, especially when they'd managed to put him in Zoey's orbit, but he felt he'd outgrown his usefulness. If the job was simply being a figurehead and mouthpiece, someone else would be more effective. He'd had enough of that as an officer to last him a lifetime.

Chapter 16

For the first time in a long while, Zoey was having a wonderful Monday. It had started in the morning when she found Ryan's note tucked under Mr. Coffee.

Indie snores. Bella farts in her sleep. Corky is the quiet one. Go figure. Call you tomorrow. R

Ryan had also left the night-light on that she'd forgotten about last night. You had to love a man who noticed details. There had been no issues with her pets in the morning, and this with them having been locked out of her bedroom all night. After Ryan left, she'd decided to keep them out since she thought they might as well get used to the fact. With any luck, there wouldn't be any room for them in her bed for the foreseeable future. No guarantees but fingers eternally crossed.

There were no packages blocking her way into the store. No skin cream from Mami and no botched product deliveries. No fires in the dumpster. Fred, too, seemed in a particularly good mood, waving to Zoey as she opened her store and flipped the sign from Closed to Open.

"That was a good picture of you and the sheriff," Fred called out.

"Thanks."

She'd made the decision to no longer be humiliated or embarrassed since Ryan returned her feelings. After all this time, he saw her as a woman. Someone besides his little sister's best friend. She was sexy. Wild. It sounded like someone else but it was her. Zoey Castillo, sex symbol. Exclusively for Ryan Davis.

The morning went swiftly with some of her regulars. She sold parakeet food and specialty cat food, two leashes and two dog beds. Carly came in with cute baby Grace to pick up dog food for Digger, their Chihuahua mix.

"You went to the anniversary party with Ryan?" Carly asked, as Zoey rang her up.

"Yeah, he offered."

"I met Levi right after I went to a wedding with Ryan."

"Yeah, I'd forgotten about that but Jill reminded me."

"Isn't he a perfect gentleman? He gave me a hug at the end of the evening. It was kind of like going out with my older brother, if my older brother was super hot."

The differences between the two experiences confirmed, Zoey's heart fluttered and did a little somersault. She wanted to tell Carly about how her date with Ryan had gone much differently, but Grace started fussing and took Carly's whole attention. Then something happened that Zoey really should have been prepared for but wasn't.

"Hey, guys," Jill said as she walked into the store and gave Grace a squeeze. "I need more of that organic food you say is so good for Fubar."

"Of course," Zoey said and left the register. "See you later, Carly."

As she located the specialty bag in the back of the store, Jill came up behind Zoey.

"You realize you can't talk to me about this. Ever."

Zoey startled. "W-what?"

"I just talked to Ryan."

"Oh. I was going to call you."

"Look, I'm happy for you. Really. But if you ever tell me anything romantic about you two, like how he kisses or, ugh, other stuff, I'm going to stuff fingers in my ears and start singing 'Baby Shark.'"

"Geez, anything but that."

The song was from a show that Grace listened to on a regular basis. Once Zoey and Jill had been over to Carly's and the repetitive three-note song was more than they'd been able to bear. They'd left the house with their ears bleeding, swearing that they'd never let their kids listen to such junk even if it did keep them quiet.

"And one more thing." Jill pointed. "You can't hurt him, or I'll have to kill you."

"I would never!"

"You say that now but you may not have a choice."

"What's that supposed to mean?"

"You have to support him. Are you going to be okay dating the sheriff? There are going to be parties, dealing with the media and elections, all the stuff you hate."

Jill cleared her throat. "You might have to buy a few fancy dresses even."

"Actually, Ryan says he's not going to run again."

"And you fell for that."

Zoey's stomach dropped. "Why? You think he's lying?"

"No. What I'm saying is, Ryan does what he needs to do. If he has to run again, he will. Anyway, is this a relationship? Is it a fling? What is it?"

"It's not a fling! Why? What did Ryan say?"

"Calm down. He didn't say. As it turns out I barely got a word out of him. I know that he wouldn't do a fling with you, but Lauren really screwed him over. She basically abandoned him when he took this job. Like being a small town sheriff just wasn't cool enough for her."

"That's horrible. Poor Ryan. All I told him is that I just want to see where this goes."

"So…no pressure."

"No. We're dating."

"Well, I wasn't sure about the two of you, but you do look good together. And I was beginning to wonder about you."

"What about me?"

"I was worried that you'd grow old, being known to everyone as the cat lady."

"But I just have the store cat."

"You know what I mean." Jill shrugged. "Maybe you have too many animals."

"I basically have dogs that have been abandoned. And I was trying to find a home for Boo. Corky, too. Do you know how many people don't want to own a pot-bellied pig?"

"I just hope they don't keep you from being in a serious relationship."

Zoey crossed her arms. "Any guy who would break up with me over my dedication to animals is not worth having."

"That's not what I mean, Z." Jill went palms up. "I just think sometimes...you might be afraid to be hurt again. And it's safer to be with pets that won't abandon you than it is to be in a real relationship where you have to take a risk."

"You're wrong." Zoey huffed.

"Okay. I'm glad I'm wrong."

"And also? I never did talk to you about my boyfriends. That was you. And Carly."

"See, you never said anything so that's where I got the idea that you were so sweet and innocent."

Zoey scrunched up her eyebrows. "Wait. How do you know I'm not?"

"Ryan said something." Jill slapped her forehead. "Look what you made me do!"

Despite Jill's disgust, Zoey couldn't help but smile. To Ryan, she was definitely no longer sweet and innocent, which was good to have confirmed yet again.

"Gah! Don't smile like that. You're making it worse." Jill plugged her fingers in her ears and sang the "Baby Shark" song.

Zoey did the same and sang at the top of her lungs as protection. She had the sudden unnerving desire to stick toothpicks in her eyes. Anything to make the song stop. That's when Zoey noticed her ninth grade music theory teacher, Mr. Olson, standing in the cat food aisle staring at both of them like they'd taken leave of their senses.

She hip checked Jill, who followed Zoey's gaze.

"Oh, hello there," Jill said, stopping the song. "We were just…just…"

"It was a bet. That's what it was. We bet each other."

"Yeah, and I lost the bet. So I had to sing a song I hate."

"And I had to listen to it." Zoey nodded.

"Listen, I don't care what you girls were singing," Mr. Olson explained, moving down the aisle. "Just so long as you stay in key."

"I'm sorry." Zoey turned to Jill. "I didn't mean to smile."

"That's okay," Jill said. "You're allowed to smile."

"Aw, thanks."

"It's just… I don't know, weird." Jill cringed. "I was never friends with any of Ryan's girlfriends. Or stupid Lauren. So…this is weird. Different. Did I mention weird?"

"I can see that."

Still, Jill was going to have to get used to the idea that her brother was a hunk of a man who was going to have sex with Zoey. Often, if she was lucky.

"Alright," Jill said, helping Zoey lug the bag of dog food to the front. "I'll talk to you later. I need to get back up to the ridge."

"By the way, how are the wedding preparations going?"

"We've finally decided to have it on the ridge. It's official."

"You'll save money on a venue."

"And I've always wanted to get married outdoors. Turns out, so did Sam."

"But you're not going to do that first thing you were thinking about doing." Zoey hoped. There was, after all, something to be said for tradition.

"No." Jill sighed. "My mother had a conniption fit."

"Getting married while wakeboarding could be a little tricky."

"You'd be surprised. We found a minister who would do it. I'm getting so much better, and we already practiced. Anyway, guess we'll have to do it the old boring way. I don't mind as long as we get married."

"I'm still on the lookout for a dog tux for Fubar. Is he still your ring bearer?"

"That's the plan. But we're still working on training him."

After Zoey cashed Jill out at the register and she was off, Zoey got busy adding dog treats to the display she had in the front. They were ordered in bulk from specialty vendors, looked like biscuits and biscotti cookies, and once during a particularly rough day, Carly had mistaken one for the real thing.

The store phone rang and Zoey ran to answer it. Could be Ryan, though he had her cell phone number. "Pimp Your Pet, how can I help you?"

"How was the dinner?" Tia asked. "Did he love Tio's rice and chicken?"

Ahem. "Oh, yeah. He really did. Thank Tio again. He's such a lifesaver."

"*Ay, mi amor,* don't you know by now he'd do anything for you?"

Zoey did know. She sniffed a little bit, not wanting to cry when nearby a customer was looking for the perfect collar and leash combo.

"Your *mami* called. She wants us all to have dinner together before she goes back. Isn't that nice?"

"What? Where? When?"

"Next Friday night. Here. Bring your young man with you if you'd like."

"*Next* Friday? Oh, I can't. I'm busy."

There was a long silence from Tia. Zoey rarely turned down an invite for dinner with Tio and Tia. "What's wrong?"

I can't handle seeing my mother again so soon, that's all. I don't know if I'm ready to tell her yet. But Tia wouldn't understand, and why would she when Zoey had never explained? She'd kept Tia in the dark, which wasn't fair. But now so much time had passed, it might hurt her to know Zoey had never felt comfortable confiding in her. It had just been easier to stop dwelling on what had happened. To forget.

Of course, look how well that had worked.

"Is Jorge coming, too?"

"I assume so, since he's her fiancé. But I didn't ask. Why?"

Zoey couldn't do this over the phone. And she didn't want to make a scene on Friday either. So she'd just have to come over before then and explain everything to Tia.

"I don't like him very much."

"Ah, so this is the problem between you and Veronica. No wonder she wouldn't say anything about your disagreement. But honey, you aren't likely to appreciate any man that she chooses. And I agree it's hard to think of anyone good enough for her, but you and I must trust her judgment."

Zoey swallowed and fought the urge to be sick. Tia wouldn't say that if she knew what Jorge had done.

"Fine, I'll come to dinner."

She'd have to talk to Tia first. Explain everything. Even if this meant a fracture in her family, a crack that might never be repaired, it had to be done. She'd waited

too long and protected both Tia and Mami without realizing she'd inadvertently protected Jorge.

Zoey glanced down at her smartphone. Still no calls
or texts from Ryan. He was probably having a crazy-
busy Monday, and she knew he had his basketball game
at the Boys and Girls Club tonight. She barely resisted
sending him a text of her own, even if he'd said that
he'd call her.

While she had a tendency to be old-school, preferring guys to make the first move and call or text, it was
different with Ryan. Everything between them was out
in the open and she'd shared something with him she'd
never even shared with her best friends. It was sort of
empowering to have this kind of freedom. To be able
to call the guy instead of just waiting. And waiting.

Her finger was poised just when Hud came in, holding his little dog, Rachel, in his big arms. He didn't
look happy.

"Where are the dog diapers?"

Zoey got back to work.

Chapter 17

Ryan had a hell of a Monday, with a complicated morning dispatchment in which he had to explain to Deputy Corwin that no, they couldn't just pull random teenagers out of class and grill them about their interest in fire. There were more nuisance calls interspersed with hiring interviews, media interviews regarding the fires and a meeting with the mayor. He hadn't had a chance to call Zoey, and before he realized this, his day had ended.

To top off a bad day, at the meeting of the Boys and Girls Club, Ethan didn't show.

"He's out of town," one of the boys offered.

"Nah, he's taking care of his grandma," Mark said.

"He's sick," yet another one said.

Good to know Ethan had friends. Nobody seemed to know a damn thing. Either way, Ryan, Aidan and the kids played a loud and raucous game of pickup basketball with the sharp pounding sound of heavy-footed boys on the waxed wood floor mixing with the squeak of rubber soles as they dashed from one end of the court to the other.

The losing team, of course, had to complain loudly that they would have won had Ethan been there tonight to play on their side. Clearly, they had their priorities straight. Later, as Ryan helped Aidan gather basketballs to put into the net, he was paged. So was Aidan.

At the same time.

Ryan glanced at his pager and recognized the number. It was the station. He wasted no time phoning. Aidan waited nearby, certain they were both being paged for the same reason.

"Had another fire tonight. This one nearly burned down an old shed near the school. We've got a suspect in custody down at the station," Deputy Corwin said. "You'll want to come down."

"You page Aidan, too?"

"Figured it was an 'all hands on deck' situation."

Ryan slid Aidan a nod. It was as they'd suspected. Someone had been arrested. Maybe they could relax knowing that no wildfires would be set with intent. Now they could simply worry about the heat and dryness of the hills, which sometimes lit up with no human help at all.

"Suspect name?"

"Ethan Larsen."

Ryan cursed under his breath. When he got in his Jeep, Aidan following, he couldn't drive fast enough. He wanted facts. Solid information. As much as he'd wanted Ethan to open up, he'd never suspected him. Not every troubled kid wound up an arsonist. But if this was Ethan's doing, he'd be in serious trouble. If there was still no actual damage, the charges would likely be misdemeanors. The important thing was to get the kid some help.

"Where is he?" Ryan asked as he arrived at the station, still dressed in his sweats and T-shirt.

"In the interrogation room," Corwin said.

"How did this happen? Last we talked this morning you had few leads."

"Well, we now have eyewitness testimony from three people."

Ryan held on to his patience by a thin and unraveling thread. "Was one of them Fred?"

"You know that. He was the first one to report seeing Ethan at the fire down by the hardware store."

"Yeah, I talked to him. Fred didn't see shit."

"He said he did. Now two other people have come forward."

Ryan didn't waste any time asking why he hadn't been informed of that immediately. "You call his parents? He's a minor."

"Of course I called his parents. They're on their way but he wanted to talk to you."

"He asked for me?" Corwin could have hauled off and slugged Ryan and he wouldn't have been more surprised than he was with that news.

"Said he knows you." Corwin lifted a shoulder.

"He's one of our kids," Aidan added, referring to the proprietary way they'd taken to referring to the boys they were mentoring.

Ryan hesitated only a moment. If he went in there and the kid confessed because he felt an odd sense of security with Ryan, he'd hang himself. Ryan couldn't fully protect him within those four walls. Ethan might need an attorney. At the least he had to talk to his parents. On the other hand, if Ethan wanted to open up to him—and wasn't that what Ryan had wanted all this time?—he had to show up for the boy. Even if, as sheriff, he was never off duty.

Opening the door to the interrogation room, Ryan held his breath, hoping his instincts were right. Eyewitness testimony was the least reliable evidence of all. People often got it wrong even with the best of intentions. And he hoped like hell they had this time.

Ethan sat in a plastic chair at the steel table, arms cradling his head, which was facedown. He looked up when the door opened, and the look he gave Ryan was enough to make him believe all those evenings with pickup games hadn't been wasted time. There was hope in his gaze, pure and undisguised. It hit Ryan hard because whether or not he could actually help would depend on a lot of things.

But he would sure in the hell give it everything he had. "You asked for me?"

Ethan stood to his full height of six five and burst into tears. "I didn't do it."

Ryan hadn't expected that, and all the air whooshed out of him. He was back to his days as an officer in the army, witnessing recruits who were not much older than Ethan fold under the pressure of combat. He'd been unable to help or even sympathize because that was not his job. He was the tough-as-nails officer of his company, part of the infantry. A leader. Those who couldn't hack it had to go. And he'd rather they go early than wind up on the field where the risk was life and death. Their lives. His.

But the whole situation had never sat well with him. A leader should be able to help and encourage those who were weaker. Had there been more time and less war, he might have. Ethan looked like the child that he truly was, his body shaking in big heaves, the fear etched on his face far too real.

"Where were you tonight?" Ryan asked, because his absence from the club that night did not exactly make his case for innocence.

"I was on my way to see my g-girlfriend." Ethan shoved large hands in his pants pockets and spoke between uneven breaths. "But I'm not really allowed to have a girlfriend. Anyway, I saw the shed go up in flames. I—I'd never seen anything like that in my life so I stopped to watch. I could already hear the sirens coming."

"Did you see anyone else in the area?"

"No, it was already pretty dark." He sniffed and wiped his nose on his sleeve.

Ryan shoved a hand through his hair. "Okay. Don't talk to anyone until your parents arrive."

"But you believe me, right?"

"Do you enjoy watching fires?" Ryan asked, knowing he probably shouldn't. Afraid of the answer.

Ethan lifted a shoulder. "Not really. It's not like I see a lot of them, and I don't spend much time outside anyway. My grandma is the one who forces me to go play basketball."

"Stay here." Ryan turned to leave the interrogation room but Ethan stopped him, a hand on his shoulder.

"I swear I didn't do this."

"I believe you."

The whisper of relief showed in Ethan's blue gaze.

"We'll straighten this out. Just be honest. Tell your parents, and if they say it's okay, then tell the deputy who comes in here after me."

"Thanks." Ethan sniffed.

"You're going to be alright." Ryan clapped him on the shoulder.

Best of all, Ethan appeared to believe it, if Ryan could go by the tentative crack of a smile.

Ryan didn't leave until Ethan's parents, his mother and stepfather, council member Nick Jacobson, showed up. He didn't leave until Ethan's parents insisted on taking him home, stating that if the deputy had any more questions he could contact their attorney. He didn't leave until he saw Ethan, walking slowly between his parents, turn to give Ryan something between a salute and a wave.

Only then did he feel it was safe to leave.

Chapter 18

"Should I call him, or is it too late?" Zoey asked Bella, Indie and Corky.

They were giving her the stink-eye, obviously, because she still hadn't brought Boo back to them. But none had an opinion on calling Ryan.

Zoey sat on her couch, a bowl of salted caramel ice cream in her lap. She wouldn't be the kind of desperate woman who had to hear from a guy every day. They were still in such an early phase of…whatever this was. Crazy as it seemed, Zoey already missed talking to him. He was so easy to talk to and a good listener.

She'd almost wanted him there when she confessed to Tia, but this was too much of a family matter. Not to mention terribly uncomfortable. She wouldn't do that to Ryan. One mention of it and he'd want to be there with her. He was just that kind of a man. She'd known that for a long while, too, but she'd never known that protection to be directed at her. It was nice for a change.

"He said he would call but maybe he just got busy."

Corky snorted and Zoey tried not to take offense since he tended to snort for any reason, good or bad. Zoey had just taken her bowl to the sink when her phone buzzed with a text from Ryan.

You busy?

Not unless one considered licking, um, rinsing out her ice cream bowl busy. She replied that she was just having a quiet evening at home with her pets, hoping that didn't sound too pathetic. It was one of many quiet evenings she'd spent alone in the past two years. There was an old Spanish saying that went, roughly translated, *Better off alone than in bad company.* She had become accustomed to such nights, but now she wasn't as satisfied with being alone.

I'm in front of your house.

What? Zoey shot up. She tiptoed to her front window and looked through the blinds to see Ryan's Jeep parked at the curb. He was serious. What was he doing sitting out there instead of ringing her doorbell?

Get in here, she texted back.

He was at her door within seconds dressed in sweats and a T-shirt with Fortune Boys and Girls Club printed on it. "Sorry I didn't call first."

She tugged him inside as Indie, Bella and even Corky came to greet him. Ryan seemed almost disheveled, in a way she'd never seen the always put-together sheriff.

She took one look at him and thought maybe he had bad news for her. She wasn't ready for this thing between them to end. Not yet. He had to give them a chance.

"Is something wrong?"

"You could say that," he said as he pulled her into his arms. "I had to see you."

"Why?"

"That's it. I had to see you, and I'm not used to that."

"Not used to…what?"

"I'm not used to having to see someone. Anyone. Like my day isn't complete until I do."

Oh. My. God. She sucked in a breath, thinking that this was really good news. This was better than she could have imagined. This was salted caramel ice cream on a hot summer day. Hot chocolate on a lazy, rainy afternoon.

"I wanted to see you, too. I thought about you all day."

"Yeah?" He gave her a slow smile. "What did you think about?"

"I thought about last night. I thought about your tongue and how much I like it." She smiled at him, shocked at how bold she was being.

His gaze darkened. "You are killing me here."

"Not yet but give me a chance."

His hands slid from her waist to her butt. "Where were you hiding all this time?"

"Me?" She touched her chest.

"Who are you and what did you do with shy Zoey?"

"C'mon, you had to know that I had a crush on you. Ever since I first saw you."

"Crush, yeah, but not…not this." He met her gaze, his hot and stormy eyes melting her heart. "I used to watch you and wonder what it would be like to be with you."

Oh, boy.

"When?"

"Different times. Like at Carly and Levi's Christmas party. Lou was drunk off his ass and trying to kiss you under the mistletoe, and you kept moving away. It took everything I had in me not to clock him."

"And I thought you never even noticed me."

"You're hard to ignore, babe." His gaze was pinned to her mouth; a thumb circled and played with her bottom lip. "Noticeable."

"I don't try to be."

"I know. But you can't help that. You're beautiful, Zoey."

He kissed her, the kiss going from tender and tentative to wild, plundering and wet within seconds. She clawed at him, trying to climb him like a tree. Bella barked, which made Indie yark. And that was the second time Zoey had forgotten all about her dogs for a few minutes. She was almost another person with Ryan. And she didn't mind this woman. This woman who knew *what* she wanted and *who* she wanted. With him, she was letting go of her inhibitions with someone she could trust.

She moved him toward the bedroom, and as he walked with her he tugged off his T-shirt with his free hand. "Need a shower first. I'm all sweaty."

He went into the bathroom off her bedroom, leaving the door ajar. He hadn't invited her in with him, so she decided to give him his privacy. Well, sort of. She gave him as much privacy as she could while she watched like a voyeur as the steam rose inside the shower's glass doors, artfully framing his incredible and muscular backside. His arms were braced against the shower wall, the muscles in his arms bunched and tightened. He dropped his head under the nozzle and the water poured over his beautiful body. She suddenly decided that this new and improved Zoey, this she-devil that had sex on her brain 24/7, wasn't going to simply sit on her bed and drool. Maybe he'd welcome some company.

Stepping inside the bathroom, she discarded clothes as she went, tossing them on the floor near where his had landed. She'd never done shower love either, but like all new things with Ryan, this too felt safe. Comfortable.

She opened the shower door and he turned to her, wearing a slow sexy smile.

"Need some company?" she asked.

"What took you so long?"

A couple of hours later, Zoey lay tangled in Ryan's legs and arms, sated and satisfied. Yet she wanted something more. Something deeper.

"Stay with me tonight. Sleep with me."

He went up on one elbow. "I have a hard time saying no to you."

"Then don't."

"Are you actually going to let me sleep?"

"That depends. Are you going to let *me* sleep?"

"It's going to be hard." He gave her a wicked smile. "See what I did there?"

"Ha, ha." She tenderly kissed his pec.

"What are you doing next Friday?" he asked.

"Why? You want to take me on a date?"

"Might be a good idea. And I have a party at the mayor's house I'm forced to attend."

Zoey sucked in a breath. She could tell him the truth, that there was a family dinner to attend, but then he'd wonder about Jorge. He'd want to be there and feel guilty that he couldn't be.

"I'm…supposed to go out with the girls."

"Ah, guess I have been monopolizing your time lately."

"No, you haven't." She sat up and turned to glance back at him. "So will you go alone?"

His hand slid down her back causing a tingle. "To the party? Yeah, I've been going stag to these things for a while now. No big deal."

"Do women hit on you there?"

In other words, as they did all the time? Pet stores, pet washes, and she'd heard the rumors about his being invited into homes for sexual favors, too. Word got around. People talked.

He quirked a single brow. "Are you jealous?"

"What? No!" She snorted like Corky but more sophisticated. "Don't be ridiculous."

"Is it? Ridiculous?" He went up on one elbow.

"For me to be jealous? Yes, because I don't have a jealous bone in my body."

So that was twice now she'd lied to him. She was going to hell.

He reached for her and pulled her back. "Remember when I told you I'd never tell you something that wasn't true, especially in bed? Thinking you might want to do the same."

Her conscience got the better of her. "Okay, okay. I have lots of jealous bones in my body. About two hundred and six, to be exact."

He chuckled. "That's better. For the record, I'm also a jealous man. I don't want to share you with anyone."

"Of course not, and you won't." Her heart now squishy and warm and, she had to face it, just a pink puddle of goo, she had to confess. "I'm not going out with the girls Friday. I'm supposed to go to my aunt's for dinner."

"Now why wouldn't you tell me that?" His brow furrowed, and he appeared genuinely confused.

"Because...my mother is going to be there, too. And probably that man."

"And you're worried I'll want to knock him out."

"Maybe a little?" She sighed against his neck. "I'm finally going to tell her."

He squeezed her tight. "You have to.

"But I don't want you to think you have to be there. You have obligations as a sheriff for a while longer and this party sounds important."

"If you need me, I'll figure something out."

"I'll be okay." She had a new strength inside she hadn't believed existed. It was going to get her through this thing with Jorge and her mother.

"Yeah?"

"Really."

"Okay, let's go to sleep."

She shut off the light on the nightstand and he pulled her back to his front, spooning.

"Hey, so who's your kindred animal? I don't think I ever heard."

Oh, no. She had to tell him. This was the Truth Bed.

"I'm a mama bear. Which surprises no one."

"Doesn't surprise me. Should have guessed. Funny," he said, his deep voice sounding ragged and sleepy in the dark. "We're both bears."

"I know, right? That's funny."

And then, somehow, even while being held this close in the dark by the man who'd headlined so many of her fantasies, she was able to find sleep.

Chapter 19

"Time for lunch," Ryan said, grabbing his keys.

"Sure, what do you want me to have brought in?" Renata said.

"No, I mean I'm going *out* to lunch." He was sick of working through lunch and being chained to the desk far too many hours of the day.

Time to get a life.

"My goodness, but you've never done that." Her jaw gaped.

Was he really that predictable?

"Yeah? Well there's a first time for everything."

"Tell the truth, sheriff," she said. "Is there finally a woman in the picture?"

"There might be." It wasn't any of her business.

For the past week, he'd spent nearly every night with Zoey. They'd started to make plans for things they'd do after he was no longer the sheriff. Trips they wanted to take together. Movies they both wanted to see. Restaurants they wanted to try.

He was falling hard for her, and it was easier than he'd ever thought it could be.

She didn't make anything complicated. She didn't ask for or demand all of his time. She understood who he was and accepted him. She knew that he wasn't the "hero" he'd been cast to be by their hometown. He came with warts like everyone else.

She'd learned that he couldn't cook, once actually burning water. He preferred the New York Yankees over the San Francisco Giants (which had caused a minor fight— their first). Among his many faults were the fact he wasn't particularly romantic, though she brought it out of him more than anyone ever had. And for the life of him, as much as he tried, his socks never wound up in the hamper.

This was the first instance where he could remember actually enjoying being exclusive with someone. He no longer had the dreaded FOMO, Fear of Missing Out. With Zoey, he believed there could be no better. He was convinced of that even if she'd done nothing other than be herself. It was all him. His idea. He liked that a whole hell of a lot.

It struck him that this could be what he'd been missing all along. A woman who wanted a no-frills guy. Zoey was a loyal friend who didn't just like him because of his accomplishments. Hell, she didn't know half of them, and he sure wasn't going to tell her.

She was a private person, too. But she was someone who could easily attend events with him, holding her own. Already he'd noticed that she was no longer blending into wallpaper and hiding in corners. She wore sexy dresses and shoes, and the panties...well, she might have always worn sexy underwear and he'd just never known about it.

Okay, so he realized he was probably an ass for appreciating that she wore sexy underwear. And at the moment he didn't care. This was exactly why he didn't deserve to be put on a pedestal by anyone. He was a perpetually horny guy.

Horny Guy drove to the bagel shop, picked up two sandwiches and was on his way to deliver one to a sexy temptress when he was stopped by Fred.

"Heard you arrested someone. Finally."

"You heard wrong. A kid was brought in for questioning."

"You didn't arrest him?" Fred bellowed.

"We can't do that without evidence. That's all you need to know."

Fred tried to keep him discussing the case, and the so-called eyewitnesses. So far two of them had already recanted and admitted they couldn't really see much in the dark except that it seemed to be a tall kid. Ryan didn't discuss open investigations with anyone, and he had places to go. And besides, it was his freaking lunch hour in case anyone cared.

"Gotta go." He pushed the door open with his back.

When he walked into Pimp Your Pet, Zoey wasn't behind the register so he placed the bag on the counter and went to find her. She was in the back of the store near the Pimp Your Pet dog T-shirts display, hanging them up.

"How can I hel—" She turned and when her eyes

registered him, they lit up in a way that made his chest tighten. "Ryan."

"Brought you lunch. You can help me by taking a break." He pulled her to him, and her hands wrapped around the nape of his neck as they always did.

"You brought me lunch?" She gaped. "No one ever brings me lunch."

"What do you do for lunch usually?" Threading her fingers through his own he tugged her toward the register.

"I bring something from home. Okay, confession time. I don't always take a lunch break."

"Thought so. Neither do I, but I'm going to start."

"I usually eat at the register and I'll stop if I get a customer."

"And I mostly eat at my desk. In meetings. Fun stuff."

"You're chained to that desk, are you?"

"Told you, I'm a desk jockey most of the time. Until they drag me out and put me in front of a camera or a reporter or some such thing."

"I don't know how you can do it." Zoey unwrapped her turkey sandwich. "Fred told me you arrested a suspect a few days ago."

"Maybe Fred should join the department. I am hiring."

"He's a busybody." She frowned. "Did you arrest someone?"

He hadn't really wanted to talk about work but Zoey had reason to be worried. She'd been at the shop during the dumpster fire, and she was likely concerned about Jill and Sam on the ridge, as well.

"We didn't. But we have some leads."

"Is it really a kid doing all this?"

"We don't know that either. But the profiling leans

toward that." They finished eating with zero interruptions. Small miracle. "Are you going to be okay Friday?"

She went up on tiptoes and framed his face. "I am. But I'm going to miss you like crazy."

Though they'd spent most weeknights together, on the weekends he was still working his renovation project from sunup till sundown. Progress was slow, and he'd had to hire a plumber since the work appeared to be more extensive than either he or Sam could handle.

"Let me know if you need me." He bent to kiss her, slow and lingering. She had the sweetest taste, like ripe cherries. "I'll duck out of the party."

"You won't have to do that,"

"I know," he said, pulling on her pouty lower lip with his thumb. "You've got this."

Chapter 20

Zoey decided that her best course of action was to come over to Tia's unannounced on Thursday after work. She didn't want Tia to worry before she had to, because she'd be doing enough of that when she found out what the man her sister was marrying had done. One thing Zoey did know was that Tia would believe her. With that in mind, Zoey had to break it to her gently.

She found Tia vacuuming. Zoey was about to announce herself by gently patting Tia's back when her aunt suddenly turned, threw a hand to her chest and crossed herself.

"*Madre de Dios*! Zoey Gloria Castillo! You scared me!"

Uh-oh. She was in trouble when Tia used all three of her names. Zoey bit back a laugh. "I didn't mean to, but you couldn't hear the doorbell so I let myself in."

"Of course, you're always welcome. This is your home." Tia gasped, rolling up the vacuum cord.

"Take a break and let's sit down for a minute." Zoey walked to the living room couch. "Where's Tio?"

"He went to the store." Tia joined her.

"Will he be gone long?"

"I don't know. Why? Do you need him? I can just call and he'll—" She reached for the cordless phone on the coffee table.

Zoey stayed Tia's hand. "No, it's just that I wanted to talk to you. Alone."

"Alone?" Her aunt quirked a brow and then some type of universal motherhood understanding flashed in her brown eyes and she smoothed her skirt. "Ah, alone. Go ahead."

The last time Zoey had asked to talk to Tia alone it had been to break the news that she'd be moving out. Tio had taken it about as well as if the nightly newscaster had announced World War III. But Tia had calmed his jangled nerves and assured him their Zoey would be just fine because they'd raised her properly.

Even though they'd let her go to Mexico to see Mami.

That mistake was on Zoey, who had insisted. Begged.

Suddenly Zoey's breath hitched.

"Mija, what's wrong?"

She couldn't look at Tia. "I—I'm a terrible daughter."

She was thinking of Veronica now, and how Zoey didn't want to be her daughter. She'd been fun, like a beautiful older sister or good friend. Not a mother. Never a mother. Which was so wrong. Zoey loved her mother in theory, but she didn't know how to be close to someone who'd essentially abandoned her. After all this time maybe it was too late anyway.

"What? No, no." Tia patted Zoey's hand.

Zoey spoke through choked back sobs. "But I am, be-cause…because I always wanted you to be my mother. Not Veronica."

Now Tia's eyes grew misty and she embraced Zoey. "*Mi amor*, you *are* my daughter. No matter who gave birth to you, you're mine."

"But you're always so nice to Veronica."

"Well, I love her too. She was like my first daughter. You are my second."

"She's not a very good person."

"Let me tell you something, honey. Your Mami is just different from the rest of her family. She always was, but that doesn't make her bad. She tries, she really does. You were her life for the first twelve years. And something else you might not know…because she's al-ways asked me not to say anything. But she's generous. For years, she's been helping us. Even though we ask her not to, and we refuse her money, she finds a way. She paid off our mortgage and we didn't know until we sent in a payment and it was returned."

"She did?" Zoey wiped a tear away.

"All that money we spent sending you to private school? She called it her way of paying us back. Even though we didn't ask for it."

Her aunt and uncle were very proud, so Zoey was shocked they'd accepted the money but happy they had. It was no less than they deserved. Feeling worse be-cause she was about to change the way Tia felt about her younger sister, Zoey bit her lower lip. Somehow she had to do this anyway.

"Something happened to me when I went to Mexico to visit her."

"What do you mean?"

"You have to promise not to tell Tio."

Tia hesitated and pinched her lips together. "If you think that's important."

"I do. At the movie party, I wanted to be glamorous just once. Like her. We went to a party all dressed up and her director…he got me alone and said awful things to me. Sexual things."

The fear and shame that had pulsed through Zoey that night went through her all over again.

Tia gasped. "*Dios mio*! Did he hurt you?"

"No. Someone interrupted him."

"Who is this man?"

"It's her fiancé, *Jorge*."

A hand went over Tia's mouth and she squeezed her eyes shut. When she opened them, they were watery. "I'm so sorry I let you go."

Zoey's chest pinched. "No! It wasn't your fault. I wanted to, remember? I begged you to go."

"Still, I knew better. So did Raul. We were so worried, but it was more about drinking. Drugs. Movie star stuff. Not this." She wiped her brow. "Have you told Veronica yet? You must. She can't marry this man."

This was the next toughest part. Zoey hitched in a breath.

"I don't want her to marry him either, but I'm afraid she won't believe me. She won't want to. You see how happy she is and how much she loves Jorge. He practically made her career." Zoey took a deep breath. Her throat was raw and clogged with emotion. "So now you know why I don't want to come over tomorrow night for dinner. Please understand that I can't be around that man."

She stood. "And you think I can?"

"Wait. Where are you going?"

Tia picked up the handset from the coffee table, dialed and walked with it into her bedroom. But the door wasn't shut and Zoey could pick up the words on Tia's end.

"Daughter…talk to you immediately…alone."

Zoey followed Tia to the doorway of her bedroom. She was just hanging up the phone, more tears in her eyes.

"What did she say?"

Tia wiped a tear away. "She'll be right over. Without Jorge."

"Now?"

"I won't have that man in my home, and she needs to know why."

But Zoey didn't want this confrontation. Didn't want this huge stone lodged in her throat. There was the worry that Mami wouldn't believe her, and also of what would happen if she did.

"Mami hasn't had anyone since my father." Her gaze dropped to the newly vacuumed rug. "She loves Jorge. I can tell. Maybe he wouldn't ever do this to anyone else again. He might have changed—and… I'll ruin their relationship."

"It was bound to ruin itself eventually. Don't you dare think for a moment this is your fault. You were a child."

All of this was true, so why did Zoey feel like a scurrying rat instead of a mama bear? Didn't her protective instincts extend to herself? What was wrong with her? Life and love were so complicated and filled with pain and loss, so was it any wonder some days she only wanted to go home to her pets and hide from the world?

Her thoughts went to Ryan and she wished she'd put this off and taken him up on his offer of coming with her to dinner tomorrow night. With his quiet strength to support her this would have all been easier. He was so strong and capable, both inside and out. Loyal and steady. She'd already fallen for him.

Her poor mother. Zoey didn't even want to think about what she'd do or feel if someone tried to rip this love for Ryan away from her the way she was about to do to Mami. But if she married a man like Jorge without really knowing what he'd done it would be Zoey's fault for keeping it a secret.

Mami showed up twenty minutes later, alone as Tia had requested. Zoey did a double take when she took in her disheveled appearance. She wore little if any make-up at all, her hair shoved under a Giants baseball cap. For the first time Zoey noticed that her mother had aged, and her heart ached. Mami was no longer the beauty she'd been ten years ago. She was nearly fifty now. Deep worry lines creased her forehead.

She stared from Tia to Zoey with wide eyes. "I got over here as soon as I could. You scared me. What's wrong? Who's sick?"

"No one is sick, *querida*. Your daughter needs to speak with you and it's important," Tia said, giving Veronica a hug. "I'll be in the kitchen if either of you need me."

"What? No." Above all else Zoey needed the woman who'd raised her to stay with her now.

"You can do this." Tia patted Zoey's shoulder and left the room.

Veronica's eyes followed Tia as if she too didn't want her to go. No wonder, because she'd been like a mother to Veronica, too.

Abandonment had turned Veronica and Zoey practically into strangers. Zoey stared into caramel eyes so like her own.

"What's this about, *querida*?"

"I have to tell you something about Jorge."

She sighed and plunked down on the leather sofa. "Oh, and it's this urgent? Gloria made it sound—"

"It's something I should have told you a long time ago but I'm only now brave enough."

"Tell me."

"The night of the party where I dressed just like you?"

"We were just discussing that not long ago."

Zoey swallowed hard. "I'm—I'm sorry to tell you— but that night wasn't so wonderful for me. Jorge cornered me when we were alone. He said nasty things to me that no grown man should say to a fifteen-year-old girl."

"Alone? When were you two alone?"

Zoey's throat burned and she ignored the first doubt. She was all in now. Because Jorge marrying her mother had raised the stakes. Zoey made a fist and let the fingernails drive into her to distract from the pain in her chest.

"He said sexual things to me, like what he'd like to do to me if we could be alone together for a few hours."

Veronica's jaw gaped, and her eyes narrowed. In her movies, this was the look the camera captured when her character was stricken with terrible, life-changing news.

"What are you saying? Are you sure? English isn't his first language and he often gets things wrong."

Zoey managed to keep her cool but just barely. "The way he looked at me? I couldn't get that wrong. He didn't need words for that."

Veronica's face flushed to a deep magenta. "I don't understand. He's always been such a gentleman. We should all talk about this at dinner tomorrow night. You'll see he's a reasonable man. He'll have an explanation, I'm sure. We'll straighten this out."

Zoey's stomach rolled and pitched. An anger she hadn't anticipated rose inside her like a tidal wave. "No. I don't want to talk to him. I don't want to be around him."

"But *querida*, he's my intended. We need to work this out. There's some mistake, I assure you."

Zoey swallowed hard, her pain diffusing through the solid stone lodged in her throat.

Her mother didn't believe her.

"There's no mistake."

Veronica plucked at her blouse. "I don't know what to do if you won't at least talk to him about this."

"I won't to talk to Jorge. I want you to believe me!"

"How can I when you're telling me such a horrible thing about a wonderful man?"

"Because I'm not saying this to hurt you!" Zoey exploded.

All of the raw pain and anger over missing her mother, over wondering why she hadn't been enough to bring her home, just let loose. "If I wanted to hurt you, I would tell you that you're not a good mother. You left me."

"But I knew that you'd be fine with Gloria and Raul. You were very happy."

Zoey's breaths were coming short and sparse. She

seemed to be yelling a little. "No thanks to you. What do you think it was like, knowing my mother wasn't coming back, after she said she would?"

"But...you never said—"

"I used to worry I'd wake up some morning and Tia and Tio would also be gone!"

"Mija, stop screaming at me." Veronica's voice rose to match Zoey's in volume. "I'm your mother."

"Yes, you are." Zoey forced some calm into her voice. It scared her to feel so out of control with rage. This wasn't her. She was calm and didn't make scenes. "But you didn't raise me. Because if you had, you would know me. Then you might believe me."

Tia came out of the kitchen as if she'd been quietly listening the entire time. "Veronica, tell your daughter that you believe her. Now."

Veronica looked from Tia to Zoey and back again. Her face crumpled and she fell back on the sofa, cradling her face in her hands. "*Dios mio*, what am I going to do? What am I going to do?"

And that's when Zoey realized that Veronica did believe her.

By the time Zoey walked home from Tia's, she was spent. Every ounce of emotion had been poured out. Just drained from her and wiped clean. She needed the walk to calm down and breathe evenly again. Walking slowly, she noticed every summer flower and blossoming tree. Counted cracks in the sidewalk. Breathed in the beautiful mild summer night. Waved to her neighbor Mr. Levin as he sat on his front porch. But when she rounded the curve, she saw Ryan's Jeep parked in front of her house.

And she ran the rest of the way home.

Zoey threw open the door. Ryan stood between the separation of the living room and the kitchen. Indie, Corky and Bella were sitting calmly on their haunches, their backs to Zoey.

"Where were you? I brought take-out from Mr. Wong's." He held up a carton. "That's probably why they haven't stopped tracking my every move since I got here."

Ryan. He wore loose basketball shorts, a tee and a backwards baseball cap. She loved him so much. He fit right in with her and her little family. Just clicked into place like he'd always been a part of them. How she'd been through the first twenty-six years of her life without him she had no idea.

He quirked a brow and the easy smile slipped off his face. "You okay?"

But she didn't want to talk about tonight anymore. She felt lighter than air. Running to him, she launched herself into his arms. He caught her easily, sliding his arms around her butt, his lips twitching into a smile.

She wrapped her legs around him. "God, I missed you today."

"Love this reception, but you realize I didn't cook any of this?"

"Baby, I'd be very afraid if you'd cooked. You opened the cartons, didn't you?"

"I did." He kissed her, both sexy and tender. "Do you want to eat?"

"Yeah," she said, nuzzling his warm neck. "But later. Much, much later."

Smiling, Ryan carried her to the bedroom.

By the time they ate dinner, it was cold.

Chapter 21

When Ryan didn't hear from Zoey on Friday night, he assumed she'd gone to the family dinner. At the party, council member Pullman had announced his candidacy for mayor in the next election, going against the current mayor. The politics and positioning games were just beginning, and they were still a year away from the mayoral election.

Ethan's stepfather, council member Nick Jacobson, pulled Ryan aside. "I won't forget what you did for Ethan."

"It was nothing, Nick," Ryan said. "I'm glad I could help."

Jacobson clapped Ryan on the back. "What you did for Ethan was everything."

Ryan let those words settle into him. He'd had a lot

of appreciation and gratitude over the years, but this felt different. "Well, it's my job."

"No, it isn't. You reached out to Ethan when you didn't have to. He's had a rough time. But he had you when he was scared and alone, and that matters."

"Ethan is a good kid."

Jacobson winced. "Sometimes. Mostly, yes, he is. Look, I hope you'll run again. I know you don't need it, but you've got my full endorsement. We need more people like you in small-town politics. People who aren't out to make a name for themselves."

Ryan hadn't ever thought of it that way.

He schmoozed away the night, hating every minute of it. Two women approached him, asking if he was free after the event. But tonight he only noticed the women's appeal in the way he would a particularly gorgeous sunset. Detached and from a great distance.

Saturday morning, he and Sam attacked the project house, stopping only when Jill brought them sandwiches and lemonade. They were back at it for the rest of the afternoon. Then, as daylight drew to a close Ryan noticed what appeared to be a small horse on the neighboring ranch. He hadn't paid much attention to the goings-on with his neighbors except to be vaguely aware they owned horses and goats, even a rooster, to his amazement. This former agricultural area was still zoned for it. But now, staring in the direction of this small horse as the sun dipped behind a hill, there was no doubt in Ryan's mind.

It was a Great Dane, not a horse, and he'd bet his shorts it was Boo.

"I'll be right back," he called to Sam, who was gathering tools and cleaning up.

"Getting myself out of here," Sam said. "Your sister is going to kill me if I don't get home soon."

"Understood."

If this was Boo, he'd have him back to Zoey by tonight. If his neighbors gave him any shit at all, he'd have to consider hauling them in. But, generally speaking, he hoped this would be one of those so-called nuisance matters he should be able to resolve with his supposedly great gift. While he knew most of the residents in Fortune, he certainly didn't know all of them. And as he approached the home, the entrance to which bore a huge wooden sign that read The Dawsons, Established 1985, he realized he wasn't personally acquainted with these residents.

A middle-aged-looking man was leading the Great Dane to the backyard. A Great Dane that was obviously Boo. Damn. All this time, right under his nose. What were the odds of his hiding in plain sight and why hadn't these people applied to adopt Boo? They certainly had the land. It was a perfect situation, other than the fact that they'd stolen him right out of Zoey's backyard.

"Hey," Ryan called out and the gentleman stopped in his tracks. "How's it going?"

"Great. You must be the one that bought the old Turner house."

Ryan held out his hand. "I'm Sheriff Ryan Davis."

"Mike Dawson." The man blinked and accepted the handshake. "Is there a problem?"

"Hope not." Ryan eyed Boo, who sat regally next to the man, oblivious he'd been stolen. Happy, even. He pointed to Boo. "That your dog?"

Even if Ryan hadn't been good at reading people,

he would have noticed the man's absolute defeat. His shoulders slumped. "It was."

"Was?"

"My wife always hated my dog. She said Andre the Giant was too big. I reminded her we practically have a ranch out here. But the house is small and Andre likes to sleep inside near me. When I was out of the country for work he supposedly 'got out.'" He made air quotes. "Turns out my wife had given him up to the shelter. When I came home two months later, my dog was gone. I heard Zoey had adopted him."

"The shelter has her on speed dial. He's one of her many rescues. She adopts, then tries to find a good home if she can't keep the dog."

Dawson shoved hands in his pants pockets and cast his gaze down. "I know. But you think she would have given him back to the family that let him go in the first place?"

"She might have." He'd like to think Zoey would understand that shit happened. The man's wife sounded like a shrew, but this man obviously loved his dog.

"I know I wouldn't have. There's no excuse for what my wife did. Zoey screens her prospects thoroughly and she would have done her research. We gave him up, or, my wife did. Love my dog, sheriff. I'm ashamed of what my wife did."

This technically wasn't a robbery and yet it was. "I'm going to have to take him back for now. I'm sure you two can work something out."

"Maybe you could put in a good word for me."

"I'll do my best." He meant it. Ryan could see the regret in the man's eyes. Zoey had a big heart and she'd have compassion for the situation. "But you shouldn't have taken him. Zoey's been worried sick."

Mike hung his head. "I imagine so. Like I did until I heard she had him safe and sound. Maybe should have left him there, leave well enough alone. But hell, I missed the big guy. Had him since he was a pup."

Together they walked the dog back to Ryan's Jeep and helped Boo/Andre into the back.

Mike gave Boo one last pat and then closed the door. "It's all my wife's fault. Damn ungrateful woman. You can screw a man out of a lot of things, but you don't mess with a man's dog."

"Once I explain the situation, I'm sure he'll be back. You have the room here, and you obviously love him."

"Thanks, sheriff. I heard you were a nice guy. You get me my dog back and you've got yourself a vote next election."

Once Ryan locked up the house, he drove a surprisingly morose-looking Boo back to Zoey's. The mystery was solved. She'd know that Boo was okay, and best of all he already had a home ready and waiting for him.

Chapter 22

Zoey was just sitting down to watch Cesar Millan, the real dog whisperer, when she heard her doorbell. She hadn't been expecting Ryan tonight, because he'd been working at the house all day with Sam. She peeked through the peephole before opening the door. What she saw there shocked her to the marrow.

"Oh my god!" Zoey threw the door open. "Boo! You found him."

Ryan stood next to Boo, giving her a satisfied smile. The smile said *I told you so.* And he'd found Boo and brought him back, just as he'd said he would do. He was not only the most handsome man she'd ever seen but he was also the most efficient. Clearly. She wanted to hug him and kiss him at the same time.

"I thought I'd lost you forever!" She squealed as she bent to hug the big lug's massive neck.

Ryan stepped inside and then unclipped Boo's leash. Indie, Bella and Corky descended on their lost pal. Corky, Boo's favorite, gave loud snorts of excitement. Indie yarked and launched himself at Boo. Bella sniffed around him, as though trying to make sure it was the same Great Dane and not an impostor. For his part, Boo looked somewhat confused and Zoey sensed he wasn't completely over the shock of being taken from her. God knew what he'd been through these two weeks, but she'd guess that eating out of garbage cans might have been on the menu. Poor, poor deprived Boo.

"Where did you find him?"

"This is the tough part," Ryan said.

"Go ahead. I can take it. He looks good so it can't have been too bad." She closed her eyes and prepared to hear the worst. "Was he wandering the streets trying to find his way back home? Was he eating out of trash cans?"

"No. He was at his first home."

"What do you mean?" That didn't make any sense. The first owners had given him up.

"He was just down the street from the property I bought. He has a good piece of land there, at least five acres. The Dawsons."

"I know. They gave him up. Irresponsible dog owners." She led Boo to the kitchen. "You must be starved. I'll get you dinner."

"Thanks, baby, but I already ate."

"Not you, silly. I meant Boo. I imagine he hasn't been fed any healthy food all this time. Irresponsible people would rather spend their cash on a café mocha than a few extra dollars for the premium food." Zoey brought out a small bag, measured water and heated it in the microwave. Then she added the water, and mixed. She set a timer.

"The others already ate. Boo, you know the drill. This takes a few minutes." She flitted about the kitchen, grabbing a bottle of olive oil and a can of sardines.

When the timer went off she mixed again, added olive oil and some of the sardines. "This is for the protein."

"You do this for all the dogs?"

"And Corky." She picked up the bowl of food. "Boo is the only patient one. I'm sure he's waiting on his pillow."

"Here you go." Zoey set the bowl down and squatted in front of him. "I don't usually feed them in here but tonight is an exception."

Boo wasn't having any of it, not even raising his head to smell. Meanwhile, the others were circling, waiting for an opportunity to move in for the spoils. Bella was panting. Indie was salivating. Corky was doing his snorting thing.

"Huh." Zoey said. "Maybe he isn't hungry after all."

"Yeah?"

"Does he look okay to you?"

"Got to be honest. Not really. Can dogs get depressed? Because he looks sad to me."

"Of *course* animals can get depressed. Corky wandered around here like he'd lost his bestie." She bit her lower lip. "What did they do to him? Something is wrong."

Ryan pulled Zoey toward the couch and into his lap. "Babe, let me talk to you here for a minute."

She worried a fingernail between her teeth, studying Boo. "Gosh, I'm worried."

"Look." He rubbed her back. "There's something you should know."

Zoey listened as Ryan explained the whole sordid tale of wicked wife versus helpless husband. By the time he was done, Zoey could barely control her temper. If Mrs. Dawson were here right now, Zoey would…she'd spit on her, or something.

"What a horrible woman. I should put her name on my list of people who should never be allowed to adopt a dog. Ever."

He stroked her thigh and kept talking. "But you see how it wasn't really the husband's fault. He didn't abandon Boo."

"No, he didn't. But he did *steal* him, Ryan."

"Yeah, I know. That was wrong. But he seemed to think you wouldn't be able to excuse his wife's actions. Either way, his wife gave him up to the shelter. Mike didn't do it but he still feels guilty."

"He could have talked to me instead of stealing him."

"Would you have given him back?"

"That depends on whether he's still married to that awful woman. Whether he's prepared to deal with a dog this size. Whether he has the room."

"Babe, he raised Boo since he was a puppy. And they have land."

She blinked. "Still, I don't know if he could be trusted. What if he goes out of town again and she does the same thing? And how can I trust someone who *stole* from me?"

"I'd say there were extenuating circumstances."

She stiffened in his arms. "Ryan, you're the *sheriff.* How can you take his side?"

"I'm not the badge, Zoey. Told you that. He's not exactly a threat to the town's residents. And you didn't see the man. He's heartsick about losing Boo again but he put up no resistance to my taking him back. He knows he was wrong but he didn't see any other way to get his dog back."

"What are you trying to say? I'm too strict with how I screen for my adoptions?"

"What I'm saying is that you need to think about whether you ever wanted someone else to have him."

"Of course I want Boo to have a good home. With plenty of room."

"You don't have the room. But the Dawsons do. Maybe a little forgiveness goes a long way."

No longer content to simply sit stiffly in his lap, she climbed off and stood before him, hands jammed on her hips, anger simmering. "You don't think I can *forgive*?"

He crossed his arms. "You tell me."

"Of course I can. And I'm going to prove that right now by forgiving what you just said about me not being a forgiving person."

He raked a hand through his hair, staring at the ceiling. "Didn't say that."

"You implied it."

"Zoey, I had a long day." He stood. "I don't want to fight."

"Me either." She took a tentative step toward him. "You found him just like you said you would. You're my hero."

"I'm not a—"

She shushed him with a finger to his mouth, the other hand wrapping around the nape of his neck. His eyes switched from their annoyed expression to a more heated one. "I know you're not a hero, but tonight can you just be my hero?"

"Yeah," he said and lifted her into his arms. "I can do that."

Chapter 23

Zoey couldn't sleep.

Ryan lay next to her, naked and sleeping soundly. The evidence of their making up was scattered all over the floor in pieces. Her bra and panties, his shirt and pants. Their sex tonight had been passionate, even a bit angry at times, maybe because Ryan wasn't fully satisfied with her explanation. And she still wasn't sure he understood that she couldn't give Boo back to the family that had abandoned him. They were at an impasse.

Unable to sleep, she quietly crawled out of bed, glancing back to Ryan, the sheets folded just below his abs at the V of muscles, looking like nothing less than a blond Adonis in her bed. He had one arm thrown over his face, the other stretched out. She studied him for a minute like a voyeur, still stunned by his utter maleness.

Tonight, they'd had what could probably count as

their first fight. She'd have to say they'd managed alright, even if they hadn't technically resolved a thing. But maybe there was nothing to resolve. She had Boo back, he'd eventually recover from the trauma and she'd go about finding him the perfect home. It had to be done. But Ryan's words came back to her in the dark and still night.

Did she secretly want to keep Boo? If so, this was selfish. Unfair. She'd never thought of keeping him permanently because he'd be better off in a bigger house. Possibly as the only dog, she'd considered regretfully, because he really was an introvert. Shy and preferring to keep to himself. This would make sense if he'd been the only pet in the Dawson home, but she understood they had a nonworking ranch on their land. Horses, pigs, chickens. He had to share attention with more pets than normal there. Another reason not to give him back.

Corky really was his best friend because she left Boo alone and let him have his space. That part often made Zoey feel guilty. Boo was putting up with a lot in her crowded little house. Indie occasionally biting at his ankles, Bella attempting to steal his food. It really was taking forever to find him a home, but she couldn't even think of giving him right back to the man who stole him. Stole him, right out of her own backyard! Why? Because he was afraid she wouldn't understand? Please. She was the most understanding person in the world.

She threw on her robe and tiptoed out of the bedroom so as not to wake Ryan and walked into the living room to check on everyone. All lay in their beds, Indie snoring loudly for a small dog. Boo wasn't sleeping but he also wasn't moving. He was just lying on his pillow, eyes opened, head down. So, yes, for the first time since she'd met Boo, he did look...*depressed* for lack of a better word. There was just no other way to describe the despondent look in his soulful brown eyes.

Sitting cross-legged in front of him, she patted his head. "Hey, boy. What's wrong?"

He simply gave a doggy sigh. Unfortunately, Zoey couldn't read his mind this time. She didn't know if he meant *It's good to be home* or *I miss my old home*, or *I'm tired.*

He hadn't eaten his dinner. Maybe the Dawsons had been feeding him junk like hot dogs. The stuff dogs loved but was bad for them. It would go right along with the Dawsons being irresponsible owners. Being a fur parent wasn't easy. It meant denying fur babies what they wanted because it wasn't good for them.

It meant hanging in there when they smelled from disgusting farts or taking them for a walk in the arid heat of the day if necessary. For her it had often meant sacrifices. She wouldn't buy the brand of ice cream she loved but chose the bargain brand so that she could afford the premium dog food.

She couldn't get away much because no one wanted to house sit three dogs and a pig for an entire weekend. Jill was busy and so was Carly. A baby. A wedding to plan. Mrs. Martinez would do it, except her cat really was bonkers. Tio and Tia were against her having so many dogs, too. They'd always had one family dog at a time and spoiled it rotten.

It was time to consider that Tia was right and she was also being irresponsible by having too many dogs. Zoey had to split her attention with them. And Jill had implied that Zoey hadn't made room in her life for a man because she'd hid behind her pets avoiding intimacy.

No. That wasn't right. She could always make more room in her heart, for Ryan or for more pets. Abandoning was never the answer.

"We'll get through this, Boo."

He gave a slight whimper.

"There you are," said a deep and raspy voice behind her.

She turned to see Ryan, hair adorably mussed and disheveled, unshaven, wearing nothing but his boxer briefs. They rode low on his hips, exposing all that delicious tanned and taut skin.

"I didn't mean to wake you up."

"You didn't. I rolled over and you weren't there." He sat behind her, pulling her between his long legs, and jutted his chin in Boo's direction. "He okay?"

"I don't think so. You're right. He's depressed." She leaned her head into the dip of his shoulder.

"Meant to ask. How did it go at dinner yesterday?" Ryan asked.

"Oh, no. That didn't happen." She closed her eyes, hating to rehash it all over again. "Thursday night I decided to tell Tia about Jorge and why I didn't want to come to dinner. She had Veronica come over so I could tell her."

"Good."

"I was right. She didn't want to believe me. But by the time I left, she did. I don't know what she's going to do, but now she knows."

"I'm sorry, baby."

"I wish you could have been there."

"Wait." He shook his head. "So then you were free Friday night?"

"Um, yes."

"You didn't call, so I assumed you'd gone to dinner."

"I knew you were busy with your party."

He cocked his head. "A party you were invited to."

Instead of a stuffy party, she'd gone up to the Ridge to see Jill, Sam and check on Fubar. She'd needed a mental health break and had to remind herself there was still so much to be grateful for. Family.

Good friends.

Ryan.

Now, she blinked with what she was certain had to be barely concealed guilt. "I didn't have a dress. I didn't—"

"You didn't want to go," he finished for her. "I get it. I didn't want to go either."

"I'm sorry."

"No, don't be sorry. It's just that I have to go to these events. And I missed having you there with me."

"Really?"

The knowledge that he wanted her with him wrapped around her heart. And realistically, he wouldn't be doing this job much longer. In less than six months, someone else would have to run for sheriff.

Ryan would be happier, and she'd have him all to herself.

"I promise I'll go to the next party," Zoey said.

She turned her attention back to poor, sad Boo.

"What are you going to do with him?" His warm breath teased her neck as he spoke.

"I'll pay him extra attention."

"That might work. I know I like that." His voice was smooth and deep and sexy.

That made her laugh and she turned in his arms. He was such a man. Which, of course, she happened to love. "Aw, baby. Am I not paying you enough attention?"

He grinned, both dimples showing. If she ever had a child, she'd want him to have these dimples. And that smile. His heart. *Whoa. Slow down, woman. You're going to see where this goes.*

"You paid plenty of attention to me tonight," Ryan said.

"I wouldn't want to be a slacker."

He nuzzled her neck. "Trust me. You are no slacker."

"That's good to know." She stood, and he followed her up.

Then she took his hand and led him to the bedroom where she continued to show him just what an overachiever she could be.

Chapter 24

Sunday was day one of Boo's recovery and Zoey took him to work. She'd decided he would be tethered to her for a while until he adjusted again. It's what she'd done when she first brought him home from the shelter. He'd been skittish and so frightened that Zoey took him with her everywhere she could. She'd taken him along to Friends and Family Day on the ridge, to the pet store and even to The Drip, the coffee shop where she, Jill and Carly had once worked together.

"Mommy, Mommy! Look, it's a horse!" A little boy pointed to Boo, who sat to the side of the register where Zoey had cleared a spot for him. It meant she'd had to do some rearranging of displays—and move the cat so she wouldn't freak out.

"Honey, that's a Great Dane," the mother said, holding her son's hand. "Aren't they beautiful dogs?"

"He's good with children," Zoey piped up from behind the register. "And one of my dogs looking for a good home."

"I don't think he'd get along with our little terrier. He's our only dog and not too friendly with others," the mother said, bending to pat Boo. "He's beautiful, though."

The morning progressed, and everyone asked after Boo, but no one had any idea of who would be interested in an extra-large dog. Three weeks ago tomorrow he'd been stolen and now she couldn't find any takers. But Mr. Dawson couldn't be the only person in Fortune who wanted a Great Dane. When Hannah came in the afternoon to relieve Zoey, she took Boo to the dog park, where he walked with his head hung low, as if the energy to even hold up his neck was now too much for him. Maybe he needed a trip to the vet. Dr. Rick would know what to do.

After getting a call from Jill, Zoey wound up at The Drip after the dog park. Carly was already sitting next to Jill. Boo had to wait outside as usual, which irritated Zoey to no end.

She slid a look to the big picture window where she could see him sitting on his haunches, looking like he'd lost his best friend. "I don't know why he can't come inside—"

"We know, we know," Jill interrupted. "He's better behaved than some children."

"Well…he is."

"Speaking of children…" Carly said.

"How's Grace?" Zoey asked the obligatory question. By now she understood that Carly took offense if no one asked about her stepdaughter. This was interesting for many reasons, not the least of which was when Carly first met Grace she hadn't much liked her.

"She's great. Very excited."

"About what?" Jill asked. "Are you all going to Disneyland?"

"I can't stand it another minute!" Carly said. "I just have to tell you guys. We're pregnant. We're having a baby."

"Oh my god, honey!" Jill squealed. "That's so great. Better than Disneyland, even."

"Really? Another one?" Zoey asked.

Far be it from her to say, but there was an overpopulation problem in case anyone cared. Not just among dogs and pets of all kinds. If only more people "fixed" their dogs and cats there wouldn't be so many unwanted animals, some of which were euthanized every day across the country. The thought made Zoey want to cry. No way would they all be saved. She shook her head. They were talking about babies now.

"Yes, another one," Carly said. "Levi hopes for a boy this time, but of course I will happily take another little girl. I never had a sister. She and Grace would be the best of friends."

"I bet I'll be right behind you after we're married. Sam and I want kids, of course."

Of course? Sometimes she didn't understand her best friends. Why was it so important to reproduce? As if one's genetic makeup was so special it had to be replicated. Passed down from generation to generation. Adoption was the only reasonable choice. On the other hand, wasn't she the one fantasizing last night about children with Ryan's dimples and smile? Whoops. Seemed her womb had hijacked her brain.

"How many does Sam want?" Carly asked.

"He said as many as I want would be fine," Jill said. "I'm going to see how the first one goes. I'm not a big fan of pain."

"Levi said he'd like four. Can you imagine? I don't think so!"

"Four?" Zoey gasped. How incredibly selfish of the man. And she'd thought Levi was a nice guy.

Jill laughed and caught Zoey's gaze. "That's how many Ryan wants."

"He does?" Zoey couldn't believe her ears. Ryan! Four children.

"Yeah, why don't you know this?" Jill said. "You probably just haven't talked about that yet. But he and Lauren had talked about kids. Apparently, she claimed she doesn't have child-bearing hips. I have to agree."

Zoey looked down at herself. Someone had once said she had child-bearing hips. She'd had no idea what they'd meant until this moment.

"Now, *you*." Jill pointed to Zoey. "You've got an ass on you."

"W-what?" Zoey said.

"You're freaking her out." Carly laughed. "She doesn't mean you're fat, Z."

"Of course not!" Jill said. "Not that there's anything wrong with that. But you're not fat. You just have a very shapely behind."

"And I'm sure you could squeeze out all those babies," Carly said. "If you want to, I mean."

Zoey thought about squeezing babies out, which she very well knew didn't come out of her *ass*, and flinched. "We haven't talked about any of this."

"They're still new," Jill said to Carly. "And taking it slow. Seeing where it goes."

"That's right." Only that wasn't completely true considering she'd already fallen for him.

She had no idea where Ryan stood on this subject and now felt a little stupid for not asking. He'd wanted four kids with Lauren. She felt a hot spike of jealousy, which didn't make any sense at all.

"He talked about all this with Lauren?"

"They *were* engaged," Jill said.

Zoey gulped down some ice water. Yes, that was true. People talked about this kind of thing when they were getting ready to be married and start a life together. It made sense she and Ryan hadn't discussed it because they weren't in that place. This made her both mad and sad. So she was *smad* over something ridiculous.

"How are you and Ryan doing?" Carly asked, stirring her herbal tea.

"Great," Zoey said. "He stayed over last night after he brought Boo back."

"Okay, that's enough of that," Jill said. "We don't need any more details. He stayed over. For all I know he slept on the couch. Yes, that's where he slept. I've decided."

"You're ridiculous," Carly said, laughing and elbowing Jill. "Like Zoey would ever share anything saucy."

"But…well, I really like him. A lot," Zoey said nervously.

"What's not to like?" Jill asked.

"Exactly," Carly said.

He wants four kids. He wants me to give Boo back to a bad person.

And still…

"He wants me to give Boo back to the man who stole him."

Both Carly and Jill exchanged a look.

"That doesn't sound like Ryan," Jill said.

Zoey was forced to explain the whole sordid tale of the Witchy Wife and poor Boo, who'd never done anything wrong but be born supersized.

"Oh, wow," Carly said. "That poor man."

"To think someone would be so cruel," Jill added, shaking her head.

"So cruel to the dog," Zoey said.

"That too," Jill said. "You mean he wants the dog back?"

Zoey nodded.

Carly and Jill exchanged another look. Zoey didn't like the fact they were having an entire conversation without her. *Rude.*

"What?" Zoey finally said, slapping the table.

"Well… I mean, he didn't do anything wrong. Did he?" Jill asked.

"Sounds like he loves his dog and wants him back," Carly said.

"It doesn't matter. Boo deserves stability and a happy home. Can you imagine what it's like in that house with a woman like that? What if she does it again?"

"I doubt he'd let that ever happen," Carly said. "Sounds like he learned his lesson."

"You both agree with Ryan?"

"One thing I know about my brother is that he's tough. When it comes to crime, he's the first one to want someone who did the crime to do the time. He was a detective, for coffee's sake. If he thought for a second the man didn't deserve another chance, he wouldn't hesitate to tell you."

"You think I should give his dog back. Give him another chance."

"But we'll support you in whatever you decide." Carly elbowed Jill.

"Of course," Jill said, rubbing her arm. "Maybe you should meet the man, and that sixth sense you have about kindred animals might tell you something. What if, even with this strike against him, he and Boo are a perfect match?"

"Well…" Zoey rapped her fingers against the table. "I want to do the right thing."

There seemed to be no one else on the horizon for Boo, and unless she wanted him, she had to consider this obvious option.

Chapter 25

Repairs on his personal money pit were proceeding as well as could be expected. Ryan spent Sunday installing the new kitchen cabinets with Sam. The new estimates for the countertops they'd ordered wouldn't break the bank but they weren't his happy place either. Said happy place remained in the bed of Zoey Castillo—he even found her fiery temper attractive.

He guessed that was because there had been plenty of people in his former life who'd demonstrated the worst in human behavior.

But Zoey was not even in the same galaxy. Her anger was a righteous indignation he understood far better than she realized. She was protective of those that needed a voice and he found that enticing him more each day. It didn't hurt that she had a heart bigger than the Pacific Ocean.

And a rocking body. Yeah, he wasn't too noble to ignore that.

The sun was heating up the valley and another trickle of sweat rolled down his back to join all the others. Sam had just taken a break for lunch and left with Jill to bring back sandwiches for them all when Zoey pulled up in her car. In the back passenger seat he caught Boo strapped into his dog car seat, the window rolled down. She'd said she'd be taking him everywhere with her until he readjusted and obviously she'd meant it.

"Hey," he said as he met her on the sidewalk. "What are you doing here?"

"I wanted to say hello." She shoved her hands in her back pockets and tipped her face up to smile at him. A ray of sunlight caught her eyes and she blinked once, gazing at him with one eye shut.

He pulled her to him by the belt loops of her jeans. "Glad you're here."

"It's not to bring Boo back."

"Didn't think so."

"But I am thinking more about it."

"Great."

"Wow, you guys are making some progress here." She looked over his shoulder to the house.

"When it's safe, I'll take you for a tour."

"Is…is Sam here?" Lightly, she let her fingers drift up and down between his chest and his abs.

"Not right now." He cocked his head. "Why?"

"It's just… I… I…"

"Spit it out, babe. Just tell me."

"I don't want to have four kids!"

"O-kay. We're having that conversation."

He chuckled a little because it had come so far out

of left field. Shockingly, instead of being struck dumb with terror, his usual reaction, he felt oddly flattered she'd even consider him as the father of her children. Someday.

"How many do you want?"

"One, probably." She shook her head, wincing slightly as though the thought injured her brain. "I'll have to see how it goes. But one child is reasonable."

"Sounds good." He didn't know where she was going with this.

She cocked her head and studied him, eyes wide and curious. "Why do *you* want four?"

"Wait. Who said I want four kids?"

"Jill said. You and your ex talked about it."

"Ah." Now he understood, though why Jill would be talking to Zoey about his ex he had no idea. He wanted Lauren firmly in his rearview where she belonged and he hated the thought of her being mentioned to Zoey even in passing. "That was a joke."

"A joke?"

"Yeah, I used to say I wanted four kids just to freak her out. It was fun watching her cringe. I'm not sure she even wanted one child though she claimed she did. And why are we talking about *her*?"

"I don't know," Zoey said, casting her eyes down. "She was important to you."

"Was."

"How important?"

While others might say that she was important enough to consider marrying, Ryan no longer knew if it was that simple. He was coming to some realizations that surprised him. When he'd returned stateside, he'd had some work to do on himself. PTSD, the counselor had called it. Ryan didn't know if that was true, but by the time he applied to the Oakland PD those episodes were behind him and it was now simply a part of his life he'd learned to handle.

The people he was surrounded by in the homicide division were good for him. They didn't cut him any slack, coddle him or think he was special in any way. Same with Lauren, who'd helped him through a difficult time. She'd been a work friend and then she'd become more.

"Not as important as she should have been, it turns out. She was a good friend. We had a lot in common."

"That's so romantic," she said dryly.

"No, I guess it wasn't." He tweaked the shell of her ear. "You don't have anything to worry about with her. We're done and have been for some time."

"I wasn't worried."

Liar. She was worried and he liked that.

"Well, except the part about the four kids. I thought I should come right out and tell you, in case that was a deal breaker." She lifted a shoulder.

"Of course. You know, there's another event next month so you can make Friday up to me. Because people are starting to ask about us."

"Who? What are they saying?"

"They want to know who the woman is that I'm seeing."

"It's none of their business!"

"Zoey, babe. This is a small town. Unfortunately, everybody knows me."

He hated *that* part. Hated that maybe just by being who he was, he'd called even more attention to the job.

But he was beginning not to hate the rest.

She stroked his arms, her fingers gliding from his biceps to his forearms. "That's alright. It won't be much longer before the election and you won't have to do the events and all this stuff you hate anymore."

Right. A jab of fear coursed through him as he wondered what Zoey would think once he told her he was considering running again. But no, this was Zoey and she was loyal to the core. She accepted him for who he was and not his job or what he'd achieved. He hoped. Because this time, the stakes were higher for him.

It would matter. Too much.

Chapter 26

Three days later, Boo was still depressed and Zoey was out of options. She'd taken him to Dr. Rick, who gave the dog a clean bill of health. He hadn't seen any major physical changes in Boo and he was qualified to judge because he'd been Boo's original veterinarian. Before today, Zoey would have never asked, but now she had to give it some consideration.

"Were the Dawsons responsible pet owners? Did they bring him in regularly?"

"Mike brought him in. It was his dog and they were quite attached. Honestly? When he came in to tell us the news that Andre/Boo had a new owner, I thought he might burst into tears. It was terrifying. I've never seen a grown man cry and I sure didn't want to start then."

Zoey explained the situation, and Dr. Rick admitted that he hadn't known all the details.

"He must have been too humiliated to tell me. Man, I feel awful for the guy." He patted Boo's ginormous head. "To lose a beautiful dog like this."

"What do you think I should do?"

"He's your dog now, Zoey. But I think soon Boo needs to be in his forever home. If that's you, great. You know I'm your biggest fan. But if it's not you, he needs to find someone else and soon. He needs the permanence."

As usual, Dr. Rick was correct. He hadn't been voted Fortune's most popular vet ten years running for no reason. Zoey drove home, knowing she had to make a decision. Could she responsibly own three dogs and a pig when she was already extending herself too far? Maybe Ryan was right and she wanted to be Boo's forever home. A part of her did because she'd become too attached, as usual. But the bigger, more reasonable part of her heart understood it was dangerous and unfair to take what you wanted without regard for the consequences.

She needed to talk to Ryan again. He might not think his opinion mattered, but in the past few weeks he'd become increasingly important to her. He was essentially her best friend. Whenever one of her customers had a funny pet story to tell her, Ryan was the first person she wanted to share with. He was the first person she thought of in the morning and the last person she thought of at night. She believed with all her heart he was one of the best people she'd ever known. And he was very resourceful with his hands, mouth and tongue. But his very best feature was his heart.

Ryan was in a fresh hell.

Today both the mayor and the city councilman running against him had asked for his endorsement in the next election. He was seriously considering endorsing neither of them. He'd just hung up with the current mayor, who'd reminded him that they had a long history and a "deep" friendship, when Renata announced he had a visitor. Not expecting anyone, Ryan was about to turn the visit down because he was off the clock and wanted to see Zoey when said guest appeared in the doorway.

"Lauren. What the hell are you doing here?"

"She said she's your fiancée," Renata said, lips pursed, opinion formed.

Ryan got the message—it wasn't a good opinion. Fair enough. "Ex-fiancée."

Renata glared at Lauren and crossed her arms. "You forgot the *ex* part. That's an important part to forget."

Lauren batted her eyelashes. "Force of habit."

"Thanks, Renata," Ryan said.

One thing he wouldn't do was leave this station with Lauren so he was here for the duration. If they were seen together it would start a rumor all over town. Zoey would hear about it and get the wrong idea. The protective streak in him with that one was strong.

Lauren closed the door to his office and took a seat.

He got up, opened his door wide, gave her a significant look then sat back down behind his desk. "What can I do for you?"

"Cut the crap. It's me. You know why I'm here."

"Shit, Lauren. Did I say anything to encourage you to come down here?"

"I couldn't just let you go without seeing this for myself. You're different. I can see it already." Rather than a happy tone, it was accusatory. Apparently, he wasn't supposed to be happy here. He should have come crawling back to her and a cesspool of crime. Because that's what he deserved.

"Believe it or not, I'm making a difference right here."

He'd helped Ethan, who'd seen a familiar face when he was terrified and waiting for his parents to arrive. This had been simply because he'd cared to start a relationship with him. He was working on a house that would be occupied by a veteran when they were done with it. He'd only been able to get the property before hard-core investors because the owner knew him and had been willing to listen to his idea. That would have never happened in Oakland. For once, he'd used his advantage as "hometown hero" to help someone else.

Then there was Zoey. He didn't know if he'd helped her but maybe he wouldn't know that for some time. Maybe one never knew they'd really helped significantly unless they stuck around long enough to find out. Unless one made connections in a small town where it was possible to watch kids grow into teenagers and then adults. The work he'd done since he moved back to Fortune might not be sexy or exciting, but it was deeply satisfying.

He hadn't expected that.

"Making a difference as a small-town sheriff? That can't be enough for you."

"You'd be surprised." He cleared his throat and got ready to admit a truth he had not realized until this moment. "The job's been good for me."

"Says the man who didn't want to lead anymore, just a year ago. A man who thought he'd die of boredom in Mayberry. What happened?"

He shrugged. "I changed."

"But what about me? I don't believe you and I have nothing left to salvage."

After a year he would have thought she'd have realized they'd never connected in any place but the job and it had been a mistake to ask for more. But the short time he'd had with Zoey had him realizing what he'd wanted all along. A woman to tell him he was done with all other women forever.

"We're done."

He'd made sure of it. Waited a year to make sure he'd notice any pangs of longing or regret. Nothing had happened. He didn't miss Lauren. When he didn't see Zoey for a day, he longed for her.

"I disagree. Look, couples have problems all the time. Issues that pull them in different directions. That was you and me."

"A year ago," he stated significantly.

"You wanted to go in a new direction and I didn't. But it doesn't mean we should have thrown us away."

He took a deep breath and lowered his gaze. "Look, Lauren. I haven't been fair to you. It took me a while to realize this myself, but part of the reason I took this job was to get away from you. To end us once and for all. I knew you wouldn't come with me and I didn't want you to."

She gave him a hostile look, the same one she threw to harried and overworked public defenders. "I'm supposed to be the bitch but that's not very nice."

"And you and I were never *nice* to each other." He leaned back in his seat, ready to give her the harsh truth he'd avoided for so long. "I was still in a dark place when we met and you, and the department, were exactly what I needed then."

"I still am. I happen to be exactly what you need. Someone who's honest with you and tells you when you're screwing up. When you're feeling sorry for yourself. Someone to kick your ass every day and remind you that it's time to fight."

"I'm actually tired of fighting. Done enough of it in my life. What I need is to be with someone who gives me the sweeter side of life. Someone who makes me feel deserving of that. I never thought I'd have that, but now I do."

"There's someone else." Lauren scowled.

He nodded. Someone with whom he had a chemistry and passionate connection he'd never had before. It was new to him, this push and pull to her, this inability to stay away even when he believed he wasn't good enough for her. There were a thousand reasons he should stay away from Zoey. But none of them seemed to matter when he weighed them against the simple fact that he didn't want to. She'd broken down walls he hadn't even realized were still up. All with her sweet smiles and loving ways. When she looked at him, he actually felt deserving of love again.

Even deserving of the damned medal. Which meant he could finally stop trying to earn it.

He was so in love with her. Unbelievably, it was one beautiful girl and her menagerie of pets who had convinced him he *deserved* to be happy. He deserved to have some of what he wanted out of life—and what he wanted more than anything was her.

Ryan didn't usually go straight from work to Zoey's house, but he headed there now like a thirsty man searching for water. For a long while after the war, he hadn't wanted anything or anyone beautiful, sweet or kind. Punishing himself because no one else would. He resented the calls from his mother and Jill with their kind words and concerns. His father was better since he always focused more on what Ryan should be doing, rather than on what he felt. His dad didn't talk about feelings, which worked for Ryan.

The Oakland PD and the friends he'd made there had been good for him because in his mind they were down in the gutter right along with him. No one gave him an ounce of sympathy or kindness. Every day was filled with the chaos of crime and a complete absence of warmth. A bit like war. It had been where he wanted to be. His wheelhouse, where he felt at home. What he deserved.

When he'd come back to Fortune, leery of being a leader again but ready to escape the mistake he'd nearly made to make his punishment permanent, one of the first people he'd run into was Zoey. He still remembered the day she'd shown up at the station. She carried with her a cherry pie that she'd picked up from Sweetums Bakery.

"Welcome home," she'd said, laying the pie on his desk, giving him a shy smile.

She'd remembered his favorite pie. The utter guilelessness in her shimmering eyes, that warmth he'd so long avoided because it touched him in places he'd shut down long ago, became something he now craved. So without even bothering to drop off his gun at home, he found himself at Zoey's doorstep. Because, much as he loved her, he'd also made a decision about the work. And she was the first person he had to tell.

For reasons he didn't fully comprehend people followed him. Depended on him. Maybe that wasn't always such a terrible thing. It was satisfying to take on burdens when someone else could not. It wasn't a punishment but an honor to serve. Ryan didn't always have to get everything right or be perfect. Zoey more than anyone had shown him that. He simply had to do what he could every day to help in the smallest of ways.

Sometimes it wouldn't be enough, but the point was that it could be. He'd failed to save one of his men, but he'd saved three others. To focus on the one he lost instead of the men he'd helped wasn't honoring the survivors. Sometimes failure was not just an option but the way life rolled no matter how hard you tried.

He didn't like it but it was true. Everyone alive was nothing less than human and imperfect, which meant errors would be made. In some cases, lives would be lost. He'd always known that but now he was learning to accept his shortcomings one day at a time.

One mistake he hadn't made was Zoey. Taking a chance with her.

She greeted him at the door with a warm smile, wearing a short yellow dress he'd never seen on her before. It was the type that left her creamy shoulders bare and irresistible. Her wavy dark hair framed her neck and shoulders.

"I was just thinking about you."

He would ask her what she was thinking, but the last time her answer had stopped his brain from processing simple rudimentary thoughts. Tonight he had to focus. Find the right words. Because this was *Zoey* and she more than most people would understand. She understood duty and compassion for the least fortunate so she would understand it for everyone.

Indie and Bella came to greet him and he dispensed pats and chin scratches before Zoey came into his arms.

"Boo?" he asked, looking past her to the dog bed where he lay next to a docile Corky.

"Still not good."

The fact that she hadn't yet made the decision to give him back to his original owner didn't concern Ryan. She would get there. Her heart was too large to watch the big guy suffer for long. He allowed her to pull him past the dogs still sniffing him as if they could smell the roast beef sandwich he'd had for lunch. No doubt they could. But when she ordered them to lie down, they all obeyed reluctantly.

"You do that so well," he remarked, letting his fingers drift down her spine and settle on the small of her back.

"They're good dogs. And trained." She waved a hand at Corky. "Sorry. I called you a dog again. But honestly, I think *you* believe you're a dog."

He followed her into the kitchen.

"Are you hungry? Because I can make you a sandwich."

That was another thing. Zoey was forever feeding him. Taking care of him. Asking about his day. He wasn't used to this kind of treatment.

"Babe, you don't always have to feed me. I can dress myself and everything."

She snorted. "I want to."

He understood. She'd been raised by Gloria, who lovingly cared for her family without complaint. And Zoey was more like her aunt than even she realized. She might look like Veronica, but from what he had seen firsthand she was nothing like her.

"Okay." He took off his holster and set it in a safe place on the counter.

As she worked, she told him about her day. Former Haight-Ashbury hippie Mrs. Mitchell had wanted Zoey to figure out her kindred animal, and when she'd said that it was a bird Mrs. Mitchell chuckled and said she'd known all along. He loved listening to her, mostly because of the lilting sound of her laugh. And he loved watching the way she moved because she was finally comfortable in her own body and with him. And they had this. An ease together. Something he could get used to.

Damn. He was addicted to Zoey.

After he'd eaten his sandwich with her on his lap (she did everything but feed it to him) he rose and drew her into her warmly lit living room.

"Can you stay with me tonight?" she asked softly, her voice a whisper as she buried her face in his neck. "You have some clothes here."

He'd been staying with her so often that he'd half moved in with her. Whether or not she realized this, it had happened with every intention on his part. He'd wanted to be with her, to crowd her space, make her love him. That probably made him a lovesick man. He might have prepared for this moment when he could lose everything had he seen it coming. Now it was too late.

Because he'd made plans with her for a future that didn't include him continuing to be the sheriff. And he didn't know if she'd want him to stay at all after he told her he was running again. But he could hope.

Chapter 27

"Sure, babe," Ryan said. "I'll stay."

Zoey simply gazed at him in his uniform of beige cargo pants and white button-up, sleeves rolled up his sinewy forearms. Took him in. Every inch of him. He had shadows of beard bristle on his chin and jawline, his mossy green eyes were warm and inviting, and he looked good enough to eat. She would now put her heart on the line with a little bit of truth. Revealing some of just where *this* was going for her. Showing him how accustomed she'd become to being with him nearly every night. How much she counted on him to hold her and make her feel safe. Desired. She'd never had a man to depend on before unless you counted Tio. Never a man she could trust with her heart and her body.

And her life had worked that way for years, her expectations lining up neatly with the results. This was different. So different that some nights she couldn't breathe.

"I almost can't sleep anymore without you."

The man now had a direct line to her heart and given the way his gaze heated, she'd told him exactly what he wanted to hear.

He drew her into his arms on the couch and squeezed her waist tight. "That's good."

"Did you get many nuisance calls today?" She ruffled his hair.

"Not many, unless you count the mayor and city councilman Pullman as nuisances, which wouldn't be wrong. Both want my endorsement in the next election."

"It's nice to be wanted, but they should really have the endorsement of the next sheriff. Right?"

He shifted next to her. "Yeah, that will be me."

"What do you mean?"

"I mean, if the good people of Fortune reelect me, I'll be their sheriff again."

The floor dropped out from under her. No, no. This wasn't the plan. *Wait. Hold on. He's going to explain in a minute and it will all make sense.* He didn't lie. He didn't change his mind once he'd made a decision this important. She could trust him. This was *Ryan.* He was steady and rock-solid, and they had a plan.

Her fingers froze in the middle of trailing through his hair. "Why? You hate it. You weren't going to run again. That's what you *said.*"

"When I first got elected, I resented being put in a leadership position again. I did it because I had to, because I was asked to help and because I was needed. Like I've done so many things in my life. Out of duty. Obligation. This was supposed to be temporary because

the last time I led anything of real importance, I failed
one of my men. It cost him his life."

Okay. This was the problem. He still felt guilty after
all this time over something that was not under his control. But Jill's words resonated in Zoey's mind: *And
you believed him? Ryan will do what he needs to do.
That's who he is.*

"Ryan, that wasn't your—"

"Fault. I get it now. All I can do, all any of us can do,
is try. Being the leader that the residents of this town
need me to be is not the worst thing that could ever
happen to me."

"But—"

You don't want that life. I don't want that life. They'd
made plans. She'd forgotten to see "where it went" and
she'd gone ahead and made plans with him. Counted on
him. Stupid. She'd allowed herself to fall for him. Like
she was careening down a hill at breakneck speed, she
moved from hurt and confusion to anger.

He should have told her *sooner*. The moment he'd
started to change his mind.

He was so quiet, so very calm, and she wondered if
he wanted her to react. Wondered if he wanted her to
scream and cry and remind him that he'd essentially
lied to her. The pebble lodged in her throat made it dif
ficult to speak, but she dislodged it by leaping off his
lap and facing him.

"You said you're not the badge! You said that."

"That's true. I'm not."

"But we made plans. We were going to go on trips
together."

"We can still do all those things, baby."

"Being the sheriff is more than a job. You'll never

get away from it. It's a career, and it's a calling. It's politics and endorsements. It's the pedestal. Everyone always watching you."

"And that bothers you?"

Bothered *her*? It had bothered him!

"You know it does and you know why!" She went hands on hips. "When did you change your mind?"

"Does it matter? The point is I'm still the same guy. I haven't changed."

"Yes, you have. How can I trust anything you say to me?"

"Wait. You don't trust me? Is that what you're saying?"

She had trusted him. Trusted him more than she had any other man. A mistake. Ryan wasn't any different. He was simply a better person, but he didn't care any more about her than the boyfriend who loved small towns and planned to stay until he left for big city life. No different than Veronica, who went to Mexico for a short while but never came back.

She needed rock-steady. No risk. An assurance that whoever loved her was never going to leave. Would never turn her life upside down. She'd believed Ryan to be that man. A man who wanted quiet, calm and privacy.

"I see now that I can help people here in bigger ways than I'd ever realized. It's the small things. But you know I'll always protect you. No matter what I do. If I dig ditches or build houses or have to endorse the damn mayor, no one will hurt you on my watch. Ever."

God, she realized that. But she'd have to protect herself this time. "Y-you can't always be around to protect me."

"Do you know what I think this is really about?" He moved to face her. "You're afraid. It's the reason you have so many animals taking up all of your time. Your work and your life. They're in your heart and your bed."

"Don't be ridi—"

"Think about it. You didn't make enough room for me."

"No way. You don't get to psychoanalyze me. I showed you real intimacy in there." She pointed to her bedroom. "Did you forget?"

"Not at all." He got close enough to touch her, to simply lay his hand on her heart. "But this is what you're holding back. From me."

No, that couldn't be true. She'd opened her heart to him. She'd—

"You, Zoey Castillo, put your pets between you and anyone who might ask more of you. It's the reason you tell yourself you want to find Boo a home, but you actually want to keep him."

He might as well have thrust a poisoned arrow into her heart. She'd thought he understood her dedication.

"Not true! I just want him to have a good home."

"He has one."

She couldn't meet Ryan's eyes. He believed Boo'd had a good home and she was clinging to him for spite. Because people didn't get to make mistakes when they included abandoning their pets.

"He doesn't get to—"

"Make a mistake?" He slid her a gaze so filled with pain that she almost couldn't breathe. "Because I've made some myself."

"That's different. It wasn't a mistake. You tried. You didn't want to fail anyone."

"But I did anyway." He took a deep breath. "I had to make a quick decision and followed all my training. It was the toughest decision of my life and one I'll never forget."

And he'd made another decision, as well. One that again put everyone else before him. Serving his town, even in a capacity he hated.

"Then why keep punishing yourself?"

"Because it doesn't feel like punishment anymore." Two large hands framed her face. "You know this better than most. This town is filled with good people I can help. If they insist on seeing me as their hero, maybe I can show them what a hero looks like. He's someone who doesn't take credit for the good he's done because he doesn't need the credit. And I might add that working in law enforcement for a small town is a lot less dangerous than it is in Oakland. Which is a good thing for a man who might one day want to start family."

She swallowed hard. He wanted a family.

"You know that I've already had someone in my life who told me one thing then did another. People around me are always changing. Leaving. We made plans for a different kind of life. If you'd said something sooner…"

"You would have stopped seeing me?" He traced then tugged her bottom lip.

She wouldn't have, but she would have certainly guarded her heart. Surrounded it with a barbed wire fence, because he was staying in a life that she wanted no part of. She thought back to the day of the pet wash and the photograph of the two of them, her obvious affection for him displayed for anyone to see. A future with him would mean many more of those photos, more parties and events, and a public life with a private man.

She dropped her gaze, her eyes watery. "I feel like you've made this decision because you want to let me go."

He forced her chin up to meet his heated gaze. "Absolutely not. Right now I'm looking at the only woman I've ever wanted. But it's up to you to decide if this is a deal breaker. I never meant to choose between you and this job."

He was asking her if she loved him enough. And god, she did, but she was still so afraid, which pissed her off. She was afraid of a life where appearances mattered too much, where people got too caught in the glamour. Life on a pedestal, where everyone always looked. Probably because they didn't want to miss it when you fell off.

She'd been that girl once before, enthralled with beauty and attention. She didn't want to make another mistake. She didn't want to lose sight of what was important. Real. A simple and quiet life. Family, home, her pets. Even though she also saw before her the only man who'd ever owned her heart, it would be a mistake to take what she wanted without regard for the consequences.

No, that was Veronica. She took what she wanted and didn't care what that meant for anyone else.

"I don't want you to do that either," she admitted. "I want you to have what you want."

"Why do I think that's not good news for me?"

"I don't know why," she said, and this time the tears spilled. "But I just can't do this."

"I think I know why," he said, his own eyes wet. And she fell a little bit deeper. "But if you change your mind, you know where you can find me."

Chapter 28

Zoey and Boo were such a pair. They were officially two of a kind. For a week, both of them lay around the house moping. Zoey crying, Boo sighing. They both wanted something they shouldn't have. These two things weren't good for them in the long run and they'd lead to more heartache eventually. Right now Boo couldn't see that.

"Did I mention your former owners gave you up?" she said to Boo one desolate morning over her second or tenth cup of coffee. Who could keep track anymore?

She needed a lot of it to keep her awake since she wasn't sleeping well at night. Or, you know, not at all.

Okay, to be precise, Boo's fur daddy hadn't given him up. His wife had given Boo up and Mr. Dawson had been too much of a coward to fight for him. Or too ashamed. But Zoey hurt for him too because his wife had taken the dog that he loved and given him away like he was nothing more than trash. It was up to Zoey to make certain Boo would never be abandoned again. No one would fault a mama bear for wanting to take care of her cub.

"You should be with people who want you as much as you want them."

Boo had no response but to lift his massive head, sniff the air and lie back down with a sigh. Corky did the same, ever the supportive friend. Ever since Boo had returned, Corky didn't leave his side. This sadness was catching and they'd all been infected.

For the past few days Zoey had stayed home from work, and Hannah was covering at the shop. Tonight was Friday and Zoey might actually show for Tio and Tia's standing invitation to dinner. An invite she'd turned down when she'd been otherwise occupied with one handsome, heartbreaking sheriff. Ironically, this week she'd planned to ask Ryan to Friday night dinner for the first time. Now she was alone again. Well, alone with her pets. Bella and Indie had reclaimed their side of the bed and were happy about it. For the record, Zoey was not.

Ryan had made his choice. She'd made hers and even though she was miserable it still seemed like the right thing to do. Sooner or later he'd have come to resent her when he realized she wasn't the right woman for him. He wasn't the right man for her if he wanted her to give up the life she'd planned and lived for so long. That life was safe. Calm. It was what she wanted and where she had to remain.

The following week Zoey took Boo with her to Friday night dinner, hoping Tia would understand. At the door, Tia's brows quirked in surprise but she accepted Zoey's explanation that Boo was too depressed and despondent to leave alone.

"Fine, let's take him to the backyard. I just vacuumed in here," Tia said.

Zoey stepped inside with Boo following and came to a full stop when she saw Veronica sitting on the couch in the living room next to Tio. As an added surprise, she wore beige slacks with a black cap-sleeved blouse, her hair in an elegant bun. Zoey had never seen her look so plain and it was a little…disconcerting.

"Hi, Mami," Zoey said. "What are you doing here?"

She had zero doubt that Jorge was not in the vicinity. Not in Tia's home. And evidenced by the serene expression on Tio's face as he sat easily next to Veronica, Tia had respected Zoey's wishes and left him in the dark. Good. His blood pressure was high enough.

Veronica stood and took a step back, eyeing Boo with more than a little wariness. "I wanted to see you before I went back."

Zoey led Boo to the well-manicured yard through the open sliding glass door. She shut it and accepted Veronica's hug. Then she was quickly herded into Tio's arms. These hugs were much needed tonight and she accepted them easily.

"The rice will be ready in ten minutes," Tio said, and headed to the kitchen.

"It will be more than ten minutes," Zoey said and both Veronica and Tia laughed.

"I do remember that," Veronica said.

"Just like old times," Tia said. "The four of us together again."

Zoey gave them both a tight smile. She hardly remembered the old days. They'd lived with Tio and Tia for a while, but it had been up to Tia to do most of the cooking and cleaning. Of course, she'd never complained.

"I'll be right back," Tia said. "I have to help Raul in the kitchen or we'll still be waiting to eat by midnight."

Now it was Veronica giving the tight smile. Sometimes it was a little like looking in the mirror. Unnerving.

"I'm so sorry, *mi amor*," she said, reaching to stroke Zoey's cheek. "I've never seen that side of Jorge. That night…he might have been drinking but that's no excuse."

"No. It isn't." For the first time, Zoey noticed that Veronica's engagement ring was missing. And her heart hurt for Veronica because now Zoey, too, knew what it was like to lose someone you loved. For whatever reason.

"I'm sorry, too. I didn't want to ruin this for you, but I just…"

"There is no sorry. You were only trying to protect me. Sometimes I forget that I have family here and people who have my best interests in mind. I've been waiting for a long time to find a man like your father and I simply believe now that he doesn't exist."

Zoey didn't want to believe that either—that her beautiful mother would remain alone for the rest of her life because she'd already met the love of her life and lost him.

"Someone else will come along," she said.

It was the one thing she was trying hard to believe and not that she'd given up the one and only man on earth right for her in every way except one.

The problem was, she knew better. She would never find anyone better for her than Ryan.

"I'll keep believing that," Mami said, squeezing Zoey's hands. "And your young man? Will he be joining us tonight?"

"No, that didn't work out," Zoey said, glancing outside to see Boo sitting on his haunches, the light of the half-moon reflecting off his gray fur, making him appear translucent.

"Oh, I'm sorry. He seemed very nice."

Zoey bit her lower lip until it hurt. "He was."

When the rice was finally ready, Zoey sat to eat next to her mother and did her best to enjoy a meal with her family. If she weren't such a coward, Ryan would have been seated next to her tonight. He'd probably be talking to Mami about her movies, or with Tio about learning how to cook. Because Ryan couldn't cook. She'd laughed about this often. He loved to eat, her food especially or so he said, but he could barely heat a can of soup.

She said her goodbyes to Mami, who promised to visit more often now, and walked home with Boo in the moonlight. There was someone sitting on her outside steps again as she approached, but this time it wasn't Ryan holding a barking box.

It was another Davis, and Jill didn't look happy as she turned and fixed her gaze on Zoey. "I did tell you if you hurt him I'd have to kill you, didn't I?"

"Yes," Zoey said, hanging her head. "But—"

"No buts! What did you do, Zoey? He's gutted."

"W-what?" Her hands trembling, she dropped Boo's leash. "Why? What did he tell you?"

"Well, nothing of course!" Jill threw her hands up. "But I can tell. I'm his sister."

"He told me he wasn't going to run for sheriff, and

then he changed his mind, just like that." Zoey snapped her fingers. "What else is he going to change his mind about? Huh? What if he wakes up one day and decides he hates the color of my wallpaper, or one of my dogs, or—"

Me. What if he changes his mind about me? What if he leaves me?

"What are you *talking* about?"

"I don't know," Zoey admitted. "But I know I was going somewhere with this before you interrupted me."

"That place better be the loony bin because you're not even making any sense."

"Oh yeah? Well, try being in love with a guy who wants to help everyone. Who wants to fix everything. Who thinks he *has* to. Try being—"

"Wait. You *love* him?" Jill gaped.

Suddenly Zoey couldn't speak but simply nodded her head and swallowed the sob in her throat. She loved him so much her heart ached.

"I didn't know, honey," Jill said, pulling her into a hug. "I thought you screwed him and then just threw him away."

"*Me*? Think about who you're talking to!"

"I am. I know you're afraid of being dumped, but you're the one who left him. Just because he's going to run for sheriff again?"

"It wasn't just the job. I need someone who's stable. Who won't change."

"Are you kidding me? You won't ever find that. Life is change. And you've changed, too."

"No, I haven't."

"You're happier than I've ever seen you."

That was true or had been. "I was, and look at me now!"

"You created your own misery this time. My brother is the most solid dependable guy I know. All his life he did what was asked of him and more. Even our parents had unreasonable expectations of him. I've always thought what he wanted was someone to love him simply for who he is, like I do."

Oh, god. A piercing pain pulsed through her. Zoey was the most selfish person on earth. How was she any different from Mr. Dawson's wife? She'd wanted to get rid of a dog her husband adored because he was inconvenient for her.

She looked to Boo, ready to commiserate with him, but he was gone.

"Boo!" she said, turning in the direction she'd walked from.

"Not again," Jill said, following. "What is wrong with him? Can't he realize a good thing when he has it?"

"Don't worry, he can't be far the way he walks. Plus, he's depressed."

"What's that supposed to mean?"

"He'll be even slower," Zoey said and hoped.

They walked down her street, both screaming out his name.

Zoey realized she could have chosen him a more dignified name when Mr. Levin, her eighty-year-old neighbor sat on the rocking chair on his porch, and called out, "And boo to you girls! You don't scare me."

"I'm sorry. Mr. Levin, did you see a Great Dane come by this way?"

He pointed in the other direction, away from her Tia's home. "He went thataway."

Of course. It was the direction of the main road and the way to the Dawsons. Zoey took off and saw Boo in the distance, running faster than she'd ever thought him capable of. Not running. More like galloping, his long legs giving him a clear advantage. Zoey knew better than to chase a dog, but what other option did she have? If Boo got to the main road he could encounter traffic.

"There he is!" Zoey pointed, and Jill started to run.

These days she was much more physically fit than Zoey and she'd definitely always been faster. There was a reason her kindred animal was a horse.

"I've got this!" Jill said, her voice carrying as she galloped ahead. No, ran.

It took everything in Zoey to catch up to them, and when she finally did Boo sat on his haunches, panting, Jill holding the leash triumphantly, not panting. "Settle a bet. Which is faster? A horse or a Great Dane?"

"You…got…him."

"I sure did," Jill said, handing Zoey the leash.

"For whatever good that's going to do me. I guess I've just saved him from a long and probably dangerous run." She squatted in front of Boo and met his eyes. "Okay, boy. Message received loud and clear. You're going home."

Two hours later, Zoey had packed Boo's belongings with Jill's assistance. This time, he was going home with everything he could possibly need. Including, if Mr. Dawson would have him, Corky. The two best friends shouldn't be separated, and if Mr. Dawson had the room and the inclination, she'd let Corky go, too. The little pig needed Boo more than he needed her.

"Why are you being so nice to me?" Zoey suddenly asked Jill, who'd wanted to kill her earlier.

"Because," she said, slamming the full trunk's lid. "You said you love him."

"I do. More than I ever thought possible."

They drove in silence and Jill said she'd wait in the car with Corky since the jury was still out on that. Despite the fact that Corky needed Boo and he needed Mr. Dawson, she wouldn't unload Corky on someone who didn't want him. But maybe after Mr. Dawson heard the rest of her reasoning, he'd agree with Zoey that Corky actually belonged here, too. Holding Boo's leash, Zoey walked up the stone pathway to the front of the Dawsons'—Established 1985—home and rang the doorbell.

And if Zoey had any doubts at all, they were erased when Mr. Dawson took one look at Boo and his eyes got weepy. He didn't have to crouch to pet him. "Andre. How've you been, boy?"

It was as if Boo had been asleep for a week and suddenly woke up. He went up on his hind legs, clearing a height well above Mr. Dawson. Easily he commanded Boo to sit and Mr. Dawson hugged his neck.

"He misses you," Zoey said without preamble. "And I'm guessing you miss him, considering you stole him out of my backyard."

"Not my finest moment." He straightened to his full height and bent his head. "I'm sorry."

"I know what it's like to miss someone so desperately," Zoey said, thinking of Ryan.

"It was so wrong of me. I was desperate. But you were worried about him, I know."

Oh, he thought she meant Boo. Yeah, him too.

"I didn't think you deserved him back, but then Ryan

told me what happened. I'm sorry, too. No one deserves that. Can you make sure it never happens again?"

"Never again," he said. "It's what I told the sheriff. You can rest assured."

"I'll take you at your word." Zoey stuck out her hand and they shook on it. "But if you ever need him to go to a new home, just give me a call first. No judgments. Promise."

"Don't worry. It won't happen."

"I've got his personal items in the trunk of my car, if you'll help me with them."

She unloaded the pillowed bed, his dog food and water bowls, a month's worth of feed, his vitamins, his special brush and his oatmeal dog shampoo.

"I think that's everything." Zoey said.

Corky snorted from the back seat and Jill shushed him.

Mr. Dawson ducked to see through the rear window and cocked his head. "Is that... Is that a pig?"

"That's Corky, a potbellied pig, fully trained, and Boo's best friend. If you'll have him, I'd like to give him to you, as well. I hate to see them apart again. Plus, Mr. Dawson, I hope you don't mind but I took a little time to figure out Mrs. Dawson's kindred animal. This usually takes me a lot longer, but I almost feel like I know your wife. Her kindred animal is a pig, so I think she and Corky would really get along."

"I'll tell her you said that." Mr. Dawson gave her a wide grin. "I'd love to take him. We certainly have the room here."

After that it was simply a matter of saying goodbye to both Corky and Boo. For now, anyway. Of course, this took longer than it should have. Mr. Dawson assured her she had visitation rights and that he'd be bringing them by her store from now on to get everything he'd normally shopped for online. So she had a new customer. This didn't make her feel any better about leaving them behind.

"C'mon, let's go," Jill finally said after several minutes. "It's getting late and I need to get home before Sam worries."

As they drove back to Zoey's house, she managed to contain the tears she knew would fall when she was home and trying to explain tonight's events to both Bella and Indie. They'd understand, she was sure. It had always been Boo and Corky, Bella and Indie. Oh, who was she kidding? Indie would be ecstatic and at least Boo would never have his paws nipped again.

She'd tried to save every animal so that she'd eventually save herself, too. But she'd stunted her own growth by refusing to take a risk with her heart...until Ryan.

Now she had to love him without conditions. It might be the scariest thing she'd ever done but he'd be worth it.

"Do you think Ryan loves me?" Zoey asked as Jill pulled up to the curb.

"I don't know," Jill said. "He doesn't exactly tell me about that stuff. Very private guy. But I've never seen him look quite so miserable as he's been this last week. Never. So if I was a betting woman, which of course I am, I would have to say yes. He must love you. I mean, what's not to love? Right?"

"Plenty," Zoey said with misery. "I let him down. I made him think I didn't love him enough. I didn't even *tell* him that I love him."

"Lucky for you, that's an easy fix."

Chapter 29

The night's basketball game had been the one bright spot in Ryan's long-ass week.

Ethan was back, playing hard and enjoying himself, actually talking to Ryan and Aidan, and understanding that not all authority figures were his enemy. He'd been so scared, he'd privately admitted to Ryan, that no one would believe him. That no one would have his back. Scared he'd be arrested and hauled off to prison to be tried as an adult. Ethan didn't know the difference between felonies and misdemeanors and he'd been one scared kid. But Ryan had been there for one tall, gangly and troubled teenager. He hadn't known whether Ethan was guilty or innocent, but he'd simply given him the benefit of the doubt until all the evidence had been collected.

And two days after Ethan had been brought in for

questioning, Aidan caught a kid in the act of throwing a lit rag into a dumpster and that mystery had been solved. Put to rest. So Ryan was good...sure he was, even if his chest ached with a kind of constant heartburn no matter what he ate. Day and night.

"See ya," Aidan said, clapping Ryan on the back as he left the gym.

Ryan was the last one out. He was in no rush to get home to his apartment. Tonight maybe he'd head on up to the ridge for the nighttime star-gazing zip-line tour at Outdoor Adventures. It was a monthly event and quite popular with their clientele. Jill had been bugging him to attend and god knew he wanted something to do tonight. Anything to take his mind off *her*.

Disappointment had plagued him for a week after Zoey chose her safe life over a life that included him. It hit him harder than he'd expected. Even though she'd never said the words to him, he'd believed that Zoey loved him. He'd obviously been wrong because she didn't love him enough.

But this was why he didn't do relationships well. You always had to give something up to make it work. He didn't want to know what he'd have to give up to actually make it *last*. Too much. If he and Zoey didn't work, and she had his heart, he now knew it wouldn't work with anyone. End of sad story.

Move on, soldier.

He locked the doors to the gym, clicking the key fob as he approached the Jeep. It lit up the dark parking lot that, due to a broken streetlight, tonight only had the benefit of a full moon for illumination.

Zoey sat on the hood of his Jeep, legs crossed like a pretzel.

What the hell?

"What are you doing out here alone in the dark? This area isn't safe."

Now he was irritated. Angry. No, he was tired. Exhausted.

No, damn it. He was *hurt*. It was difficult to admit even to himself.

After everything he'd been through in his life, how shocking that one small woman could single-handedly pierce his heart.

"Hi," she said shyly.

"Get down," he ordered and offered his hand.

She took it, jumping down and straight into his arms. He'd been about to step back when he saw the tears in her eyes. Despite all the anger and resentment that tightened his chest and made it hard to breathe most days, his heart rate sped up in fear that something or someone had hurt her.

"What's wrong?"

She didn't answer, shaking her head and biting her lip.

"Zoey. Talk to me." Hand on the nape of her neck, he tugged her up to meet his gaze.

"Y-you said I'd know w-where to find you."

If you change your mind.

He didn't trust himself to speak, so he just studied her gaze.

"I gave Boo back, and he took Corky, too."

"You didn't have to do that—"

"No, you were right. It was the thing to do. People make mistakes and he should be allowed a second chance. And I… I did surround myself with my animals not just because I didn't want them to feel abandoned but because I didn't want to be abandoned."

"Zoey—"

"I'm the luckiest girl in the world to have my aunt and uncle, who mean the world to me. But I've always had it in the back of my mind that people leave me eventually."

His chest pinched uncomfortably. "Your father. Your mother."

"Yes, and I was afraid when you changed your mind about the job, that you might eventually change your mind about me, too. I couldn't bear that thought." Her eyes were watery and shimmering in the moonlight.

"Look at me. You never have to worry about me leaving you. Ever. I lo—"

"Wait," she said, a finger to his lips. "I want to say it first. I thought I loved you from the moment I first saw you. But now I know you, and I know what love is. It's knowing that someone is so good that they're everything you want to be, too. When someone completes you. When you fit together. I love you, Ryan. I love you like crazy."

"Can I talk now?" He chuckled, pulling her closer. "I love you, Zoey, and I take you right along with all your animals. I'm never going to ask you to give up anything that you love. I love your heart and I love the way you love me."

In the arms of the man she loved more than she'd ever believed possible, Zoey felt light enough to float away and join the moon above in the black velvet sky. She'd waited for him outside the gym on the hood of his car, the full moon her only company. Somehow, she'd have sworn, the moon had given her the courage to stay and wait for him. To say what she needed to say. Jill was right. It was, in the end, an easy fix. The truth.

He loved her. She loved him. Could anything on earth be richer than this? A coil of warmth rolled through her as she clung to Ryan's broad shoulders.

"You're going to have to give me a little direction on how to be a good and supportive girlfriend to the sheriff. I have no idea what to do."

"You don't have to do anything but love me."

"That part is easy. But I want to be everything you need."

"Just be yourself." He tugged on a lock of her hair. "Everyone will love you like I do."

"Promise to hold my hand when we're at a big party and don't leave me alone for too long until I find a friend."

"You got it, baby."

Then, as a ray of moonlight lit up his beautiful face, Ryan Davis bent to kiss her.

And once again, just like the very first time, it was everything she'd always dreamed it would be and more.

Epilogue

Six months later, election night

Throwing the sheriff a party on his election night was in some ways a lot like a family party given by Tia and Tio, who knew how to celebrate. Zoey and Ryan could have made the party bigger and far more glamorous. They could have rented a hall, since they certainly had enough well-wishers. But neither one of them had a need or desire to make the occasion any bigger than necessary. Besides, the election wasn't exactly a nail-biter since Ryan had run unopposed.

Tia emerged from the kitchen with a full plate of Spanish rice. She set it on the serving table with all the other food friends and family had brought. A two-tiered cake with a blue-and-white theme from Sweetums, caramel brownies and an assortment of mouthwatering hors d'oeuvres. Jill was busy setting up the buffet line. The pregnant Carly was near ready to pop and pouting that she couldn't have any champagne. She sat with Sam and Levi, who was bouncing Grace on his knee.

This was her new life. More entertaining and attending parties than she'd ever imagined, but Zoey was going into this new life on her own terms. Yes, she now owned pantsuits, dresses and shoes (turned out Zoey loved shoes—who knew?) and only wore her denims and Chucks to work these days. Ryan didn't ask her to do this, but she did it for him anyway. She wanted to.

Life was comfortable and easy, the way it should be. When the stress of small town politics and mayoral endorsements got to Ryan on some evenings, Zoey would simply make out with him, then deposit a pet in his lap and all was well. Therapy, cheap and easily available. She was still rescuing dogs and cats but she'd now signed up with a foster agency she trusted, who actively helped to find them a home, too. She had a stricter policy on how long she would keep them in her home. This helped attachment issues (hers) and ensured responsible pet ownership. Besides, since Ryan had moved into the house there was less space because she'd made room for him. Plenty.

Boo was doing well and quite happy again with his owner, and Corky was still his constant sidekick. Zoey checked in, though it was clear she'd be doing less of that. On one visit Mrs. Dawson had apologized in person for letting her kindred animal take over in a negative way. Well, she hadn't put it quite that way, but claimed a raging case of PMS and the fact that Boo had eaten one of her favorite shoes. While this was no excuse, Zoey did accept the apology.

"A toast to our sheriff and his lovely wife, Zoey," said city councilman Ted Pullman, holding up his glass of champagne. "And thank you, Raul and Gloria, for hosting in your lovely home. Thank you, Zoey Davis, for putting up with all of us in Fortune's government. We can be a difficult bunch."

Oh, yes, they were married. Maybe it had seemed quick to some, but not to them. Zoey had been pining away for the man for at least a decade. And Ryan joked and claimed he had to get her tied up before she changed her mind. As if. The wedding had been a small and intimate affair held at the local church in front of close friends and family. Ryan's parents attended, as well as Jill and Sam, and Tio and Tia. Carly and Levi. Even Mami flew in.

Though the wedding was small, his proposal had been large and romantic. Ryan went down on bended knee, which she thought was so sweet and had made her cry. He slipped a gorgeous diamond solitaire on her finger and claimed he'd never been romantic until she'd turned him into a first class sap. (His words.) He might be a first class sap, but he was *her* first class sap.

"Speech! Speech!" friends and well-wishers called out.

With the ease of the natural leadership that was his gift, Ryan strode to the center of the room. "Well, once again I'm your sheriff. I'll admit it was a tough race, neck and neck to the end—me, myself and I."

Laughter from everyone.

"It's an honor to serve again."

"There's no one better!" A man's voice from the back of the room called out.

"Thanks, Dad." Ryan held up his champagne glass.

Hoots and more laughter.

"Thank you all for the warm way you've treated my wife, Zoey. She's a private person, as I am. And she really does not know when the light on Main and Third will be installed. Half the time, neither do I."

Zoey didn't know if she'd ever stop smiling when she heard Ryan call her his wife. There were many parts of her new life she was still getting used to, and this was by far the sweetest one.

"Being part of law enforcement in a small community like ours is the most rewarding part of my life. I will get to know your kids as they grow up, and they'll get to know mine. We'll all work together to make this town a place we can call our home. I will admit I never wanted to be a hero. Be assured that I still don't call myself a hero and I never will. But I have to thank you from the bottom of my heart for making me your hometown hero. There's no greater honor."

At those words, everyone cheered and drank a toast to Ryan Davis, the newly elected sheriff of the town of Fortune. Her husband, the love of her life. Ryan caught her gaze and winked as he raised his glass.

Next to her, Jill, her best friend and sister-in-law, pulled her in for a hug. "Thank you for making him so happy."

Heart full, Zoey made her way to the center of the crowd and into Ryan's waiting arms.

* * * * *

As a child, **Soraya Lane** dreamed of becoming an author. Fast-forward a few years, and Soraya is now living her dream! She describes being an author as "the best job in the world." She lives with her own real-life hero and two young sons on a small farm in New Zealand, surrounded by animals, with an office overlooking a field where their horses graze.

For more information about Soraya, her books and her writing life, visit sorayalane.com.

Books by Soraya Lane

Harlequin Romance

The Soldiers' Homecoming

The Returning Hero
Her Soldier Protector

Bellaroo Creek!

Patchwork Family in the Outback

Heroes Come Home

The Army Ranger's Return
Back in the Soldier's Arms
The Navy SEAL's Bride
Mission: Soldier to Daddy

The Larkville Legacy

The Soldier's Sweetheart

Visit the Author Profile page
at Harlequin.com for more titles.

THE RETURNING HERO

Soraya Lane

For Hamish & Mackenzie. I'm so fortunate
that you both share my love of dogs!

In Dogs We Trust
The unofficial motto of the soldiers
within the Explosive Detection Dog Service

Chapter 1

Brett Palmer leaned against the door of his vehicle. Visiting had seemed like a great idea before he'd left home, but now he was here...turning up unannounced wasn't so easy. Perhaps if he'd planned what he was going to say, had a good reason for not touching base with her before now, but he'd just jumped in the car and decided to chance it.

He sucked back a big breath and forced himself to walk forward. He'd known Jamie Mattheson for years, so it wasn't like she'd get a shock to see him, but still. It wasn't as if he'd ever spent time with her on her own, either.

Brett swallowed the memories, refusing to go back in time, and jogged the last few steps to the front door. He knocked. No one answered. There wasn't even so much as a shuffle from inside. Brett knocked again.

He could either get in his car and leave, or head around back to see if she was there. The sun was already out in full force, typical of Sydney at this time of year, and he had more than a hunch that she could be out in the garden.

Brett stepped back down and walked around the side of the house. It was looking nice, but then he knew Sam had painted the weatherboards before he'd left for their last tour, had made sure he'd done all the maintenance so Jamie had nothing to worry about while he was gone. He'd put money on it that she'd prefer the house to be falling down around her if it meant she could go back in time and have her husband back.

Brett pushed the side gate open and looked around the corner. *There she was.* Standing with her hands on her hips, like something was really frustrating her. Then he saw the something, sitting in front of her, alert, nose pointed in the air.

Bear. She had Sam's dog. How the hell had she ended up with Bear so soon?

"Jamie," he called out, not wanting to startle her but not wanting to be caught staring at her, either.

The dog had given up sitting patiently and was now barking and thundering toward him. He'd been his best mate's dog, but right now he was protecting his new owner, and Brett wasn't exactly game to take the massive canine on.

"Bear, it's me," he called out, as the black dog hurtled toward him. "Bear! It's okay, boy."

The dog slowed, still looking protective, but Brett was comfortable that he was no longer about to be attacked.

"Brett? What are you doing here?"

Jamie was suddenly rushing across the lawn to him, arms outstretched.

"Hey, sweetheart." He held his own arms out, one eye on the dog, until she threw herself against him.

Brett held her tight, holding on to her like his life depended upon it. He'd been best man at their wedding, vacationed with them, had dinner at their house…and now he was comforting a widow.

"It's so good to see you." Jamie stepped back, but she held on to his hands, firmly, like she'd never let go.

Brett looked into her eyes, saw tears there that she was bravely holding in check. This woman had been his best friend's wife, and he'd never, ever wanted to be in this position. He was just grateful that he hadn't been the one to tell her the news when it had happened.

"You've got Bear." He knew he was stating the obvious but he still couldn't believe it.

He turned half his attention back to the dog, who was keeping a close eye on them.

"And I have no idea what to do with him," she admitted, stepping back and letting go of Brett. Jamie had her hands back on her hips as she stared at the dog. "I'm doing my best, but he's, I don't know, smarter than me, I guess. We're not communicating that well."

Brett dropped to his haunches, eye level with the canine. "Hey, Bear. Remember me, bud?" The dog let out a low whine, looking up at Jamie then back to him again. "I know you do. Come here."

Bear slowly walked over to him and sat down on Brett's feet. He gave him a scratch, liking that the dog had accepted him. God only knew they'd spent enough time together when he was serving.

"I'll teach you everything I can, Jamie. He's a pretty

special dog, but he's used to certain commands and lots of them."

She laughed. "Yeah, sometimes I wondered if Sam thought he was more special than me. Probably showed off photos of him to everyone and forgot all about his wife."

Brett reached for her, took her hand again as he stood to full height. "You know that's not true. You meant everything to Sam." He chuckled. "To be honest, we all had to tell him to knock it off most of the time. He talked about you *way* too often."

She laughed, gripping his hand tight. "You always were the charmer."

He put his arm around her, needing to hold her, to show her how much he cared. "I miss him, Jamie. I miss him so bad that I can't..." Brett blew out a breath, dropping his chin to the top of her head. "I just needed you to know that I'm here for you. It's taken me a while, but I'm back now."

Jamie looped her arm around his waist and steered them toward the house. "How about we have brunch?"

"Here?"

"Yeah, why not," she said. "Besides, I haven't had anyone to make pancakes for in a while."

Brett signaled to the dog to follow them, and walked behind Jamie as she went into the house. She was dressed in a tiny pair of cut-off denim shorts and a loose-fitting T-shirt, and he wished she were covered up. She was his friend's widow. She was beautiful. Her legs were so long and tanned.... He forced his eyes to the sky. *Jamie was Sam's wife.* Just because he'd loved her from the moment he'd met her, thought she was the most caring, gorgeous woman he'd ever spent time with, didn't mean it was okay to start giving in to his feelings now.

Sam had been gone only a little over six months. He'd been his best friend. And Jamie was his widow, he reminded himself again.

But deep down, Brett knew exactly why he'd put off coming for so long.

Jamie hadn't stopped moving since they'd walked inside. She couldn't. Because if she stopped even for a second, she'd either start crying or throw her arms around Brett and never let him go.

Having him here was unexpected, unusual, and yet exactly what she needed all at the same time. Since Sam had been gone, she'd had an emptiness inside of her that had ached every single day, but seeing Brett...? It was like the pain was finally easing. Because she could talk to Brett about her husband, really talk about him, and he made her feel like Sam could still walk through the front door, hassling Brett for chatting her up like he usually did. Jamie took a deep breath.

"Maple syrup?" she asked.

He laughed. "Yes, ma'am."

Jamie flipped a pancake and turned around to look at the man seated at her counter. He looked like he always did—handsome and tanned—but there was something different about him now. Something she couldn't pinpoint, except for maybe a hint of unhappiness that kept crossing his face, that made his smile never quite reach his eyes like it once had. There was so much she wanted to ask him, but she wanted to wait until the time was right.

"So tell me how you ended up with Bear?" Brett asked.

She smiled at the dog lying near her feet. He might be hard to communicate with, but he sure was loyal and she loved him for that.

"The detection dog unit contacted me, told me that he had to be retired after the accident, and they wanted to offer him to me first." She shook her head, turning her attention back to her pancakes. "Sam loved him so much, so I couldn't say no. And it is kind of nice having the company, even if we haven't quite figured each other out yet. He's only been here a few weeks because he had to be in quarantine for a while."

She knew Brett had lost his dog in the same explosion that had killed her husband, that he probably wasn't ready to go there yet, but...

"I know I should have come by sooner, Jamie, it's just..." Brett's voice trailed off.

Jamie held up her hand. It seemed like they were both struggling to find the right words. "No apology necessary. We just do what we have to do to cope, right?"

He nodded, looked grateful that he didn't have to explain himself. Instead of asking him anything further, she flipped the last pancake and placed it in front of him, adding it to the stack.

"Looks good enough to eat," he said, grinning as he poured syrup over them.

Jamie sat down beside him, reaching for the coffeepot she'd left just out of reach. It seemed right having Brett here, even if it was just the two of them, because being alone these last six months, she'd started to forget the person she was, the happy, easygoing person she'd always been. Brett was making her remember how nice it had always been to open their home to friends.

She chanced a quick glance at him, wishing she could resist but unable to. When they'd first met, Brett was dating another woman, and then when he was single she'd already been seeing Sam. *His best friend.* Just because they'd been attracted to one another before didn't mean anything, she knew that, but she had a notion that she should be feeling guilty, shouldn't feel so comfortable in his presence.

"Do you still have your house here?"

Jamie watched as he finished his mouthful before setting his fork back down on the plate. "I decided to put it on the market a while back, and it sold while I was deployed."

"Oh." She hadn't known. "So where are you staying?" She'd been wanting to get in touch with him for months, had presumed he was away again, because he hadn't even been able to make it back for Sam's service.

"I've been at a recuperation clinic. My leg was burned pretty bad when the…" His sentence trailed off. "It's kept me away for a while, then I traveled around for a bit to come to grips with everything, and I only just arrived in yesterday."

She swallowed, taking a deep breath before she asked a question that needed to be voiced. "You're staying in a hotel, aren't you? You only came back here to see me."

Brett looked guilty. "You were Sam's wife. I could only stay away for so long. He'd want me to look out for you, Jamie. You know that. He even asked me as much."

Unspoken words hung between them, words that would never be braved by either of them. Because before it had just been flirting. Now that Sam was gone…

It was too soon for either of them, wasn't something that could ever happen. But it didn't mean she wanted Brett to leave, and it didn't mean that he was here for any other reason than because he loved her for being Sam's wife.

"I want you to know that I'm here, no matter what you need, okay?"

Jamie stared at him, raised one eyebrow as she looked into his eyes. "You really want to be here for me? To help me?"

He nodded. "Of course."

"Then help me with Bear," she said. "Turn me into a worthy owner of the dog who meant the world to my husband."

Brett was playing with his fork, looking at the half-eaten breakfast on his plate.

"You're sure you want me hanging around?" he asked. "I mean, you don't have to say that just because…"

Jamie reached for his hand, squeezed it and stared straight into Brett's eyes. "You weren't just his friend, you were mine, too," she confessed. "I've missed you guys—you, Sam and Logan. I miss you all. I didn't just lose my husband, I lost having you two here all the time, too."

Brett grunted. "Bet Logan's been better at staying in touch."

She shook her head. "He's phoned me a couple of times, but I haven't seen him, either. It's been—" Jamie shrugged "—weird. But he did say he was back in town soon, so maybe he's back now?"

Brett looked surprised, but she didn't say anything. He went back to eating his pancakes and so did she.

"Well, if you need help with Bear, I'm here," he said. "How about we start with a few basics today, and I'll come past tomorrow and we can take him out to a park or something."

Jamie stood up to clear their plates. "That sounds like a good plan," she told him.

A niggle in her mind was telling her she should have asked Brett to stay, that her husband would have been horrified that his best buddy was paying to stay at a hotel, but she wasn't ready for that. Wasn't ready for a man to be sleeping in her home, under her roof—a man who wasn't her husband, even if she did hate being on her own at night. Being alone…it took her back to her childhood, brought the ice-cold fear back, and she hated that as much as the reality of waking up without Sam beside her.

And if she were honest with herself, she was feeling nervous about being with Brett too much, just the two of them. They'd always flirted, it was just how he'd always been with her, but back then she'd also been in love with her husband, which meant their joking had always been nothing more than fun. Now?

She just had to take one day at a time. Having Brett here was better than being on her own, and she knew it was what Sam would have wanted. Even if she was having feelings about Brett that he wouldn't approve of.

Chapter 2

Brett didn't know what he'd expected, but being with Jamie was…different. He always knew it wasn't going to be the same without Sam, and he was pleased he was here, but it didn't make it easy.

Thank God they had Bear to deal with. He would have felt weird coming over again without a good reason, without a purpose to help her.

"So did Sam ever teach you any of his commands?"

Jamie shook her head. He could tell she loved the dog, and it looked as if the canine reciprocated—the trouble was plain simple communication. Bear was sitting faithfully beside Jamie, and her hand had fallen to the top of his head, which told him that there was no reason they weren't going to form a good team. They just weren't in sync yet, and that's what he was going to help her with.

"The thing with this dog is that he's extremely easy to teach, so long as you make your commands and actions clear and consistent," Brett told her. "You don't have to be Sam, but you do have to understand how he learns."

"Do you mean like how they need to be rewarded by play?"

Brett grinned. "Exactly. This dog was chosen for the dog detection unit because when we tested him as a youngster, his commitment to a game of ball was unwavering."

"So I need to play with him?" she asked, staring down at the dog.

"Yeah, you need to play with him, and you need to let him be with you all the time, because that's how Sam treated him whenever they were together."

Jamie was laughing and he loved seeing her happy, as if for a moment they were both here for any reason other than because of what had happened—that they were just two friends catching up under the sun, like old times.

"You guys always act so tough, but when it comes to your dogs, you're like marshmallows."

"It's part of the bonding process, you know that," he told her, pretending to be offended. "And we *are* tough, I'll have you know."

"Yeah, that's what you all tell each other, but really? You're just lonely when you're away and want a warm body in your bed to snuggle up to."

Brett laughed, unable to help himself. "How did you figure us all out so fast, huh?"

Jamie held up her hand to shield her face from the sun. "So are we just going to start with the basics?"

He nodded. "Why don't we run through sit, stay and heel, then I'll teach you how to play with a ninety-pound canine. Sound good?"

The smile she gave him made him drop his gaze, focus on the dog instead, because he was walking a dangerous line between helping out a friend's widow and wanting to be here because he'd always liked Jamie and still did.

And if he were honest with himself, it's why he'd taken so long to come back. It hadn't just been about his injury, it hadn't just been because he was struggling to come to terms with losing his best human friend *and* his canine best friend, it was because when it came to Jamie, he didn't trust himself. He could have all the best intentions in the world, but without Sam here, he was screwed.

Jamie watched as Brett moved across the grass, Bear running along beside him and then bounding ahead to catch the ball.

"You just need to have fun with him," Brett called out. "Let him know you love playing just as much as he does."

She couldn't help but laugh at them as they charged around her small lawn.

"It's not about the space, it's the quality of time you spend with him. He wants you to guide him, to be his leader and his equal, too. He will always look to you for direction, because that's what he's been trained to do."

"So in other words he wants me to be his wife?"

They both laughed and she watched as Brett nodded to the dog to follow him.

"You must miss your dog," she said, wishing she could take the words back the moment they left her lips.

Brett's mouth fixed in a hard line, his jaw clamped before he took a visibly deep breath. "Every goddamn day," he told her, running a hand through his short brown hair. "Teddy hardly left my side in four years. It was like he always knew what I was thinking before I'd even thought it myself. And then..."

Jamie felt like her breath had died in her throat, her lungs refusing to cooperate. The day Teddy had died had been the day Sam had died, too.

They stared at one another. She watched as Brett swallowed. Neither of them wanted to talk about that day, because somehow Brett had made it home and her husband and Brett's dog had been killed. She wished the comment had never come out of her mouth, but it wasn't like she could take it back.

"Have you had any ongoing veterinary care for Bear? I'm hoping after all he did for the army that he's on a full pension."

He'd changed the subject but only just, although she wasn't complaining.

"When I collected him he was pretty much healed, on the outside at least," Jamie told him. "He had a bandaged paw still and lots of missing or singed fur, but they made sure he was almost back to health before letting me take him. And they seemed to look after him pretty well when he was quarantined."

"I was the one who carried him back to the truck," Brett told her, his voice low. "He managed to come toward me, but the ringing in his ears must have been as bad as it was in mine because he couldn't even walk in a straight line, and his paws and legs were badly burned.

There was no part of me that could have tried to get away without helping him, and it was like he wanted to do the same for me."

Jamie refused to look away, no matter how uncomfortable the conversation was making her, because she knew how hard it must have been for Brett to talk about what had happened, even just a little.

"I can't believe you even managed to lift him, after what had happened to you," she said softly.

Brett dropped to his haunches and slung his arm around the dog. "If it hadn't been for this boy," he said, stroking the dog's fur as he spoke, "everyone in that truck would have died that day. It wasn't until I collapsed that I realized why my body was burning so bad, what a mess my leg was, and then I passed out from the pain and shock. Bear was braver than any of us."

Brett was staring past her now, and Jamie didn't want to make him uncomfortable. It was so nice having him here, having a familiar face to chat to, that she wanted to make sure he stayed for the afternoon.

"What do you say we take him for a walk?" she suggested.

Brett smiled, clearly relieved she'd changed the subject completely.

"Do you usually take him out?" he asked.

She grimaced. "It's not that I don't want to, but he's kind of massive and I'm worried I won't be able to control him if we come across another dog or something."

Brett shook his head. "Did that husband of yours teach you *nothing* about this dog?"

She laughed. "No, because it was like they shared the same brain! Bear just did what Sam wanted him to do, like they had some silent communication thing going on, and he went everywhere with him so it wasn't like I was ever in sole charge."

Brett sighed. "Fair call." He followed her inside and stood back as she locked the doors. "How about you tell me what you'd like to do with him?"

She checked the side door was locked before gathering Bear's lead from a drawer and facing Brett.

"I guess I want to be able to walk down for a coffee and sit without worrying how to handle him if there's another big dog coming toward us. And walk through the park, throw a ball for him and know he'll come back when he's off the leash, that sort of thing."

Brett opened the front door and held it open for her, waiting as she clipped the leash to Bear's collar.

"He's too well-trained to have a fight with another dog, and he will never, *ever* chase a ball and not bring it back to you. It's why he made the squad in the first place."

"Were you with Sam the day he chose him?"

Brett shook his head. "No, but I remember him being so excited that he'd finally found the perfect partner. Bear was with a family who loved him, but they were moving overseas and had put him up for adoption. When Sam went to see him, he tested him out with a ball and he knew straight away that the black giant was going to be his sidekick."

They fell into a comfortable rhythm, walking side by side.

"Is it okay to talk about him?" Brett asked, his voice an octave lower.

The question took her by surprise. "Yes." They walked for a bit more before she continued. "I mean, it's hard, it's always hard, but it's nice talking about him with you."

"I half expect him to be at the house when we get back," Brett said with a smile. "Waiting to give me a telling off about hanging out with his wife."

"Yeah." Jamie was smiling, too, but it was bittersweet. "I guess I'd become so used to him going away on tours, so for me it just seems like this has just been an especially long one. Like I'm just waiting for him to fly home and pick up where we left off." It had been the same when her dad had never come home from deployment—like one day he'd just walk through the door again and everything would go back to normal.

"If it's too hard having me here…"

"No," she blurted. "Having you here is the only good thing that's happened to me in a long while, so please don't think you're making me uncomfortable. It's the complete opposite."

Brett was pleased she wanted him here, but every time they talked about Sam made him feel plain weird for being with Jamie, just the two of them. Lucky they had the dog as a distraction, because it meant they had something to focus on other than the fact that nothing was like it had been the last time they'd seen one another.

"So you just give him a gentle reminder if he walks ahead of you by pulling the lead back," he told her, closing his hand over it and showing her, "and telling him to heel, but you're probably not going to need to do that very often."

Brett didn't move his hand when Jamie's brushed past it, fingers almost closing over his before she realized. It was stupid—they'd touched plenty in the past—but having her warm skin against his reminded him of all the reasons why he shouldn't have been here. Because there had been a time when he'd wished he'd asked Jamie out, before she'd met Sam, and they were dangerous thoughts to be remembering now that she was his friend's widow.

"Brett, I don't want to bring up what happened again, but I need to ask you one question."

He cleared his throat and turned to face her. "Shoot." So long as he didn't have to relive what had happened again, he'd tell her what she needed to know. Those memories caught up on him enough without voluntarily calling on them.

"I keep thinking about the army sending Bear back, once they'd made the decision to retire him. Is it normal for them to care for a dog like that, even though their career is over, and then pay to send them home?"

Brett couldn't help smiling at her. Trust Jamie to have figured out that it wasn't exactly protocol, especially when the handler was no longer alive and able to fight for his dog.

"Let's just say that me and the other boys put a fair amount of pressure on our superiors to make sure Bear had a good retirement. I didn't know he'd be given back to you, but there aren't that many dogs in the world capable of what he did on a daily basis, and it wasn't exactly a tough call to send him home a hero."

Jamie reached out to him, took him completely by surprise as her hand stayed in place on his shoulder.

"Well then I guess I owe you a pretty big thanks," she said, throwing him a smile that made him want to look away, because that smile had always teased him and he didn't want to think about her like that, not now. "It means a lot to have him here, even if I'm kind of hopeless at the whole business of looking after a dog."

Brett fought not to shrug her hand off, and was pleased when it just dropped away.

"So which café are we going to?"

"Skinny latte?"

Jamie looked up. "How did you guess?"

He chuckled and ordered, before peering into the cabinet with her. "And I'm also guessing that you want something sweet. Maybe the chocolate peppermint slice?"

Jamie kept staring at the rows of food, trying to ignore the slice so she wasn't completely predictable. In the end she gave in to her sweet tooth. "Okay, how about we share a piece?"

She walked back outside to where they'd left Bear, not liking the idea of just tying him up and leaving him beside a table.

"He's fine," Brett said, pulling her chair out for her and then taking the seat opposite.

"I can see that. It just seems foreign to me," she told him.

"This dog won't let you down. Trust me. His manners will be better than most of the people in here."

Jamie rolled her eyes, but she knew he was probably right. And she also knew that Brett pulling her chair out for her was the kind of gentlemanly thing that not many guys did anymore. Her husband had, so she was used to it, and she liked being treated like a woman.

Brett's mobile rang and he punched a button to silence it before answering and mouthing *sorry* to her.

Jamie touched Bear's head, stroking his fur, not looking at Brett. But she couldn't help but take notice of
what he was saying. The fact that it was Logan, her
husband's other best buddy, made her want to frown
and smile simultaneously.

Part of her was liking being with Brett, but another
part of her, like a pang of hunger gnawing at her stomach, wanted Sam back here, too. So she could sit and
listen to them talk and laugh and be boys, like she always had. Her husband, Brett and Logan.

Brett cleared his throat and Jamie's eyes snapped
up to meet his. She had no idea whether he was waiting for her to say something, or whether he was just
watching her.

"Jamie, what do you say?" he asked.

She raised her eyebrows, wishing she hadn't been
daydreaming. "To what?"

"Logan's in town for the next week and he wanted to
know if you're free tonight. We thought we'd go grab a
few drinks, catch up."

Jamie liked that they were trying to include her, but
she didn't want to be a third wheel. "You guys just hang
out. You don't need to ask me along."

Brett put his hand over the phone and leaned toward
her, eyes never leaving hers. "Please come," he said,
reaching for her with his other hand, fingers closing
over hers. "I'll pick you up on my way and drop you at
your door at the end of the night. Come out and have
fun, we both want to take you out."

She looked from his eyes to his fingers over hers,
wished that it was just a platonic gesture, that his skin
against hers wasn't sending a shiver up and down her
spine.

"Okay," she said, not needing any more convincing.

Brett grinned and pulled away, leaning back in his chair again and discussing details with Logan. She was pleased their coffees arrived at the same time as he hung up, needing something to distract her. Somehow she'd gone from hanging out with her husband's friend, to being on edge about agreeing to a night out. It was only supposed to be an evening with friends, so why was her stomach twisting like she was going on a first date?

"Sugar?"

Jamie nodded and reached for it, careful not to touch Brett's hand again.

"So Logan's back for a while, too?" she asked.

"He's still working, but he's based in Australia indefinitely."

"And you're sure he was okay about me tagging along on a boys' night?"

Brett cut the chocolate peppermint slice into two pieces and nudged one in her direction. "Since when are you not allowed to tag along on a boys' night? I don't recall Sam ever leaving you at home when we used to catch up."

"True." Brett was right, she *had* always hung out with them. But now that it was just her, she didn't want them feeling sorry for her and feeling like they had to include her.

"When was the last time you went out?" he asked.

"Can I pass on that question?" Jamie laughed and took a bite of the slice. "It's been a while."

"If another guy so much as looks at you he'll have me to deal with, so you're in safe hands."

Jamie picked at some chocolate and then took a sip of coffee, because she didn't want to make eye contact with Brett. There was only one guy she was worried about, and he was sitting directly across from her. He might trust himself, but she wasn't entirely sure that her thoughts were as pure.

Chapter 3

Jamie padded barefoot into the kitchen and fed Bear. She poured herself a glass of water and leaned on the counter, slowly drinking it, concentrating on the cool liquid and how it felt as she swallowed. It was the only thing she could think of to calm her nerves, other than going for a run, and after the time she'd spent in the shower and doing her hair, she had no intention of getting sweaty.

What was she doing?

It wasn't the fact that she was going out that was making her feel guilty, because she was in desperate need of doing something fun that got her out of the house. Her problem was that she couldn't stop thinking about Brett, and it was making her feel things that she had no right to feel.

She'd dolled herself up, made more of an effort than

she had in months to look good, and it was Brett she was trying to impress. It was as if all the years of flirting had finally caught up with them, and with Sam not here, things were starting to feel awkward, fast. Or maybe not so much awkward as *exciting*.

"Brett is forbidden. Brett is my friend," she muttered, realizing that she was looking at her dog as if he were part of the conversation. "Tell me I'm crazy, Bear. I'm crazy, aren't I?"

He just stared up at her, pausing, before going back to eating his dinner.

Jamie sighed and dumped her water glass in the sink before walking back to her bedroom and looking at the clothes she'd thrown on the bed. She had her little black dress, a pair of satin pants and a sexy top, and her favorite skinny jeans. She reached for the dress and held it up, looking at her reflection in the floor-length mirror behind the door.

She wanted to wear the dress. She wanted to make Brett notice her. *She wanted to feel sexy.*

Jamie stripped down to her underwear and slipped on the dress. She was about to reach for a pair of five-inch black heels that she'd never worn before, that were just stuck in her closet, when her hand stopped moving. Everything stopped. Because just above her shoe rack, hanging on a little hook, was her husband's dog tag on its silver chain.

Jamie slowly reached for it, fingers clasping the cool metal, tracing over the tag that she'd spent so many hours staring at since he'd gone. The same tag that she'd often touched when they'd been lying together, in bed on a lazy morning….

"If anything ever happened to you, would they give me this?"

Sam frowned. "Nothing's going to happen to me, baby, but yeah. They would."

She reached for it again, turning it over and reading the inscription out aloud. "Samuel Harvey Mattheson. O positive."

"Are you going to recite all my vitals, too?"

Jamie lay her head on Sam's bare chest, still holding his tag as she shut her eyes.

"Don't ever leave me, Sam. You have to promise to come home."

He kissed the top of her head. "Baby, I'm coming home. Haven't I always told you that nothing could keep me away from you?"

"How can you be so sure?" She kissed his chest, lips against his warm skin, before moving up and kissing his mouth, trying to stop tears from falling down her cheeks and onto his face.

"If I don't, then promise me you'll wear this. I don't ever want you to forget me, Jamie...."

Jamie had sunk to the floor, tears pricking her eyes then falling in a slow, steady trickle down her cheeks and into her mouth. What was she doing? How could she even be *thinking* about Brett like she had been? What was wrong with her?

But she knew. Deep down, she knew.

There had been a spark between her and Brett for years, a spark that could have easily turned into something more if they'd met at the right time, and now he was here and she was a widow. Her feelings were only natural. But they were also wrong. Being lonely wasn't an excuse to give in to any of those feelings, not now, not ever.

Jamie reached back up for the tag and took it down, slipping it around her neck. She needed Sam close to her, wanted him close to her, and she was upset that she'd forgotten the promise she'd made to him that she'd wear it.

She also slipped back out of the dress, suddenly not wanting to make Brett notice her like that. She reached for her skinny jeans instead, paired them with heels and pulled a scoop-neck tank over her head. Jamie finished the look with a biker-style leather jacket and hoop earrings, before going back into the bathroom to fix her makeup. She smoothed foundation over her tearstains, put on some more mascara and touched up her lip gloss, before running a hand through her smooth hair—courtesy of her straightening iron.

When the doorbell rang and Bear started barking, she took one final look in the mirror and kissed Sam's dog tag.

Tonight, he was with her, looking out for her, just like his friends were. She couldn't stop her feelings for Brett, but she *could* stop herself from acting on them.

"Bear, it's just Brett again."

He stopped barking as soon as she spoke, but he stayed by her side as she opened the door, like he had no intention of not protecting her, even if he wasn't allowed to bark.

"Hey," she said, opening the door to find him standing a few steps back from the door, hands jammed in his jean pockets.

"Hey," Brett replied, moving forward. "You look, well, *wow*."

Jamie smiled, knowing she shouldn't be so pleased that he liked the way she looked but unable to pretend otherwise. She reached for the dog tag, fingers closing around it as she looked at Brett, needing the reminder.

"You don't look so bad yourself," she heard herself say.

"Yeah? Well you look like you're going to need a bodyguard to stay safe tonight."

Jamie laughed. "Well, lucky I have two of them, huh?"

It was true—she could have worn the dress if she hadn't been feeling so guilty, because Brett and Logan would act like her overprotective big brothers if a guy so much as looked at her too long, let alone if anyone tried anything on her.

"So shall we go?" Brett asked.

"Just let me check I've locked everything, and I need to grab my purse."

She disappeared back into the kitchen and then the living room, double-checking all the locks.

"You know Bear would maul any strangers who even tried to come in here, right?"

Jamie glanced across at Brett, knew he was watching her. He quickly looked up and met her gaze when she caught him out, but it sent a ripple of delight through her body that he *was* staring at her, no matter what she'd been telling herself as she stood in the closet.

"So not only do I have personal bodyguards escorting me tonight, you're telling me that I have one living in my house now? A big, furry, ninety-pound one?"

Brett held up her purse for her and waited for her to walk ahead of him down the hall. Her face flushed as she realized he could be checking out her butt.

"I'm saying that you're safe with Bear here, and you're definitely safe with me," he told her, his voice a note lower than it had been earlier.

Jamie glanced over her shoulder and waited for Brett to follow her out the door. Then she locked it and looped her hand through his arm. She could have so easily dropped her head to his shoulder, given him a hug, but she didn't want to blur the lines of their friendship. Once she wouldn't have thought twice about touching him like that, because before it had never meant anything, but she knew he was feeling the change between them and the spark that seemed to have ignited since he'd walked back into her life.

"Thanks for taking me out tonight," she told him, ignoring everything else and saying the one thing she needed him to hear. "I feel like I've been alone for a really long time, and it's nice to just get out of the house and have fun."

The taxi was waiting for them, and he opened the door for her to slide in before sitting beside her.

"Here's to a good night," he said, covering her knee with his hand.

But as soon as he did it, he backed off. Fast. Because the way he looked at her, the way she couldn't help but look back at him when he touched her, must have scared him as much as it damn well terrified her.

Chapter 4

"This feels weird," Jamie said as they walked through the door of the bar.

Brett couldn't have agreed more. He felt like they were on a date, the two of them heading out for the evening, and it didn't help that he was thinking things he wished he wasn't about Jamie. The music was loud but not overpowering, and because it was still early it wasn't completely packed with people yet.

He looked around for Logan, desperate to see him. Once they found him, he could go get some drinks, leave the pair of them to catch up and deal with getting his head in the right space. It was bad enough that he'd spent the day before with Jamie, but seeing her again tonight was too much, too soon.

"There he is."

Jamie was leaning into him, talking into his ear over

the noise and the music. He looked where she was point-
ing, groaning as she took hold of his hand. He got it;
she was probably nervous about being out on the town
without her husband, was reaching to him for support.
But the way he was feeling right now, he didn't need her
hand thrust into his, fingers interlaced as she walked
slightly ahead of him toward Logan.

When they reached him Brett pulled his hand away
and ran it through his hair instead. He needed to get it
together, and fast. Logan would notice straight away if
anything was going on, and he didn't want to be inter-
rogated by anyone   especially not his best mate. Logan
would be the first person to call him to task if he knew
even the half of what he'd been thinking.

"Hey, Jamie." Logan jumped off the bar stool and
wrapped his arms around her, giving her a big hug.

When he let go, Brett stepped forward and greeted
him, grabbing hold of one of his hands and slapping
him on the back at the same time. They hadn't seen
each other in months.

"How are you, stranger?"

Brett shrugged. "Better now I've seen you."

They stared at one another, so much unsaid, but it
only lasted a moment. Logan knew what had happened,
would be the only person in Brett's life who would ever
come close to understanding what he'd experienced,
although even he couldn't imagine how disturbing it
had been, how violent. They hadn't seen each other in
a long while, had a lot of catching up to do.

Brett shook off his thoughts. "What are we drinking? My shout."

"Start with a beer or straight to bourbon?" Logan
asked.

Jamie laughed, and Brett angled his body to better include her. He'd been so wound up in seeing Logan again that he'd almost forgotten about her. Brett touched his palm to her back, moving her forward between them and taking a step back to make room for her.

"I think we'll start with beer. How about you?"

Jamie smiled. "Um, maybe a cocktail for me."

Logan raised his eyebrows and Brett laughed. "So maybe we'll start with bourbon then, if you're hitting the strong stuff straight away."

Jamie leaned over the counter to reach for a menu. "It's been a *looong* time since I've been out. Can't you tell? The only cocktail I can think of is a Cosmopolitan from *Sex and the City*, but there must be something else...."

"Long Island iced teas," Logan announced. "Three of them."

Jamie pushed her shoulders up, shrugging, an innocent expression on her face. Brett needed to warn her.

"They're kind of potent," he said.

Her smile was sweet enough to make him feel dirty for admiring her cleavage when she leaned forward.

"Lucky I have you two to look after me then, huh?" She put an arm around each of them, her smile infectious. "I need a night of just having fun, so order away, boys. I'm in."

Brett did as he was told and watched her walk off with Logan, looking for a quieter, more comfortable place to sit. They all had a lot to talk about, or maybe they didn't. Maybe tonight was about letting Jamie have fun without feeling guilty, just being there for her and making sure she had a good time and got home safely at the end of the evening.

He just had to remind himself that he would have plenty to be guilty about if he ever let himself give in to the way he was feeling about her. Brett paid for the drinks and stuffed his wallet back in his pocket, before carrying their drinks to the table. He could see Jamie leaning toward Logan, talking, touching his shoulder as they discussed something that had her smiling. Logan was rock-solid, the perfect guy to be spending time with Jamie, because he would honor his word and never do anything that would jeopardize their friendship or the one he'd had with Sam. Trouble was, it wasn't Logan who was spending time with Jamie, because he was still working.

"Drink up," he announced, placing the tall glasses on the table and sitting down beside Jamie.

The way she looked at him took him by surprise, made him hope that Logan hadn't noticed it, but maybe he was just being oversensitive.

"To Sam," Logan said, holding up his drink. "A good soldier, a damn good friend and husband to the sweetest woman I've ever met."

Brett glanced at Jamie, saw her eyes were damp. He held up his own glass. "Cheers to that."

They all took a sip, but Jamie was spluttering as soon as she'd swallowed her first mouthful.

"Are you guys trying to kill me? This stuff is like poison."

Brett laughed. "It gets better. Just keep drinking."

"Has Brett shown you his new tattoo?" Logan asked.

Jamie shook her head, looking at him. "Nope." She took another sip and grimaced again.

"Brett had his done as soon as he was out of recovery, and I got mine when I touched down in Australia."

"You have new matching ones?" she asked. "Can I see?"

Logan pushed his T-shirt up, rolling his arm around to show the words marked in black ink, curling letters over four short rows.

"'Fight a battle for a cause that's worth the victory. Fight a war that's worth dying for. Remain brave in death. Honor those you love.'" Jamie stared at Logan's arm as she finished reading the words.

Brett knew she was fighting emotion, because her voice had become low and husky, a deeper tone than he'd ever heard from her. He responded by rolling up his shirt until he could show her his matching ink, only just able to push the fabric high enough for her to see it.

Jamie turned to inspect his properly, trailing her fingers across each word as if she were writing them, committing them to memory. Her touch was light, and when her hand dropped to land on his thigh, it almost made him lose the drink he'd just reached for.

"You did these for Sam, didn't you?" she asked.

Brett nodded when she looked at him, and Logan did the same.

"Well, they're beautiful," she said, dabbing her eyes with the back of her fingers. "Maybe I should get one, too?"

"No," Brett said, faster than he'd meant to.

"I don't think so," Logan chimed in, almost as quickly.

Jamie raised an eyebrow, looking puzzled. "Because I'm a girl? They're not exactly military tattoos, are they?"

Brett looked to Logan for help but didn't receive any. He cleared his throat, not wanting to dig himself a hole that he couldn't claw his way out of, but not having any intention of letting her ink herself.

"Your skin is beautiful and you don't need any ink, Jamie. Don't go rushing into anything."

"Just keep wearing that tag," Logan added. "It's what he would have wanted."

She laughed and took a hearty sip of her drink, before slowly downing the rest of it.

"Bottoms up, boys," she announced, grinning at them over the top of her glass.

Brett and Logan exchanged looks before shrugging and following her lead.

"My round this time. Another?" Jamie asked.

They both said yes and watched her walk away, like two bodyguards ready to pounce on anyone who so much as bumped into her.

"'Your skin is so beautiful'?" Logan mimicked, punching him in the arm. "Seriously, couldn't you have come up with anything better than that?"

Brett glared at him. "It wasn't like you were stepping in to help me out."

"Yeah, I was too busy watching you swooning over her. You know she's out of bounds, right? Because I'll…"

Brett gave him a playful shove, trying to laugh the comment off. "You don't have to tell me, I know."

"I miss him, Brett. I seriously miss him."

Brett leaned back in his seat, watching Jamie at the bar as she leaned toward the bartender to place her order. He couldn't believe he hadn't noticed the dog tag she was wearing around her neck, but then he'd been trying his hardest not to look at her chest, and the way the tag was being swallowed by her breasts… Brett cleared his throat. That wasn't something he needed to think about right now. Sam had been like his surrogate brother, and he would never disrespect anyone he considered family.

"I can't stop thinking about that day. It's screwed up, Logan. The things I saw, what happened, I just wish I could forget it all, for good."

Brett shut his eyes, blocked the memories out, doing what he always did. Because forcing them away was a damn sight easier than dealing with them, and he didn't want to go there, not now.

"I'm going to go help her carry the drinks back," he announced, needing to move.

Before Logan guessed that he also couldn't stop thinking about Jamie, in all the wrong ways.

Jamie leaned back into Brett, eyes shut, the room starting to spin. She'd had three cocktails, but she wasn't exactly used to drinking and it felt like three too many.

"I don't feel so good."

Brett's arm was suddenly looped around her shoulders, holding her closer to his body. She opened her eyes to look at Logan, but he was starting to blur.

"I think someone needs something to eat," Logan said.

"And water," she mumbled.

Logan jumped up and gave her what she guessed was a salute. "Glass of water and greasy fries coming up."

She tucked back tighter into Brett, starting to feel sleepy.

"Thanks for looking after me."

His chuckle made his chest vibrate beneath her ear.

"They were pretty potent," he told her, his hold on her shoulders loosening as he bent forward to retrieve his drink. "We shouldn't have let you have more than two."

Jamie groaned. "You're going to take me home, right?" She didn't want to have to flag a taxi on her own in the dark, not to mention go home to an empty house. Most nights, she tried to remind herself why she was okay alone, but tonight her brain just wasn't cooperating.

"We weren't exactly going to get you drunk then let you find your own way home."

Jamie shut her eyes again, wishing she had only had two drinks. They'd been having so much fun, and she hadn't been out in so long.

"Brett, can you stay with me tonight?" she asked.

Jamie thought she felt his body stiffen, but maybe she was imagining it.

"Ah, I'm not sure," he said. "I'll see you home, though."

Jamie shook her head and turned, hand on Brett's shoulder as she stared up at him. "Please? I just don't want to be alone tonight."

He looked down at her and she couldn't read his face. Having her eyes shut and sitting still for a few minutes had made the spinning stop, but she was still feeling less than average.

"If you still want me to stay when we get to your place, then I will," he finally said. "Just don't go saying anything to Logan because he'll go off and get the wrong idea and I don't need him getting all crazy protective over you."

She smiled up at him, leaning in to kiss his cheek. It

was warm and slightly stubbled, but where she kissed him was soft enough to make her want to keep her lips there. Jamie had only meant it as an innocent thank-you, but she could have easily moved slightly to the left, kissed his lips instead. She was staring at them, eyes unable to leave his mouth, even as his hand came up between them and gently pushed her back into her seat.

"Let's not do anything we'd regret sober, okay?"

Brett's voice was soft, but the hungry eyes staring back at her were telling a different story entirely.

"Who's hungry?"

Logan had returned with the bar food, which looked perfect and greasy.

"Me, please," she responded, her thigh pressed to Brett's as she leaned forward. She was telling herself she needed it there to anchor her in place, keep her steady, but she knew better.

She was drunk and coming on to her husband's friend. It was a hundred shades of wrong, but it felt every shade of right. Jamie reached for a fry and dunked it in ketchup, closing her eyes with delight at the salty, greasy taste.

"These are *sooo* good," she murmured.

Logan laughed. "Drunk as a skunk."

She didn't care what they said. Tonight had been better than good, it had been amazing. For the first time in forever, she felt like herself again, and it had been a long time coming.

Because for a while there, she'd wondered if she'd lost that Jamie forever.

Jamie held on to Brett's arm as she stepped out of the taxi, and she didn't let it go as they walked to her front door. He hadn't said anything about staying or not staying, and even though she'd sobered up a heap, she still didn't want to be alone. Nights like tonight brought everything crashing back to her, even though it had been over a decade ago.

It had been pitch-black outside, and she'd been tucked under a blanket, alone, waiting for her mom to come home. She knew she'd be drunk, but she wanted to wait for her to come back. When the door had opened, she'd stayed still, not made a sound, knowing her mom would just make her way upstairs and collapse on her bed.

Only it hadn't been her mom. She'd hidden, terrified, as two men in balaclavas had burgled their house, never making a noise so they wouldn't know anyone was home. Tears had choked in her throat, but she'd stayed silent, wishing that her dad had made it back. Knowing that if he'd been alive, her mom would still be holding it together, that she would have been safe.

"So here we are," Brett said when they reached the door, jolting her from her thoughts.

She fumbled in her bag for her keys and called out to Bear as his loud bark boomed through the door. Letting her memories take hold was not something she usually let happen, not that easily.

"Just me," she told her dog, "it's only me."

His barking stopped and she turned the key. Brett leaned past her and pushed the door, standing his ground as she dropped to give the dog a cuddle and then usher him back inside.

"Are you going to be okay on your own?" he asked, looking uncomfortable, hands jammed in his pockets.

Jamie wasn't going to lie to him, especially not

now. "I've never been okay on my own," she admitted. "Every time Sam went away, I'd pretend to be all brave because I didn't want him worrying about me, but when he was on tour I hardly ever went out unless I could be back before dark. I was just too nervous coming home to an empty house."

His expression changed, his face sad. "Is it better with Bear here?"

She nodded. "Yeah, a little."

"You still want me to stay tonight, don't you?"

Jamie nodded again. Relief took away the tightness in her shoulders as she realized she was actually going to have someone in the house. That Brett, one of the people she trusted most in the world, was going to be sleeping under her roof, protecting her, letting her have a good night's sleep without her worrying about every creak or rustle outside the window. Without her thinking someone might find their way into her home.

Brett smiled when she stepped back, and he walked into the house and locked the door behind him.

"I'll just bunk on the sofa," he said, following her into the kitchen.

"I can make up the spare bed," she told him, flicking on a light and fumbling in the pantry for coffee. "I don't want you being uncomfortable."

"Hey," Brett said, coming up behind her and taking the coffee. "You go sit down, I'll make us both a cup. I'm sure your head could do without all the movement, might help the pounding stop."

His hand over hers made her freeze, and she resisted the urge to push back into him, to rock her body back into his like she was so desperate to do. She craved his

touch like a desperate woman who'd never had the pleasure of a man before.

"Go sit on the sofa," he ordered, voice low.

Jamie reluctantly did as she was told, listening to
Brett as he moved around the kitchen. She flopped onto
the big sofa, tucked up against a cushion, eyes back on
him as he stirred two cups and then carried them over.
He placed them down and went to sit on the armchair.

"It's way more comfy over here," she told him.

He hesitated before coming over to sit beside her.
Jamie tucked her feet up and changed position, her body
against Brett's instead of the oversized cushion. Now
she had an oversized, warm, muscled man to lean into.

"Thanks for tonight," she told him.

"My pleasure," he responded, staying still but looking down at her.

Jamie knew she was still a little drunk, that she
needed to just sleep it off and not do anything stupid,
but ever since she'd kissed Brett at the bar, on the cheek,
she'd thought of nothing other than his lips; his full,
kissable lips.

Before she knew what she was doing, she reached
up to touch his face, tracing her fingers over his mouth
before leaning on him and putting her lips there. It was
a sweet kiss, a warm kiss, a kiss that made her skin tingle. And it wasn't easy to pull back from. Brett didn't
resist, didn't push her away, but he didn't move closer,
either. He just moved his lips enough for her to know
that he was kissing her back, that he wanted it, too. Or
at least that's what she wanted to think.

He didn't say anything when she pulled away, and
neither did she. Brett reached for a cushion, put it at the
end of the sofa and leaned back into it, letting her fall

down against him. She put her head against his chest, tucked up beside him, like a cat purring into his hold as he put his arm around her.

She should have gone and found a blanket to keep them warm, but she didn't want to move and Brett was warm and snuggly even without anything covering them. Instead she shut her eyes and let sleep catch her and wrap her in its equally warm embrace. She couldn't have fought it if she tried, and Jamie had a feeling that for once she might actually sleep through the entire night without waking, terrified, like she usually did.

Brett stared down at Jamie. She was asleep, he could hear the change in her breathing, but it didn't make him even close to being sleepy himself.

Jamie, Sam's wife, had just kissed him. And he'd done nothing to stop it and everything to encourage it.

Granted, he'd had a lot to drink, but not enough to make him drunk or to make him forget that she was forbidden. Even Logan had reminded him, just in case he'd managed to forget himself, that she was the one woman he wasn't supposed to think about, *like that*. And yet she'd come on to him and he'd willingly accepted her advances.

But then he'd known he was a goner tonight from the moment she'd traced her fingers down his inner arm, along the words of his tattoo, and he'd known he was incapable of doing the right thing when she'd kissed his cheek in the bar. The heat of her breath against his skin, her warm lips, the look in her eyes…like she wanted him, trusted him and needed him, all rolled into one stare. Into one gentle touch that he found one hundred percent irresistible.

Brett groaned, but there was no getting away from her, not now that she was clutching his shirt between her fingers and her head was tucked against his chest like it was her own personal pillow to snuggle up into.

The light in the kitchen was still on, but unless he could teach the dog how to turn it off, he was just going to have to shut his eyes and do his best to ignore it.

He caught sight of Bear watching him, head between his paws, eyebrows raised.

"Don't look at me like that," Brett told him, scowling.

He didn't need a damn dog to make him feel even more guilty than he already felt.

"And don't you be forgetting that I saved your life," he muttered, before shutting his eyes.

The truth was that Bear had saved all of them that day. He'd stopped after Sam had sent him out, body dead-still, tail quivering, head cocked to the side. It had been Bear who'd alerted them to the bomb—only trouble was that it wasn't a standard improvised explosive device. This IED had been remote-detonated, most likely from a local hiding where they hadn't been able to find him. Someone watching, in wait, to explode an entire 4x4 full of SAS soldiers, wanting to blow them all into pieces.

Sam and Brett's dog had been the casualties that day, so maybe he should be showing Bear some respect and thanking *him* for saving his life.

He shut his eyes, knowing sleep wouldn't come easily, because it never did these days. If he managed to fall asleep, he'd wake up in a sweat and twisted in his sheets, mind full of the darkness of that day he was trying so hard to forget. And then he'd lie awake, scared of shutting his eyes again because of the memories that flashed like scenes from a movie beneath his eyelids.

Chapter 5

When Brett woke up, the pain in his leg and back hit him straight away. He was all crooked from lying flat, and when he tried to move, he realized he couldn't. Because the woman he'd just been having an erotic dream about was still attached to his chest, her long hair splayed out across him, arm slung down low, cheek to his heart.

He shut his eyes again, remembering how uncomfortable it had been carrying a hundred-and-fifty-pound pack when he was on patrol with the SAS. At least Jamie was warm and… He swallowed away that particular thought. Now he just had to hope that she didn't wake up for a little bit longer, so she didn't have to wonder if it was a gun or if he was just pleased to see her when she realized where her hand was resting.

But…he'd slept. He'd dreamed about Jamie. And he

wasn't wet with sweat. Which meant that last night was the first night he'd actually slept through, without nightmares, since *that day.*

When Brett opened his eyes again, Bear was staring back at him, his nose right beside his face, as if he'd just been waiting for them to wake up.

"Hey, buddy," he whispered, receiving a giant lick in reply.

Jamie groaned then and wriggled closer against him, her arm flinging across his chest. He kept one hand on her to keep her in place, not wanting her to fall off the sofa if she stretched the other way. Another low groan told him she perhaps wasn't a morning person, or that her head was starting to thump.

"Want some pain meds?" he asked, keeping his voice low.

She went still, then put her palm flat on his chest and pushed up. Her hair was all messy, curlier than he'd ever seen it, and her eyes were smudged. She looked lazy and sexy all rolled into one.

"I slept on you."

He chuckled. "We still have our clothes on, so don't worry."

She didn't smile, so he was guessing his joke wasn't in the best taste, but she did flop back down on top of him, face buried in his chest again.

"My head kind of hurts," she muttered. "And don't even try to tell me I don't look like crap, because I know I do."

He laughed. "You actually look pretty good."

Funny how he could go from freaking out to joking with her in two seconds flat, and he wasn't lying, either.

"Warmed-up crap," she muttered. "That's even worse than straight crap, right?"

Brett pushed her gently off him and stretched, being careful to flex his leg before standing up. He'd missed a few physical therapy sessions since he'd been back, and the last thing he needed was to do damage to his just-recovered leg because he was too lazy to stretch.

"I'm going to get you a glass of water and something for your head. Where do you keep the meds?"

"In the bathroom," she mumbled.

Brett stood and crossed the room. If he were going to pretend like he was here just to protect her, to look after her, he may as well do something to actually be helpful.

Jamie excused herself, went up to her bathroom and took a long shower. She just stood there under the burning hot water, letting it pour down her face and hair. Her head had stopped pounding, thanks to the tablets she'd just swallowed, but she was still feeling a lot less perky than she usually did.

She forced herself to step out of the shower and wrapped a massive towel around her small frame, using a different one to dry her long hair. After what had happened last night she was in no hurry to rush back downstairs to Brett, not after she'd gone ahead and kissed him. Her only hope was that maybe he thought she'd been too drunk to remember it. *She wished.*

Jamie rubbed moisturizer onto her body, then applied some makeup, smoothing on some foundation, then mascara, blush and lip gloss. She didn't want to look like she'd gone to too much effort, but then she didn't want him to see her looking hungover with no makeup on, either.

She heard a noise behind her and jumped, but it was only Bear. The last thing she needed was Brett walking in on her naked, wearing only a dog tag around her neck. The dog tag that was supposed to remind her, no matter what, that a certain friend of her husband's was out of bounds.

"Hey, buddy." Bear was staring at her with his head cocked to the side, and she was pleased to think about something other than her behavior the night previous. "You hungry?"

Her stomach growled in response to her own question, so she left her hair pinned up wet and signaled for her dog to follow her. She wasn't used to drinking, and she sure as hell wasn't used to dealing with a hangover.

Jamie removed the dog tag and slung it back on the hook by her shoes, feeling like a traitor for wearing it after the way she'd behaved with Brett the night before, and pulled on jeans and a T-shirt. Then she walked down the hall to find Brett with the morning paper, sprawled out over the kitchen counter as he ate a piece of toast.

"Hey," she said as she went straight for the coffee.

He looked up and held his toast in his mouth as he shuffled the paper so it took up less space.

"How you feeling now?" he asked with a grin.

Jamie groaned. "Please don't remind me about last night." She poured herself a large cup of coffee, stirred in two sugars and took a gulp. It was piping hot and burned her tongue but she didn't care.

She scooped a cup of Bear's special dog biscuits into his bowl, aware that he'd been patiently waiting at her feet since they'd arrived in the kitchen, then went back to nursing her coffee.

"I'm feeling a bit responsible for plying you with those drinks," he said, finishing his toast. "Maybe we should have gone with beer, or just let you a have a few girly cocktails instead of the most potent blend on the menu."

Jamie held up her hand. "I'll take full responsibility for drinking them, so long as you don't ever mention the words *Long Island iced tea* to me *ever* again."

Brett laughed and held up his coffee cup. "Deal," he agreed. "You want me to make you anything for brekkie while you nurse your head?"

She groaned again, sipping more coffee. "I'll just have toast, thanks. Cold toast with jam, something easy on my poor stomach."

The way Brett was watching her told her he was thinking about something, waiting to ask her something. Please don't bring up the kiss. The last thing she needed right now was to deal with that particular conversation, especially before she'd eaten anything and had time to process it.

"Jamie, I don't know if you remember, but when we were at the bar, and then when we came back here last night…"

She gulped when he paused, and then he said, "You mentioned that you never told Sam how scared you were coming home to an empty house in the dark."

Phew. She could deal with this conversation if she had to. It might have been difficult to talk about, admitting to that, but given what the alternative topic could have been, she was relieved.

"My dad was a soldier, and he died on deployment, too." Jamie kept her gaze trained on her coffee, not wanting to look at Brett. "When he died, my mom went on a bender that lasted a few years, and I was home alone when we were burgled. I hid until they left, but I guess I've never really gotten over that fear of it happening again. Which is why I'm obsessed with locking doors and being inside before sundown, and my security alarm was always on before Bear came back to live here."

Brett was still staring at her, concern written all over his face. "So I'm guessing you told Sam about what happened, but you never told him how much it still scared you. Because you always knew that he'd be going away and leaving you alone. That there was nothing he could do to change that."

Jamie nodded.

"I can't believe he was away for months at a time, and you had to be a prisoner inside your own house every night. You should have told us."

She sighed and moved closer to him, staying on the other side of the kitchen counter and leaning forward. "I just always had that fear of going to sleep and not knowing if someone could have gotten into the house while I was out. There's nothing Sam could have done for me, except worry like crazy from the other side of the world, and that wouldn't have been good for either of us."

"But you're sleeping okay now?"

She shook her head, not wanting to tell the truth but wanting to lie to Brett even less. "Last night was the first time since before Sam deployed that I've slept through without waking. I've been better with Bear here this last month, so I'm not complaining, but being alone isn't something I've ever been good at. I freak out at every sound and then can't fall asleep again."

Brett stared into his coffee cup, which she was sure must have been empty by now. "Did you sleep better because I was here with you, or because of the alcohol?"

Jamie grinned at him. "Last night might well have been a combination of both, but I have no intentions of turning into an alcoholic just to sleep through the night. Plus I have no plans of turning into my mom."

He smiled, but he wasn't laughing at her joke. "Let me stay for a few days, let you catch up on some sleep while I'm here."

His voice was lower than usual, an octave deeper. She shook her head. "You don't have to do that. I'll be fine."

She might have been telling him no, but inside she was screaming out for him to stay. Having Brett here would make her feel safe, let her relax and just sleep solidly for a few nights at least, but she didn't expect him to do that.

And her intentions weren't pure, either. Because ever since she'd starting thinking about Brett in a certain way last night, remembering how soft his lips had been, how sensual it had been pressed against his body, she'd thought of nothing other than having him here. Keeping him close. Wondering if something could happen between them, and whether he wanted it as much as she did, even if she did know it was wrong.

She took a deep breath. "I don't want you feeling sorry for me."

That made him smile. "I most definitely don't feel sorry for you," he said. "And it's no big deal. If you want me to stay, just say so. Besides, sleeping isn't exactly easy for me these days, and I slept through the night last night, too."

"If I'm honest, Brett, having you here for a few days sounds idyllic." She wanted to stay strong, but she also wanted a man in her house again. Wanted the company of someone she could actually talk to, who wasn't afraid of the truth. Of what had happened to her husband. Because she had no one else to talk to, and no one else to turn to. She'd lost her dad and then her husband to war, and she was tired of being alone. "But only if you're sure."

She listened to Brett's big intake of breath, watched the way his body stiffened then softened back to normal again. When they weren't serving, Sam's two best friends had been as much a part of her life as her husband had, and she missed having them all around. It was like she'd lost all three of them at once.

"Then I'll stay. As long as you need me here, I'll stay."

She dropped her head to his shoulder. "He would have liked you being here, you know that, right?"

Brett shrugged, but she could tell he was finding this as awkward as she was. "You know, he made me promise to look out for you if anything ever happened to him. I just never figured that we'd actually be in that position."

Jamie smiled. "I'll never forget what you've done for me, Brett."

Brett was her friend. Nothing more. She just had to keep reminding herself of that, because falling in love with her husband's best buddy? Not something that could happen. Not now, not ever.

Brett could have been the man of her dreams—*once*. But now wasn't the time to look back. Now was about the future. The one she had to build without her husband by her side. No matter how much she was thinking about *that* kiss.

"Well, if you're staying you're definitely not sleeping on the sofa."

He shrugged. "Whatever's easy for you. I don't want to be any trouble."

Jamie poured herself another cup of coffee and gestured for him to pass his cup over for more. "You never did say how long you were back for? What your plans were?"

Brett took the now full cup from her and looked at her over the counter. "I'm kind of done with the army."

She felt her eyebrows shoot up. "What do you mean by *kind of*?"

"I mean that I've served my time and now I'm retired. Honorable discharge."

"Wow." Jamie hadn't even considered that he might have left the army, that he was done with a role he'd been in for so many years. "Did it have something to do with what happened?" She didn't want to bring it up again, but she also wanted to know.

The relief that hit her body, knowing that there was no chance she could lose Brett, too, was like a physical weight lifting from her shoulders. The last thing she'd need was to worry herself silly the next time both Brett and Logan were deployed. She'd lost too many men in her life to deal with the possibility of losing another.

"I was burned pretty bad on my leg and back, so my injuries were enough to put me out of action for a while, but to be honest I think I've given enough to the cause. I don't think I could have gone back on deployment again after what happened, after what I went through. It's changed how I'd react to a situation."

"So you'll be staying with the army, though?" she asked. "Doing something with dogs still?"

Brett shrugged. "I need to spend some time figuring my life out, what I want to do, where I want to be." He took a sip of coffee, a thoughtful look on his face as he stared out the window. "Right now I can't imagine a life that doesn't involve working with a dog all day, being deployed or training for the next task-force operation. So I just need some time to process everything."

"Can you take your time deciding?"

He nodded. "Yeah, I can. I need to focus on recovering fully, then I can figure out what I'm going to do long-term. Start over, I guess."

And he was going to be doing a lot of that figuring out here, if she had anything to do with where he would be spending his time while he was in Sydney.

"So when you say you hurt your leg and back badly…" she began, not wanting to push him but desperate to know.

"It means I should be doing physio stretches and exercises every day," Brett confessed, "starting this morning."

"Well, it just so happens that I have a heap of work to do, so how about you do what you need to do and I'll sit in my office and try to get this book finished."

Brett grinned. "Deal."

Brett smiled at the physical therapist through the computer screen. It wasn't ideal, but he'd been through rehabilitation and all the hard grunt as far as his leg was concerned, and now it was just a matter of gaining the muscle strength that he'd lost and getting his body back to full capacity.

"So you're not pushing yourself too hard yet?"

He laughed. "Not doing enough is more the problem."

"Well, best I can advise you is to do your stretches daily, and start doing some light jogging if you're up to it. Then you can slowly get back to the point where any type of exercise will be okay."

He gave her a salute. "Yes, ma'am."

She grinned. "Pleased to see you have your spark back. Obviously someone's been looking after you now that you're back home."

Brett glanced up, looked at Jamie working through the open window of her office. "I'm just pleased to be back," he told her.

"Okay, show me your leg stretches, both sides, and then you can get back to doing whatever it is that's making you smile."

He was pleased he'd decided to use video messaging to contact her, because otherwise another day would have passed without him doing the exercises. Before he'd come to see Jamie, he hadn't missed a day, but she'd been more than a little distracting. The fact that she was working and could look out at him wasn't exactly helping his powers of concentration, but he needed to block her out.

How many times had he had to just focus and get on with a task for work? Ignoring one woman shouldn't have been a struggle, but it was.

Brett ran through the exercises, lifting both legs separately, tightening and releasing and then jumping up and down as he'd been shown to do.

"What do you think?" he asked, slightly out of breath once he'd finished the series of reps.

The physical therapist nodded. "Good work. Just keep it up and extend yourself a little bit more every day. You'll get a feel for how hard you can push your body."

They said goodbye and he stood up, slowly stretching before doing some fast sprints back and forth across the lawn. His leg twinged when he stopped too quickly, but he kept it up, taking care not to strain anything. Bear was watching him from the edge of the grass like he was crazy to be using so much energy in the heat, and he had a feeling Jamie might be watching him, too. He didn't indulge himself in looking in her direction, not yet. Because staying focused was already proving to be a task he wasn't excelling at.

When he finished he dropped to the ground to do two sets of crunches, then press-ups, before shutting his eyes and just lying in the sun. Maybe he was getting old, or maybe his body had just been through a more serious trauma than he was letting himself admit. But he was definitely ready for a shower, or a swim in a cool pool would have been even better.

"You look exhausted."

Brett opened his eyes and stared up at Jamie. He rolled to his side and pulled up to a sitting position.

"I thought you were chained to your desk for the rest of the day?" he asked.

She sighed. "Watching you out here wasn't helping to keep me stuck in there."

"If you'd rather I went…"

"No," she replied, holding out a towel and a bottle of water before he could continue. "What I want is to forget about work and just enjoy the day."

He wiped his face and neck with the towel, before twisting the top off the water and guzzling it down.

"When's your deadline?" he asked as she flopped down to sit on the grass with him.

"End of the week," she said, as Bear came over and leaned against her, looking for attention. "I'll make it, I just can't concentrate today. Or at all, lately, if I'm completely honest. My brain just doesn't want to switch into the right gear."

Brett watched as she tried to push the dog away, laughing as he leaned on her and wouldn't give up. In the end she gave up and Bear laid upside down beside her for a belly scratch.

"For someone who keeps saying she doesn't know a lot about dogs, you're sure developing a good friendship with this one." Bear had his eyes closed now, in heaven at all the attention he was receiving.

"It's not that I don't love him, because I do," Jamie said, smiling with her eyes as she stared at him. "I just haven't ever had a dog before, and I wasn't confident with telling him what to do. Or what to expect from him."

"Love is a pretty good start," Brett said, wishing he'd chosen his words better as soon as they came out of his mouth.

"Yeah? Well I've never found it hard to love, so maybe we'll be okay after all."

Brett stayed silent, wasn't sure what to say. Just because he was thinking about last night, wishing that he hadn't been so damn honorable and pushed her away when she'd kissed him, didn't mean he needed to bring it up. The only consolation was that she didn't have anything to regret now that she was sober, because if he'd let things go too far she might not have the same smile on her face that she did right now.

"As much as I'd like to enjoy the day with you, I think you need to get some more work done."

She groaned. "Have you been secretly talking to my editor?"

Brett grinned. "No, but you don't need this deadline hanging over your head, and you'll feel so much better for doing at least some of it today."

"You're right, I'm just procrastinating."

Brett sat up properly and stretched his legs out in front of him. "I'll make you a deal."

She raised her eyebrows. "Let me hear it."

"I'm going to head out, run a few errands and pick up some groceries. We can cook something nice for dinner, and you can forget all about your deadline, once you've worked for a few hours."

"Promise me we can have chocolate for dessert, and you have yourself a deal."

Brett held out his hand, smiling when her palm slipped into his. He was on dangerous territory, and he was starting to enjoy it.

Chapter 6

It had been a long time since Brett had shopped for groceries and arrived home to cook dinner. He kicked the door shut with the heel of his boot and carried the bags through the house, before putting them on the ground and calling out to Jamie.

"I'm back," he called, wandering down the hall toward her office.

"Oh, hey," she said back.

He walked a couple of steps backward, looking into the bedroom he'd just passed. Jamie was tucking sheets into the bed, hair pulled up into a ponytail, wearing cutoff denim shorts and a tight tank top.

He could have done without seeing Jamie looking like that, making a bed that was presumably for him. Thank God it was down the hall from her room.

"I just wanted to let you know I was back."

She smiled and threw the duvet on the bed, followed by a couple of pillows that had been sitting on the ground.

"You were secretly checking up on me, weren't you?"

Her smile was infectious, no matter how much he wished he could distance himself from her. In the car, he'd reminded himself how he needed to behave, how he needed to think about her, but no amount of good intentions could help him when he was faced with Jamie in the flesh.

She didn't seem to notice that he hadn't replied and breezed past him, her shoulder skimming his bicep as she headed down the hall.

"Before you ask, I worked solidly almost the entire time you were gone, so I don't have anything to feel guilty about."

Brett froze before he could follow her, had only managed to turn before his feet refused to move. Because staring at him, eyes on his, was Sam. Sam's smiling photo was hanging in the hall, straight outside the bedroom, and he hadn't even noticed it when he'd walked past looking for Jamie. *For Sam's wife.*

"Brett?"

He shook his head, mouthed *sorry* to his friend, the friend he was so close to betraying, and followed Jamie to the kitchen.

"Are you okay?"

Brett forced himself to snap out of whatever the hell it was he'd sunk into. She'd been Sam's wife for years, he had known that this morning and he'd known it the night before, and yet he was the one who'd suggested he stay, who'd decided to go grocery shopping for dinner. It wasn't Jamie's fault that he was flipping out over something that was every bit his fault, so he needed to pull himself together.

"Sorry, yeah, I wasn't sure what you'd like."

"Mmmm, what are we making?"

He watched as she started to pull things out of the bags. "It's the only thing I can make that doesn't involve packets of sauce or frozen food."

Brett never took his eyes off her as she laughed and pulled out a bag of tomatoes.

"Pasta?"

He nodded. "My mom was a great cook, and it's the only thing I ever learned from her."

Jamie's face lost the rosy glow he'd been enjoying watching, her eyebrows dragging together as she frowned.

"You were only young when you lost your parents, weren't you?"

Her voice was tender and it made him want to walk straight around the kitchen and hold her, to engulf her slender body in his arms and just feel what it was like to have her pressed to him. This woman who was driving him crazy—who'd *driven* him crazy for years—was driving him wild now.

Brett cleared his throat, well past the pain of what he'd endured as a teenager, but still not a fan of dredging up the past.

"I was eighteen, and they both died in a head-on collision," he said, wishing he'd just shut his mouth and not said anything. Talking about what had happened back then was almost as bad about talking about what had happened to Sam. "I was at a party, drunk, and I phoned them to come and pick me up. Turns out they both got in the car that night, and if it hadn't been for me, they would have still been at home."

Jamie was staring at him, palms on the counter. "I can't imagine what that was like for you, Brett, but you can't honestly blame yourself."

"Actually, you're the one person who probably can understand," he said. So many people had acted like they knew what he was going through, but Jamie had only just emerged from that place of loss herself. "It's no different to you losing Sam, it's just at a different stage in your life. The only thing that isn't the same is that you had nothing to do with him dying. Me? I'll never forgive myself for making the call that took them away from me and changed my life forever."

"Brett, you were eighteen years old. Teenagers are supposed to call their parents in the middle of the night when they need them."

Brett shrugged. "Nothing anyone says to me will ever make me believe that I wasn't responsible." He stared at her, watching her mouth as it turned down into a frown. "The only thing that saved me back then was the army. I was surrounded by guys like Sam every day, and they become my surrogate family. They still are, I guess."

"So in other words you found a way to forget about what had happened."

"I'm the first to admit that I ran away from that life, but at the age I was, I didn't really have any other choice. Well, not any choice that would have been good for me."

And this was why he needed to respect Sam, even in death. He'd been family to Brett, just like the rest of his unit had been, and the last thing he needed was more guilt to carry around.

He listened to Jamie sigh before she returned to taking the groceries from the bags. "I'd run away in a heartbeat, Brett, so don't think I'd ever judge you for turning your back on the life you had taken away from you. You were brave to start over, especially in the army."

Brett should have stood his ground, just stayed still on the other side of the kitchen, but he ignored his better judgment and joined her.

"What do you want to run away from?" he asked, voice low.

"From everything about this life, from the memories, just to start over and pretend like this was all a bad dream. That I didn't choose to marry a soldier, knowing that there was a chance he'd die like my father did. I still can't believe that I lost both of them like that."

He wished he could offer it to her, wished he was brave enough to just tell her that he'd run away with her if it meant they could both forget and start over.

"I can't help you run away, Jamie, but I can help you heal."

She smiled across at him, nudged him with her shoulder. He should have resisted, but instead he slung his arm around her and pulled her in for a hug, closing his eyes when she dropped her head to his shoulder and wrapped her arm around his waist.

"I think you've already helped me," she told him, her voice laced with a softness that made him wish he wasn't thinking what he was thinking. That he was just a friend wanting to help another friend with no hidden agenda.

"What do you say I teach you how to cook Mama's tomato pasta sauce?"

She loosened her hold on him until her arm fell away, and he made himself let go of her, too.

"Was your mom Italian?"

He grinned, glanced at her before taking the tomatoes from the packet. "Sure was. And she'd kill me for buying nonorganic produce."

"Ah, well that explains the dark good looks, huh?"

Jamie was laughing and he raised an eyebrow back at her, which only made her laugh more.

"You would have liked her," he said. "And I know she'd have been impressed that I at least remembered one of her dishes."

"I have no doubt that I'd have loved the woman who raised you," she said. "Even if you did lose her young, she sure did a good job."

He looked away when Jamie leaned down to pull out the chopping board, not needing to see the way her shorts showed way too much skin when she bent forward.

"What else do you need?"

Brett reached past her for a knife from the wooden block on the counter, pleased that they were finished with their awkward conversation. He didn't mind opening up to Jamie, but going back into the past was never easy. Not for him. "You can either chop tomatoes or onions?"

"I'll do the onions," she said.

Brett went to question her, to be the gentleman and offer to do the crap job, until she reached for her sunglasses and put them on.

"Ah, smart girl."

She laughed. "Years of experience chopping these suckers. I always keep an old pair handy."

"You know this isn't going to be a quick meal, right?" he said, chopping the tomatoes into even pieces. "It needs to cook for an hour, maybe longer."

"Did you buy wine?" she asked.

"Yes, ma'am."

Jamie dropped her knife and pulled her sunglasses off. "Red?"

He nodded. "Paper bag on the floor."

She crossed the room, pulled out two big wineglasses and pulled the cork from the bottle, before pouring a little into each glass. "We may as well have fun, right? I don't mind waiting if we have something to do to pass the time."

Brett took the glass from her, wishing he didn't have to look at her, that her eyes hadn't locked on his.

"To new beginnings," she announced, holding her glass up to touch his.

"Cheers to that," he said, wishing he'd been man enough to tell her how important the past was.

Brett took a sip as she did the same, swallowing the wine slowly before putting down his glass.

"So what do we do once we're done with chopping?"

They were standing side by side, Jamie with her glasses back on.

"If I was being a purist then I should have skinned the tomatoes first, but it'll still be great like this and otherwise we'll run out of time," he told her, pleased to take his mind off her by talking food. "We need to sauté the onions first with some fresh garlic, then add the tomatoes, some chopped red capsicum and a few handfuls of fresh basil."

"Sounds heavenly."

"Wait until you taste it with freshly shaved parmesan sprinkled on top with a grind of black pepper."

Jamie's tongue flicked out to moisten her lips and he wished it hadn't. She was clearly thinking about the food, but it made his mind skip off in an entirely different direction.

"Sounds delicious."

"I also cheated with the pasta," Brett told her. "I should be making it myself, but I found a homemade spaghetti at the store."

"I can't believe *you're* teaching *me* a recipe."

He put down his knife and reached for the wine again. "You say that like I'm some uncouth caveman."

Jamie chuckled as she finished the onions and washed her hands. "I guess I just never took a special forces soldier for a cook. I mean, when have you even had time to learn culinary skills?"

"You did hear me say that I can only cook one dish from scratch, didn't you?"

"Yeah, but it's a damn good one from the sound of it," she said, pulling out a stockpot and turning on the gas. "Want me to start on browning the onions? I can be your sous chef if you like?"

He nodded and reached for the cloves of garlic he had sitting on the counter, then started peeling and slicing them. There was nothing he didn't like about cooking with Jamie, about being with her, about having her by his side.

Maybe it would have felt the same with any woman, because it wasn't like he'd ever cooked side by side with anyone else before, but deep down he knew he was kidding himself.

The way he felt for Jamie wasn't normal, which made it all the harder for him to fight. When he'd been out shopping, he'd wondered if he should just call her and say he'd gone back to his motel, that he'd see her again in a couple of days, but that thought had left his mind as fast as it had entered. Because Jamie was addictive, and right now, he was the addict.

"If we don't eat it soon my stomach is going to start roaring."

Jamie leaned back in her seat and gave Brett what she hoped was her most pathetic face. It seemed to work, because he laughed and walked himself and his glass of wine across the room and to the bubbling pot. The aroma of the sauce cooking had filled the room, and her stomach *was* starting to rumble.

"Mama will be shaking her fist up there in the clouds," he joked, turning around with the wooden spoon in his hand. "She'd be telling me that it needs two hours to reduce properly."

Jamie groaned. "I don't care." She took a final sip of wine and joined him in the kitchen. "Is this for me to taste?"

He nodded and held it out, his other hand poised beneath it to catch any drips.

"Tell me what you think," he said.

Jamie leaned closer and opened her mouth, letting him tip the spoon. The taste explosion made her shut her eyes for a second, instantly fuelling her angry appetite.

"Oh, my God," she managed to say after swallowing, her words all sounding like they'd merged into one. "That's incredible."

Brett dipped the spoon back into the pot and tasted a mouthful himself. "Not bad, if I do say so myself."

"I can't believe I've known you for so long and never known you could cook like that."

She reached for the spoon but he didn't let it go, shaking his head. "Just one more taste, then you have to wait until the pasta is cooked."

Jamie made a face but dropped her hand, waiting for Brett to offer her another mouthful. He was grinning when he extended it in her direction, before pulling back and leaving her openmouthed and waiting.

"Brett!"

He just laughed and gave it to her, but she moved at the same time, meaning a few drops dripped onto her chin. Brett pulled the spoon back and reached for her face, wiping gently at her chin, his fingers sweeping across her skin to catch the sauce. He licked the sauce from his finger, and she couldn't take her eyes from him, watching his face, his mouth, his tongue.

They were standing closer than they should have been, and now they were staring way longer than they should have been, neither blinking, just watching.

Brett moved his body slightly but Jamie stayed motionless, eyes still never leaving his. She couldn't think of anything else except for Brett; suddenly he seemed to fill the room with his presence. It was like he was towering over her, his body blocking out everything, his eyes stopping her from seeing anything else, his masculinity calling out to her, making her want to close the distance between them and end up wrapped in his big arms.

"Ah, I should put that pasta on, right?" he asked.

Jamie cleared her throat, took a step backward to put some distance between them, to force a space between them that would stop the magnetic pull she was feeling toward him. Toward a man she couldn't feel like that about, not yet. Not now. She'd lost two soldiers in her life already—there was no way she was going to let a third one break her heart.

"I'll, ah, go set up the table outside," she told him, nodding her head like she was trying to convince herself. "We may as well eat alfresco."

Brett turned away and pulled out a big pot, filling it with water and setting it to boil. "This won't take long. I'll bring it all out when it's ready."

Jamie swallowed a lump of something—maybe it was just pure emotion but it felt like pure pain to her—and pulled out place mats and cutlery. She could come back for the wine, but right now she needed some space. A moment to breathe. A moment to think about what she was so close to doing.

Because if she did it, if she gave in to her feelings, then there was no going back. And she didn't want to spend the rest of her life regretting ruining the one friendship that meant the world to her, and had meant even more to her husband.

Jamie walked outside and set the table, before wandering around to the side of the house and leaning against it, out of view of the kitchen. She needed to feel the air on her face, shut her eyes and just think.

About Sam. About the fact that she was still wearing her wedding ring, that she still loved the man she'd married five years ago, that she didn't want to be unfaithful to him even though he was gone.

And the fact that her feelings for Brett were starting to consume her.

Because friends or not, widow or not, she wanted

to know what it felt like to kiss Brett again. To be held in his arms. To have his big body pressed against hers, protecting her, *loving her.*

"You okay?"

Jamie's eyes flew open and she smoothed her hands down over her shorts.

"Yeah, fine. I just needed a minute."

She turned to find him standing by the table, not coming into her space, but concern was written all over his face. He'd brought the wine and their glasses out, along with some napkins.

"Jamie, are we okay?"

She took a deep breath. "Yeah, we're okay." Jamie paused. "We are, right?"

Brett nodded, smiling, but his eyes told a story of concern. Of not knowing what to say, of what to think about what was happening.

Because they weren't okay and yet they were, all at the same time.

"How's that pasta looking?" she asked.

"Your stomach still growling?"

She reached for the wine bottle and poured a little more into each of their glasses. "It just so happens that I'm ravenous. I can't wait."

Brett gave her one last, long look before turning around and heading back inside. "Give me two minutes. Then you can eat until you can't fit another mouthful in."

Comfort food was exactly what she needed, and if the taste of sauce she'd had inside was anything to go by, it might even take her mind off how she was feeling. At least for a few minutes.

Chapter 7

Jamie leaned back, glass of wine in hand, staring up at the stars. It was only nine o'clock, but the sun had gone down long ago and the only light around them was the artificial kind. She'd lit the large candle in the center of the table, and the small flame was making her smile with its constant flicker against the glass, but it wasn't doing enough to distract her entirely from Brett.

Their dinner had been amazing, and things seemed to have simmered down between them. There had been no awkward silences, no difficult conversations, just a pleasant night eating alfresco in good company. She was full and content from the huge bowl of pasta she had, the tomato taste still lingering even now. She'd never tasted homemade tomato sauce like that, and now she had, she knew she'd never be satisfied with the bought kind again.

"You know, when you're away like we were, the stars are the only constant. The one thing you can look up at, and know that someone else in another country will be staring up at that same sky."

She turned her head slightly so she could see Brett's profile. The light was playing off his features, making him look even more handsome than usual. His dark hair looked black, shadows across part of his face making his features seem even stronger, more masculine. Jamie had always thought him handsome, but sitting out here with him tonight, watching the kind and thoughtful expressions on his face, she knew she'd never realized quite how gorgeous he really was. They'd spent so much time together over the years, but never alone like this without the other guys around.

"Did you wonder sometimes why you were there? Wish you weren't?" Jamie asked him. "I mean, it must have been hard dealing with being away so often, doing what you were doing."

He chuckled. "There were plenty of times I wished I wasn't there, but that was usually because of boredom, or missing things from home." He paused, took a long sip of his drink, clearly deep in thought. "I never lost sight of why we were there, though. And without us? So many soldiers would have been losing their lives. There would be convoys blown up everywhere without our dogs detecting IEDs. Men coming home in body bags. The young guys standing on those bloody things is enough to make you physically sick. Just kids, in their twenties, and having to have prosthetic limbs fitted just to be able to walk again." He sighed. "And besides, the army was like my family. They were all I had."

"I can't even imagine what you went through. How

you could put your life and your dogs in danger…" She froze, catching her lip between her teeth. "I'm sorry, I didn't mean…" Jamie wished she could have crawled into a hole and died. She knew why they did it, she just couldn't imagine dealing with it, living it. And she hadn't meant to bring up his dog dying again.

Brett smiled, but she knew the reminder of his dog must have hurt.

"It's okay, you don't have to worry about offending me," he said. "We all know the risks when we go in, but nothing prepares you. Especially for the hatred, of how desperate they are to blow each and every one of us into pieces. It's kind of hard to understand until you're there, and once you are, you just have to stay focused on the job."

"I heard about that dog they found. The one that survived despite everything she went through." Jamie sighed. "I should be embarrassed by how much I cried when I read it."

He laughed, his smile wide. "Yeah, she was injured, survived one of the harshest winters and summers on record, and managed to be spotted by troops more than a year later. Sarbi is the poster dog for never losing hope. And better still, she's an Australian citizen."

They sat in silence for a bit, and Jamie hoped she hadn't ruined the night by bringing up war and death. She'd been trying to avoid mentioning Sam, but somehow the conversation had reverted to soldier talk, which seemed to lead straight back to her husband.

"Do you think I'm going to make it? As a dog owner, I mean?"

Brett had been leaning back, his chair on two legs,

but when she spoke he pushed in closer to the table and leaned toward her instead.

"Sweetheart, Bear is in love with you and you're desperate to look after him properly. If there was ever a partnership destined to work, it's this one. And besides, you were already doing well, it was just that he was a bit confused by your signals."

The smile that spread across her face was genuine, because if Brett thought she could make it, then maybe her chances weren't so bad after all. Especially with his help to make her understand her new canine—she wouldn't have ever given up on Bear, but they sure could have struggled for a while trying to figure one another out.

"Talking of partnerships," she said, digging her fingers into her palm to force herself to continue. "Are you sure I'm not keeping you from seeing anyone? I mean, I don't want you to feel that you have to be here babysitting me."

He stared at her, face expressionless. For a moment she wondered if she'd offended him, wished she hadn't said anything, until he shrugged and grinned at her.

"I'm not seeing anyone, if that's what you're asking," he said. "And for the record, I have no plans to *babysit* you."

Jamie fought the blush that was heating her neck and cheeks, refusing to give in to it. "I didn't mean to be nosy, it's just you've been spending so much time with me, and I didn't want you to feel so sorry for me that you were missing out on seeing someone else. Someone…" *Special* was what she'd been thinking of saying. He might have said he wasn't seeing anyone, but it didn't mean he wanted to spend all his free time with her.

Now his expression was serious, completely different than before. "I'm not here because I feel sorry for you. Don't ever think that for a second."

She stared back at him, lost in his dark gaze, his eyes stormy and almost black in the half-light. She'd thought he looked beyond handsome before, but all riled up he looked even more irresistible.

"Don't get me wrong, I love having you here, but I feel guilty about keeping you from what you want to be doing," she said. "I know I need to stand on my own two feet, learn how to be alone." Just because she knew it, didn't make it any easier.

"Jamie, I only came back to Sydney for you."

She swallowed, not quite sure what to say. He wouldn't have come back to his home city if it hadn't been for her? Maybe she'd heard him wrong.

"I'm the one who should be feeling guilty, for taking so long to get back here. For not being here for you when you needed me," he said. "I've been beating myself up about deserting you for months, so believe me when I say that this is exactly the place I want to be. Sam was family to me, and that makes you family. I should have been here sooner."

"Oh, Brett, you were injured and you'd lost your best friend and your dog. You have nothing to apologize for," she told him. "I just appreciate seeing you again, having you here, but I wouldn't have judged you if you'd decided not to come home at all."

He cleared his throat, leaned across the table toward her and then seemed to change his mind, clasping his hands and staring back up at the sky.

"I didn't come back for no reason, Jamie."

When he looked back at her, she had to force herself

not to hold her breath. Because she had a feeling that what he was struggling to tell her was something that would change *everything* between them. More than a touch or a drunken kiss ever could, which meant this was something she wasn't sure she wanted to hear.

Just because she was having feelings for him, knew that the way she felt about him had changed, didn't mean that she was ready to hear him admit the same to her.

"You don't need to tell me," she heard herself say, afraid..

"You know when we met, all those years ago? Before you had even met Sam?"

She did remember, well. It wasn't something they'd ever really discussed, but it wasn't something she'd ever forgotten, either. "You were dating that gorgeous blonde."

"She *was* gorgeous, but I finished with her that night."

Jamie felt her eyebrows pull together. "Why?" Now she *did* want to hear what he had to say. Why would any man end things with a woman that beautiful?

"Because after I met you, you were all I could think about. I didn't want to ask you out while I was involved, because I wanted to do it right, but by the time I found you…"

No, he couldn't have. Jamie gulped. "I was already with Sam," she finished for him.

"You were already with Sam," he repeated, "and he was happier than I'd ever seen him in his life, so there was no way I would have ever stepped in, even at the start. Sam was like my brother, and I'd have sacrificed anything for him. *And I did.*"

"But you were looking for me?" she said, voice low, almost a whisper. "You actually came looking for me after that night?"

"Yeah." He chuckled. "Kind of ironic, huh? It all just blew up in my face like I'd never even met you, like that night had never even happened."

"And you never told Sam? You just let us…" She didn't even know what to say.

The night she'd met Brett, at a party where she'd hardly known anyone, she'd been drawn to him immediately. But their flirting had been nothing more than that, because he'd had a girlfriend, although she'd be lying if she said she hadn't been thinking about him afterward. That she hadn't wished he'd been single.

And then she'd met Sam. Gorgeous, kind, loving Sam, who'd she fallen in love with and married within a year. Leaving Brett as a pleasant memory of what could have been.

"I told Sam that I'd never found the girl I met at that party, the one I'd talked about nonstop, because when I saw him with you, I knew he'd found *the one*." Brett blew out a breath. "I never stopped kicking myself for letting you walk away that night, and I got to see my best friend marry my dream girl. And all these years I just kept my mouth shut and never said anything, because no good could ever have come out of me being honest about my feelings, about what had happened."

She couldn't stop staring at Brett, could hardly believe what he was telling her—the words that were coming out of his mouth. She'd been insanely attracted to him, too, but thinking about what could have been wasn't something she'd ever really considered, until now. Because she'd been happy with Sam, she'd *loved*

Sam, and Brett had always been his best friend. His best friend who'd loved to flirt with her and make her laugh, who she'd always thought could have been someone more to her at a different time, different place.

"So what did you come back for this time, Brett?" she asked.

Brett shrugged. "I told myself I was coming back to look out for you, to stay true to what I promised Sam, but honestly? That's not the reason I'm still here."

Jamie's hand was shaking slightly as she reached for her glass, clutching the stem to steady it, for something to do to stop herself from staring at him. For the first time in her life, she was absolutely speechless—couldn't even grasp what he was telling her. She took a sip of wine.

"So why are you still here?" Her voice was so low she wondered if he'd even heard what she'd said.

"Because I've never forgotten how I felt that night I first met you, and how I felt every time I saw you with Sam over the past six years. Every single goddamn time, Jamie."

She'd be lying if she didn't admit to always liking him, too. Because the truth was, she'd never forgotten how she felt the night they'd met, either. And they'd always been so comfortable with one another, so easy.

"And how do you feel now?" she asked, feeling brave and needing to know how he honestly felt about her right now.

He reached for one of her hands, turned it so her palm was facing up and stroked his fingers across her skin before closing his hand over hers. "Honestly?"

Jamie nodded, needing to know, to hear what he had to say.

"I wish to hell I didn't feel so damn guilty, but my feelings for you haven't changed, and I don't think they ever will. No matter how many times I tell myself that it's wrong, all the reasons I have for it *to be wrong*, I can't change how I feel."

Which meant the ball was in her court. It was up to her to decide where this conversation was going, what would happen next. And just because she wanted something to happen, didn't mean she was ready for it.

"I…" Her voice trailed off. "I don't know what to say."

"Then don't say anything," he said. "Just don't say anything, or forget I ever told you, if you need to. I don't want things to be weird between us, but I couldn't keep this to myself any longer."

"Do you ever think about what might have happened? What could have been if I hadn't met Sam, if you'd found me before then?" she asked, her voice almost a whisper. "Even the day before I met him, that could have changed everything."

"All the time," he said straight back. "I know things would have been different, but I was too slow to find you. We can't look back, Jamie. Trust me, I've been doing it for years and it's done nothing but infuriate me."

Jamie knew he wasn't going to make the first move—to him she was still Sam's wife, *forbidden*, out of bounds. He'd as good as told her that Sam had been the brother he never had, part of his surrogate family. But this was Brett. This was a man she'd loved as a friend for years, a man she could trust, and a man who was making her heart race like it hadn't in so long. A man whose arms, *lips*, she'd dreamed of; whose touch she'd often fantasized about. It was something she'd never admitted, but it was true.

She pulled her hand away from his and stood up, then slowly walked around the table to stand in front of him. She watched as he pushed back his chair a little, so he was facing her, the expression on his face hard to read. But his body language was more than obvious, telling her that he wanted her to come closer, that he wasn't going to say no. That he was ready and waiting for her to make a move.

Jamie moistened her lips, eyes on his as she closed the distance between them, arms hanging at her sides as she stared down at the man in front of her. She was going to bend down, had intended on sitting on his lap, but suddenly her confidence was waning. She wanted to be the confident, brazen woman who knew what to do and didn't hesitate, but it wasn't something she'd ever had to do before, especially after years of being with the same man.

Brett made it easier for her. He pushed up to his feet and now stared down at her, a good head or more taller than she was. Jamie placed her hands on his chest, feeling the heat of his body, the muscles of his body, through her palms. But it was nothing compared to the heat in his gaze.

She could hear her heart beating, her breath coming out in shallow bursts, but she wasn't going to back down, wasn't going to pull away when she was the one who'd started this. Brett was standing still, arms at his sides, but when she leaned into him, tilted her face up to him, his arms came up to circle around her waist and hold her.

They both hesitated, until her gaze hit his lips—his

full, tempting mouth—and she suddenly couldn't wait any longer. Jamie stretched up, on tiptoes, lips meeting Brett's in a soft, luscious kiss that had her wrapping her arms around his neck to lock him in place.

She relaxed into him as he drew her closer, tucked tight against his big, warm body. Everything he'd just told her was running through her head, sending goose pimples down her arms and back at the thought of him wanting her all these years. And if she were honest, maybe she'd always felt the same, it just hadn't been something she would have ever acted upon. Until now.

"Jamie, are you sure about this?" Brett murmured, lips brushing hers as he spoke.

She nodded, arms still looped around his neck, and gazed up at him even though she was flushing all the way to her toes at the way he was looking back at her. Just because she was nervous didn't mean she wanted to shy away from how she was feeling—she wanted to enjoy it. Ever since Sam had died, she'd been lost, sad, alone. Brett was making her feel alive in ways she hardly remembered. It was like she'd become an old spinster, and now she was…well, now there was a fire back in her belly. It might have been wrong in so many ways, but at this moment, it was also right.

Jamie moaned as Brett kissed her again, his lips moving softly and then with more urgency, making her want to rip his clothes off him where he stood. She was conflicted, part of her unsure about being with another man, but the other part…? Maybe it was the wine giving her confidence, but Jamie wanted Brett like she hadn't wanted anything in a long time. And she'd barely consumed a glass, anyway.

She pushed up his T-shirt, wanting to touch his skin,

but his hands left her waist and closed around her elbows, stopping her.

"Hey," she whispered, mouth still firm against his.

"No," he said back, and she could feel his smile against her mouth.

Jamie dropped her hands, took a step back. "I'm sorry, I thought…"

He collected her hands and put them firmly back on his body, his arms looped around her waist again, and he tugged her closer.

"You thought right, I just think we need to take this slow," he said, mouth murmuring against hers. "Let's not rush into anything we could regret."

Brett tucked a finger beneath Jamie's chin, tilting it so she was looking up at him again. He could see the confusion swimming in her gaze and he didn't like that he was the cause of it.

"Sweetheart, you mean too much to me for us to ruin our friendship in one night. I'm trying to be the good guy here, and there are only so many times I'm capable of saying no."

She looked embarrassed. "You're, ah, right. I mean…"

He'd known Jamie a long time and he'd never heard her stutter, or be lost for words. But then he'd never been intimate with her, either.

"Jamie, look at me," he said, voice husky as he stared into her blue eyes.

She obliged, eyes finally locked back on his like she'd given in to the fact that she needed to watch him back.

"I meant everything I said, but I'm not even sure we

should be doing this," he confessed. "I just don't want you to have any regrets."

Jamie sighed. "I know. You're right. It's just…" She blew out another breath. "Well, it's hard and confusing, but it also just seems natural. Like we're supposed to be doing this. It should feel wrong but it doesn't."

Brett smiled and dropped a slow kiss to her lips. "Don't take my being a gentleman as not wanting you, okay? Because if I had it my way I'd be dragging you to your bed and not letting you out of it until morning." He kept his lips only inches from Jamie's, teasing her. "Or maybe the next few days."

They both laughed, and he wrapped his arms around her for a proper hug, holding her tight. Brett inhaled the fresh orange scent of her shampoo, enjoyed the softness of her silky hair against his face, the feel of her slender body against his. He wasn't lying about wanting her, but he was also between a rock and a hard place.

Sam had been his best bud. He'd have taken a bullet for him, and if it had been a choice, he would have traded places with him in a heartbeat if Sam could have been alive to come home to Jamie. But now that he was here, with a lonely widow he'd been in love with for longer than he cared to admit, walking away, resisting her, was proving to be more difficult that he could have ever imagined. All he knew right now was that he was in love with a woman who should still be off-limits to him. And instead, he'd almost been at second base with her, and he'd had to stop things before they went a lot further, and fast. So much for being in control of his feelings.

"What do you say we head inside? Call it a night?"

he suggested, even though it was the exact opposite of what he wanted to be doing. To what he was thinking.

Jamie nodded against his shoulder, but she wasn't letting go. Her arms were tight around him, face nestled against his neck.

"Am I a terrible wife?"

Her words were so low, such a whisper, that he wondered if she'd even meant him to hear them.

"You were a great wife, Jamie. But if you don't want something to happen here, it's your call." He wouldn't push her, and if she said no, then that would be the end of whatever had just happened between them. "I'll be here for you no matter what, okay? I want you to do what feels right for you. And I don't want us to do anything without thinking it through properly."

She didn't say anything, just kept holding on to him. When she finally stepped back, her hand came up to his face, warm against his cheek.

"You're a good man, Brett Palmer," she said, tears swimming in her eyes as she smiled up at him. *"The best."*

Brett just watched her, jaw clamped tight as he looked into her eyes. She was more than just a beautiful woman to him—she was a friend; she was Sam's widow; she was the woman he'd lusted after for weeks until he'd seen her in the arms of another man, then wondered every what-if about since. And now she was the woman he could have a chance with. *A second chance with.*

He cleared his throat, unsure of what she was trying to say. Was she letting him down softly, or the complete opposite?

"I think you're right, we need to call it a night," she said, her hand falling away as she stepped backward.

Brett nodded, but he quickly reached for her fingers before she moved too far, squeezing them before letting go.

"I'm going to stay out here a while," he told her, "clear my head a bit."

She grinned. "If you need any help with that, there's still almost half a bottle of wine sitting there."

He gave her a mock salute, smiling as she laughed and walked backward.

"'Night, Brett," she called out. "Oh, and thanks for the most delicious dinner I've ever eaten. You would have made your mama proud."

"Good night, Jamie," he said.

He watched as she glanced at Bear sitting under the table, but she didn't call out to him.

"You keep him for company," she said. "Just make sure he comes in before you go to bed."

Brett didn't take his eyes from her figure until she'd disappeared inside the house, and once she did, he poured himself a large glass of wine and sat down on the deck beside the dog. He would have preferred a beer, but wine would have to do.

"Do you think he'd kill me?" Brett asked the dog.

Bear raised his head and whined.

"Yeah, I know." Brett gave his head a rub before using that same hand to prop himself up. "He'd probably give me a black eye."

Sam wouldn't begrudge either of them happiness, but he'd only been gone six months and already Brett was moving in on his girl. And Jamie was more than Sam's girl, she'd been his *wife*. But he'd stood back once to let them be happy, done the right thing, and now maybe it was his turn. If something happened between them, if she really wanted it, then he wasn't going to push her away. Because he couldn't. And there was a part of him that thought maybe he finally deserved to be happy after everything he'd survived, that he needed to stop blaming himself for every bad thing that had happened in his life. That maybe he needed to accept that something good could happen to him....

The noise was deafening. The boom that hit his ears, the explosion, was still echoing in his head, until it started to ring—a high pitch that seemed to get louder and louder, and it was the only thing he could hear.

He picked himself up, staggered backward like he'd lost his balance, and realized his leash was still hanging from his hand. Only there was no dog attached.

He looked around him, tried to call out to his dog, but he couldn't hear his own voice. Then he saw the fur, parts of his dog's body. He was screaming but he still couldn't hear himself, just knew his mouth was open and his throat was raw, even as tears fell down his cheeks.

Sam. He couldn't see Sam either. He yelled out, spinning around and staggering, feet colliding. And then he realized Sam was gone. That the men back at the 4x4 were waving to him, he could see their mouths moving, and then he saw Bear. Sam's dog. He was dragging his leg, falling over, but Brett wasn't going to leave him. Couldn't leave him.

Then everything went black as arms reached out to him and he crashed to the ground....

Brett lay back on the deck and stared at the sky, trying so hard to fight the memories, to push them away and not go back to that dark place. There was nothing he could have done for Sam, he knew that. But he could do something about Jamie—he just had to figure out whether the right thing for her was having him around, or the exact opposite.

It would have been so easy for him to stop her from going to bed, to have asked her to stay with him for a while. It would be almost as easy for him to follow her, to take her hand and tell her how he really felt, tell her what he wanted, see if she wanted the same without offering her time to think about it. But something was holding him back, and he knew it probably always would.

Because no matter how good that kiss had been, no matter how much he wanted her in his arms, she wasn't his to want. She still wore her wedding ring, and she still loved her husband. So no matter what she might think or feel right now, he *needed* to give her time. Time to figure out what she wanted. He'd told her the truth, and now he just had to wait

For some reason, he had to be the good guy around Jamie—he'd felt the same way that first night when they'd just met and spent hours chatting. There was something about her that brought out the good in him, and he liked it.

He just hoped that it was something about her house that had helped him sleep the night before. Otherwise? He'd have yet another reason to want her in his arms. It had been months since he'd been able to shut his eyes and just relax into blackness, to sleep without thinking, and he didn't want to go back to that dark place ever again. Not if he could help it.

Chapter 8

Jamie sat on her bed, legs curled up beneath her. She didn't know what to do. Part of her wanted to march straight back out to Brett and tell him that she'd often thought of that night they'd first met. Maybe not in recent years, but after she'd first been with Sam, she'd often wondered: *what if*. Sam had been the love of her life and she'd never for a moment *not* wanted to be with him, but Brett...well, Brett was Brett. He was a man she'd been physically attracted to from the moment she'd met him, and she'd also been charmed by him, too.

Until she'd realized that he had a girlfriend. A girlfriend she now knew he'd finished with so he could seek her out.

Argh. There was nothing about this that was easy.

Sam's smiling face, from a collection of their wedding photos, was staring at her from the dresser, a reminder to a life that no longer existed. A memory that would always make her happy, but one that wasn't a reality anymore. Just like her dad had become only a memory, so, too, would Sam. Because he was gone, and nothing she could do would ever bring him back.

But Brett was real. And he was sitting outside her house, on his own, instead of with her. Waiting for her to tell him what she wanted.

She uncurled her legs, stretched, then stood. She slowly walked toward the window and parted the blinds, knowing that she'd be able to see him. Sure enough, he was sitting where she'd left him, only now his arm was slung around Bear as he stared up at the sky. No doubt looking at the stars and remembering a time when he wasn't home, when things were different. Maybe he was even thinking about her.

Jamie longed to go to him, to be with him, but she didn't want to make a mistake with a man who meant so much to her as a friend—she'd be lost without him.

She touched her forehead to the window and watched him. Just stared at his silhouette—his broad shoulders, his dark hair, his muscled forearm resting over her dog—and the coolness of the glass gave her flushed skin some relief.

But instead of going to him, she went to her bedside table and pulled out her leather-bound notebook, the one she kept close in case she had an idea for a new story or illustration.

Suddenly she knew exactly what she needed to do. Jamie pulled the cap off her pen and tucked up under the covers, pen poised. When Sam had been away, they'd always written to one another. Even though they'd been able to talk via video chat, they'd written so they had something to look forward to, something to anticipate in the mail during the months when they were parted.

She needed to write to him now. Needed to get her feelings off her chest and tell him…how much she still loved him, but how much she needed to let part of that go so she could move on and be happy.

Dear Sam,

This is the only letter that I've ever written to you, knowing it will never reach you. But part of me believes that you're still here, in some shape or form, and if you are, I need to tell you how I'm feeling.

I know in my heart that I will never stop loving you, no matter how much time passes or what happens in my life from this day forward. I know you'd be so proud of how Bear and I are getting along, and I wouldn't give him up for anything. But there's something I need to tell you, something I never thought would even be a possibility.

You've been gone now for just over six months, and Brett came to see me. I don't know how or why, but something has changed between us. I think I'm falling for him, Sam, and I need you to know that if you were here, this would never have happened. But you're not here, and Brett is, and I believe that you would want me to be happy. We're both holding back, stopping anything from happening, *because of you*, but I don't want to be alone just to prove to your memory that I loved you.

So I need you to know that I'm falling in love with your best friend. I trust him and I know he'd never to do anything to hurt me, and I need to see if we could be happy together.

I love you, Sam, with all my heart. Not a day goes past that I don't wish that you were still here, but I've had to accept that isn't ever going to happen. I always thought you were the one, but now I'm realizing that maybe there is more than one person out there in the world for each of us. I will never stop loving you.
Jamie xx

Jamie wiped away the tears that had spilled down her cheeks and ripped the page from her notebook, before folding the letter in half. She tucked it into an envelope, sealed it, then scrawled Sam's name across the front of it.

She had no idea if Brett would still be outside or not, but she needed to go to him before she lost her confidence. Because if she didn't act now, maybe she never would. And part of her believed that she deserved to be happy, no matter what.

Brett shut the door and locked it, before flicking the switch and plunging the living room into darkness. He'd sat outside feeling sorry for himself for so long that even the dog had tired of keeping him company, and now he needed to crawl into bed and just sleep. No amount of thinking, of questioning himself, was going to help him to make a decision, and now he just wanted to crash. Otherwise he'd just let old feelings of guilt start to seep back into his mind, and he was over dealing with the emotional baggage he'd carried for the last decade.

"Brett?"

He squinted into the dark, trying to figure out where Jamie was. Then she flicked on a light and he could see she was standing in the hall, facing the living room.

"Hey," he said, not having expecting her to still be up. "Did I wake you?"

She shook her head. "I never went to sleep."

Brett crossed the room but kept his distance, not wanting to tempt himself after the hard talk he'd been giving himself outside. Jamie was out of bounds and he had no intention of crossing that line again, no matter how much he wanted to. Unless she came to him, it wasn't even something he was going to consider. The ball was firmly in her court now, and he wasn't going to budge from *that* particular resolution.

"Can I, ah, get you anything?" he asked. He knew how stupid it sounded the moment he said it—what kind of question was that to ask somebody in their own house?

She didn't say anything, just stared at him. Why was she down here when she'd gone to bed almost an hour ago?

"Jamie, what happened before," he began, not sure how to tell her what needed to be said, what he'd been thinking about. "I'm sorry if I crossed the line, because I never meant to do anything to make you uncomfortable."

Jamie shook her head. "No, Brett, you didn't cross the line and you didn't do anything that I didn't want you to do. Sam is gone. We both know that, and we both need to understand what that means."

He swallowed, wishing this was easier, wishing he didn't feel the way he did about her. Because then he wouldn't be tempted by her lips, or her hair, or the way she was watching him.

"Jamie…"

"You said you'd be here for me, no matter what," she told him.

Brett never took his eyes off her, and he also never moved, even when she started to come closer.

"I meant that if you needed me…" he began, the rest of his sentence disappearing when her finger touched his lips to silence him.

"I need you, Brett," Jamie said, standing on tiptoe at the same time as she looped her arms around his neck. "I need you now. We can't punish ourselves for how we feel, because we're not doing anything wrong."

Brett never moved, kept his hands at his sides, scared of what would happen if he let himself touch her, if he gave in to what was so close to happening. He was only a man and if she pushed him there was no way he'd be able to walk away.

"Jamie…" he murmured, but he wasn't committed to telling her no, so he never did. He'd said if it was her choice then he'd let it happen, only he hadn't expected her to act quite so soon.

"Kiss me, Brett. That's what I need you to do."

He stared into her aqua-blue eyes, knowing he was a lost man. No amount of good intentions was ever going to be enough to resist Jamie, not when her body was skimming against his, her mouth so close.

Damn it! Brett's hands flew from his sides to her waist, locking her in place against him as he crushed his mouth to hers. Her moan only spurred him on more, made him yank her hard to his body, one hand leaving her hips to caress her back, to feel her long hair and fist into the soft curls.

"Jamie," he forced himself to say, his mouth hovering over hers, unable to back off even if he wanted to. "Are you sure? We can't go back from this. It changes everything."

She tipped her head back and looked into his eyes, her fingers tracing down his chest, before she grabbed hold of one of his hands and led him out of the room. Jamie flicked the switch in the hallway and walked them both to her bedroom, stopping at the door and leaning against the wall.

"I've never been so sure about anything, Brett," she whispered into his ear, her hand clutching his T-shirt tight to keep him near. "Take me to bed."

He stared at her, long and hard, before reaching past her and pushing the door open. There was only so long that he could play the good guy and keep telling her no. So what if he'd made himself a promise, if she was supposed to be forbidden? Jamie was holding his hand and inviting him to spend the night with her, and he'd lost all power to turn and walk away from her. This was her choice, and he wasn't going to try to change her mind. He'd told himself all along that he wouldn't fight it if she was sure it was what she wanted, if she came to him, and now she had.

Jamie laughed and walked backward into the room, holding both his hands. When she bumped into the edge of the bed, she stopped and pulled his hands around to settle on her waist again.

"Brett," she whispered, fingers stroking up and down his face, before she held onto his shoulders and reached up to kiss him again.

He broke the kiss only to push her back onto the bed, watching as she fell back before bending to settle over her, his thighs locking her in place as he straddled her. She reached out to him, pulling him down, but he needed a moment to drink in the sight of her—to see her long hair splayed out around her, her full lips facing him, the rise and fall of her breasts as she lay on her back beneath him. For years he'd wondered what it would have been like if things had been different, fantasized about having her in his bed, and now she was sprawled out beneath him.

Brett dropped his upper body over Jamie's, careful not to crush her with his weight, and kissed her mouth, before trailing kisses down her neck and back up to her lips again. For something that was meant to be so wrong, it felt so damn good.

"Don't stop," she whispered, sounding breathless.

He chuckled, smoothing the hair from her face before stroking her cheek. "I have no intention of stopping," Brett told her.

"Good," she replied, claiming his mouth again as she cupped his skull to force his head down, gripping on tight, fingers twisted in his hair.

Her lips moved gently, her tongue exploring tentatively at first, before becoming bolder, colliding with his.

All the best intentions in the world couldn't have made him say no to this.

Jamie let Brett push her T-shirt up and she wriggled out of it, left in only her bra and her shorts. She gulped when he immediately reached down for her button, before unzipping the denim and pulling it down her legs—

slowly, as if he were trying to tease her. She pointed her toes so he could slip off the jeans completely, and laughed.

"Why do I have all my clothes off, and you're fully dressed still?" she asked.

He grinned and shrugged, but she wasn't going to let him sit there in his jeans and T-shirt while she was left in only her underwear.

"Off with it," she ordered, pushing his T-shirt up, eyes feasting on his stomach and chest muscles.

Brett obliged, taking it off and then standing to shed his jeans, too.

She sucked back a big breath as she watched him, looking at his big body, eyes glued to him as he lowered himself back on the bed. Jamie reached out to touch the tattoo on his left arm first, and then his other shoulder, fingers tracing over both of them. Years ago, she'd hated tattoos, but she'd grown to appreciate them now. And Brett's ones meant something to him, told a story of who he was and what was important to him, and the ink stretched over his muscles gave him a tough edge that was at odds with how gentle and kind he'd always been to her. If ever she needed reminding of the soldier he was, of how he could protect her if ever she needed it, his tattoos made that crystal clear.

Jamie slipped her hands onto his shoulders to stroke her nails down his back, but his whole body tensed, went rigid.

"What's wrong?" she asked, dropping her hands, knowing that he hadn't even remotely liked the way she'd just touched him.

Brett gave her an unconvincing smile. "My back's kind of off-limits," he said.

"You mean because of your injuries?" she asked, voice soft, knowing how difficult it must be for him to talk about.

"Yeah."

"You don't have to be embarrassed, Brett," she said, leaning up to press a kiss to his shoulder, gently touching his lower back this time and avoiding where she'd almost touched before.

"Jamie…" He said her name as if it were a warning.

But she wasn't going to take no for an answer, not after all they'd been through together. She wanted to touch every part of Brett, and she wasn't scared of what had happened to him or the marks that had been left on his skin. It wasn't like they'd just met and he had to hide who he was from her.

"Let me see you," she whispered, pushing him gently back down to the bed, "There's nothing I could see right now that could change the way I feel about you."

Chapter 9

Chills ran up and down Brett's body just at the mention of his scars, of her seeing them. He hadn't let anyone other than the medical team that had worked on him see how he looked now, to really see what had happened to him. Jamie looking at the mess that was his skin wasn't something he ever wanted to happen, but the way she was staring at him, like he was doing something to hurt her by not just opening up, was telling him that he may not have a choice. He didn't want to hurt her, had no intention of pushing her away, but this was something that he needed to prepare for.

"I can't," he muttered, rolling firmly on to his back.

Jamie tucked her knees up to her chin and wrapped her arms around her legs. The mood had changed, was no longer about sex and suddenly included a whole lot of stuff that Brett wasn't ready to face. Gone was the fun, flirty vibe they'd had happening between them, replaced by a serious, we-need-to-talk session.

"You've never talked about…"

"And I don't want to," he said, voice firm as he interrupted her. There was no way he was going to start talking, not now. That he was going to ruin what had been an otherwise perfect evening by dredging up exactly how his skin had become so disfigured.

"Can we just pick up where we left off?"

"You don't need to tell me, Brett, but let me see. *Please?*" she asked.

He shut his eyes, not wanting to get angry with this woman who'd been through so much, who he so genuinely cared about. Who was being so brave in another way that he knew must be beyond difficult for her. It shouldn't be so impossibly hard, but it was. Opening up had always been difficult for him, yet he'd told her openly about the truth of his past, about his parents and how he still felt responsible for their deaths. This, though…this was different. The pain was too fresh.

"I'm embarrassed," he admitted, opening his eyes and looking straight into hers. "I'm no longer the guy who can go to the beach and just take off his top without thinking about it. It's not something you want to see or hear about. It's not who I am. And it's not how I want you to see me."

Now it was Jamie shaking her head, telling him he was the one in the wrong. "No, Brett," she told him, voice low and husky. "You *are* still that guy, because you're still handsome and you're still *you*. I don't care what your skin looks like, but we can't do this without you opening up to me. We can't take this further if there's any secrets between us."

He knew he was being stupid, that there was no point in delaying the inevitable, but letting Jamie see what he'd been through, what he was *still* going through, was like giving up a piece of his soul that he'd never intended on letting anyone be witness to. His skin had always been tanned and blemish-free, he'd always been the one to whip his shirt off on a hot day, but everything had changed the day he'd been burned. And not just his body, but his mind, too.

"It's ugly," he said, voice flat, knowing he was fighting a losing battle.

"I don't care," she said straight back, her gaze unwavering. "I just want you to let me in, Brett."

Jamie dropped her arms and moved closer, hands on his shoulders as she gently motioned for him to move. She couldn't have made him budge an inch if he hadn't wanted to, but he knew that the only way Jamie was going to trust him, that they were going to move past this, was if he let her in. If he trusted her to see what scared him the most.

Brett took a deep breath and reluctantly rolled over onto his stomach, hands under his chin as he lay there for her to inspect him. He was expecting a gasp, something to tell him what a shock it was for her seeing him like that, but all he could hear was silence. A long stretch of silence that had him holding his breath, wishing he'd refused.

And then she touched him. Brett dropped his head into the pillow. He'd been waiting for her to make a noise and now he was the one forcing back a groan. Or maybe it was a cry for help, he didn't know—all he knew was that Jamie was touching him in a way that was making him want to scream at her to stop, and at the same time beg her never to take her hands off of him. Because now she'd seen it, there was no going back, and all of a sudden he wanted her to see the real him. Needed her to see his pain and help to heal him, because he didn't want to be broken anymore.

Her fingers traced his entire back, dipped into the tender areas where he'd almost been burned alive, before she caressed the smooth parts of his back that reminded him of what all his skin had once looked like. What his body had once been.

Then she started to trace down his leg, too, the leg that he was so lucky to still have attached to his body, but that was disfigured from the skin grafts he'd painfully endured in recovery.

"Stop," he commanded, head rising off the pillow. His back was one thing, but she was taking things too far.

"No," she whispered, pushing him back down and straddling his buttocks instead. He still had his boxers on, but he could feel the heat of her as she sat on him. "Don't move a muscle."

Jamie put her palms over Brett's arms as he spread them out on either side of him. At the same time she dipped her head until she could press a soft, warm kiss to his back, between his shoulder blades. Here, the skin was still smooth and tanned, like his back had always been, and she wanted to start here before she moved lower.

"Jamie…" She heard him mumble her name.

She continued undeterred, moving her mouth slowly down his back. When she reached the first of the jagged edged lines that crisscrossed down his entire lower back, she made her kisses even lighter, only just letting her lips touch him, as soft as she could make them. His skin was still pink where he'd been burned, the marks a blazing reminder of what he'd been through, and she needed to show him that she didn't care, that she could deal with the wounds he'd come home with, the wounds that he'd be forced to live with forever. That she accepted the man he was today as much as she would have accepted the man he'd been before the explosion—that in her eyes he was no different.

Her hair fell forward and splayed across his back as she started to move lower again, making her way down his leg now, shuffling her body farther down the bed. His right leg was impossible to compare to his back— the scars extended all the way down his thigh and calf, enough to make her want to gasp, at least when she'd first seen them. But now she focused on the shape of his leg, the muscles still bulging from his calf, the thickness of his thigh that told her how fit he was, how determined he'd been to stay strong even through what must have been a painful recovery. Brett was a fighter, she knew that, and he'd endured what might have broken others.

"They're just marks, Brett," she told him as she wriggled back up his body and sat on his buttocks again, hands spread out over his back as she gently massaged his shoulders.

"They're marks I'll have forever," he muttered.

When he went to move, she pushed herself up on her knees so he could flip onto his back beneath her. Jamie lowered herself when he looked comfortable, staring into his eyes as she leaned forward. She tucked her long hair behind her ears to keep it out of the way.

"You're still the same, handsome Brett you were to

me before I saw them," she said. "It's part of you now, and they don't scare me."

"You have to say that now," he told her. "You can't exactly be honest with me about how much they disgust you."

Jamie frowned. "Of course I can be honest with you." She paused, touching his cheek with the tips of her fingers because she needed to connect with him, needed him to know that she was telling the truth. "Do your scars terrify me and remind me of what we've both lost? Sure. But they're just marks, Brett, and they're *your* marks, so there's no point in pretending like they're not there. Now that I've seen them, I've seen them. You don't have to worry about hiding them from me, or how I'll react."

"I hate that I have a constant reminder on my skin," he admitted, reaching up for her and stroking a hand down her hair until he reached the ends of it, skimming the center of her back.

"At least you're alive to be reminded of it," she whispered. "At least you're here, right now, in my bed."

Brett groaned, his hand falling from her hair. "I'm sorry, I…"

"Shhhh," she said, leaning down on to him, her elbows on either side of his head to prop herself up, bodies pressed together. "Stop talking."

"And what?" he asked.

"Kiss me again."

Jamie didn't wait for Brett to act, because she was already hovering above him, lips aching to close over his and feel what it was like to be almost naked and this intimate with a man she'd been attracted to for so long. *And he didn't disappoint.* Brett's mouth was firm against hers, his lips warm and soft. His hands were in her hair as she pressed herself even tighter against him, her body tight to his.

She could feel how much he wanted her, and it only made her sure in her decision. Brett wasn't just some rebound guy to her, someone to fill the bed with to keep her warm. He was a man she already cared so much about, only now…

"Jamie, I think we need to slow this down," he said, hands still tangled in her long hair as he yanked her back a little.

"No," she told him, wriggling against him until he groaned, fighting him. "Don't stop."

Jamie was being cruel to him, she knew she was, because he was trying to be the good guy and she was the one lying on top of him, forcing him into compliance. Making him be bad. But she didn't want him to be the good guy right now, didn't want him to think at all, she just wanted him to act.

"Are you sure?" he mumbled in between kisses.

"I've never been so sure about anything in my life," she whispered, before claiming his mouth again and teasing him with her tongue. There was no way she was going to let him stop.

Brett's moan was all she needed to spur her on, to make her reach behind her back and fumble to unhook her bra. His expert hands came to her assistance, and all of a sudden they were completely skin-to-skin, her breasts against his warm chest, almost as close as two people could be.

"This feels right," she told him, pulling back so she could look into his eyes. "Don't you think?"

From the way he was staring back at her, she knew

he felt the same. It was different, it was terrifying, and it was exhilarating, because it was the first time she'd been intimate with a man who wasn't her husband in six years, *but it was Brett.* And if there were ever going to be another man besides Sam she made love to, she knew in her heart that it was right that man was him.

Chapter 10

Jamie woke up and reached out an arm, feeling for Brett, but she opened her eyes instead because there was no warm body beside her. She sat up, pulling the sheet up with her to cover her breasts, and she spotted him straight away. He was sitting in the big armchair she had beside the window, his T-shirt and boxers on, staring at something that she couldn't see. Or maybe he was just staring at nothing.

"Hey," she said.

Brett turned, his big body filling the entire chair that had always seemed so roomy to her when she tucked her legs up and read a book in the sun.

"Morning," he replied.

Jamie watched the way he looked at her, like he wasn't sure, like something was troubling him. His expression was nothing like the one she'd witnessed before they'd fallen asleep.

"Brett, what's wrong?"

He shoved a hand through his hair. "You want me to be honest?"

She knew there was only one answer she could give to that question. "Yes."

He sighed. "Everything."

Tears pricked her eyes and she blinked them away, refused to let them even come close to spilling. After last night, she'd expected to wake up in his arms, thought what they'd shared was special, that they'd just pick up again where they'd left off, but the way he was looking at her...

"I don't understand," she managed to say, eyes never leaving his.

She watched as Brett stood and crossed the room, moving to the bed beside her. A low moan from Bear made her gaze flicker for a second, but the dog was still in his own bed.

Brett took one of her hands, the other still clutching the sheet and keeping her covered. All of a sudden she felt vulnerable being naked, whereas before she'd been completely comfortable.

"I feel guilty," he admitted, fingers stroking the back of her hand as he held it. "I don't want to, but I can't help it."

She understood the guilt, but if he was having second thoughts about what they'd done... "Brett, I don't regret last night, if that's what you're worried about. Not for a moment."

He moved closer, his thigh pressed to hers as he faced her. "I don't regret it, either, but what we did, what happened, it's changed everything."

"Is that the worst thing in the world?" she asked.

He smiled, but the sadness in his eyes scared her.

"If I'm honest with you, I can't think of anything I'd rather do than be with you. For the first time since the explosion, I've slept through the night, like I'm protected in your arms from the worst of my memories. And then I wake up and realize that I've taken Sam's place, that I've taken something from him, and it scares me."

She took a deep, shuddering breath. "If Sam was here, this never would have happened, Brett," she told him, her voice barely more than a whisper. "But we are here, together, and somehow we're helping each other through. Can't we just enjoy being together without feeling guilty?"

He nodded. "I've always thought of you as part of my family, Jamie. I guess I just don't want to be responsible for losing another family member."

Jamie touched his cheek, let the sheet fall away to her waist. "You're not going to lose me, Brett. I promise. But I'm also not going to lie to you and say that I don't love Sam still, because I do. So much. But the way I feel for you…"

"We can't," he insisted.

"We can," she said firmly, not about to let them ruin what had happened because they were afraid. Because he was scared of losing something that he wasn't even in danger of losing.

They stared at each other, and she knew how hard it was for him because it was just as hard for her.

"You're not betraying Sam."

"If sleeping with his wife isn't betraying him, then I don't know what is."

"Come here," Jamie said.

He looked like he was going to resist, but he obeyed, moving closer. It wasn't that he didn't want to be with her, she knew that, but she also understood that his morals could ruin what was so fragile, so new, between them right now.

"Take off your top and get under the covers."

Brett went to protest but she shook her head before he could say anything. "Just do it for me, please."

He followed her instructions and pulled the covers up over them both, but he still looked awkward. Jamie pushed him down on the pillow then lay her head on his chest, arm around him.

"I need this, Brett. After last night, I can't deal with arguing or not having you here beside me. Because then I might start to feel guilty about what we did, and I've accepted the decision I made."

She listened to his breathing, focused on the inhale and exhale of air and the way it made his chest move.

"I don't want to hurt you," Brett told her.

She traced circles on his skin, fingertips needing to touch. "You won't hurt me, Brett, and I won't hurt you. But if you walk out on me? That will hurt. Because I don't want last night to have meant nothing. If we're talking about betraying Sam, then that would be it."

"As in you don't want what we did to be a one-night stand."

"I don't want it to be a one-night anything," she admitted, moving so she could rest her chin on his chest and stare at him. "What we did wasn't because of loneliness or selfishness, it was because it felt right, and I know you feel the same."

Brett reached for her hair, stroking it. "I just don't feel right, being in this room, seeing the photos of him, knowing that I've just stepped in and somehow taken over his life. Slept in his bed with his wife. It's not okay."

Jamie smiled at him, needing him to be honest with her, needing to hear the words that he'd been holding trapped inside.

"You stepped in to look after me, and what happened between us? It just happened. But if you want me to..."

"You're not taking down his photos because of me."

She laughed at the seriousness of Brett's tone. "I'm not taking down any photos, but what I was going to say is that we can always stay in the other bedroom. If you need to, I mean."

Brett groaned. "Can we just go out for breakfast? Walk somewhere?"

"You bet," she said, leaning forward to kiss him.

What started as a light peck became deeper, their lips moving softly, brushing together, before Brett cupped the back of her head so she couldn't get away, mouth more insistent.

"It doesn't seem to matter what I tell myself," he muttered, breaking the kiss, "I just can't get enough of you."

"Breakfast," she told him, pushing herself up and dragging the sheet with her so she could escape to the bathroom without him seeing her naked in the bright light. "Before we end up staying in bed all day."

It wouldn't have been a bad thing, but they both needed to get out of the house. There were too many memories in this room that were haunting Brett, and if she were perfectly honest, in the full morning sunshine, there was something not so easy to ignore about being with another man in the room she'd shared for years with her husband. No matter how much she wanted it to feel right, she knew that going out was exactly what they needed to do. A quick shower and a little makeup and she'd be ready to go.

She'd already been through losing her father, and then as good as losing her alcoholic mom for years at a time. So losing Sam and then losing Brett? Not something she had any intention of letting happen, especially not now that they'd spent the night together.

Brett clipped Bear's leash on and dropped to his haunches, looking the dog in the eye as he ran his fingers through his fur. He missed his own dog like crazy, was so used to having a constant companion by his side.

"You're doing pretty well with everything that's going on," he told the canine.

He received a low whine from Bear in return.

"It might not be guns and explosives, but it's still tough, huh?"

"Are you talking to yourself or the dog?"

Brett cleared his throat when he realized Jamie had walked into the room. "The dog, of course. Talking to myself would just be weird."

"He saying much in response?" she teased.

Brett looked her up and down, knowing there was no way he'd ever be able to resist her so long as he was staying in the house with her. When he wasn't with her, he was thinking about her, and when he was with her… *damn*. No amount of good intentions would ever help him when they were together.

"Let's go," he said, before he had any longer to think about Jamie and the way she was making him feel.

"Are we going to walk all the way there?"

He laughed. "You make it sound like it's a hike."

"I'm the girl who always takes a car. You seem to keep forgetting that."

"You have a dog now, and a guy with you who likes to feel like he's earned a cooked breakfast. So Bear and I vote for the walk, that's you outnumbered."

Jamie sighed and took Bear's leash from him, smiling as their hands collided. "My dog, remember? I'm the one who's supposed to be up for walking all the time."

Bear was looking up at them, studying them each in turn, and he felt sorry for the poor dog, listening to them banter. There was no chance he'd ever figure out what they were saying, and he'd been so used to understanding commands when he'd been on the leash for work.

"He's all yours, let's go."

Brett waited for her to shut and lock the door behind them, before walking slow to match her pace. The sun was shining down on them already, another hot Sydney day. He'd spent days and weeks out under the scorching sun, working with his dog and the other guys, patrolling for explosives constantly, but that sun had never been enjoyable. It had drained them all and made them grumpy, made their skin dry and their throats burn. This sun made him feel free. *Alive.*

"Brett, I know you don't want to talk about what happened…."

He glanced sideways, seeing the frustrated look on Jamie's face as she clearly tried to figure out how to talk to him about something she was obviously so desperate to know more about. It wasn't that he didn't want to talk to her, it was just that dredging up the past wasn't always worth the pain, or the reality. He'd been in a black hole that could have swallowed him alive, his thoughts so dark they'd almost consumed him, and going back wasn't good for him or her.

If he shut his eyes, he could still smell the burned flesh, still feel the searing pain of the fire as it shot up his leg and across his back.

"I just…" She paused and stopped walking, arms crossed like she didn't know what to do with them. "I just want to know if it happened fast? If he suffered. I'm sorry." She blew out a big breath. "I've been wanting to ask someone that question for so long, and I think you're the only one who can answer it because everyone else just wants to fob me off and pretend like it wasn't anywhere near as horrific as I know it was."

Brett started walking again, because if he was going to talk then he needed to keep moving, needed something else to focus on to help him say the words. He'd thought she wanted to know about his experience, what he'd been through, but she wanted to know about Sam and he could hardly hold that back from her. She deserved to know.

"When we were working that day, it was just like usual," he began, wondering how the hell he was going to say what he needed to say, but continuing anyway. It wasn't something he'd ever talked about, but it was a scene that had run though his head constantly ever since it had happened. He could see it as if it were yesterday—shut his eyes and pretend like it was that day all over again. "We were with a unit of SAS guys, providing support, and I was working with Sam. We both got our dogs out and started doing our drill, but we knew there was something off almost immediately."

He was staring straight ahead when Jamie slipped her hand into his, and he didn't resist. Because talking about that day was beyond hard, and it was something he'd never done before. Brett needed her strength.

"His dog identified the explosive immediately," he continued, ignoring her because now he'd started talking he needed to get it all out. "His dog went dead still, and for a split second we looked at one another, because we knew it was bad, that we were in a hot spot, that Bear had only frozen like that for one reason. We called out to the guys not to move, and then Teddy indicated another one." He paused. "You have to understand that sometimes, most of the time, our dogs just raise their tails slightly, move differently, in a way that only their handler would ever notice. But we all knew what Bear had detected that day, and we all knew how badly things could end. That we might never see another day."

Brett swallowed down the lump of emotion choking his throat and blinked to force the tears back. He didn't want to cry, didn't want to *feel* again, but the memories were crashing into him like they'd only just happened.

Jamie was squeezing his hand tight, like she wanted to take some of the pain for him, but he knew she already had enough pain of her own to deal with. He just wanted to tell her like it was, explain to her what had happened so they could both move forward and never have to talk about it again.

"From that moment, it was like everything moved in slow motion, before becoming such a fast blur that I don't even remember the details." He looked at her, saw that Jamie's eyes were filled with tears, just like his were from going back in time to that day. "All I know is that I was blown back so far my body was slammed down close to the 4x4, and Sam was gone. So was Teddy. To this day, no one can understand how

Bear managed to survive the blast, or how either of us didn't lose limbs. But it was fast, so fast that I don't know how or why I ended up so far from the bomb."

Jamie's hand in his stopped him from moving as she pulled him to a halt. She had the leash in her other hand, and she let go of Brett's hand for a second so she could loop her arm around his neck and draw him into an embrace so warm, so loving, that he was powerless to pull away. *And he didn't want to pull away.* Because no matter how guilty he felt, this felt so right, too. He needed Jamie as much as she needed him. He liked that he could be honest with her when he needed to be, that they understood what the other had gone through, on some level at least.

"Thank you for telling me," she murmured, pressing a kiss to his cheek. "Thank you, for being honest with me when no one else could."

Brett shut his eyes. Sam's blood covered him, bits of his best friend burning and blasted all around them. There were so many pieces of him, so much flesh that when Brett had woken up, he'd vomited until there was nothing left in his stomach. And his dog, his beautiful dog had been killed on impact, too.

But they weren't memories he was ever going to share with her. If he ever needed to get them off his chest, he could tell Logan, a fellow soldier who'd seen enough on his tours to cope with what he'd hear. He'd never let Jamie suffer through those particular memories with him, the blatant truth of that day. There were some things she needed to be protected from, and that was top of the list.

Jamie pulled back then, looked into his eyes and didn't break contact even as she kissed him.

"I need you to know that I want you here, Brett. It might be weird, that we're together and all that, but all I know is that this is right. That having you in my life seems right and I don't want to lose you."

He nodded, but he still wasn't convinced that what they were doing was any part of okay or right. It wasn't that he didn't have feelings for Jamie, because he did. His problem was that he felt too much for her, and he knew that he'd never, ever want to walk away. That this wasn't just about comfort or friendship.

"When you say you want me here, do you mean that we keep this just between us, or…?"

She ran her hand down his arm before looping it through so they could walk arm in arm. "I think we should tell Logan. I mean, I don't want to lie to him and I don't want to come between your friendship. We need to be honest with him."

Brett blew out a breath. "Logan is not going to be okay with this."

"I know, but we need to tell him. *I'll tell him.* I just don't want this to be any more awkward than it needs to be, and the longer this goes on, the harder telling him will become, because he'll think we've been lying to him all along if we don't come clean."

"Maybe we should text him, tell him to meet us for lunch or something after our walk tomorrow?" Brett suggested. "He might take it better if there's a lot of people around. You know, so he can't knock out every tooth in my mouth." After the way Logan had warned him off the other night…it wasn't going to be pleasant, no matter how or where they did it. Logan was going to be furious, not with her, but with him.

Jamie laughed but he shook his head.

"What?" she asked.

"I don't think you know Logan like I do," he said. "There is nothing about this that's going to be easy. He's like a teddy bear around you, acts like he wouldn't hurt a fly, but the Logan I know isn't going to deal with this well."

"I lost my husband, Brett, and now something has happened between us. I'm not intending on acting like you've taken advantage of me, if that's what you're worried he'll think."

Logan was going to kill him. Actually kill him.

Jamie couldn't stop laughing as Bear ran after the stick she'd just thrown like his life depended on it. Having fun with him had changed the dynamic between them, and she was pretty sure her dog was enjoying it as much as she was.

"I told you, he made the squad based on his determination with balls and sticks," Brett said, grinning straight back at her.

"Why did I never realize how much fun he was before?"

Brett came up and put his arm around her. "Because you were both trying to figure the other out, and everything had become too serious. It was like a child living with you who wasn't allowed to have fun, so he was bored and didn't understand what was being asked of him."

Jamie gave Bear a hearty pat when he dropped the stick at her feet for the umpteenth time. "Good boy," she praised, before throwing it again.

"We used to call Bear the branch manager and my dog the deputy branch manager," Brett said, pressing a kiss to her cheek. "The two of them used to have a blast when we let them play."

Jamie leaned into Brett, enjoying his arm around her and the sun beating down on her shoulders. She moved only when he had to reach into his back pocket to retrieve his mobile.

"Is it Logan?" she asked.

Brett tapped a message into his phone before turning his attention back to her. "Yeah. He's said yes to lunch tomorrow."

"What do you say we just grab something to take away this morning?" she asked him, shaking her head at Bear as he faithfully retrieved the stick again. He looked disappointed that their game was over, but it wasn't like they hadn't let him have a heap of fun. "I know a place nearby where they do a mean bacon-and-egg sandwich, and we can sit in the sun and relax."

Brett's gaze met hers. "That's exactly what I need to take my mind off things."

"You mean Logan?" she asked, tucking under his arm and pulling him along with an arm around his waist.

"Yeah." He hugged her back as they walked. "So where is this amazing food place?"

"Ah, it's more like a food shack, but I promise you it's good. They do great coffee, too."

"So it'll kind of be like our first actual date?" he asked, raising an eyebrow when she looked at him.

"Yeah, I guess it will be. That okay with you?"

"Sure is. But I'm guessing we might have to buy for Bear, too. I doubt he's going to tolerate us eating greasy food in front of him without sharing."

Brett knew he needed to just shut his mind off, but it was easier said than done. Meeting Logan was seriously playing with his head, and he knew better than Jamie how tomorrow was going to go down. But there was nothing he could do about it right now, so he needed to shake off his worries.

"My shout. Want the same as me?"

Brett returned her smile, not wanting to ruin her happiness. "Whatever's good, but order me two."

"Typical boy," she muttered, spinning around to go in and order.

He watched as she disappeared then came back with a number on a piece of brown paper.

"Oh, this is a really classy place, isn't it? I was thinking of taking you somewhere nice for our first date, not to a takeaway joint."

She giggled. Jamie actually giggled, and the noise was infectious enough to make him laugh straight back at her.

"Trust me, it's worth overlooking the surroundings for the food. And the coffee. Did I mention the coffee?"

"I think you're being paid to do PR for this place," he said to her, grabbing her hand and pulling her in against his body. "I don't believe you for a second."

"Well, you should," she whispered, tipping her chin up and brushing her lips against his.

She jumped away when their number was called. Brett couldn't take his eyes off her as she walked away—and he couldn't have forgotten her smile even if he walked away and never returned. Jamie was getting under his skin, and there was nothing he didn't like about it.

"Here you go," Jamie announced as she emerged once again. "Coffee for you, and the food is wrapped up in here. Let's go find a spot somewhere nice."

They walked the five minutes back to the park and sat on the grass, Bear sprawling out beside them. Jamie reached into the bag and pulled out massive sandwiches wrapped in paper, passed one to him, then unwrapped one for Bear and put it on the ground, before taking one for herself.

"Well, it at least smells good," he told her, taking his first bite.

She did the same, watching him, like she was expecting a reaction. He took another bite, and ketchup and sauce oozed out down his hand, along with runny egg yolk that tasted incredible.

"Amazing or what?" she asked, eyebrows raised as she kept eating hers, hands tilted up to keep the sauce from running onto her skin.

"You win, it's amazing," he told her, mouth full as he tried to talk. He kept eating, not able to stop for the juice running out of it.

When they'd both finished and cleaned up as best they could, using only paper napkins, Brett lay back on the grass beside Jamie, his elbow propping him up. He looked at Jamie, and she at him, both nursing their coffees.

"Thanks for this," he said, reaching out to run his hand down her hair, tucking a few loose strands behind her ear.

"For greasy food and damn good coffee?" she teased.

"No, for showing me that we can just hang out and enjoy being together. That it's simple things like this that are important, just…" He didn't even know what he was trying to tell her. "I guess what I'm really badly attempting to say is that being with you isn't easy for me, but it's worth it. It's worth the pain just to have you with me."

Jamie brushed the back of her fingers against her eyes, and it was only then he realized that she was trying to disguise her tears.

"Don't cry, Jamie. Please don't cry," he murmured, taking her hand and squeezing it tight.

"Just ignore me, I'm all emotional," she said, smiling and squeezing his hand back. "I'm happy, Brett, I promise you I'm happy."

"Good. If you're happy, then I'm happy."

And it was true. He might be finding being with Jamie hard to wrap his head around, to deal with, but her being happy was what was important.

Chapter 11

The sun shone brightly through the window and onto Jamie's face as she struggled to open her eyes. She reached out a hand and found an empty space beside her again, which was the only reason she forced herself to sit up, to see if Brett was sitting across the room in the chair again.

He wasn't. But when she glanced toward the door, he was standing there watching her.

"What are you doing up so early?" she mumbled, dropping back down into the pillows but not taking her eyes off of him.

He laughed, crossing the room and carrying a large tray. "First of all, it's almost nine o'clock, so it's not early, and second, I was getting you breakfast."

She pushed herself back up again and flattened the bedding out so he could put the tray down.

"Did you make this?"

Brett chuckled again. "No, I took Bear for a run and picked it all up at that place down the road. Turns out they do fresh fruit salads and muffins for people like me. All I had to do was put them on a plate and walk them upstairs for you."

She leaned in for a kiss. "Well, it's the thought that counts. And I'm starving."

Brett carefully settled himself across from Jamie, obviously trying not to tip the tray, and reached for a bowl of fruit. "It scares me to even say it, but I could get used to this. Being with you, the whole domestic bliss routine."

When she smiled he grinned straight back at her. "Me, too," she said. "But maybe you'll feel differently when you realize I'm not *that* domestic."

"When I say domestic, I wasn't exactly referring to housekeeping."

Now it was Jamie laughing at him, waving a piece of fruit on a fork in his direction. "So you mean you like bedding me and dining with me?"

Brett shrugged. "Well, when you put it like that…"

She grinned and settled back against the pillows to devour her fruit, before reaching for the coffee and muffin he'd brought for her.

"So we still on to meet Logan today?" she asked.

Brett wished they could have just stayed in their nice little bubble without involving Logan, but he knew there was little he could do to get out of it now. Trouble was, it wasn't so much how Logan would react that was troubling him, it was that he knew what he would say. And Brett knew that every word that came out of his friend's mouth would be the truth, exactly what he'd already struggled with, and he didn't want to second-guess what he was doing with Jamie when it already felt so fragile.

"How about we finish breakfast, you get yourself ready, then we take a walk before we meet him."

Jamie took a sip of her coffee. "Deal."

Jamie looked at Brett. He was staring into the distance. "Everything okay?" she asked.

He turned to meet her gaze and smiled, but she could tell he had something on his mind. The kiss he dropped to her lips told her the problem wasn't her, but she still wanted to know. She was pleased they'd decided to walk Bear before meeting Logan for lunch—it gave them time to relax and just enjoy being together.

"It's Logan, isn't it? You're worried about telling him," Jamie stated as soon as he pulled away.

"It's not that I don't want to tell him, I can just see how this is going to go," he said, his hand stroking her hair as he looked into her eyes. "Part of me thinks we should just pretend like everything is normal, then go back to this when we return to your place."

Jamie sighed. On some level she agreed with him, but she didn't want to lie to Logan, and she didn't believe he was going to take it that badly. Not if they were honest about how everything had happened between them, that it wasn't something they'd ever have acted upon if the circumstances had been different.

"Let's just see how it goes. Maybe we're overthinking it."

He didn't look like he agreed, but he took her hand and tugged her in the direction they needed to head in. "For my sake, I hope you're right."

"Your sake?" she queried.

"Yeah, my sake. Because he'll never believe you could do any wrong, which means that I'll be the villain. He'll hate me and he'll feel sorry for you."

Jamie hoped he was being dramatic, even as her heart started to race at the thought of things going bad. Was she being naive to think Logan would behave like an adult and hear them out?

"Come on, Bear. Let's go," she ordered, giving him a hand signal to run on ahead. He bounded off, cheerful and content, just like she'd been before they'd started talking about Logan.

"Why don't you take my mind off everything by telling me about your book project," he said.

Jamie giggled. "I thought you were going to suggest something else entirely."

He pretended to look horrified. "We're in the middle of a public park, Jamie. Shame on you."

She just kept laughing and he wrapped his arm around her so she could loop hers around his waist. "I'm writing about happy things. Fairies and flying ponies, and little girls who can achieve whatever they dream."

"Sounds good."

"I just wanted to write about a fun little world that was a happy place. So I could escape each time I sat down at the computer or sketched the illustrations. Although I can't say the topic of the book has compelled me to work on it for any decent stretch of time."

"There's nothing wrong with wanting to escape reality," Brett told her, kissing the top of her head when she leaned her cheek against his shoulder. "We all have to do what we have to do."

"Which is why you didn't want to tell Logan," she remarked.

"Look, we can deal with Logan. Let's just not let it ruin this, okay?"

"I couldn't have said it better myself," she said. Because she had no intention of letting anyone or anything ruin what was happening between them.

Jamie stood up when she saw Logan enter the restaurant. They were sitting outside so Bear could be with them, and she didn't think he'd see them. Brett hadn't bothered to stand—he seemed more interested in shredding his sugar packet into a thousand pieces than looking out for his friend.

"Hey!" she called out when she spotted Logan.

He wrapped her in a big bear hug, holding on tight. "We don't see each other in months and now twice in a week. How lucky am I?"

She gave him a kiss on the cheek and stood back as Brett rose and the boys did some handshake-backslap ritual.

"You two hanging out a bit?" Logan asked.

Brett cleared his throat and she jumped in to answer for him. She'd hoped for a relaxed coffee first, that they could just hang out and enjoy catching up, but it seemed they were diving straight into it.

"Brett's actually staying with me, keeping me company," she said. "It's nice to have someone in the house again."

"Oh, yeah?" Logan answered, waving over a waitress and ordering a latte before picking up the menu.

"So you've been working? How's your dog?" Brett asked. "Jamie's doing really well with Bear."

Jamie frowned at him, not wanting to change the subject yet. She just wanted to get everything out on the table, deal with the two most important men in her life by being honest. Then they could get back to chitchat and food, but they needed to get this out in the open now, especially since they were already on the topic.

"We should let the dogs get together for a play, take them to the beach or something," Logan said, before turning to Brett. "And you can stay with me if you need a place to crash once Jamie kicks you out, because we both know she'll be sick of you soon, right?"

Both guys laughed, but she didn't. Jamie tapped her fingers on the tabletop, trying to figure out how to get what she needed to say out there without Logan completely losing the plot.

"I thought you'd be staying at the barracks?" Brett asked.

"I've rented a place not far from there, and no one seems to mind me living off-site. They're putting me on some local work, security and bomb checks for the celebrities they have coming in over the next few months as part of the Visit Australia tourism campaign."

"Logan, there's something we need to tell you," Jamie blurted, interrupting their talk about Logan's work. It wasn't that she wasn't interested in what he was saying, about what he did, but she couldn't sit here pretending like they didn't have something major to discus with him.

He put down his menu, looked from her to Brett and back to her again. "Is everything okay? It's not Bear, is it?" he asked, diverting his gaze to study the dog sitting at her feet, before reaching down to pat him. "You look good, boy. Jamie looking after you, huh?"

"We didn't mean for this to happen, especially not so soon after Sam passing away, but Brett and I are, well, we're close. We're, um, well we've become more than friends, and we wanted you to be the first to know." Damn it! That hadn't come out well at all, not as she'd planned, not like she'd practiced in her head. She didn't want to stuff this conversation up, and that was exactly what she'd managed to do.

Logan's fists had clenched on the table and she could see a tick at his temple.

"Logan, I can explain…" Brett began, before Logan cut him off straight away.

"Our friend dies, and instead of looking after his wife, *like we both promised to do,* you decide it's okay to sleep with her? To just slot into Sam's life like you can take his place?"

"It wasn't like that," Jamie told him, reaching for Brett's hand. "This wasn't planned, it's just…"

"So you *are* sleeping together?" he demanded.

"Logan, I can explain," she stuttered, emotion clogging her throat and making it near impossible to speak.

"Jamie, this is between me and Brett. You're a widow and we promised Sam we'd look after you, and instead he's has taken advantage of you?"

Her hands were wet, clammy from the tension at her table, and she was starting to flush hot. *This was not good*. There was no part of this that was good. Brett had been right, they should never have told Logan, they should have just stayed in their own little bubble of happiness.

"Logan, I didn't want to tell you, but we…"

Logan laughed, but it was a harsh sound that made

Jamie cringe. "Please don't insult me or Sam by using the word *we* when it comes to Jamie, Brett."

Jamie didn't know what to say, hated that they were starting to have a conversation about her as if she weren't present, as if she couldn't hear every single word they were saying. She'd known pain, plenty of it lately, but this cut straight to the bone.

"Logan, why don't we go and talk about this somewhere private?" Brett asked. "Leave Jamie out of this."

"Oh, I have every intention of leaving her out of this," he said, seething.

Jamie watched as they both stood. They were big men, tall and muscled, and the testosterone surrounding her was enough to make her head spin. She knew this wasn't looking good, that at least one of them was about to explode, but she'd never seen either of them be violent before. Surely they wouldn't...

Jamie's mouth went dry. She swiveled in her chair to watch them as they walked down the steps. It seemed too calm, too orderly, but the heated exchange that began when they were on the footpath was anything other than calm, and deep down she'd known it was coming. As soon as she'd seen Logan's expression, when she'd told him, she'd known. Her hand dropped to Bear, kneading his fur as she stayed seated.

Logan was in Brett's face, and he wasn't doing anything to stop him. Until he said one sentence. One sentence that Jamie heard even from where she was sitting, her hand now resting on Bear's head as she stared at the pair of them arguing. Her heart was thumping so hard she could hardly concentrate, a ringing in her ears making her head pound.

"I love her, Logan."

She froze, her hand stopping its back-and-forth stroke of her dog's head. There was nothing that could have prepared her for that moment, the second that she heard Brett say those three little words that sent her mind spiraling, that made it almost impossible for her to breathe.

He loved her.

Only the moment was shattered by the crack of Logan's fist hitting Brett square in the jaw. Jamie screamed, or at least she thought it was her because all she could hear was the ringing of a scream in her ears as she watched Brett stagger backward and Logan stand there, staring down at him, disgust written all over his face. Brett stood, not moving even as Logan raised his fist again, obviously deciding he wasn't going to engage, that he didn't want to fight his friend. In less than a minute, Logan stormed off down the footpath without a backward glance, disappearing before she even thought to call out to him. Before she was even capable of acting. Before she could do anything to right the wrong that had just happened because of her. Because she was as much in shock from what Brett had said, not just because of what Logan had done.

She flew down the steps and reached for Brett, gasping at the blood pouring from his nose and dripping into his mouth.

"Brett? Oh, my gosh…" The words came out like they were all connected, a complete jumble. "I don't, are you…?"

This couldn't be happening. Her hands were fluttering in the air with no idea what they should be doing to help him. And she still couldn't stop thinking about how it had felt to hear those words—*he loved her.*

"I'm fine," he insisted, wiping at his face then cursing when he covered his shirtsleeve in blood.

"No, you're not fine," she managed to say. "I'll cancel our lunch and then we can…"

"No," he said, staring down at her with a coolness in his gaze that sent shivers down her spine. This was not the same man she'd made love to, the same man whose hand she'd held as they strolled through the park earlier. The man who'd just confessed his love for her. "There can be no *us*, Jamie, don't you get that now? This is why I didn't want to meet Logan, because I knew that he'd tell me what I already knew, what I've been trying to ignore this whole time."

She stood dead-still, feet rooted to the spot, unable to move even if she wanted to. "Just because Logan didn't understand doesn't mean this is wrong. He'll get his head around it, eventually. We knew this wasn't going to be easy for him to digest, Brett, we knew it was going to be tough."

"It's not about Logan accepting us or not, Jamie, it's about him being *right*. Maybe this is me taking advantage of you, doing something that is so wrong it shouldn't have even crossed my mind that any part of it was okay." He stared at her. "Sam was my best friend, Jamie, and he trusted me like he trusted no one else. Except for Logan. And now I've lost both of them, because I did something that I've known was wrong every step of the way." He stared at her, his expression empty. "It doesn't matter how I feel about you, Jamie. I should never have let this go so far between us. I shouldn't have told you about looking for you, about seeing Sam with you. None of it."

Jamie stared back up at him, digging her fingernails into her palm, determined to stay strong.

"So what are you saying, Brett?"

He looked at her then looked away, like he couldn't even make eye contact with her anymore. "I need to think," he said, walking a few steps backward, putting enough space between them that it felt like they'd never be close, that he'd never hold her in his arms or kiss her ever again. "I'll see you later."

Jamie stood and watched him—the man she'd just opened herself up to, the man who'd only moments earlier said he loved her—walk away. Instead of fighting for her, fighting for their right to be together, he'd just given up and left her. And she had a feeling that he wasn't just walking away from lunch, he was walking away from *her. For good.*

She squared her shoulders and forced herself to walk back up the steps and into the restaurant, hating that the other people seated outside in the courtyard had witnessed the scene and no doubt heard some of what was being said. Bear's wagging tail made her smile, though, and she dropped a kiss to his head before sitting back down again, trying to stay calm. Her dog was at least loyal, would never leave her side unless she wanted him to. Bear was the only constant in her life right now, no strings attached.

"Ma'am, would you like to cancel one of your orders?"

She nodded bravely. "Yes, just the eggs benedict for me, please. And another latte. Make it strong."

There was a newspaper at the empty table beside her, so she reached for it and started scanning the articles. She wasn't interested in reading, but she was interested in doing anything she could to take her mind off Brett. To try to keep things normal and pretend that everything was okay for a little while.

If that meant sitting alone with her dog to eat brunch, then that's what she'd do. She needed to be grateful for her life, for the fact that she was sitting here, alive, in the sun. She could go home and cry later, but right now she was going to eat her eggs and drink her coffee.

Because she'd put herself through enough, *been* through enough, to just take a moment for herself and pretend like everything was okay. Inside, she wanted to fall apart, but her mind was strong, and she wanted to keep it that way. Life didn't get much tougher than losing a husband, but she'd survived that, and she would survive this. Just like she'd survived losing her dad when she was a teenager and dealt with a mom who'd been more interested in drowning her sorrows in a bottle of wine than comforting her only daughter.

She was a fighter, and she wasn't going to lose her strength, not ever.

Chapter 12

Jamie was tired. She was tired of waiting, tired of thinking, tired of everything. She'd read through the final draft of her latest manuscript, played around with all of her sketches to send her editor, but nothing was inspiring her. And now here she was, curled up in her favorite chair again with a cup of coffee, staring out the window. She'd spent a lot of time sitting in the same spot and thinking after Sam had died, after the men had come knocking at her door and told her the news, and it was the only place she felt like sitting now. She didn't know why, but whenever she looked out the window it helped her to relax.

Bear's low whine broke her trance, and she smiled over at him. He'd been through so much, which made them perfect companions, but she also knew that the only reason she was doing so well with the dog now was because of Brett.

Brett. She couldn't stop thinking about him if she tried. He was the only person who'd made her feel alive, who'd made her feel like *her* again since Sam had died, and now he'd gone and walked away. Not to mention the wedge she'd driven between him and Logan—a wedge she was worried might be irreparable.

I love her. They were the words that had echoed in her head since the fight. Maybe she'd heard them wrong, maybe he'd said something else, but the way her heart picked up speed whenever she played that moment over in her mind told her that she'd been right. That there was no mistaking what he'd told Logan, before she'd heard the smack of Logan's fist against his face. How could he feel that way about her and still walk away?

It excited and terrified her in equal parts, because this was Brett. Her friend, Brett. Her husband's friend, Brett. And he was also the man she'd made love to the night before and couldn't stop thinking about. The only man other than her husband who she could ever imagine being with, and the only man she wanted to be with. But now he was gone, and she'd never have the chance to hear the words from his lips, or say them back to him.

Jamie sighed again and reached for her phone, checking to make sure she hadn't missed a call or a text. Eventually she was going to have to admit that Brett wasn't coming back, at least not tonight. She was alone, again. Just her and Bear, and what she'd shared with Brett might be over for good, just a memory.

"Want a cuddle?" she asked the dog. She moved to the sofa and grabbed a blanket to tuck around herself.

He pricked his ears and watched as she settled herself, flicked on the television and patted the spot beside her. It didn't take him long to decide to join her—he padded over and jumped up, taking up more space than she was. But she didn't care. He was a warm body and he loved her, and that was all she needed right now. Bear was her oversized cuddly blanket—not to mention her protector at night.

Her dog was someone who wasn't going to leave her, someone who was supposed to be by her side, no questions asked. Someone who'd be in her life for as long as was possible.

Someone she could love without feeling guilty about what her heart was telling her.

Brett leaned both elbows on the counter and stared down into his drink. The warm brown liquid didn't have any answers, and it wasn't a vice he'd ever indulged before, but after what had happened with Jamie, he'd decided a bourbon might help clear his head. Not that it was doing the pounding any good, or helping the purple swirl that was starting around his eye and across one side of his nose. He'd taken one look in the cracked bathroom mirror and decided that he was best not to look at the reminder on his face.

He held up the glass and took a small sip, cringing as the liquid burned a fiery trail down his throat. It was only early afternoon, and he never drank straight spirits at the best of times, let alone on an empty stomach.

Brett glanced around at the other people in the bar—all men. It was dark and dingy, an underground dive that made it almost impossible to remember that it was a bright, sunny day outside. The kind of day he should be enjoying, rather than sitting around feeling sorry for himself.

He swallowed a larger gulp of his drink this time, finding the second taste smoother than the first.

"You ready for another?"

Brett looked up as the bartender spoke to him. "Ah, no. I think just one will do me."

He received a nod in response. "I haven't seen you here before."

"And hopefully, at this time of the day at least, you won't see me again."

The bartender chuckled. "You don't exactly look like my kind of lunchtime regular. The type who only ever consumes liquid for lunch, that is."

"Heaven help me," Brett said, tipping back the rest of the glass and closing his eyes as he swallowed it down. The drink had made his stomach swirl with a heat that felt better than the cold dread he'd been experiencing earlier, but he still didn't want to be tempted by a second.

"Woman trouble?"

Brett nodded. "You could say that."

"Don't be an idiot, that's my advice. If you love her? Tell her you're sorry and make it up to her. The guys that don't do that…?" The bartender raised his eyebrows. "They're the ones who turn into my regulars, and it's a sad story from then on. Although women troubles are pretty good for business down here."

Brett stood and put his wallet into his back pocket. "Thanks for the advice. It's not quite that simple, but you're right."

He walked to the entrance, feeling like a desperate man as he stared at the light filtering through the door. Suddenly the confines of the bar, the darkness, even the smell, were all telling him that he needed to run, and fast. Before he turned into a depressed creature who needed bourbon and darkness to deal with his life on a daily basis.

Brett's memories would forever haunt him—that last day with Sam like a scene from a movie playing on repeat sometimes—but he wasn't ever going to give in to them. He had been part of Australia's most elite special forces team, was trained in active combat, even how to deal with being captured and held by an enemy, and that training had instilled a strength in him that he wasn't ever going to let disappear from his mind.

The trouble was, that training had also taught him that there was nothing more important than his fellow soldiers, *his men*. And Sam had been his wingman, his buddy, the person he trusted with his life on a daily basis. Part of the family that he'd created after losing his parents.

So did he maintain that loyalty even in Sam's death, or did he give in to his feelings for Jamie and try to tell himself that *that* was the right thing to do? Because the broken, hurt look in her eyes when he'd walked away from her earlier might end up haunting him for the rest of his life, too. He loved her, there was no denying that, but he also had a loyalty to his family, and that meant respecting Sam even in death. What Logan had said was what had terrified him all this time with Jamie— words that he'd told himself before giving in to the way he felt. Before making love to Jamie and knowing it was so wrong, but also so right.

Brett held up his hand to shield his eyes from the bright sunlight and started to walk, because he had nothing else to do and nowhere else to be. He just followed his feet, needing the time to think. He hadn't been lying to Jamie when he'd told her how he'd felt that first time they'd met, or about how he'd come looking for her, and part of him knew that she deserved to know the truth about the past. About how he'd felt and what he would have done if she hadn't already met Sam.

That night, that first time they'd met, they'd spent hours talking. Two people at a party, not part of the crowd around them, they'd sipped champagne, laughed and talked like he'd never talked to anyone in his life before. And then his girlfriend had interrupted them, told him off for leaving her even though he'd seen her dancing and having fun without him, knew she'd been fine on her own.

He'd walked away from Jamie, tugged in a direction that he'd known had been wrong, but knowing that he didn't have a choice. The look in her eyes, the way they'd looked at one another, was a moment he'd never forgotten. His hand held by one woman, and everything else held by a woman he'd only known for less than a few hours.

Ten minutes later, from across the room, he'd watched her leave, and the next time he'd seen her, she'd been laughing and in the arms of his best friend. *Sam*.

Brett stopped walking and stared up at the sky, eyes adjusted to the sun now

He'd fallen in love with Jamie from the moment he'd met her. So what if it wasn't the right thing in everyone else's eyes? If it wasn't what he'd planned? He'd stood back and let his friend be with the love of his life, and now it was his turn, wasn't it? It was his chance at a happiness that he'd never known, his time to see if he and Jamie could be together. Did it mean he didn't love

Sam like a brother, now that Sam was gone and he and Jamie had the chance to fall in love?

If Jamie wanted him, then he was a fool to walk away, he knew that. Logan might be his friend, but Jamie could be the love of his life, the woman who'd be at his side for the rest of his life. And that wasn't something anyone else had the right to tell him he should give up. Not Logan, and not Sam's memory. Because no matter how much he respected his friends, he needed to respect himself and what was important to him, too. If they were truly his family, wouldn't they want to see him happy?

The only person who had the right to push him away and end whatever it was that had happened between them, was Jamie. He just needed to tell her that before she changed her mind and didn't want him back.

He'd spent so long worrying about what other people would think was right, about being faithful to those he loved, that he'd forgotten what was most important. What was right by Jamie. What would make Jamie happy.

What would make him happy.

And there was only one thing that could make him happy right now, and that was Jamie, in his life, in his arms.

He wanted to give her enough time to think, to deal with what had happened, but he didn't want to leave it so long that she thought he didn't care.

Brett headed toward a café he could see across the street and decided to have a late lunch, just sit for a while and eat, think about what he'd say to her. Because this could be the most important thing he ever prepared for in his life, and he didn't want to screw up the one chance he might get to prove himself to Jamie.

Chapter 13

Brett crossed the street and looked at Jamie's house. It was like the first day he'd arrived, when he'd been so uncertain about coming, about what he'd say to her, and now he was feeling just as awkward.

Only this time, he actually had something to be awkward about. Not to mention something to say that he couldn't even rehearse right in his mind, let alone out loud in front of Jamie.

It was getting late but the streetlights raised the canopy of darkness. She would no doubt already be asleep, but he was ready to come back and if he didn't do it now he might never do it. He'd needed to take his time, to think and be sure about the decision he'd made, and now there was no doubt in his mind that what he was about to do was right.

Brett slid his key into the lock and turned it, quietly

opening the door and shutting it behind him. Jamie had given him the key, willingly invited him into her home, but he still felt weird about just letting himself in and treating it like his own place. Especially after what had happened. She'd probably hear him and think he was an intruder, not expecting him to ever show his face again, and the last thing he wanted was to fuel her memories of what had happened in her childhood home.

"Just me, Bear," he called out in a low voice, not wanting the dog to attack him thinking he was a stranger.

He walked through the house, flicked the light on in the kitchen, and it was then he heard the low growl. Brett looked around and realized the noise was coming from the sofa.

"Hey, boy, just me. It's Brett," he whispered.

The growl turned to a whine, and he stepped toward him so Bear could see him. His eyes adjusted to the half-light and he saw that the dog was snuggled up to, and protecting, Jamie. She was sound asleep, head tucked into a large cushion, blanket half over her, half over Bear. He knew better than to approach him too quickly.

Brett didn't want to wake Jamie and give her a fright, either, so he quietly moved toward the sofa, pulled the blanket up to her chin without disturbing her or the dog, then walked back to turn the kitchen light off. He made his way in the dark into the living room again and slumped down in the armchair. It wasn't the most comfortable place to sleep, but he'd experienced far worse, and he wanted to be there when Jamie woke up.

He didn't want her to think he'd spent the night somewhere else, wanted her to know that he cared enough

to come home and deal with what a jerk he'd been earlier in the day. And most of all, he wanted to be near
her. This last week had made him feel alive again—
being around Jamie and Bear—and he wasn't going
to give that up without a fight. Not to mention the fact
that he'd finally been able to sleep since he'd been in
her home with her. And if she asked him to leave in the
morning? At least he could tell himself that he'd tried,
that it wasn't his own fear than had driven a wedge between them. He'd respect her choice no matter what
she decided.

Brett was starting to be thankful that he'd had the
glass of bourbon, because without it, he may have ended
up sitting awake all night. But the heaviness in his eyes
told him he needed to sleep, and he wasn't going to
deny himself. Not with Jamie asleep on the sofa opposite him. There was nothing he could do until she
woke up, which gave him a little longer before he had
to pour his heart out and convince her that what he'd
said earlier, the way he'd behaved, had been him acting way out of line.

The truth had been how he'd held her in his arms
the night before, what he'd said to her these past few
days. Today, he'd just been plain scared, and that wasn't
something he would ever have admitted to in the past.

Jamie woke to the sun shining on her face and a big
body pinning her down. She could hardly feel her legs.
When she opened her eyes it was to a large black nose,
with Bear resting his head on her chest.

"You're squashing me," she muttered, pushing the
hair from her face, trying again to stretch out her legs
and failing. He either didn't hear her, or didn't care,

because he didn't budge an inch and she was suddenly claustrophobic.

"Morning."

Jamie's heart stuttered into a superfast beat. Brett? What was he doing here? She locked eyes on him.

"When did you get back?" She hadn't been expecting him here, let alone waking to find him in the same room as her.

"Ah, last night. But you looked so comfortable on the sofa so I left you there. Sorry if I woke you."

She pushed Bear off and stretched, making an attempt to push her hair down, knowing how terrible she must look. She'd curled up without washing any of her makeup off, so her hair was probably the least of her worries compared to her panda eyes.

"You don't have to make breakfast," she told him, standing to watch Brett as he moved around the kitchen.

His dark brown eyes met hers, and she couldn't help but smile at him. *This was Brett.* No matter what had happened yesterday, he was still the same Brett she'd always loved as a friend, and now...what? She didn't know how to describe what had happened between them, how she felt about this gorgeous, kind man cooking in her kitchen. But she did know that she didn't want to lose him from her life.

"I want to make up for yesterday's lunch disaster," he told her, cracking eggs into the pan as he spoke. "I know it's going to take more than eggs to apologize, but it's a good start, right?"

Jamie nodded, smiling back at him, but she needed a moment to gather her thoughts, to be alone. To deal with the fact that she'd gone to bed thinking she might never hear from him again, and now she was about to sit down to breakfast with him. Thank God she hadn't woken in the night and tried to attack him, thinking he was breaking in.

"I'm just going to freshen up. I won't be long," she told him.

Jamie headed for the bathroom and shut the door behind her. What she wanted to do was sink to the floor and feel the cool of the tiles against her skin, but she also wanted to hear what Brett had to say. He was either going to tell her he wanted to go back to just being friends, or that he wanted something more, and she needed to prepare herself either way. She wanted him here so badly, but she also had no intention of forcing him.

Not to mention she was terrified of losing him as a friend.

Brett had been trying to rehearse what he was going to say, but the trouble was that he wasn't entirely sure *what* he wanted to tell her. He put the eggs and bacon on the plates and walked them to the table, before returning with the toast and then the pot of coffee he'd freshly brewed. They said food was the way to a man's heart—he was the hoping the same might be true for women. Or just one woman in particular.

"It looks great."

He looked up as Jamie entered the room, watching as she first looked down at the table, then at him, before sitting. She immediately fingered the napkin he'd put beside her plate, as if she needed something to do, something to take her mind off what was happening or what they were going to talk about.

"The scrambled eggs look so creamy," she said, taking a mouthful and fluttering her eyes shut for a second as she swallowed. "And they taste *really* good."

"The trick is to not add any milk. Just whisk them all up and straight into the pan, and turn them off as soon as they're almost cooked."

"So you know more than just pasta and sauce, huh? What happened to you being a one-trick pony?"

Brett swallowed his mouthful and reached for a piece of toast. "One breakfast recipe and one dinner, that's all." He took a bite and watched her. "Now that you've tasted this, I don't have any more hidden talents to wow you with. This is me going all out to impress."

Jamie smiled, but before she could reply he cleared his throat.

"I didn't cook you breakfast to brag about my skills in the kitchen, Jamie. I wanted to say sorry. To genuinely tell you how sorry I am for what happened and for what I said. I was a jerk and I never should have behaved like that."

She shook her head. "You don't need to apologize. I should never have insisted we tell Logan, not so soon. It was stupid and I have no idea what I was thinking."

Brett put down his fork and leaned toward her, both arms on the table. "If we hadn't told him we would have been lying, and telling him later would have been worse. He would have felt betrayed, so you were right. I just wish it had happened differently, and if I could do anything to change that, I would."

"So what are you trying to tell me?" she asked, picking at small bits of egg as she glanced up at him.

"What I'm trying to say is that no matter how badly it went down yesterday, telling Logan was the right thing. He's been with me, with us all, through thick and thin, and I don't want to lose him. The way I reacted was unacceptable, but everything he said just kind of fueled what I'd been worried about all along."

Jamie was looking at her food, eating little mouthfuls like she wasn't really hungry, but he waited her out, knowing she'd look up eventually. What he hadn't said was that he didn't want to lose her, either, but right now he wasn't even sure she was his to lose.

He picked up a piece of bacon between his fingers and crunched on it, never taking his eyes from her, and when she looked up he was ready. Or at least he was ready for the connection. What he wasn't ready for was the bright blue of her irises, the way they looked as if they were bathed in water from the tears glistening in them, the sight of her bottom lip tucked under her teeth, like she was having to bite on it to stop from crying—it was almost enough to break his heart.

"Why did you come back last night, Brett? Was it just to tell me that, or something more?"

Brett put the piece of bacon down that he'd been holding and wiped his fingers on his napkin. This was his moment, this was the chance he'd been waiting for, and he wasn't going to blow it.

"I came back because I was a coward yesterday, and that's not the man I am."

"I know you're no coward," she told him, a smile curving her lips and taking the sadness from her face. "You're one of the bravest people I know, and the fact that you didn't punch Logan back, and that you walked away from me? Neither of those things makes you a coward, it just makes you a person who doesn't want to do the wrong thing by the people you care about."

"I deserved the bloody nose, it's not that, but walking away from you?" He shook his head. "That was the worst decision I've ever made in my life, and I need you to know that I will never walk away from you like that ever again. I was stupid to let fear stop me from doing the one thing in my life that I've never been so sure about. *How I feel about you.*"

Brett's voice was husky, a deeper tone than it usually was. He pushed his chair out and moved around to Jamie, taking her hands in his and dropping to his knees beside her instead of towering over her.

"You're the best thing that has ever happened to me, Jamie," he told her, staring into her eyes. "What we did, what we're doing, it might not have been planned, but I'm going to fight for you if I have to. I don't care who says no and stands in our way, if you want me here, then I won't ever leave you. And that's a promise I will never break."

Jamie had tears falling down her cheeks now in a slow, steady stream. "I only want you here if you want to be here," she whispered. "I need to know how you feel about me."

She reached out and touched just under his eye, where he knew he was sporting a nasty black bruise. Her fingers were feather-light, tracing across his skin.

"I've never wanted anything so bad in all my life," he admitted. "Or any*one*."

"I can't lose another man I love, Brett. I can't…" The words were low, almost a whisper.

"I'll promise in front of every single person we know if I have to, to make you believe me, but I will never, *ever* let you down Jamie. I'm here for you, for as long as you'll have me. You're my family, too, not just the guys."

Her fingers traced beneath his bruise again before reaching around to his ear, then to the back of his head. She pulled him toward her and leaned close, her face only inches from his.

"I think I love you, Brett," she whispered, tilting her mouth toward him, lips parted.

He didn't hesitate. Brett closed his mouth over hers, lips crushed to Jamie's and moving just enough, drinking in the taste of her, the warmth of having her body and mouth pressed to his.

He only pulled back because he had to, because he needed to tell her how he felt, too.

"I don't *think* I love you, Jamie," he whispered, mouth hovering so close to hers as he spoke that her plump lips just touched his. *"I know so."*

Jamie held on to the back of Brett's head, drawing him back to her again, her mouth taking his captive. He wasn't going to stop her, but he did want to make things more comfortable.

He dragged her hand from his hair, lips barely leaving hers, and slowly moved them down to the carpet, tugging her down on top of him.

"Sorry about breakfast," she whispered, as she put her hands on either side of his head to brace herself.

"Screw breakfast," he muttered as he flipped her on to her back, so he was braced above her. "I'll take you over food any day."

"Oh, yeah?" Her fingers grabbed hold of a fistful of his hair.

"Yeah."

Brett tried to growl but she just laughed at him and tugged him lower.

"Shut up and kiss me," she said.

"Yes, ma'am."

She laughed as he kissed the hollow of her neck, just above her collarbone, holding down her arms so she was powerless to move. His lips slowly moved up her neck, before settling on her mouth. His grip on her loosened as she submitted to his kiss, moaning as his tongue teased hers, lips soft one moment then rough.

Jamie pushed up his shirt, hands sliding against his bare skin, moving across his scars and up to his shoulders, then down again.

"That's a dangerous game you're playing," he muttered against her mouth.

"I know," she whispered back as she ran her hands up his stomach this time, taking her time so she could feel his muscles, exploring every inch of him.

"Do you want me to strip you naked here on the floor?"

Hmm. She did like the sound of that… "Is that a take-it-or-leave-it question?"

"No," he said, nose against hers as he stared into her eyes. "Multichoice."

She waited, his breath hot against her skin.

"The other option is that I pick you up and drag you to your bedroom. So I can have my wicked way with you there," he said, his voice deep and husky.

There was no mistaking what he wanted from her, and she wanted it every bit as bad.

"I'll take option two," she said, liking her newfound confidence, that she could tell him what she wanted without being too shy. "It just so happens that I have nothing else to do today, so my schedule's clear."

"So I'm just some toy to pass the time with?" he asked, holding her down by the wrists again and kissing her, before hauling her up and scooping her up into his arms.

Jamie slung her arms around his neck, loving that he was strong enough to just pick her up and carry her, like he was her protector. She knew she could take care of herself, but knowing she had a man in her life who'd stand by her side no matter what was something she loved.

"No, I'm saying you're my lover, and I want you to…" She didn't finish the sentence, the heat in his gaze making the words stall in her throat.

"Lover, huh?"

"Unless you don't want to be?" she asked, catching her bottom lip beneath her teeth.

"Oh, I want to be," he said, forcing her lips to his in a kiss that left her breathless. "Just don't expect me to let you out of your room anytime soon."

Jamie pressed her face into his chest as he carried her down the hall and kicked the bedroom door shut behind them.

Last night she'd been miserable, and this morning she was so happy she couldn't stop smiling.

Brett put her carefully on the bed and stared down at her. "I love you, Jamie," he said, all hint of playfulness gone, his tone serious. "I'm *in* love with you."

"I'm in love with you, too," she said back, not hesitating, loving that she was hearing the words straight from his mouth as he looked into her eyes, rather than secondhand, as he had admitted them to Logan.

Brett lowered himself over her and kissed her again, softer this time, more gently.

It was time for her to let go of the past and make a new future with this gorgeous, kind man, and there was no part of her that wasn't sure. She wanted to be with Brett, and no one was going to take that from her. Not ever.

Sunlight was pouring into the room, and Jamie was fighting to keep her eyes open.

"You know, I don't think I've ever been in bed at this time in the afternoon before," she mused.

Brett laughed, which sounded like a weird kind of rumbling from where she had her head pressed to his chest. She was curled up beside him, the sheet half-covering them, as she basked in the way he was stroking his fingers across her skin. Jamie felt like a well-petted cat, so content she could have purred, loving that he couldn't seem to take his hands off her.

"It feels good, doesn't it?"

"What?" she murmured. "You touching me like this? Because you can keep doing it until it's dark out, or forever, for that matter."

Brett moved his hand to stroke her hair. "Just being together. Not fighting it anymore."

"You know that Sam wouldn't have been angry with us," she said, wishing she didn't have to break the intimate moment between them, but needing to say what was on her mind. Jamie pushed up and stared down at Brett. "It doesn't mean I didn't love him with all my heart, but I think we met all those years ago for a reason, Brett. Because I met two men I could have fallen for, two men I might not have been able to decide between if I'd known that you'd come looking for me, and it's our time now. It's never been right before, but it is now."

Brett had an expression on his face that she couldn't read, but she could at least tell that he wasn't angry.

"I'm not scared of facing Sam one day," Brett told her, his lips kicking into a half smile. "He knows I would have traded places with him if I could have the day that bomb went off, and by the time I do see him, he'll be able to tell that I loved you just as much as he did."

Jamie dropped a slow, casual kiss to Brett's lips. "So are we just going to live in bliss for a while and never leave the house, take baby steps?"

Brett's face turned more somber and he sat up and propped himself against the pillows. "I know it didn't go well the first time, but I think we need to try to talk to Logan again."

Her eyebrows shot up. "You do?" The thought terrified her, especially how things had turned out, what she'd gone through thinking that Brett had left her.

He ran his fingers through her hair and tucked a few wisps behind her ear, his eyes never leaving hers. "Nothing is going to scare me off or change the way I feel about you Jamie, but Logan is important to both of us, and I want to try to make amends. Make him see that this is real, that this isn't something that's going to go away just because it makes him uncomfortable. I want to explain to him why everything he said is flawed, why this is right."

She nodded, sighing as his hand cupped her cheek and she relaxed into it. "Okay. I just don't want to burst this perfect little bubble we're floating in right now. I want to stay like this forever."

"We won't ruin this, not this time," he said. "I promise."

She trusted him, but she also knew how Logan's disapproval could affect them both if it went bad again.

"So if he punches you again or tries to make us feel disgusting for what we've done?"

Brett leaned forward to drop a kiss to her forehead. "Then we tell him that his friendship means a lot to us, that he's family, but that we're in love and we need him to respect that. We're not going to change who we are or how we feel for anyone."

Jamie found herself nodding. "And when exactly are you proposing we do this?" she asked.

"Tomorrow."

"And everyone else in our lives?" she asked.

"We can take telling the rest of the world a little slower, I think," he said, pulling her closer so he could put his arms around her. "Logan can be our first step, and then we'll just take it one day at a time. Do what feels right, when it feels right."

Jamie shut her eyes and relaxed against Brett's bare chest, happy that it was warm enough that they could just lie naked, with only the light sheet covering them.

"You have a plan for how we convince him to see us again?"

He tightened his hold on her. "You can organize to meet him, say you want to talk with him, take the dogs to the river or something," Brett told her. "No matter how angry he is with me, he'll never say no to seeing you."

"You sure about that?" she mumbled against his chest.

"I'm sure," he said. "When I turn up, too, he'll have no choice other than to see me, to hear what I have to say."

"If that's how you want to do it, then that's how we'll do it."

"Good," Brett said, hands stroking her back and disappearing beneath the sheets, against her skin. "Because now that that's sorted, I want to forget about everything else for the rest of the day and just think about you."

"Oh, really?" She laughed, wriggling as he held her, teased her.

"Yes, really," he said, capturing her mouth in a kiss that made her turn into liquid against him. "And that's only the start of it."

Chapter 14

Jamie had a flutter in her stomach that wasn't doing anything to help her nerves. She opened the back door of her car and signaled for Bear to jump out, just like Brett had instructed her to do with him, and he obediently hopped out and waited beside her.

"Don't overthink this."

She stared at Brett over the top of the car, where he was leaning. "I'm starting to think this wasn't such a good idea, that's what I'm thinking. Why didn't we just tell him that you would be coming?"

Brett sighed and walked around the car to her, and pulled her into his arms. "Because he would have said no, and he would have been angry before he even arrived."

She held on tight to him before stepping out of his embrace and clipping on Bear's leash. "Come on then, let's go and get this over with."

"You'll be fine. Just be yourself, and I'll deal with Logan if things don't go as planned."

Jamie shut her eyes, took a deep breath, then walked off through the park and to the river where she'd organized to meet Logan. For all her talk originally about wanting to be honest, about wanting Logan to know, she wasn't feeling so confident anymore. She would do anything to protect her relationship with Brett, and this felt like doing the exact opposite of what she should be doing.

"Once bitten, twice shy," she muttered to herself.

She looked across at Bear, wondering why he'd stopped walking, why he had his head cocked to one side, watching her. Jamie dropped to her haunches to give him a cuddle.

"I'm sorry, boy. I keep forgetting that you're always trying to figure out what I'm saying." She unclipped his leash, knowing it was about time she trusted him. "Let's go find your friend, huh? Off you go," she instructed, flinging her arm out in the signal Brett had taught her.

Bear gave her a look, like he was making sure he'd understood her properly, before trotting off ahead. She might be feeling more confident as a dog owner, but her knees were positively knocking over the idea of seeing Logan.

"Jamie!"

She looked up and saw him, standing by the river, hand held up in the air. Bear paused, looked back at her, clearly asking if he was allowed to run over to the other dog.

"Go see," she told him, walking faster herself and watching as he bounded off to say hello.

It was now or never.

"Hey, Logan," she called out when she was near.

"Hey," he replied, closing the distance between them and kissing her on the cheek.

It didn't feel anywhere near as awkward as she'd been expecting, seeing him after what had happened, but she knew everything would change when Brett appeared.

They both watched the dogs sniffing and playing, happily getting to know one another again.

"Do you think they remember each other?" she asked.

"Yeah," Logan said, jamming his hands into his pockets. "They've spent months at a time in the same place, and I don't think they forget. They probably have better memories that we do."

"Want to take them for a wander?"

Logan nodded and gave the dogs a whistle. "Jamie, about what happened . . ."

"Logan, I don't want you to apologize. There was nothing about the other day that went as planned." Jamie touched her hand to his shoulder, squeezing slightly. "I'm sorry I put you in that position. It was wrong and we should have thought it through better instead of just springing the news on you."

He stopped and stared at her, like he wasn't sure what to say.

"You're going to hate me for saying this, but Brett? He deserved a black eye. I'm only sorry about the way I spoke to you."

She sighed, shaking her head. "But that's it, Logan. Brett didn't deserve it. I'm as much to blame as he is for what's happened between us. You can't not attribute some of your anger toward me."

"Jamie, sweetheart, you're a widow. You're probably

lonely." His expression was kind but it also annoyed her, like the fact she'd lost her husband meant she couldn't make up her own mind about how she felt or what she did. "Brett took advantage of you, so it is his fault."

She knew she had to tell Logan the truth, now, before Brett turned up, because this conversation wasn't exactly going as planned. "Logan, Brett and I met before I even knew Sam. Pretending like us being together isn't partly my fault is just patronizing."

His eyebrows shot up and his face seemed to visibly harden. "I'm not sure I'm following you."

"Do you remember, years back, Brett telling you about a girl he'd met? A girl he spent weeks looking for?"

Logan laughed. "Yeah, and he never found her."

"But he did," she told him, voicc low. "That girl was me, and I'd just started seeing Sam when Brett finally tracked me down."

"You two weren't…"

"No!" Jamie said, not wanting him to imagine the situation being worse than it was. "I remembered him, of course I remembered him, but he never said anything about looking for me, about the night we'd met. Because he could see how happy Sam was, and he took the high road and walked away. Until recently, he never even told me what had happened."

Logan shook his head. "I think we need to keep walking."

Jamie fell into step beside him, wanting desperately for him to understand what she was trying to say.

"Brett and I have always had feelings for each other, but nothing would ever have happened while I was married to Sam." She took another deep breath. "I loved

Sam so much, and nothing could have jeopardized our marriage, but with him gone and Brett back?"

Logan didn't say anything, but she knew he was listening.

"The fact that something has happened between us now is okay, Logan, because we've done nothing wrong."

"Sam has only been gone…" He shrugged. "Whatever I say isn't going to make a difference, is it? You've clearly already made up your mind."

Jamie slowly shook her head, but she panicked when she saw Brett walking in their direction.

"What?" Logan asked, looking over his shoulder. "What the hell is he doing here?"

"Don't overreact, he wanted to come and make things right with you."

"I should just leave," he muttered.

Jamie looped her arm through Logan's to keep him in place. "No, you're not. Because we're all adults here, and you guys are best mates. You're not falling out because of me, and you need to promise me that you'll listen to what he has to say."

She watched as the dogs ran over to Brett, running circles around him then bounding back off to the river to inspect the ducks again.

"Hey," Brett called out.

Logan stiffened, but she didn't let him go.

"Geez, your eye really came up," Logan said.

Brett shrugged. "Guess I deserved it." He passed them each a coffee from the cardboard tray he was holding. "I just want this coffee to go better than our last attempt, so can we all keep our fists to ourselves?"

Brett had angled his body slightly to watch the dogs, and Jamie knew Logan was watching him.

"You must miss Ted even more when you're around these two," Logan said.

Brett's eyes were nothing short of honest when he turned back, the look in them enough to break Jamie's heart. "It's easy for someone else to tell me he was just a dog, but I miss him like hell. All the time. I don't think I'll ever stop thinking about the way he died, about what I lost that day."

They all stood and sipped their coffee.

"Jamie told me, about her being the girl from all those years back."

Brett took another sip of his coffee before sending a smile in her direction. "I need you to know that I would never have come between Jamie and Sam, but I love her, Logan. I always have. This isn't something new for me, it's just something I've never acted on before."

Jamie could hardly breathe, she was terrified of what was going to happen now. Of what Logan was going to say. How his reaction could change everything.

"Did you come here wanting my blessing, or do you not care either way?" Logan asked.

"If I didn't care, I wouldn't have told you the other day, and I wouldn't be standing here now," Brett told him. "I'm not going to walk away from Jamie, but then I'm not planning on walking away from you, either. Not after all we've been through. I just want you to try to understand."

Logan started to walk, slowly, and they both started to move, too. The dogs were having a ball and they followed them along the gentle curve of the river.

"I think I just need some time to get my head around

all this," Logan confessed, running a hand through his short hair. "It's not that I want to be the one that comes between you two, I just need to process it. It's a lot to take in."

Jamie couldn't help the smile the spread across her face, and the wink Brett gave her made her heart race. It was a baby step, but it was a step in the right direction.

"You both mean too much to me to lose either of you. So if you need time?" she said. "Take as much as you need."

"And you really think Sam would have been okay with this? That he wouldn't want me to do everything and anything to protect you? To stop you from making a mistake?"

"Logan, you don't need to protect her, because I'm not going to hurt her," Brett said, stopping at the same time Logan did. "Me walking away? That's what would hurt Jamie. And I love her." He smiled at her, eyes connecting with hers. "I love her, man."

Logan tipped his head back, eyes closed, before shaking his head and looking first at Jamie and then at Brett. "Just give me time. I just need time to wrap my head around all this."

Jamie knew when to change the subject, and that time was now. They'd told Logan what they needed to tell him, and it had gone down without anyone having their teeth knocked out, so now they just needed to hang out.

"Want to let the dogs have a swim?" she asked.

Logan laughed. "You ever had Bear in your car, soaking wet?"

Brett was laughing, too, and she couldn't not join in.

"A quick swim and then a long walk so they can dry off, then," she suggested.

The guys exchanged looks and kept laughing, even as she told Bear to jump in and he did so with a massive bound, like he was a professional lifesaver. Ranger was barking on the sidelines, glancing back at Logan, waiting for the command. When he got it, he launched into the water, too, both dogs swimming toward a group of ducks.

"What's so funny?" she asked.

Brett's cheeky smile made her glare at him. "You. For thinking for a moment that you'll ever get your dog out of the water."

"What do you mean? He's so obedient." she said, annoyed with the way they were both grinning at her. "You told me he'll obey me at all times, Brett. Was there something you neglected to tell me?"

"Even Sam couldn't ever convince that dog to get out of the water. You? Not a chance."

Jamie threw her hands up in the air. "Maybe you could have told me that *before* he showed off his dive?"

"Nah, this is going to be way more entertaining," Brett said with a laugh.

"The joke's on you, *Brett*," she told him, hands on hips. "Because you're in the back with him if he's still dripping wet when it's time to go home."

Logan was almost rolling on the grass he was laughing so hard.

"On second thought, he won't be wet, because we'll be using your T-shirt to dry him," she said.

"I take it all back," Logan said, still smiling. "You guys are perfect together. I've never seen Brett bossed around like this—ever."

Jamie grinned, but she had to move fast when Brett burst into a sprint and hurtled toward her.

"Don't you dare!" she squealed, running as fast as she could to get away from him. "Logan, help!"

Brett grabbed her around the waist, almost knocking the breath from her, before tossing her over his shoulder and leaving her powerless to do anything other than try to kick him.

"Take me anywhere near that water and I'll kill you," she hissed.

"Oh, baby, I like it when you talk rough," Brett whispered, slapping her on the backside.

"I mean it, Brett. Logan!" she screamed for him to help her again, but he never came to her rescue. "Logan!"

"Hey, you told me not to interfere," Logan called out. "This is me not interfering."

"Bear!" she yelled. "Bear, help me. Get Brett. Get Brett now!"

The dog who was supposed to be impossible to get out of the water leaped out with as much gusto as he'd leaped in, his big bark echoing around the park.

"Good boy, Bear!" she told him, still upside down over Brett's shoulder.

Brett stopped moving and put her back on her feet, watching the dog as he wagged his wet tail and kept barking.

"Jamie?"

"Get him, Bear!"

Bear launched at Brett and knocked him to the ground, giant paws landing square on his chest before he took him down.

"Just licks," she told him. "Lick Brett."

Her dog did as he was told, and now it was her laughing, watching Brett pinned to the ground with Bear lying on top of him, soaking wet, pleading with her to make it stop.

"Who's wet now?" she asked.

Logan held his hand up for a high five, and she gave him one back. This was how it was supposed to be—Brett and Logan getting on like they always had. And she felt good. Ever since Sam had died, she'd been like a fish out of water, but all that had changed, and she couldn't have been happier.

"Come on, Bear, let him go," she commanded. "That's no way to treat your new daddy."

Epilogue

Jamie looked around the large table and couldn't wipe the smile from her face. A year ago, she'd been a widow, and even her friends had struggled to know what to say to her, or how to treat her. And now? Now she was married to a man she could be herself with. A man who wasn't scared by the fact that she would always love the husband she'd lost, who was okay with her wearing her old wedding ring on her other hand, because Brett had loved Sam, too. Perhaps even as much as she had.

A tap on a glass made her turn to her new husband, eyes locking on his as he grinned and leaned sideways to give her a quick kiss.

"What are you doing?" she whispered to him.

"I'm about to do my speech, unless you want to go first?"

A speech? She hadn't even thought about speeches,

had been so preoccupied with her vows that she hadn't even considered having to speak in front of everyone at the table.

She watched as Brett stood up beside her, their friends and family lowering their voices until they were eventually surrounded by silence.

"I guess I need to start by thanking you all for being here," Brett said, one hand holding his champagne flute, the other falling to rest on her shoulder. "This was a day we only wanted to share with those people closest to us, and there is one person that isn't here today that I would like to acknowledge."

Jamie reached for Brett's hand, her palm covering his fingers. She didn't want to cry, but the whole day had been so emotional and now she had tears caught in her lashes again.

"We all know I wouldn't be standing here today with Jamie if Sam was still alive," Brett began, taking a big breath before continuing. "Sam was my best friend, and I always promised that I would look after Jamie if anything ever happened to him. I know he wasn't meaning it quite so literally when he said that—" Brett paused as a few of their guests chuckled "—but I also know that he would have wanted us both to be happy in his absence."

Jamie stood then, needing Brett to know that she wanted to hear what he was about to say, what he was already saying, and not knowing how to. She looped her arm around his waist, holding him tight.

"Sam was the only one of us who was married, and no matter how much we teased him about marrying so young, we loved Jamie as much as he did. I just want to say, Sam, if you're up there—" Brett wiped his eyes with the back of his hand before holding up his glass "—that I will look after this woman until my dying breath."

Jamie had tears falling fast down her cheeks, curling into her mouth. There was nothing she could do to stop them, and she also didn't want to. Because she had loved Sam with all her heart, and now she loved Brett, too, just as deeply but in a different way. And she needed to hear what he had to say.

Brett turned toward her, putting down his glass and taking both of her hands into his.

"I always told Sam he was the luckiest guy in the world, and I mean it when I say I will look after you. One day, I might have to give you back to Sam, because I don't want to be fighting him in the afterlife, but while we are here, on this earth, I will never let you down, Jamie. I will always be here for you, and I will do anything to be the husband you need me to be. I love you."

Brett wiped away the tears that had stained her cheeks, before leaning in and kissing her softly on the mouth. She put her arms around his neck and held on tight, not wanting him to stop, but the clapping and clinking of glasses around them forced the kiss to an end.

Even though her throat was choked up still and her eyes wet with tears, Jamie turned to face the table. She needed to say something, and they were *her* family, *her* friends. They were here to celebrate, and if they saw her cry it didn't matter.

"I don't have anything planned to say, and I'm sure you're all ready for dinner to be served, but I'd like to say thank you to all of you for being here today." Jamie looked at the light hanging above the table, needing a second to gather her strength and force her emotion back as best she could, so she could get the words out. Brett took her hand and squeezed, and it was all she needed to find the strength to continue. "When I married Sam, I knew I'd found my soul mate, but it seems that I'm one of the lucky ones." She squeezed Brett's hand back. "Brett was our friend for so many years, and now he's my husband. Life has a way of throwing us curveballs, some so bad that we wonder how we'll ever live through them, but Brett has proven to me that sometimes we have more than one soul mate in the world. I am so grateful to be standing here today, with the man I love."

Jamie reached for her glass and held it up. "To Brett, for being the love of my life, and teaching me that falling in love for a second time might be a miracle, but it was one that I deserved."

"To Brett." The words echoed around their table as everyone raised their glasses.

"I love you, Brett. So much," she whispered to him.

"And I love you, too, baby," he said, dropping a kiss to her forehead.

As they sat down, two waiters appeared with the main courses, but it was the tapping against a glass again that had Jamie's attention, followed by a deep *huh-hmm*. She scanned the table and realized it was Logan, sitting directly across from them.

"I'll make this quick because dinner is being served," Logan said, standing. "For the past ten years, the two most important people in my life have been Sam and Brett. When Sam died, we were all hit hard, and thinking about Jamie being on her own was almost as hard as losing him." He gave her a wink across the table. "I might have given Brett a black eye when I first found out, but I honestly believe, now I look back on what happened, that Sam would have told me what a jerk I was being. Because looking at these two today, it's obvious they were meant to be together." He held up his glass. "And let's not forget Bear, Sam's loyal dog, who has taken up the role as Jamie's number-one protector. If anyone didn't approve, it would have been Bear, but even he seems to accept this union." Logan laughed. "To Brett and Jamie, two of my favorite people in the world."

Jamie smiled at Logan—the man who had been her first husband's best friend and was undeniably Brett's best friend, too—and held up her glass. She took a slow sip before looking at every single person seated around the long table again. The white tablecloth was set with low candles from one end to the other instead of flowers, because she'd wanted to be able to see and talk to everyone, and she loved watching the smiles and chatter as she looked at them all now.

Brett nudging her broke her trance, and she switched her attention to him.

"You okay?" he asked.

"More than okay," she assured him, looking down at the plate of food in front of her.

"Then eat up, Mrs. Palmer," he said, waggling his eyebrows and making her laugh. "Because you'll need *all* your energy tonight."

Jamie elbowed him in the ribs but he was having none of it, swiftly grabbing her arm and pulling her in for another quick kiss.

"I'm so pleased I married you," he said, his mouth hovering over hers.

"Ditto," she said, laughing as he kissed the tip of her nose instead of her lips.

She reluctantly turned her attention back to her food—king prawns, calamari and scallops tossed in her favorite linguine with garlic.

Life didn't get much better than this.

* * * * *

"We need to get our story straight," she reminded him.

His smile faded. "It's best not to offer too many details. We met in Atlanta, and now we have Ben."

She turned to face him, adjusting the lap belt as she shifted. "Your family's not going to question you showing up with a six-month-old baby? Like maybe you would have mentioned it to them prior to now?"

One bulky shoulder lifted and lowered. "I told you we aren't close."

"Your mom not knowing she has a grandchild is a bit more than 'not close,'" Cory felt compelled to point out. "Will she be upset we aren't married?"

"I'm not sure."

Her stomach tightened at his response. "Will she want to have a relationship with Ben after this weekend?"

"Good question."

"I have a million of them where that came from," she said. "I don't even know how your father died."

"Heart attack."

"Sudden." She worried her lower lip between her teeth. There were so many potential potholes for her to tumble into this weekend, and based on the tight set of his jaw, Jordan was in no shape to help navigate her through it. In fact, she had the feeling she'd be the one supporting him and he'd need solace well beyond a distraction.

"Can you answer a question with more than two words?" She was careful to make her voice light and was rewarded when his posture gentled somewhat.

"I suppose so."

"A bonus word. Nice. I'm sorry about your father's death," she said, giving in to the urge to reach out and place her hand on his arm.

Don't miss
His Secret Starlight Baby *by Michelle Major,*
available March 2021 wherever
Harlequin Special Edition books and ebooks are sold.

Harlequin.com

HARLEQUIN

Heartfelt or thrilling, passionate or uplifting—Harlequin is more than just happily-ever-after.

With twelve different series to choose from and new books available every month, you are sure to find stories that will move you, uplift you, inspire and delight you.

Love Harlequin romance?

DISCOVER.

Be the first to find out about promotions, news and exclusive content!

Facebook.com/HarlequinBooks

Twitter.com/HarlequinBooks

Instagram.com/HarlequinBooks

Pinterest.com/HarlequinBooks

YouTube.com/HarlequinBooks

ReaderService.com

EXPLORE.

Sign up for the Harlequin e-newsletter and download a free book from any series at **TryHarlequin.com**

CONNECT.

Join our Harlequin community to share your thoughts and connect with other romance readers!
Facebook.com/groups/HarlequinConnection

HSOCIAL2021